THE RISE

RICK BETTENCOURT

THE RISE OF THE NORMALS
BOOK 1

Published in the United States by Bettencourt Concepts, LLC.

ISBN (paperback): 979-8-9987866-0-0

ISBN (ebook): 979-8-9987866-1-7

First Edition: September 2025

Contents

Part One

Nurturing

Chapter One

Victorian Volley

T HE VAMPIRES AND SHIFTERS gathered in an open field, barely visible under the dark, cloud-covered sky. Diesel and Bence marked the boundaries of the Victorian Volley court with black and red flags, then moved off to the sidelines.

"Vamps or Wolves?" Diesel asked his best friend. "Who do you think'll win tonight?"

Victorian Volley, a game played by both vampires and shifters, where two teams faced off in the pitch black of night to hit a glowing ball fused with magic energy, was popular in New England in the fall.

Bence shrugged. "Last time it was the Vamps. Maybe shifters'll finally get a chance."

"I'll bet you my *PEOPLE* magazine we won't," Diesel said.

"We?"

While Diesel and Bence, too, were wolf-shifters, unlike their brethren, they preferred their more human-like, less magical traits. As the game relied solely on the players' enhanced senses to navigate the court and detect the ball, they weren't qualified.

"We're technically shifters," Diesel replied.

Bence and Diesel's fondness for humans received much ridicule in Hubbard Forest. According to scripture, embracing one's supernatural nature was the way, and those who sought refuge with humanity were scorned.

The team captains, a sleek and muscular werewolf and a tall, pale vampire, shook hands before taking their places on the field.

Behind them, the crowd of onlookers cheered at the toss of the glowing ball, which hovered in the air and signaled the start of the game.

Victorian Volley relied solely on the players' enhanced senses to navigate the area. As the game progressed, the ball flickered and then disappeared altogether.

Diesel took out a set of gaslight visionaries—goggles made of sleek, black metal, with small, glowing red lights along the sides. He handed a pair to Bence. With a few adjustments, the goggles came to life, revealing the hidden field and the action on the court.

The game was fast paced and intense. Both sides showed impressive agility and skill. The Wolves shifted midair to intercept the ball, while the Vamps used speed and precision to outmaneuver them.

Near the end of the fourth quarter, the score was tied when the moon emerged from behind the clouds and bathed the field in a warm glow. The Wolves advantage became apparent as they grew stronger and more aggressive under the moon's light.

"I might be out my magazine," Diesel said to Bence.

Bence snickered. "It ain't over."

Unable to see the ball in the moonlight, Diesel relied on the grunts and groans to follow the game. He adjusted the gaslight visionaries with its inscription, "Crafted in Yorkshire, 1898," along the frame. He had given Bence the banned, newer pair, from the 21st century.

"Thanks for the modern technology," Bence said, following the game without regard as the rest of the onlooks made their adjustments to the lenses.

"Shh," Diesel said. "We're not supposed to have them."

Bence smiled and watched unwaveringly.

As the game proceeded, the players became more aggressive, trying to gain an advantage in the in-and-out of visibility to the game. It was chaos on the field, with players colliding and falling to the ground, yet the Wolves still led.

Abruptly, the referee blew his whistle. "Foul!"

The crowd fell silent as the referee rushed over to the Vamps lead net defender, Ketch. A shifter lay on the ground with his leg bleeding, and he growled in pain. His teammates barked angrily at the vampire.

The referee sternly addressed Ketch. "No biting allowed. That's a foul, and you know it."

Ketch protested. "I was just playing the game. It's not my fault the shifters are so fragile."

The referee shook his head. "That's not an excuse. You broke the rules, and now you're out of the game."

The shifter limped off the field, aided by his teammates, and Ketch was escorted out by two large, imposing ogres.

But the Vamps weren't ready to give in.

At the reset of the game and a swift and graceful move, the team captain volleyed the ball past the werewolf goalie, scoring the winning point. The stands opposite Bence and Diesel erupted in cheers as the vampire team celebrated their victory.

"Guess I get to keep this." Diesel opened his coat to show Bence his forbidden magazine.

CHAPTER TWO

"Humansexuals!"

I n Hubbard Forest, Maine—two hours from the coast and another two to Canada—lay a swath of land occupied by supernatural and paranormal creatures locked in time by a barrier system placed over the region in the nineteenth century.

At the edge of the woods stood a tree portal, one of many throughout the land. It beckoned the vampires and werewolves to return from feeding in the contemporary, human realm with its bursts of orange and blue lights.

Not far from the tree, at the end of the dirt road, Diesel and Bence ogled glossy pictures in *PEOPLE* magazine strewn across their thighs. A copy of their village's newspaper, *The Gas Lamp*, which had originally hidden the prohibited human publication lay on the ground beside them.

A cacophony of voices sounded as the hunters returned.

A cool evening breeze slid over Diesel's exposed torso. "They're coming back."

"We should hurry," Bence said. The wolf-shifter redressed and grabbed his dark-brown leather coat but left his duffel to retrieve later.

A British voice grew closer. "I'm sick of eating moose and deer. No humans come 'round here no more." Diesel recognized the voice as Ketch's—the pain-in-the-ass vampire.

His compadre Pedro, in his squeaky tone, replied, "The queen won't let us out past the second barrier."

"I know, numbskull," Ketch said. "But they can still get in. The queen, that bitch, just needs to lure more into the eating zone."

"Is that really The White Queen's responsibility?" Mitsy, Diesel's sister, said.

"Listen to her. Since she's become pregnant, she thinks she's all that and a feminist doctrine."

"Shut up, Ketch," Mitsy said. "I'm just saying, the queen can only do so much with the virus going on."

"She can do more." Ketch met up with Diesel and Bence on the dirt road heading toward the portal. "Oh, look who we have here. The humansexuals!"

"Leave them alone, Ketch," Mitsy said.

"All dressed in their human clothes like real people."

"Hey, huma," Pedro chided.

Diesel tucked in his shirt.

"Guys, I said enough." When the vampires caved, Mitsy stepped closer to her approaching brother. "You two eat anything?"

"We're fine." Bence, blond and bluish-gray eyed, was a half-foot shorter than the tall, shaggy-dark-haired Diesel whom he now stood by.

A massive pine tree on the other side of a dented, metal barrier at the end of human realm, beckoned the group's return, and a blue beam emitted from its trunk.

"It's always a time warp to go back in," Bence said. "I can't wait to live out here, full time."

"Shush. Our plan. Don't let anyone—"

"Oh, hey humas!" Ketch, a vampire, said. "Look at you two dressed like it's the twenty-first century."

"It is, idiot."

Ketch pursed his lips, making fun of the verbal insult. "In Hubbard Forest we respect the past. You know that."

"We do know, blood breath," Bence said. "We don't need you to remind us. We do what we want."

"And that's why you'll never fit in." The vampire smiled.

Wolves emerged from the depths of the forest and transformed from their canine state.

Elder Bainbridge, the oldest wolf-shifter of the community, handed the naked shifters loincloths. "Single file! Single file."

"Time to return home, fed and filled on fur." Ketch smirked and rubbed his belly. Black pants, a pressed white shirt, and a black vest, embroidered with thin, red stitching, covered the vampire's thin frame.

"You nervous?" Diesel said to Bence.

"Shh. Let's not raise suspicion."

The pine tree's trunk opened, and a neon light cast psychedelic-like colors on the hunters: Blues. Teals. Greens. Purples. Reds. Yellows.

"Saturday's the mating ceremony," Buck, Mitsy's husband, said to Diesel, while waiting their turn. "Your father needs you to mate this year."

Diesel nodded. Options for a young, male Super in Hubbard Forest—especially one in his twenty-first year, finished with university, and the
last male in the family line of a dying shifter species—were slim.

"Some of the clan think you and Bence are gonna ask to mate each
other," Buck said. "That would definitely go against tradition."

"We're not going to mate each other." Diesel inched forward in line. "I
won't let the pack down. I never have."

"Since you've graduated college, you're a changed Super."

"I learned a lot at UPS."

"The University of Paranormal and Supernatural is a good school. Your
dad and stepmom are proud."

"Yes, sir." Diesel didn't think they were proud, but didn't want to be-
labor the point. No one majored in Humanity—the study of the human
species—nor dressed and acted like one, like him and Bence.

"They just don't show much emotion," Buck said. The wolf-shifter,
while several years older than his new bride, bore the title of stud of the
pack—the only male shifter to pass on the pack's genes in many years.

Bence stopped to tie his shoe.

Buck shook his head. "No wonder humans are such a mess. All those
laces and unnecessary add-ons." He held his wife's hand, helping her step
over a tree root and into the portal. "Careful there, Mits. You're carrying
my precious cargo."

Diesel let a witch couple and few wolf-shifters go before them. When
the haphazard line grew thin, Bence stepped in first. Diesel followed.

With flashes of light, snaps, and buzzes, the portal recorded their return from the human realm. The decade-long toll tracked the comings
and goings of Supers who inhabited the region. While the portal had the
ability to send them far away—through a vast subway-like network to other

realms—this trip was a register-only one to let them through the protective barrier to the other side.

Central Maine's Hubbard Forest spanned many acres—covering miles of both human and supernatural worlds. The same species of trees and animals occupied both sides. Even humans could bypass the dual barrier system—the Double Bubble—Supers could not. While humans could easily wander in, they seldomly left.

As the group dispersed to their abodes and places of worship, Diesel and Bence lingered behind.

The tree's blue beam faded, and a red one took its place.

"Well, this is it," Bence said.

"What did Luke say, about two-three minutes after burn down?"

"Maybe five."

"What do you mean *maybe* five? There's a limited time to go back. You should know the exact time."

"He texted me the coordinates." Bence thumbed a cell phone, one he acquired from the Trash Heap boneyard months back.

"He must be loving Salem and life with humans."

"He is. He met a nice girl, a real girl. She doesn't care that he's a witch. In fact, it's pretty common for witches and real people to coexist there. Supers can go undetected."

"Must be beautiful."

"Beautiful?" Ketch shot out from the dark. "You two human-lovers play love-dovey again."

"Ketch, give it a break," Diesel said.

"Oh, the big, bad wolf-shifter who never shifts is speaking up for himself and his boyfriend."

"We're not boyfriends, Ketch." Diesel felt the sting of Bence's glare. "And if we were, what the hell do you care?"

"Not boyfriends? I hear you two can give a Super some good relief," he walked closer. "I thought you might want to play with a vampire and satisfy his needs." Ketch grabbed his crotch.

The tree's center light shut down, leaving only the glow of the waxing gibbous moon.

Ketch ripped the *PEOPLE* magazine from the inner pocket of Diesel's jacket and laughed. "You two boys tossing off to humans again?"

"Give me that." Diesel attempted to grab it, but the vampire's speed was no match.

Ketch paged through the old magazine. "Human-lovers. You guys are evil you know that? An abomination to the Dark Lord, Darthius."

"And you're so pious," Bence said.

"You like men? Women? How about Blacks? Asians?" The vampire paged through the magazine. "I think they all taste divine." He tore a page out and bit it, as if savoring flesh.

"Cut it out, Ketch." Diesel resisted the impulse to shift. The fur on Diesel's neck bristled.

"Human-lovers are despicable."

Diesel sneered and trembled. "You are an ass—"

"Oh. Am I pissing you off? Huma! Huma! You don't want to go and shift now, do you? You might ruin your human clothes." The vampire radiated a static charge that nipped at Diesel's skin in heated jabs.

"Enough, Ketch." Bence tugged at Diesel's jacket. "He's not worth it, Dee."

Diesel's emotions waffled between anger and embarrassment. Watching the vampire ruin his prized link to the human world pissed him off and knowing Ketch was on to Bence and him using the magazine to fuel their people fantasies—like with their recent sexual escapade on the other side of the barrier—mortified him.

"Human-sexual . . . human-sexual!" Ketch bit a piece of the magazine's page, and it clung to an incisor as the vampire chided. He tore out another picture, one of celebrity Carolyn Sohier, Diesel particularly liked and ate it as well. "When are you going to grow up and act like a real Super?"

Diesel's mouth quivered. He bit his lower lip and gnashed his teeth. The urge to shift strengthened, bringing him to the edge. His jaw snapped.

"Yo, Ketch! Ketch!" Pedro's squeaky voice called out. "Dude!" The pudgy vampire burst out from the forest. "We spotted a human!"

Ketch tossed the magazine to the ground. "Where?"

"By the Hawkins' cabin."

The vampires vanished, leaving behind their scent in metallic, cool waves.

Diesel picked up his magazine and shoved it back in his coat pocket. The pain in his jaw eased to a sting. His nose throbbed.

"Diesel." Bence's back was to him. The tree hummed. "It's time."

Bence placed a hand on the pine's trunk. "Luke said when it vibrates . . ."

"Is it?"

Bence nodded. A red-orange dot glinted in the hollow of the tree.

"You gonna miss this place?" Diesel asked.

Bence looked back at him. "I'm gonna miss you."

"Bence, c'mon now. You'll meet a nice human and fall in love. Isn't that what this is all about anyway?"

Bence frowned. "You said you're coming after me. And we could live together."

"I will." He drew him in.

"Maybe I should wait. Your sister will have her baby in a month, and you'll feel free to leave." The blond wolf-shifter stepped away from the portal.

"No, Bence. You must go now. The Howling Moon is near, and they'll make you mate a she-wolf."

"But they'll do the same to you. You and I . . . we can live together, openly, in Salem."

Diesel removed his totem from around his neck.

"What are you doing?" Bence asked.

Diesel placed the large wolf tooth and the rope it dangled from in Bence's palm. "I want you to have it."

"But—"

"Take it. Without it, they can't make me mate."

"But it's your essence. You're giving it to me . . . is a . . . it's a sign of commitment."

"I'm committed to you, Bence. Please, take it."

Bence removed his own, similar looking totem. "I want you to have mine. It'll serve me no good in the human realm anyway." He placed it around Diesel's neck. "Besides, they'll really think you lost your marbles running around the forest without one."

"I'll meet you in Salem. I promise."

Bence shook his head.

"I will." Diesel touched the tooth resting against his chest. "I won't ever let you down, Bence Derringer."

"You don't let anyone down. That's your problem." Bence put Diesel's totem on and tucked it in his shirt, then he stood on tiptoes and kissed

Diesel on the cheek. "You're a good man, Dan Diesel Cade. That's why I admire you."

"I'm not a man. *That's* my problem. I'm a wolf-shifter."

MAT KWAN, WITH ELBOWS on his thighs, held a cigarette loosely between his fingers. Its smoke furled, stung his heavy-lidded eyes, and roused him from reverie.

"Damn it!" The cigarette burned his fingers. Ash littered the cabin's wide floorboards. He stubbed out the Marlboro in an ashtray beside a glass of Jim Beam.

Across from him, a tousled blanket hung from the double bed's side from which he had arisen. The other half of the covering draped on the floor. The nightstand's lamp lit an open bottle of Xanax.

He sank back the rest of the bourbon.

From his suitcase on the bench at the end of the bed, a Delta tag—stamped BGR—swayed in the open window's breeze.

A rap at the door startled him. "The hell?" He grabbed a clean, white T-shirt and slid it over his mahogany chest.

Long feet spanked the floor as he covered the short distance out of the bedroom and through the living room. Before he could check the visitor through the three small windows atop the entrance, the door flung open.

He sprang back. "Jesus!"

"He ain't he-ah." Two men, dressed in black cloaks, barged in. The tall one smiled, revealing incisors the length of a fork tine, while the short, pudgy one held Mat back by his wrists.

"Bite him. Bite him," Shorty said.

Numbed from Xanax, terror, or both, Mat froze. Thoughts of Madeline, his wife, and son, Ty, raced through his mind. Better times. When they were alive. 'Take me,' he thought. 'I'm better off dead.'

"Lucifer in hell!" The tall one held his hand to his mouth. Blood trickled down his fingers. "A friggin' cement block."

"What?" Shorty asked.

The tall one spit blood. In his hand he held his cracked incisor.

Shorty laughed. "Problem with your dent-chiz, Ketch?" He flung Mat around and grabbed the man's wrist to his mouth, gagged, then hopped back. "A goddamn Metanormal."

Ketch swung a punch to Mat's face.

Mat flinched, felt nothing.

Ketch's jaw dropped, and he gripped his fist. "What the? Let's get the hell outta here."

CHAPTER THREE

The Fight

T HE SUN ROSE OVER the wolf den.

In the middle of Hubbard Forest, Mitsy and Buck's small hollow lay under a bank of tree and rock. The simple home, common for a religious wolf-shifter, was made up of a mix of natural elements—rock and tree-root walls, dirt floors—with simple, modern amenities that were sanctioned by the scriptures.

Honoree III, Diesel and Mitsy's father, stood in the center of the couple's living area. "It's not okay!" A large tiger's tooth hung from a chain around his neck and a gray loincloth clung to his waist. The alpha ripped the laptop from Diesel's hand.

Diesel sprang for it. "Give me—"

Honoree barrel-chested in front of his son. "I said, it's not okay." His breath reeked of rotten meat. His beard came to a tip at the chin, combed from constant strokes in meditative thought. Brown, unkempt hair—scattered with bits of grass and twigs—hung past the patriarch's shoulders.

Diesel trembled with anger. The laptop served as his only means of connecting to Bence and Salem.

"Were you out playing human again? Or maybe you were shopping at the boneyard looking for human clothes and . . . these types of modern contraptions?" Honoree held up the laptop.

"Guys, please," Mitsy held a hand beneath her baby bump. "We're not here to argue. We should be celebrating."

"Celebrate?" Diesel asked.

"You missed the midwife visit. Again." Jezebel, their stepmother, leaned back on a chair, crossed her legs, and sipped coffee from a mug. She wore a chocolate brown silk dress with a beaded applique and decorative buttons on its bodice. "For Satan's sake, give it a rest, Honoree." Jezebel slurped.

"I'm not giving it a rest!" Honoree faced his son. "You were out in that damn horseless carriage again." As alpha, Honoree saw to it that his pack adhered to the Regency's demands to preserve history—remaining locked in a perpetual nineteenth-century .

Diesel's rage intensified. He needed the laptop. *Fuck culture!*

"Weren't you?" Spittle hit Diesel's eye.

"I drove to the edge of the forest to get reception, Sir." He left the mode of transportation, his diesel jalopy, out of his statement."

"Drove. Normal wolf-shifters *shift*. They don't drive," Buck said.

Honoree forced Diesel to the ground with his knee.

Diesel was accustomed to his father's display of dominance over his beta spirit with such acts, but this time something clicked. "What do you care what I do? I'm not hurting anyone." Diesel tried to get up, but his father kneed him in the stomach.

"Look at you. Pathetic." Honoree hovered over him. "Dressed like some sort of modern freak. No wonder no she-wolf wants you." He ripped the baseball cap from Diesel's head and flung it to the ground.

Diesel scuffled toward it, but his father stepped on his hand. Diesel's mouth filled with dirt from the floor as his father pressed a foot onto his neck.

"Your sister is having a baby. You were to be here when the midwife and Witch Lena performed the gender reveal. And instead, you're out playing human! And playing with their satan-forsaken contraptions."

"I . . . I . . . .forgot." Diesel spit a mix of blood and grit.

"My son . . . the last male in my line . . . shows no respect for our heritage. Tradition is sacred!"

"Tradition . . . makes us weak." He said it. He'd been holding it back for years. The pressure on his neck grew. "Look . . . at all the things humans have brought to the world."

"Dad, stop!" Mitsy shouted.

"They could advance our species." Diesel gasped for air. "Instead, we're dying." His lessons at university educated him in more ways than one.

"UPS was a waste if that's what they taught you," the alpha said. "You were to learn how to fight them."

Jezebel huffed. "His majoring in Humanity has many benefits to our society. He knows them well."

"Enough, Jezebel!" His father never liked being put in his place by a female.

"I have a manicure, Honoree. Are you done?" she added.

"No. I'm not done."

"Humans are inferior." Buck went to Honoree's side. "The supernatural species is the highest class of all beings that ever inhabited the Earth. Didn't they learn you that in college, boy?"

"What they *learned* me, is that Supers … shall die … when humans take over."

"They will never take over." Honoree's foot gave way, and Diesel gasped for air.

"They are taking over," Diesel said. "There are normal human beings developing into Metanormals as we speak."

"Hogwash! That's a myth."

Jezebel examined her nails. "Not that I am a religious woman, sorry Buck, but their scriptures do say, 'the meek shall inherit the—'"

"Quiet, woman!" her husband chastised. "We don't speak of the human's scriptures in my daughter's home."

Jezebel rolled her eyes. "Yes. Sir. Your daughter's home is sacred." Despite his distaste for his stepmother, her spunk sometimes played in Diesel's favor.

"Here, Super scriptures rule," Buck said. "We're at the end of human time. Lord Darthius shall rise and they will see that the supernatural truly rule the planet."

"Satan, hear our prayer," the group muttered as Diesel dusted off his baseball cap.

Honoree fumbled with the laptop to open it but knew not how. "These damn human contraptions." He flung it against the wall. "Tradition is sacred!"

Mitsy gasped.

Diesel snapped. He lunged at his father's legs, tumbling him over his back. "You son of a bitch!" Diesel pinned the alpha to the ground.

"Don't you talk to me like that!"

Diesel's jaw cracked as the shift took hold. Fur sprouted across his arms. With a snarl, he burst upward—seizing his father by the mane—and drove him into the wall. "Alpha. Fuck that!"

The portrait of Mitsy and their great-great-grandfather, Honoree I, toppled beside the ruined laptop. The frame splintered, and the glass burst, the old bloodline fracturing with it.

"Diesel, don't!" Mitsy rushed him.

Diesel's shirt ripped as his torso grew. His Levi's split. Like most shifters, his wolf was larger than his human form.

Before Honoree shifted in defense, Diesel flung him by his mane to the ground, then leapt back upon him.

"Lord Darthius!" Buck tugged at Diesel's fur.

Mitsy pleaded with her brother to stop.

Jezebel tidied her coiffed hair.

Diesel preferred not to shift: It ruined a good pair of hard-to-come-by, thirty-two-inch-waist jeans. More so, he hated caving into magic and losing control of his emotions.

With his father cowering in an ugly, awkward mid-shift, Diesel managed his anger and switched back.

Pieces of his ripped, Red Sox T-shirt clung to his torso. Half naked, he dragged the ruined jeans clutched to his ankle as he retrieved his baseball cap and put it on. His body pulsated with rage.

Jezebel rose and stopped in front of Diesel. "You know, stepson, you have an obligation to this pack and to your father to perpetuate the species." She gripped his chin. "You are the last male in the line. Don't screw it up for us."

"Why do you care? I'm not your blood," Diesel said. "What do you get out of it?"

She sneered. "A happy husband."

"You haven't cared about me for the first twenty years of my life . . . sending me off to boarding school . . . making sure I went far away for university."

"If you remember, I was the one who let you major in Humanity at UPS instead of other, more traditional things such as Shifting, Vampirology, or Artificial Intelligence."

"Let me?"

"C'mon, Honoree. We're done here. My manicure is waiting."

Buck escorted them out. "Mitsy can't have all this turmoil. It could disturb her pregnancy."

"Tradition is sacred." The words left Honoree trembling.

When they left, Mitsy handed Diesel one of her husband's loincloths.

Diesel sighed and wrapped it around his waist.

"Dad is off his chain lately," Mitsy said.

"Sorry about Great-Great Granddad." Diesel chinned in the direction of the refuse on the floor and sat in the chair opposite the one Jezebel abandoned.

"Did Bence leave?" she asked.

"How'd you know?"

"Because you're off your chain worse than Dad."

"I'll be all right."

Mitsy placed a hand on his shoulder. Its warmth calmed the jitters raging through Diesel's body. "Go with him."

Diesel looked back at her.

"Go. Go after Bence."

"It's not what you think between him and me."

"First, it doesn't matter what I think. Second, I know it's not him you're really after."

"It's not that simple." He leaned his elbows on the table.

"Ever since you returned from Uni you've been depressed. I know you long to live in the human world."

Diesel downed the cold coffee Jezebel hadn't finished. "You got anything stronger?"

Mitsy reached through the passthrough, above the table, and grabbed Buck's cognac from the galley.

The alcohol eased the sting, like that from a hundred bees, rippling through Diesel's body.

"Stop pretending what's holding you back is me. The baby and I will be fine."

"So, is it a boy?" He glugged the booze. Males were all the clan cared about.

Mitsy beamed.

"Awesome. Maybe Dad will lay off me now."

"I've been praying, Diesel." She cut him off with a hand up. "I know . . . I know. You don't have to say it. I know you don't believe in our religion. But Lord Darthius—"

"Let's not go there about him." He sipped more cognac.

"Fine. We don't have to agree on everything."

"No, we don't. It's just . . . I love you, Mits. I want to make sure you and your baby are safe."

She pinched her nose. "This isn't easy for me, but I want you to follow your dreams."

"The other day you said you needed me here to help you through pregnancy and thought I should adhere to Saturday's mating ceremony to perpetuate the species."

"I know what I said. But. I want you to . . . go to Salem. You've only been talking about it ever since you were a kid. You even went off to school to study humans. I know . . . I know we don't always see eye to eye, but you're my kid brother."

"I . . . I . . ."

"Mitsy and Kiba will be fine." She rubbed her belly. "My baby boy will be fine. I have faith in the Lor— Let's just say I know we'll be fine."

"Did you have a vision?"

"You said you didn't want to talk about my . . . faith." She went to the shattered picture of their great-great grandfather and returned it to the nail on the wall. "Let's just say it came to me in a dream. Honoree the First spoke to me."

Diesel capped the booze.

She grabbed a broom. "It's taken me awhile to admit this to myself but maybe Supers aren't always meant to be with Supers."

He rose. "Are you telling me that you believe humansexuals are *not* the abomination as your so-called scripture states?"

"It doesn't matter what I believe. And, yes, I've come to be a little more liberal in my thinking, thanks to you." She smiled and leaned onto the broom handle.

"I'm glad I could expand your supernatural mind." He took the broom from her and cleaned up the mess.

"As for this so-called glitch in the portal that you talk about—"

"Quiet. Only a few of us know."

"Can it really get you to Salem?"

"Once through the portal, there's a tear in the second barrier on the southeast side. Bence and I saw it the other day."

"Lucifer, Diesel! I don't need to know all the details. If the queen found out there was a way out of the magical world, she'd have our heads."

"Did the queen come to the gender reveal? Sorry, I missed it."

"No. She just sent Lena."

She kissed him on the cheek. "Wait . . . that doesn't look like your totem?"

Diesel touched the wolf tooth dangling from a leather rope around his neck. "Oh, I gave mine to Bence. This is his."

"What? You gave it to Bence?" She clutched her belly, winced, and leaned against the couch.

"Mits?"

She held her hand up. "I'm good. That totem, Dee, is your lineage . . . your . . . your . . . everything." She fidgeted with her own necklace.

"Bence gave me his."

"Oh, dear Lord. Why did you do that?"

Diesel tripped over the ruined Nikes still clinging to his feet and retrieved his jeans from the floor.

"You know he's hung up on you. Any logical Super would interpret that exchange as a sign of commitment, Diesel."

"It *was* a sign of commitment. At the last minute, he didn't want to go through. I promised him . . . someday . . . soon . . . I would meet up with him."

"But you don't even love him. You told me that."

Diesel removed the tattered sneakers.

"You care about him, but you don't love him the way he wants you to love him. I'm not trying to put words in your mouth."

"I know. I know I told you that."

"Besides, he's not even human. Don't humansexuals want to be with humans? I don't understand this . . . this fluidity thing."

"I just hated to see him crushed. If he stayed, you know the pack would have made him mate with a she-wolf. That's not him."

"But you can't play with someone's emotions." She pressed a thumb and index finger to her temples.

"Are you okay? Do you need me to get you anything?" He propped a pillow on the couch. "Lie here."

"Diesel, stop. You don't need to watch over me. Not anymore."

Diesel blinked.

"Not that you need it . . . not that you've ever needed it. But you have my permission to go."

"What?"

"You heard me. I don't need you to look after me. I'll always be your big sister." She touched her belly. "Big in more ways than one."

They chuckled.

"But Mits . . . I . . . I . . . I don't know what to—"

She kissed him. "I love you, Dee. Go. To. Salem. Like you always wanted. Besides, you embarrassed Dad in front of his wife and best friend. You think he's going to let that go?"

"Okay. But only if you promise me something."

Mitsy cocked her head.

"Promise me you'll find me if Buck . . . or this place . . . gets too out of control for you or my nephew."

Mitsy sighed.

"Send someone for me. I know it's not easy to get over to the human world, but Elio might know."

"Dan Diesel Cade, you think a dragon is not going to cause a stir walking through the streets of Salem? The Double-Bubble has kept us contained for decades for a reason."

"They say it's liberal there."

She rose and placed a hand on his heart. "I'll be right here."

He set a hand on hers, and they hugged.

Chapter Four

Find a Wolf

WHILE A CAMPFIRE BLAZED, Mat inched the muzzle of the Smith & Wesson past his lips. The rifle stroked the roof of his mouth.

He whimpered.

His hands shook. The barrel clattered against his teeth.

Photographs of his wife and child curled in the fire before him.

He fixed, as best he could, a trembling finger on the trigger guard. The eight-by-ten of Maxine, Ty, and he at Disneyland morphed until their faces distorted into ash.

Mat shook violently. His finger scooched closer to the trigger.

Pop!

Mat flung the gun to the ground.

Pop! Pop!

"Jesus Christ. Let me be!" Mat shouted.

In the distance, a car engine burst to life. Its popping now a steady roar.

"What the hell." He rose then paced.

The cool, summer night masked the vehicle's distance. It idled rough—*Tick! Tick! Fffft! Fffft!*—and stalled.

Mat's phone rang. "For the love of God." He went to the bench to retrieve it.

The campfire snapped. Embers billowed into the air.

Trinity Hawkins, the phone read. The blue-eyed, redhead flashed on the screen.

"Yeah. What's up?"

"I should ask you the same."

Again, the engine sputtered and stopped.

"I'm just going through some things I brought with me." The photograph's ashes collapsed into the bed.

"You sound like you're outside."

"I built a campfire to keep warm."

Crickets chirped. An owl hooted.

"Mat, do you need me to come up? You sound down."

"No. I told you I'd get your parent's cabin ready for you to list. You can come up this weekend, as planned."

"Are you thinking about Maxine and Ty?"

He pinched the bridge of his nose, closed his eyes. Tears welled.

"I know what it's like to lose family," she said. "It's hard."

"It is." His voice choked.

"Mat, please. Talk to me. Isabel told us expressing our feelings helps us move past them."

He covered his mouth and quaked.

"Mat? Are you there?"

"I'm . . . I'm here. I'm still here." He looked over at the rifle next to the rocks that edged the pit.

"I can get a sub to cover class for the rest of the week."

He wiped snot from his nose with the back of his hand. "I have no purpose."

"You're a firefighter. You save lives. Of course, you have—"

"Ex-firefighter. Besides, I'm not worth saving."

"Stop the pity party."

"Pity party? Is that what you think?"

"Isabel said we need to let ourselves off the hook. It's okay to let go. We can't let guilt overwhelm us. It was an accident, Mat."

"I could've done more."

"Your family died in a fire. You didn't mur—"

"I should've been there."

"You know, it took me awhile to realize this, but it's okay to not mourn. It's okay to feel good. Feeling bad doesn't mean you loved them more. There's this false belief that if you feel really, really bad about someone whose gone it means you really, really loved them. Like you have to suffer to prove how much you loved them. That's bullshit, Mat."

"I didn't think elementary school teachers said, 'bullshit.'"

"That's bullshit." She chuckled.

Mat cracked a smile.

"Are you having visions again?" Trinity asked.

He opened his mouth to speak, then shook his head.

"I dreamt of Ginny again last night," Trinity said. "She was trying to tell me something important about my parents, but I couldn't make it out."

"While you saw your kid sister, I saw vampires."

The empty bottle of Jim Beam shattered in the fire.

"You . . . you had a dream about vampires?"

"It wasn't a dream. Probably just too much to drink."

"That's a new one. You haven't told me about seeing creatures of the night before," the latter of which she said with a ghostly affect.

Sparks hurled into the air. Leaves on a nearby maple ignited.

"Shit," he said.

"What?"

"The campfire . . ." A lit branch fell to the ground. The grass ignited.

"Is everything all right?"

"Just a small brush fire."

"No one better to put out a fire than a fireman. Wait. Are you going to be okay?"

"Yes, Trin." The fire grew. "I'll call you in the morning."

Mat grabbed a shovel, rushed to the edge of the property where flames nipped brush, and smothered it with dirt.

THE THOMPSON TWINS' "HOLD ME NOW" squeaked out from the Walkman's discarded headset on the passenger seat—the old diesel and Walkman were human detritus no *normal* Super would have been interest in.

Diesel turned the engine. *Ara-rar!*

"C'mon." He pressed the medal to the floor.

Tick! Tick! Fffft! Fffft! The engine roared to life.

"Ha ha! Yes. Yes." He gunned it to a healthy rev, then stepped out and closed the hood. The moon's location signified about an hour until the hunters returned and for him to slip out. But before that, he wanted to locate a replacement laptop and give his goodbyes to Elio and Bingham.

He pressed a foot to the brake to move it out of park when the engine's idle whirred into a high-pitched idle.

"Damn it."

Rrrrrr! Fnnnnn!

He tried to open the door, but the handle to the old jalopy fell off. "Of course."

The engine raced and screeched, and smoke billowed from under the deck lid and filled the cabin. He cut the engine.

Bam! The hood blew open. A fire ignited.

FLAMES SHOT OUT FROM a pickup truck, and smoke engulfed it. Mat grabbed the fire extinguisher he'd taken with him from the cottage. "I know I asked for a purpose, God, but you don't need to keep bringing me fires." He pulled its safety pin and aimed the nozzle at the engine. A weak stream of foam bubbled out. "Great."

"*Save the dog,*" a familiar voice said.

He spun around, then dropped the fire extinguisher. "T-t-ty?"

An ethereal image of his son hovered a few inches off the road. He wore the pink sneakers and matching nail polish they had fought over. While Mat riled against his son's effeminate side, his wife had caved in and bought him the girls' running shoes the child wanted.

Ty pointed to the burning truck. "That dog's for you."

"What?"

His son pointed.

"It's a car fire, Ty. Not a dog." He paused. "I'm not seeing my dead son. It's the pills."

Ty vanished.

"No, Ty wait!" He paused. "Maybe I am losing it."

The fire raged behind him.

He looked up to the sky. "God, I did what I could to protect my family. I hope it was enough."

Smoke billowed near, and Mat coughed. He didn't need three years of fire training with the U.S. Forest Service to know the truck was beyond help. He was more concerned about the nearby trees catching fire. He retreated to his Toyota RAV4—the one he'd driven from California after he quit the force—to dial 911, but there was no reception.

A wind roared. It rustled papers he had in the Toyota, and he had to hold onto the open door to keep steady. Branches rustled. Mat feared the squall would fan the flames.

But when he caught sight of the truck, he raked a hand over his face in disbelief as the fire went out.

The truck ticked.

Mat stood motionless.

Burnt metal radiated heat.

He moved toward it. With the smoke dissipating, he could tell the driver's side window had been kicked out, and a boot laid on the ground next to shattered glass.

"Oh my God." Mat rushed closer, forgetting not to touch the hot handle, then removed his T-shirt to use it to open the door.

"A . . . a dog . . . No. That's not a . . . It's a wolf."

CHAPTER FIVE

A Metanormal

FROM AN OPEN GARAGE bay, Jezebel dragged her stepson's limp wolf carcass by the scruff of his neck. "Come, you mongrel. I have a vested interest in seeing this wolf-shifter species survive. God forbid you make me break a nail."

As wolf, Diesel whimpered.

She looked up at the moon. "Five more days, then I don't care what the hell you do."

"Hey, Lady!" a tall, Black man yelled from the front porch of the cabin across the lawn. "Where the hell do you think you're taking that wolf?" He jumped over the porch rail and onto the grass.

"Oh, a human. How fun." Jezebel dropped Diesel—head onto the ribbon driveway. "None of your business, Homo sapien."

"Excuse me?"

"Oh, please. Mr. Man, you have no idea what you're getting yourself into."

"That's a wolf. You have no place treating it like that."

"Ew, I can smell your human stink from here."

"Lady, what the hell is wrong with you? Is this your wolf?"

"Unfortunately, he does belong to the pack."

"The pack."

"Wolf pack. Duh."

He neared. "I saved the wolf. It was injured in a car fire. He's in no position to be dragged around like a rag doll. I have a call into the wildlife rescue to get him in the morning."

"You'll do no such thing."

"It's done, lady. You know, for someone who left their pet wolf in a truck that caught fire, I don't think you're in much of a position to be telling me what to do.

She laughed. "Truck. You think I'd be caught in one of those things. Now don't let me use my shifting skills to harm you. Not that I care about your safety, it's just I hate to ruin my dress and these nails, I just had them done."

Mat shook his head. "It's a violation of Maine law to contain a wild animal. Do you have a permit?" He lowered to Diesel's side and grabbed the wolf-tooth amulet around his neck. "These are not pets, ma'am. Keep the wolf here, lady. He's injured. I'll see that he's properly taken care of."

"Dear Satan in Heaven, you leave me no choice." She rolled up her sleeves.

"Satan in—?"

She bared her snout and growled.

"The hell! Get away from me, bitch." He crab-walked backward.

She lunged full-on wolf and slammed up against an invisible barricade around him. Jezebel shrieked and retreated. "What . . . what in the hell are you?"

T WILIGHT SCRAPED THE HORIZON, and a dim hue cast on the door to Buck and Mitsy's den. Honoree knocked louder this time while Jezebel wobbled in a broken high heel.

"You should've woken me right away," Honoree said. "Why a beautiful woman like you chose to go out in the middle of the night without the protection of her man, I'll never know."

"Yes, Honoree. I was a bad wife." Jezebel fidgeted with a tear in her gown that exposed part of her olive skin.

He brushed back strands of hair that drooped over her face. "We'll get you cleaned up. This just goes to show you, you need me to watch over you. It could've been even worse. What if Diesel turned on you like he did to me? You wouldn't have been able to defend yourself. You saw what that ungrateful canine-shifter did to me."

"I know, Honoree. I know." She rolled her eyes. "You're right. What was I thinking? But I'm telling you, there was a Metanormal looking after him."

"Shush, none of that. We don't need to get the forest riled up. Now, my little lady, let's not go spreading rumors." Poised to rap again, the door opened.

"What are you doing here at this time of—Good Satan, Jezebel, what happened to you?" Buck let them in.

"The little missus went out looking for my loser son . . . on her own."

"On your own! Diesel did that to you? That son of a bitch."

"It wasn't Diesel," Jezebel said. "It was a meta—"

"Jezzy says a . . . says a human was holding Diesel hostage."

"A human? A human made it into Hubbard Forest without a vampire getting to it?"

"It wasn't just a—"

"I know, Jezzy," Buck said, "sometimes those humans are hard to take down."

"It wasn't *just* a human."

"She says he was a man," Honoree whispered.

Mitsy came out from the bedroom tying a robe around her waist. "What's going on? Did you say Diesel's in danger?"

"The traitor tried leaving the forest," Jezebel said, "but apparently his jalopy caught fire, and a Metanormal came to his rescue."

Buck leaned in. "Metanormal?"

"Buck." Honoree shook his head. "I'll go scope out the situation. The missus is just a little flustered from the situation is all."

"Yes, master." Jezebel sighed. "I've seen the error of my ways. But more importantly I need my nails fixed and a hot shower."

Buck turned toward the bedroom. "Mitsy! Mitsy! Your father and step-mother are—"

"I'm right here, Buck. Geez. C'mon Jezebel, let's get you cleaned up. What the heaven happened?"

"Don't swear, Mits," Buck said. "The baby . . . Remember, he can hear your negative vibration."

"Of course, Buck." Mitsy led Jezebel to the bathroom.

"Oh, I dread the thought of wearing acrylics, Mits. I just hate those snap-ons."

After getting Jezebel washed up, they sat at the kitchen table while the men drank from tin cups and discussed their strategy. Jezebel wore a towel, and Mitsy tended to her nails.

"Humans bad." Buck toasted Honoree.

The alpha laughed. "Long live the Supers!" He clinked Buck's cup.

"Long live the wolf-shifters!"

"You boys aren't drinking this early, are you?" Mitsy asked.

They snickered. "'Course not."

"I can do this on my own, Buck." Honoree sipped.

"Let me go with you. If there's a human in the forest," Buck said in a lowered voice, "who has lasted this long without a vampire sucking their blood and left in the boneyard, it could very well be a Metanormal."

"Look, Buck. I mean no disregard for your religion but . . . do you really believe in Big Foot?"

"Huh?"

"Big Foot. It was something Diesel told me he had learned about humans . . . at university. A mythical creature humans believe in, is all I'm saying." Honoree sank back the last of his drink, then leaned in closer to his friend. "Do you really believe in this Rise of the Normals bull crap?"

Buck swigged from his cup. "I do. The scriptures say that the normal human being will advance into a species far more magical than any Super. Their rise could be our demise. Lord Darthius is our only salvation."

"I don't know, Buck. The scriptures also say it's a sin to eat shellfish."

"Well, luckily, we're too far inland to be dining on lobster and shrimp. Plus, the double barrier should protect us."

"The barriers protect humans not us. They can get in for feeding, but we can't get out."

"Look, I don't need schooling in Barriers 101. I understand. What I meant was, the barriers do protect us. They keep us from getting too close to shore to eat shellfish for one." Buck chuckled. "The White Queen implores supernaturals to continue our cross-species alliance. Vampires and shifters mingle now. We're becoming stronger as a result."

"But wolf-shifters are still endangered. Which is why it's so important for Diesel to mate."

"Well, let's not let a little Homo sapien get in the way."

"It's more powerful than an ordinary Homo sapien." Jezebel placed her other hand out for Mitsy to file. "Easy with my cuticles, dear. They weren't that damaged."

"It's okay, love," Honoree said. "I'll take care of it."

Mitsy set Jezebel's hand in a warm bowl of water. "Guys, maybe we should let Diesel be. After all, he's an adult. He'll do what's right."

Jezebel leaned closer to the table's edge. "You really think your brother is capable of doing what's right?"

Mitsy snipped off a piece of Jezebel's broken nail.

"Ouch!"

"I know you two haven't always seen eye to eye," Mitsy said, "but he always does the right thing in the end."

"Hm." Jezebel sat back. "Oh, my dress. That was such a waste of a shift. Do you really think the seamstress can patch it up?"

Mitsy nodded.

"Maybe the vampires are just full from their feast last night," Honoree said.

"Since the White Queen banned them from transforming people in order to contain the vampire population, perhaps they're not as hungry and drinking too much." Buck set his cup down. "Honoree III, we haven't gone human hunting in quite some time. For old times' sake, let's go, then get your good-for-nothing son so he can grow this pack."

"Buck, I thought you were going to stay with me," Mitsy said.

Jezebel raised an eyebrow. "Don't you want to see your brother's return to the pack?"

"Of . . . of course."

X ANAX HADN'T QUIETED MAT'S overactive mind much, and his prescription ran low. Thoughts of his son speaking to him, vampires, a wolf inside a burning vehicle, and a crazy lady trying to steal it, kept Mat up past sunrise.

Click, click.

Groggily, Mat covered his head with a pillow to drown out the noise.

Pfft, pfft.

"The hell," he thought.

The noise from the opposite side of the cabin grew louder. He bolted upright in bed and grabbed his rifle resting against the nightstand.

A rustling— "in the kitchen?"—intensified. He pulled back the covers, crept out of bed—careful to let the bedsprings not squeak too loudly—and pointed the rifle toward the sound. "Please let it be a rat." He skulked forward.

Click, click. It sounded like someone typing. He'd left his computer at the kitchen table after looking up the number for the wildlife rescue.

With his back to the wall near the entrance to the bathroom, he peered around the corner, then burst out, rifle first, at . . .

A bristly, naked man . . . typing at the table.

"Get the hell outta here!" Mat said.

The man rocketed up with muscular arms raised. "Sorry, sir." He was tall, dark haired, solid build, and unshaven. "I was just . . . trying to reach my friend. I mean no harm."

Mat motioned with the rifle to the door for the man to leave.

The naked man shuffled around the kitchen's circular table, following Mat's prompts. "You're a real, live human."

Mat furrowed his brow.

"I saw you sleeping, didn't want to disturb you." The man backed his way toward the door. "I've studied your species for so long. I'm just . . . just honored to be in your presence."

Mat recognized the tooth amulet the man wore. "What's that around your neck?"

"This?" He touched it. "It's my buddy Bence's totem. He's the one I was trying to email. He has mine. Name's Diesel." He stepped closer to Mat with an arm extended.

"Get back!"

"I mean no harm." Diesel jumped back—hands up, junk flopping.

"Do you often go around naked, breaking into people's homes to use the internet?"

"No, sir. There are not a lot of hu . . . people . . . in fact, there are no people here. They don't last . . . never mind."

"They don't what? This friggin' place is crazy."

"It must be tough for you comprehending it all. At university they taught us most humans don't believe in . . . well, I learned that it can be a shock for humans."

"Believe?" When Mat scooched closer, a burn mark on Diesel's right foot came into focus. "Where did you get that burn?"

"I was trying to start my damn truck and it caught fire."

"That was your truck?"

"You saw it?"

"I saw it all right, plus the wolf locked inside and then some crazy lady who came to get it."

"Jezebel? She came? Why didn't she take me?"

Mat's mind raced: The lady lunging at him, then retreating. "I must be losing it. This can't be real," he thought.

"Sir, are you okay? Do you need to sit down?"

"Get out!"

"Okay. Again, I mean no harm." Diesel turned and limped toward the door.

"Why are you naked?"

"It happens when I shift."

"Sh-shift?"

Diesel faced him. "I can explain it, but I'm not sure you're ready. You should leave. If the vamp—never mind."

"The vam . . . vampires?"

"Did you see them?"

Mat grew dizzy.

Diesel rushed to his side.

The gun fell to the floor, and Diesel caught Mat before he went down with it. "Let's get you some water."

Diesel's touch was electrifying. Mat let the naked man lead him into the kitchen. He sat down while Diesel drew water from the tap and handed him a glass. "Thank . . . thank you."

Diesel sat beside him.

Mat drank. "I'm a bit weirded out is all."

"Makes sense. I would be too. When I crossed over into your realm, the few times I have, I was mesmerized too. We took a couple of field trips at university."

"My . . . my realm?"

"That's what we call it." Diesel stood. "You want some more water?"

Mat avoided looking at the man's privates. "I'm . . . I'm all set with it. Thank you."

Diesel sat.

"That . . . that wolf that was in your truck. Was he yours?"

"Sorta."

"You know it's illegal to . . . I've got the wildlife rescue coming today to check it. I locked it in my garage so that Jezebel person wouldn't harm it. She was dragging the poor thing. I didn't want her to hurt it. In fact, you should check it. Make sure it's okay. I left it some water and the rest of a ham sandwich I had in the fridge."

"It was good."

"Huh?"

"Sir—"

"Name's Mat."

"Mat, the wolf isn't in your garage . . . anymore."

A chill ran down Mat's spine. He stared at Diesel's amulet, then the burnt foot. "Where . . . where is he?"

Diesel paused, then put a hand to his chest. "He's right here. Thank you for rescuing me."

Mat passed out.

DIESEL CARRIED MAT BACK to the bed. "Oh my God, he's beautiful. A real human." He set him down and brushed a bead of sweat off Mat's forehead. The man's scent smelled like nothing he'd ever sensed before. He leaned in to relish it further. Mat's hair was cropped tight. His dark skin radiant.

Diesel sniffed the crook of his neck. He wanted to lick it, but Mat stirred and moaned.

Mat grabbed Diesel's hand as it examined his chest.

"Strong," Diesel said. "Solid."

Mat guided Diesel's hand to his abs, then toward the band of his boxers.

Diesel stepped back, noticing Mat's arousal.

Mat woke. "The hell!"

Diesel covered the launching of his own excitement. "You got a pair of pants I can borrow?"

IN MAT'S JEANS AND a loose-fitting T-shirt, Diesel swept glass from the broken window he had escaped out of in the detached garage. As he emptied the dust pan's contents into a metal barrel, the hair on the back of his neck bristled, then something grabbed him and dragged him, headfirst, out of the bay.

"You're coming with us." Honoree dropped him to the ground. "It's not a choice."

Buck stepped out from the other side of the garage. "Listen to your father, Dan Diesel. You have an obligation to procreate. You know the wolf-shifter species is on the verge of extinction. And you're the last of your father's lineage."

"I know already. I don't care about that," Diesel said. "You know what I am."

"Oh?" Honoree said. "What exactly are you?"

"I'm a . . . I'm a humansexual, like it or not."

Honoree spit. "I knew it. A Satan-damned huma."

"It's all right, Hon. We'll get through this. He can still reproduce."

Diesel brushed gravel off his knees and rose.

"Mitsy is counting on you," Buck said to him. "She needs you. Despite what she may say, she needs her brother to help her through this pregnancy and be there for her new son. You can't walk out on family. Why would you?"

Mat burst out from the cabin door and down onto the grass. "What the hell is going on?"

"Ah, there's the human I heard about," Honoree said. "None of your business, Homo."

"Who you calling—"

"He means Homo sapien." Diesel adjusted his shirt.

"I asked a question. I expect an answer." Mat stepped closer to the men. "What is going on? You're on private property."

"Private property." Honoree laughed. "The last humans that lived here never made it out alive. I'm surprised you made it this long."

Mat hitched an eyebrow.

"Don't listen to them, Mat," Diesel said. "They're just trying to scare you's all."

Honoree grasped Diesel by the shirt sleeve. "Let's go."

"Wait!" Mat stepped closer. "Where are you taking him?"

"Back to the pack where he belongs." Buck followed Honoree to the edge of the forest.

"Diesel?" Mat asked. "Are you going on your own recognizance?"

"Um, my own what?"

"Do you want to go with them?"

"Mat, I appreciate all you did for me. But maybe they're right. I have an obligation to the pack . . . to my family . . . to a species."

"I'm glad you're seeing reason," Buck said. "I told you, Honoree, it's just a phase these young kids go through sometimes. They think life is better on the other side."

"Leave him." Mat placed his hands on Buck and Honoree's exposed shoulders.

Stunned, Honoree jumped back. "For Satan's sake!" He rubbed his arm, as did Buck.

"Human, you think it's funny tasering a wolf-shifter?" Buck got in Mat's face. "You don't know what you're getting yourself into, Homo." He and Mat stared each other down. "Maybe we should have him for lunch, Hon. The pack hasn't had human meat in decades. We're supposed to leave you for the vampires—queen's orders."

Mat punched Buck in the face, and the wolf-shifter fell on his back.

Honoree dove at Mat, but, before he reached him, he slammed up against an invisible wall and collapsed backward.

Diesel stood mouth opened.

"You okay?" Mat asked Diesel.

"Humans aren't supposed to be able to do that." Diesel looked at Honoree and Buck's motionless bodies. "They're out cold."

"I don't know what came over me. I don't like them, Diesel. Something deep inside me tells me so. I've never felt such a wave of hatred before."

Buck stirred.

"You should go, Mat. You don't belong in this forest. When they wake, they're going to shift. You won't be able to fight them off." Diesel looked up at him. "Unless you're a . . ."

"A what?"

Honoree groaned.

Buck shifted first, then Diesel's father.

They gnarled and snapped at Mat. When they lunged, Mat kicked Buck in the stomach, then elbowed Honoree in the snout. Both whelped.

Honoree nipped at Diesel, landing him on his back and dragging him to the edge of the forest. Diesel kicked. Honoree bit his burnt calf. "Argh!"

Buck joined, bit his free leg, and dragged him closer to the brush.

He didn't want to shift, if he could avoid it, and ruin the borrowed clothes. "Let me go, Dad! All right, I'll come!"

"No, you won't." Mat kicked Honoree in the chest. "Get off him!"

Honoree shrieked. Buck let go of Diesel.

"What the hell kind of father treats their son like that? Let . . . let your son do as he pleases." Mat fell to his knees, head down and sobbed as the wolves ran off deep into the forest.

CHAPTER SIX

Devotion

M AT POURED THE CONTENTS of a Jim Beam bottle down the kitchen sink. "A humansexual?"

Diesel leaned against the counter. "It's a sin for humans and Supers to mate . . . to love."

"I must be losing my friggin' mind. This . . . this mystical crap all makes no sense."

"That's why you should leave. You don't belong here. The queen extended the barrier last summer to include this cabin, and others, for the vampires to—"

"I don't want to hear it, Diesel. This is ludicrous!" Mat tossed the empty bottle into the trash and headed for the bedroom.

"I don't mean to confuse you or make you feel like you're going crazy. I'm just telling you—"

"Telling me what, Diesel!" Mat shouted from the bedroom and Diesel followed. "What?" Mat stood with a prescription bottle.

"I'm a humansexual. I'm sympathetic to the plight of humanity. It's not a very popular opinion in these parts."

"So, I should be grateful you haven't eaten me?" Mat shook his head, went to the bathroom, emptied the contents of the bottle in the toilet, and flushed. "The booze and pills. That's what it is. There's no friggin' magical world in Hubbard Forest. I'm seeing things. Maybe you're just a figment of my imagination. Is that what you are?"

"Huh?" Diesel followed him into the bedroom.

Mat rushed and shoved him in the chest. "Are you real? Are you friggin' real?"

DIESEL GRASPED HIS WRISTS, and they tussled. Mat fell back onto the bed with Diesel atop him. He pinned his arms over his head. "I know it's hard to believe," Diesel said, inches from Mat's face.

Mat's heavy breath and strong human scent enticed Diesel. He rolled off him to prevent shifting and ravishing the man as his instinct to hunt reared.

Mat's breathing quieted. "My friend, Trinity, this is her parent's place. She needs to sell it. They left her saddled in debt." Mat stared at the ceiling. "Wait . . . your father said something about the people who lived here never making it out alive." He got up onto his elbows. "That was Trinity's parents. They were found dead with their little one in Acadia in a slip-and-fall hiking Cadillac Mountain."

"My father. Don't pay any attention to him. He just assumed the vampires drained the prior residents and disposed of them in the Trash Heap as they're supposed to."

"Trash Heap? I don't even want to know what that is." Mat sat up. "So, this humansexual thing. You like humans?"

"Yes."

"Have you ever been . . . ? How do you know?"

"I just do. Ever since I was a kid I longed to live like a human and was . . . attracted to them. I'd find old human magazines at the Trash Heap, a boneya— um, junkyard for discarded . . .things. My friend Bence and I liked to look at the people."

"But you look human. Well, when you're not a dog—"

"Wolf."

"When you're not a wolf, that is. And your father, his friend, and your stepmother. They're not human?"

Diesel laughed. "Far from it. We look human, in our non-canine form. It's an evolutionary thing to blend in so we can hunt undetected amongst humans."

"Comforting."

"But you can tell the difference between a Super and a Pure—a human that is. Pures, real humans, are much more delicate and beautiful. It's hard to describe." Their eyes locked for a moment, till Mat looked away.

"Over a century ago, the Wizard War's resolution saw the creation of the dual barrier—or the 'Double Bubble,' as some of us call it. It was placed over the forest to contain and protect us since Supers are dwindling. The thought being it would make Supers stronger to fight against the rise of what's called the normal . . . ordinary human."

"The rise of the human?"

"We call it the Rise of the Normals. It's been feared for millennia. It's written in the scriptures that humans could threaten Supers' existence by becoming more powerful than any supernatural or paranormal creature before it."

Mat rose and went to the window. "I'm sorry. And you're saying I'm one of those mega—"

"Meta . . . Metanormals."

"Metanormals who will overthrow vampires and wolf-shifters?"

Diesel sat up. "And mages, wizards, witches, fairies—all Supers. You see, humans fall into a couple of categories. I love this stuff . . . studied it at uni. Graduated with honors."

"They teach this to . . . to Supers?"

"Of course. You see, most humans or Pures do not exhibit magic. They're called Normals."

"Normals? Normal Pures."

"Uh huh. Then there are those Normals who develop . . . and the jury's still out on how . . . . They develop the capacity to manifest magic without the wands, potions, and things Supers need to create it. They're similar to a wizard but even more powerful."

"This is a lot to take in."

"The Rise has increased substantially over the last century or two. It baffles superkind. Normals becoming Metanormals. Most Supers feel threatened by your existence, while some of us think it's cool . . . very few of us."

"And I thought being Black and Korean was unique enough." Mat chuckled.

"That's unique?"

"My dad was from South Korea. My mom African American."

"Oh."

After a bit of silence, Mat faced the window and leaned up against the sill. "So, if I'm supposed to overthrow your species why do you . . . like humans?"

Diesel rose and stood behind the man. "Some of us don't believe all that bullshit in the scriptures. Our buddy Luke got out last year and messaged us back that there's a whole world out there of supernaturals and Pures who mingle. He's a witch and settled down with a girl—a pure human."

Mat spotted the ashtray and empty glass on the nearby table. "I could use a drink . . . or a cigarette."

"Didn't you just throw all that away?"

"I know what I did, Diesel." Mat pinched the bridge of his nose. "Look, I'm sorry."

Diesel leaned beside him against the windowsill. "I was escaping. When you found me . . . in the truck . . . I was trying to get out of here. My friend Bence—"

"The one who stole your totem? The one you fantasized over magazines with?"

"How'd you know about us and the magazines?"

"I was a kid once too."

"He didn't steal my totem. We exchanged them when he left. But yes, that Bence." Diesel touched the amulet. "Bence is a humansexual too."

"And he's a wolf-shifter?" Mat chuckled. "I can't believe I'm acknowledging this."

"Yes, he is. This weekend is the Howling Moon. Bence and I were expected to take a mate, a she-wolf, and procreate as it's our twenty-first year. He and I are the last of the line. There are very few healthy males left in our pack."

"Hence your father's demands . . . not that it makes it right."

"But yes, that's why he's been such a jerk. My sister, Mitsy, she's pregnant with a boy."

"Oh, well that must float his boat."

"It does, but she's a female."

"So."

"So, women are not valued like they are in your realm."

"I'd say that's a stretch, but I get your point."

"They need the paternal line to continue."

"Where's Bence?"

"Probably in Salem by now."

"Massachusetts?"

Diesel nodded.

"In Salem, Supers and humans can coexist there. We want to love who we love, Mat. Be who we are."

Mat left the bedroom.

"What's wrong?" Diesel limped after him.

"You should go, Diesel. To Salem. And find a nice . . . human to settle down with."

"But my sister. The thought of leaving her behind with her arsehole husband, Buck. And abandoning her with her new baby . . ."

"What does she think?"

"She told me to go."

"Well?"

"I know. I'm torn between following my heart and doing what I should."

Mat pulled out two sodas from the fridge and offered one to Diesel. "Always follow your heart, Diesel. Not that I'm one to offer advice."

Diesel cracked open the drink. "Oh, a mystery. I love me a secret."

Mat smirked while sipping. "I was a shitty husband and a shittier father."

"Past tense?"

"My wife and boy . . . my kid. They both died in a fire."

"Oh, I'm sorry."

"In my heart of hearts, I wanted to be there with them. Stay behind and protect them from the wildfires, but I had to work."

"Work. I've always wanted to work . . . have a job. It sounds so purposeful. Take my truck to the shop . . . or the plant . . . or maybe even an office . . . and do something to expand human society."

"You really have a skewed sense of our . . . realm."

"Skewed? Some of your finest men and women are what you deem ordinary. I'm sorry. You were saying? I want to hear more. What happened to your family?"

"They perished in a wildfire that ravaged our neighborhood."

"Why the guilt?"

"Who said I was guilty?"

"I was a kid once too." Diesel winked. "What do you do . . . for work?"

"Is this an interview?"

"I'm human-curious, remember?"

"I used to fight fires for the U.S. Forest Service."

"Ah, hence the guilt. What do you mean 'used to?'"

"I quit last fall. It's been two years since my family perished when the Donlan Fire consumed Northern California."

"And you were off fighting it elsewhere? That's noble. Your family's death was an unfortunate accident."

Mat gazed at the floor. "There's more."

Diesel waited.

"My wife and I were on the splits. My son. We argued constantly over how to best raise him."

"How so?"

"He liked to dress like . . . like a girl."

Diesel blinked.

"You see, in our society . . . the human realm . . . that's not . . . it's not . . . people look down on it."

"I dress in twenty-first century clothes, while traditionalist wolf-shifters and werewolves wear animal fur and hides."

"Werewolves? Wolf-shifters? There's a difference."

"Think of us as a subset of werewolves. Werewolves have no control. Wolf-shifters do."

"Control?"

"Over shifting."

"I can't believe I'm having this conversation."

"It's fascinating if you think about it. Over the last few centuries, we've comingled with other Supers. It's supposed to make us stronger . . . as a genus. Werewolves are believed to be the lowest of species. I don't really buy all this shit. I just live here."

"Jezebel . . . she had on a dress."

"The women have more leeway, as long as it's period."

"Period."

"A costume from what you would call the nineteenth century, Victorian."

"I won't ask why."

"It shows one's devotion to the Dark Lord, to the period we lost out to human's rise . . . so it's believed. Modern clothing . . . actually, anything contemporary, is an affront to our religion, which I don't buy either."

"You're quite the rebel."

"Bence was . . . is too. Societal norms are sometimes best broken. How else can we grow?"

Mat soaked it in for a moment. "Go to Salem, Diesel. Be who you are. *Us* humans," he laughed, "don't always do that. If you've got the chance, take it. Don't look back."

Diesel sat at the kitchen table. "I ain't gonna get far with this." He put his foot up on the empty chair.

"Oh, damn. Your father made it worse. Let me get some more bandages."

Mat returned with some salve and dressed Diesel's foot.

Diesel relished the human's caring touch. "This should at least get me to Elio. He can heal me up, then I can catch the portal's opening at noon."

"Dare I ask?"

"Elio. He's a dragon."

Mat shot up, and the chair he had been sitting in slammed up against a cupboard.

"It's complicated, but Bence and I discovered a way out of the Double Bubble, but you got to catch the portal when it's opened. If I leave now, I should be able to get to Elio for dragon tears. No doubt he'll cry when I tell him and Bingham I'm leaving."

"Dragon . . . dragon tears?"

"Bingham's not a dragon."

"Of course not. Why should I think—?"

"He's an abandoned wolf-shifter. Elio takes care of him. He's what your society would call 'intellectually impaired.' Bingham suffered a birth defect, stunted in mid-shift—part human-looking and part wolf. He ain't pretty, but he's a great guy."

"Someone abandoned him at birth?"

"Supers don't take kindly to those of us who don't fit in."

"Sounds like SoCal."

Diesel tied the sneakers Mat gave him. "Bence and I are humas. Remember?"

"But you look . . ."

"Yeah, I don't look like a humansexual."

"That's not what I meant. I just meant you're pretty strong . . . good . . . good looking. I would think you'd be an asset to—"

"Not if I can't get it up for a she-wolf." Diesel stood. "And good-looking? I think you need your eyes checked."

"You don't think you're attractive?" Mat's phone rang. "That's Trinity. The one whose parents owned this—"

Diesel's mouth fell open as he eyed the red-head's image flashing on Mat's phone. "Wow, she's beautiful."

"So, you like . . . girls?"

"I like humans."

They stared at each other while the phone danced across the table.

"You gonna answer it?"

Mat grabbed the phone. "Trin, hold on one sec." He covered the receiver.

"I should let you go." Diesel took his free hand. "Thanks again for everything. If you're ever in Salem, look me up. I'll return your clothes . . . buy you a beer." He chuckled. "I always wanted to say that, 'buy a—'"

Mat inched closer. "My son said you were for . . . that you were important for me." He moved in. "He wasn't wrong."

"Mat?" Trinity's voice peeped out from the phone. "You there, Mat?"

"Your son?" Diesel asked. "I thought he—?"

"It's a long story."

"Mat," Trinity said. "Do you want me to call back at another time?"

"Bye, Mat." Diesel embraced the man.

Mat dropped the phone. They both reached for it and hit heads. "Sorry, I can get . . ."

"No, allow me." Diesel handed him the phone, then went for the door. "You were important for me too, Mat."

Mat grinned, then eyed is his phone and his face blanched. "Trinity! I didn't know you had me on video chat."

From the cabin's other bedroom, Mat held his phone over a box he had removed from the closet so Trinity could see its contents. "This it?"

"Yes, that's the one," Trinity said. "Thank you. I had hoped my parents left it there. My brother will be happy. We loved playing those old games, and looking through the old photographs."

Mat closed the lid. "I'll leave it out to take back to Elk."

"I'll take it with me when I come up this weekend."

"About that. Maybe you should—"

"Hold on." As displayed on Mat's phone, Trinity rose from her desk and the chalkboard behind her came into view. "Good morning, Sarah." She smiled. "Mat, my aide just arrived, and the school busses will be here soon."

"I can let you—" he said.

"I'm gonna grab a coffee from the cafe, you want something?" her aide asked.

"That would be awesome. Thank you."

"Green tea?"

"You know what I like," Trinity said. The door closed. "So, Mat...who was that?"

"Who was what?" Mat left the main bedroom with the box of memorabilia and games in hand.

"Don't play dumb. The guy you were . . . you were talking to when you answered the phone."

Mat plunked the box on a barstool at the kitchen island. "Some guy . . . lives nearby."

Trinity set the phone on her desk and erased the chalkboard. "Some *hot* guy."

Mat smirked.

"You like him?" Trinity smiled, hand on hips.

"Trinity! No. For God sake."

"Mat, it's okay."

"There's nothing to be . . . to be okay about, Trinity." Mat huffed.

"Look, all I'm saying is that maybe the reason you were so harsh on Ty wasn't so much about who *he* was but about—"

"Enough, Trinity! Gosh, between you and Isabel I don't know who's worse."

"We just want you to be happy."

The classroom door opened beside her, and the aide backed in with a wheelchair. "They're here. Coffee's going to have to wait."

Chapter Seven

The Meeting

I N AN OPEN, GRASSY area surrounded by large maple trees, an impromptu clan meeting convened outside the wolf dens.

"It broke my friggin' tooth!" Ketch yelled, his shattered incisor visible to the cluster of vampires, shifters, ogres, and others surrounding him. "How am I supposed to feed with one fang?"

"Order! Order!" Honoree banged the gavel. A diverse board of male Supers flanked him. "We mustn't panic."

Mitsy picked at her fingernails.

In the back benches reserved for females, Jezebel sat cross-legged next to Mitsy. "We need a witch!" she shouted.

The crowd hushed.

A hunched-back ogre whispered to a smaller one beside him. "This is a matter for men. She doesn't know when to keep her trap shut." His friend snickered.

Jezebel rolled her eyes at Mitsy.

Honoree clanked the gavel again. "I'm afraid my wife is right."

"Afraid?" she mouthed to Mitsy.

Mitsy leaned into her. "Jezebel, we shouldn't involve Lena. It's danger—"

Jezebel rose. "It's a woman's job to ask for the White Queen's assistance."

A she-wolf beside Mitsy muttered to her friend, "It's a woman's job to know her place."

Jezebel squared her shoulders. "I shall ask the White Queen to lend us her witch and perform a Metanormal-detecting spell. A rogue, infected human could tear this village apart."

"We should dispose of it in the Trash Heap," a faerie said

"Obviously. If we could kill it, we would," said a mage.

"Not till I drain its blood!" Pedro shouted, and Ketch nodded.

"And I eat its flesh," a wolf-shifter added.

Mitsy tugged at Jezebel's sleeve. "Only Witch Lena can perform that spell," she whispered. "And if it's a real Metanormal, it might not even work. I need her to stay safe so she can protect my baby."

"Quiet, child." Jezebel worked her way through the row of women, then pushed out from the throngs of men. "My dear husband, it would be an honor for me to provide my service to the pack and this community." She faced the crowd, leaning back onto the board's table. "It's for the betterment of our clan that this Metanormal be extinguished and for my stepson to return to the pack, where he can strengthen the wolf-shifter species."

A she-wolf behind Mitsy whispered to her friend. "Diesel? Who'd want to be mounted by that huma?"

Mitsy spun around. "Quiet, bitch. That's my brother you're talking about."

The shifter's snout snapped forward, and she growled.

"Order! Order! Folks, please. We mustn't let this matter go unresolved. My wife is correct. The Metanormal must be stopped."

The vampire sitting beside Honoree at the board's table raised his hand. "I make a motion to allow Honoree's wife to summon a witch to kill the Metanormal and return Diesel to his pack."

"I second," said Buck.

"All in favor?" Honoree asked.

"Aye!" shouted the board of directors, who all rose their hands.

"All opposed?"

The hands went down.

Honoree banged the gavel. "The motion has passed unanimously. Let it be stated, Mr. Secretary, in the clan's records. I move to adjourn the meeting."

The crowd squabbled and disbanded.

When the gathering thinned, Mitsy approached Jezebel.

"I so tire of these stupid men," Jezebel said. "It's time a woman takes a stance, don't you agree?"

Mitsy twisted her wedding band. "Jezebel, you know how I feel about the safety of my baby."

"Yes, Mits. I know. Witch Lena will just cast a little spell." Jezebel let some Supers leaving pass. "Our little plan is still intact."

"You promised the safety of my child."

"I'm a promise keeper." Jezebel sashayed away and flung a hand in the air. "Have no fear, it's Jezebel's year."

A T THE OPENING OF the dragon's moss-covered cave, Diesel placed a shoe back on his healed foot. Elio blew his nose with a trumpet-like blare that shot flames down the embankment to the expanse below.

Bingham, who played ball in the field with a three-armed ogre, looked up, saw Diesel, and ran—as best he could with his one human-like leg and the other in wolf form—toward them.

Elio clicked and cooed while Diesel interpreted the dragon speak.

"I realize he's going to miss me." Diesel looked down. "I'll miss him—"

The dragon placed a paw on Diesel's shoulder and chirped further.

"Thanks, Elio. You're right. It *is* time to move on. Hubbard Forest isn't a place for me . . . for rebels."

"Tell Heel I said goodbye. I know he's not good with farewells anyway."

Elio nodded. His husband, Heel, often worked abroad for the king and had been in Yorkshire for months.

Diesel and Elio sauntered down the grassy slope and met Bingham halfway, where the boy tackled Diesel upon seeing him.

"W-what you d-do here?" Bingham's half-formed snout made it difficult for him to speak.

"Hey, kid. How's it going? I see you like the football I got you?"

Bingham nodded, then waved to his ogre friend who traipsed off into the forest. "Play?"

"Come here, fella." Diesel grabbed the boy before he could run off to grab the ball.

Elio clicked an order, and the boy faced the dragon. "'S matter, dad?" He obeyed the dragon's prompt and sat beside Diesel.

"This is difficult for me to say," Diesel said. "You know I don't like to disappoint people, but it's time to do the right thing for Dan Diesel Cade. Something he's wanted for a long time."

Elio clicked.

Diesel looked up at the dragon. "Yes, I know I'm talking about myself in the third person. It . . . it helps me separate myself from the situation some."

Elio rolled his eyes.

Diesel huffed. "I need to do what's right for me, Bingham."

The kid scrunched his furry brow.

"I need to leave the forest for a while."

Elio cooed.

"Well, maybe more than a while," Diesel corrected.

"You j-j-just back from uni." Bingham said, looking down at his half paws.

"Hubbard Forest isn't the place for a man like me to settle down in, Bing. As humans say, 'I need to spread my wings.'"

Bingham laughed. "You have no wings. My Dad's got wings."

Elio hugged the boy.

Bingham looked up at the dragon. "We go visit? Like at UPS?"

Elio clacked, and Bingham frowned.

"But Salem is accepting of Supers," Diesel said. "Why can't you visit?"

The dragon clicked.

"Yeah, I suppose a dragon walking the streets of Salem, even if they are progressive, would freak out a few humans."

Elio embraced him, and a dragon tear splashed onto Diesel's head.

A T HIGH NOON, THE tree portal glowed, and Diesel entered its hollow. "Come on, tree. You should turn orange any second now."

He had memorized the paces and steps to take once out: *About one mile from the portal, take a left onto the gravel road, then another five paces into the woods. Behind the boulder, lift the second barrier's bluish, electric screen.* It was a tight squeeze, according to Bence's email that he had read on Mat's laptop.

From there, the world awaited. "Bence. Bence. Bence. Let's get this party start—"

The red light flickered, turned yellow, then black.

"Tree?" Diesel pounded the tree's core. "Come on. Not now." Bark splinters rained onto the ground.

"It ain't working," a voice said from behind.

Diesel faced Pedro.

"None of them work." Ketch stood beside him. "Rumor has it the White Queen shut the tree portals down until after the Howling Moon. Thanks to the wolf-shifters." Ketch snickered, and they walked away.

Diesel sat on the tree's root and covered his face with his John Deere cap. "This isn't happening. There's got to be a way out of here." He leaned his head up against the trunk. "I should've gone with Bence. I shouldn't have waited."

Ahead of him, someone screeched in the distance.

He jumped to his feet. His fur raised, like antennae detecting a signal. His T-shirt ripped up the back.

WOLF BLOOD RACED THROUGH Diesel's body, and his paws pounded the dry, dusty terrain. With the surrounding's scents more heightened, he could smell the fear nearing. He followed it, rushed past Ketch and Pedro who strolled the footpath, and nearly toppled them over.

Sunbeams glistened through the canopy. Pine trees. Maples. Rocks.

Traces of the fear drew closer. When Diesel burst out into the grassy expanse, Mat's screaming stopped.

Elio scurried down the embankment. Bingham held his football and stared at the human.

Diesel shifted back into his man form. "It's . . . it's all right, Mat." He put a hand out toward Mat and shook off the buzz from transforming. "They're good. They won't harm you."

Mat stood, mouth agape with his head shifting between Bingham, Elio, and a now-shifted Diesel.

"They're my friends." Remnant hunger from his alteration attracted him to the man.

Elio clacked loudly.

"Yes, I'll put some clothes on." Diesel moved toward the cave—where he often slept in the back—but before he left, he touched Mat's arm. The human's trembling eased. "Trust me, Mat. You're in good hands with Elio and Bingham. These are the two I told you about."

Mat nodded.

"I gotta put something on. Looks like I ruined your clothes."

Mat smiled gingerly. "'s okay."

"Play ball?" Bingham asked him.

Elio walked Diesel back to the cave, while Bingham tossed the football to Mat.

In the back corner of the cave, Diesel stepped into an extra set of pants from his area. "The portals are closed. Apparently, the queen doesn't want me or anyone else getting out till after the Howling Moon."

Elio groaned.

Diesel pulled a thermal shirt over his head. "What am I gonna do, El? I got Bence's email that he made it out of the second barrier, but there was nothing else. He should've sent me another message by now. He left two days ago. We haven't been out of contact with each other this long since before we found the internet. I'm worried, El."

Elio looked out at Mat and Bingham playing catch.

"They're cute, huh?" Diesel stood beside Elio. "That man has a hold on me of sorts. I can't explain it. Around him, the pack can't get to—" He turned in Elio's direction with a wide grin.

Elio groaned.

"Yes, that's it!"

The dragon shook his head.

"I can use him to get me out of here."

Elio clacked.

"I'm not using him."

The dragon grumbled.

"Humans can get in and out of the forest. It's just us Supers who are locked in. If we're together maybe . . . yes!" He embraced the dragon.

Elio growled, and a thin wisp of smoke came out from a nostril.

"Well, I think it's a great idea!" He jumped up.

The dragon placed a paw out, but Diesel rushed past it and out into the sunlight. "Hey, Mat! Mat!"

Elio lumbered down the hill after him, chirping concern about human emotions, vulnerability, and Mat's attraction to him.

"Don't worry, El. This isn't like the time Luke and I tried to break the portal trying to get out."

Elio clacked.

"I don't care that it got witches banished from the kingdom. They're better off in Salem anyway."

Elio stopped.

"I know what I'm doing, El. I graduated summa cum laude in Humanity at UPS. I know all about human emotion."

Chapter Eight

A Witch

T HE WHITE QUEEN'S THRONE was covered in royal-blue velour and matched the drapes hung along the diamond-paned windows behind her. The afternoon sun glistened on the chalky cobalt marble floors. She cocked an eyebrow, cracked a smile, then burst into laughter. Her face was pasty white, hair in a gray bouffant, and traces of the black lipstick she wore specked her teeth.

"Say it again." The queen fought back hysterics. Her chubby body jiggled.

Jezebel folded her arms across her bosom and sighed. "There's a human in the forest. We need witch powers to exterminate it."

"And . . . and you . . . you are coming to *me* for help." Another jiggle besieged her.

"I know it sounds funny," Jezebel raised her voice over the queen's roar, "on the face of it. But apparently . . ." Jezebel jerked her head. "Apparently, even Honoree and Buck can't take it down."

The White Queen settled some and grasped the glass-globed cane that rested against the throne's arm rest. "And you, Jezebel, need a witch's assistance in doing . . . what exactly?"

"I'm following my wolf-shifting, wifely duties." Jezebel smirked. "It's a woman's obligation—is it not?—to procure assistance from you."

The White Queen tapped the cane against the alabaster floor and waited.

"From your Majesty." Jezebel smiled widely.

"That's better. Now, if there's a human roaming around the forest. Why haven't the vampires killed it."

"It broke Ketch's tooth."

"What! Preposterous." She leaned forward. "Why would he not tell me himself? He's my lead vampire."

"Pride, I imagine." Jezebel placed a hand on her hip. "May I?" She pointed to a button-tufted stool. "The flight over here on that smelly dragon was brutal."

The queen nodded, and Jezebel sat.

"We . . . the clan thinks it might be a . . . a Metanormal."

The queen perked. "In Yorkshire, we've heard rumor about an infection, of sorts, to the Homo sapien."

"They're called Metanormals, according to the scriptures."

"Oh, please. The scriptures. Who believes that crap anymore?"

Jezebel rolled her eyes. "You have no idea what I'm living with."

"I know exactly what you're living with!" The queen slammed her cane to the floor. "Your fate, Jezebel!"

"We need not repeat my fate, your . . . Majesty. I know what I'm up against. I know what I need to do."

"Then do it!"

"Well, there's a little problem."

"The meganormal?"

"Meta . . . Metanormal. It has its hands all over Diesel."

"Hm." She strummed the band of her sapphire ring against the cane's globe. "Very well. I will lend you Witch Lena, Jezebel. But just this once!" She sat back. "I can't believe Ketch and Pedro can't handle a simple human being."

"The man called Mat is a little complicated."

"Oh, I like that name; it's like the rug I rest my feet on when I use the crapper."

The two laughed.

"Oh, Jezebel I do miss your old, wicked ways."

Jezebel chuckled. "You could always unleash me." She revealed the metal bands around her wrists.

"I don't think so, deary. Witch Lena! Lena! Out here."

The door behind Jezebel creaked open.

Witch Lena donned a red, white, and black dress that puffed out below her knees. She wore blood-red shoes that matched the same-colored speckles in the noisy costume coming Jezebel's way.

"Jezzy, problem with Mitsy's child?" Her long, blond hair draped her bare shoulders. "The reveal said it was a boy. You must be pleased." She leaned into Jezebel. "One more trick and you're free?"

"Lena!" the White Queen said. "Don't taunt her. The wolf den apparently needs your help."

"Oh? Again."

"From the sounds of it there's a human roaming the grounds, and no one can kill it."

Lena laughed. "Are you serious?"

"It's a Metanormal. Lena." Jezebel patted the matching stool beside her for the witch to sit.

"Girls, King Winston is in Yorkshire investigating the Rise over there. The university has seeded his research centre to study the matter further. He'll be interested to know the infection has spread."

"Perhaps that scripture isn't such crap after all," Jezebel said.

"You've been living with inferior Supers too long."

"Not by choice, may I remind you," Jezebel said.

The White Queen rapped her cane. "Jezebel, one day you may learn that all species have a place in our society. Even lowly shifters."

"That's why you made me one."

"You're a one trick . . . *wolf*?" Witch Lena squinted in a hard smile.

"We need not repeat history," the White Queen said. "Lena, take Jezebel to the wolf dens and exterminate the human. Use an apparition spell to get there. It'll be quicker than traveling by dragon. Diesel must procreate the wolf-shifter species. After all, some animals are needed to scrounge the forest floors and pick them clean. If this mega . . . Metanormal thing is getting in the way, get rid of it."

"If it's not?" Lena asked.

"It is," Jezebel said.

"Very well." Lena rose, smoothed her dress, and curtseyed. "Your Majesty."

The White Queen's eyes trained on Jezebel.

Jezebel sighed, rose, and bowed. "Your Majesty the White Queen of Hubbard Forest, you have my allegiance."

The queen rolled her eyes. "Don't play kiss ass, Jez. I know who you are. You think getting Diesel to mate will free you?"

Jezebel spun and sneered. "It'd better."

"Jezebel, you were cursed to live out the rest of your life as a wolf-shifter. It's your only trick."

Jezebel rushed her. "If I have to live in squalor for the rest of my days I shall die!" She trembled, then, after a moment, tended to her bun of backcombed hair. "I was promised a second chance at his twenty-first year."

The White Queen leaned back and clacked her ring again. "Play nice, and we shall see."

"I've been playing nice for decades."

"Some things are beyond my control, Jezebel."

Jezebel sashayed her way toward the door. "Powers or no powers. We witches are evil."

J EZEBEL AND LENA CRACKED out from dusk's ethers behind Mat's cabin. The smell of fresh cut grass hung in the air, and a rust-colored tractor was parked in the open bay of the garage.

Jezebel smoothed her dress and fixed her hair. "If I had my witch powers back, I could kill the damn thing myself."

"You really think the White Queen will restore your powers after you finish your time with Diesel?"

"No. I don't think it's her call unfortunately. If it had been, I would have killed the bitch myself years ago."

"Jezebel!"

"Oh, Lena. Let's not pretend we like her."

"I didn't say I liked her. It's just that killing things put you in this predicament in the first place."

"I needn't a lesson in morals from you, Witch Lena."

Lena gazed into a crystal globe at the end of her wand. "They're on their way."

"Get Buck and Honoree, they need to see what powerful women can do. Plus, they'll want to feed on its carcass, and I need to play the dumb Mrs. Wolf-Shifter I'm supposed to be."

From Lena's globe, Mat and Diesel strode the road leading to the cabin. "Oh, what I'd do to have one of those again." Jezebel reached for the orb.

Lena clapped her hands, and Buck and Honoree snapped out from behind the barn.

Honoree toppled onto the ground beside his friend. "For Satan's sake!"

"Hello, husband. Look who I've brought."

Buck staggered on all fours. The cup he had been drinking from spun on the ground, and its contents dripped from his face. "Honoree, where are—? Oh."

"Lena," Honoree said. "So, glad you could help us out. It's a small matter that requires a touch of magic."

"Honoree, darling. Your son is approaching with that man. We must be quiet."

Honoree nodded as Buck picked up the tin cup and emptied any remnants into his mouth.

Diesel and Mat rounded the corner of the cabin's property, where the grass grew wild by the property's line, and a water well stood nearby.

"It shouldn't be that much of a problem," Diesel said. "You just need to drive us through the barrier."

"Are you sure it's safe?" Mat asked.

"Sure as can—"

"Halt!" Jezebel yelled.

Lena flung a bolt of lightning their way, but they dove into the brush. The well's roof and winch collapsed onto its stone base.

"Don't you have better aim?" Jezebel drew Lena by the arm toward where the boys had disappeared. "You should've waited till they were closer."

"You should've warned me with your halt."

Honoree followed. "You need us to help, ladies?"

"No, husband. This is a matter for wit— It's a matter Lena can handle on her own, right Lena?"

"Whatever you say."

"Didn't you put a tracking mechanism on your hex?" Jezebel muttered.

"If you had given me a second to home in on him, maybe I would have."

"You young witches."

Lena spun around. "Listen, do you want my help or not? Maybe you'd rather live out your life as a wolf-shifter."

"Everything all right, ladies?" Honoree said.

"All is good, deary. We're tracking the boys now."

Buck tossed his tin cup to the road. "Let me sniff 'em out." He transformed and dashed off into the woods, and Honoree did the same.

Jezebel huffed. "Always got to prove themselves."

While the men howled off in their pursuit, Jezebel and Lena stepped up onto the cabin's front porch for a better look out into the forest.

"Dad! Buck! Back!" Diesel yelled.

"The boy never did take much to his father." Jezebel rested a hip on the porch railing.

"Can you blame him?" Lena studied the light emanating from her fingertips. "I'm getting a bead on the human." She cupped her hands together. The light intensified and piqued Jezebel's interest.

"What do you see?" Jezebel asked.

"I think it is a Metanormal. A very powerful one."

"No wonder I couldn't penetrate it. I may be a dormant witch, but I have a ferocious bite." She sneered.

"Let us be!" Diesel's voice grew closer.

"They're on their way," Jezebel said. "Aim for the Black one. Not Diesel."

"I know what Diesel looks like, Jez. Did you say Black?"

"Did I stutter?"

"He could be one of the originals."

"Pardon?"

"One of the original Metanormals from the Civil War."

Jezebel shook her head. "Lena, humans don't live that long. Seventy . . . eighty years. One hundred max."

"Humans carry over into their next lives."

"I didn't know they suffered additional lives."

"They do."

"Oh, that's tragic. You mean, if we kill the damn things they'll come back. No wonder King Winston's all over this Rise.

"The infection's gone mad."

"I didn't think race or gender carried over," Jezebel said. "At least they don't for us. Thank, Satan."

"No, they don't for humans either. It's just a hunch I have that he's one still clinging to a past life."

"Oh, now you're a psychic?

"Let it rest, Jezebel. Your jealousy is palpable."

"Well, let's kill the ole' Metanormal now so I can get my wings." Jezebel chuckled. "Maybe Queenie is right. Wolf-shifters may serve a purpose, scrounging the forest floors, that need perpetuating after all."

A canine's whelp erupted from the forest. Mat rushed out onto the lawn with Diesel in tow.

"Witch Lena." Diesel stopped. "What are you doing here?"

"Sorry, darling," Lena said. "I know you like playing house with your lover boy here, but you have an obligation to uphold." She flicked the glowing orb off her fingertips, and it radiated out in Mat's direction.

Diesel shifted midair, jowls open to snap at it, but he was too late.

The ball of light slammed into Mat's chest and knocked him against the side of the well. The orb ricocheted back at Lena and brought her to her knees. She clutched her chest and fell face down.

"Lena?" Jezebel lowered to the witch's side. "Lena, are you—? Lena!" She flipped her over and slapped her face. "Lena!"

The wolves gnarled and barked.

Jezebel laid Lena's head on her lap. "Speak to me . . . speak!"

Lena opened her eyes; blood dribbled from her mouth. "The Metanormal is too strong."

"You're going to be okay. Let's get you up."

Lena grabbed her hand. "No, Jezebel. I can't."

"What do you mean you can't? You're a witch. With our powers, very few can—"

She coughed blood, and it speckled her dress.

"No, no. Lena, I need you . . . we need you. Mitsy's child."

"Take my powers, Jezebel."

"But . . . but . . . what do you mean? Take your powers?" Jezebel bit back a grin.

"The Metanormals are converting ordinary humans, as Winston thought. You must stop them, or all supernatural creatures will vanish."

Jezebel held her hand. "I know we haven't always seen eye to eye, but I can't be the only witch in Hubbard Forest. Who am I going to make fun of when she wears these loud dresses?"

Lena coughed. "Take my remaining powers. Put them to good use and kill the humans."

"What? Take your powers?" Jezebel placed a hand to her chest. "If you insist." Jezebel leaned over Lena, drained magic from her mouth, and breathed the life out from her.

Lena gasped. "He's . . . more . . . powerful . . . than you think."

Jezebel took one, long final breath, and Lena withered into ash onto the floorboards. A quiet wind swept her away.

More wolves had ascended onto the lawn. In a frenzy, they gnashed and fought with one another. Their attempts to get to Mat were met with discouraging whelps.

Jezebel stoked a charge at her fingertips. "Come on . . . light baby. Light." Sparks flickered, and she aimed them at her wrist cuffs. But the energy only heated the shackles. "Ahhh!" She blew at her wrists and fanned her hands. "That son of a witch is hot."

She focused and fueled the magic more. A rod of yellow light shot out from a clenched fist and punched a hole in the floorboards. "Ha! That's better."

Jezebel pointed a fist at the well cap, and it went up in flames.

Mat stumbled up onto his knees.

She aimed the magic at him. The bolt's kickback slammed her against the side of the cabin. "Yikes. I'm a little rusty." It hit Mat in the back. Like Lena's discharge, it recoiled. She ducked, and it shattered a window above her.

She peered over the porch railing. Mat groaned and tried to get up. "Well, at least I've got some juice in these old batteries now," she said.

Jezebel snapped her fingers, stared at her palms, and cocked an eyebrow. "Oh, come now." She clapped her hands. "You've got to be kidding me. You mean, I still have to walk?"

She strolled off the porch and into the forest, leaving the wolves fighting behind her.

CHAPTER NINE

Ants in the Pants

CRICKETS CHIRPED, AND AN easy breeze drifted in through the cabin's open windows, where white curtains swayed. Diesel towel dried his hair while Mat, with a blood-stained wrap around his chest, placed food at the kitchen counter.

"Wow, you made dinner," Diesel said. "It smells delicious."

"It's just to get something in our stomachs. We can head out afterward." Mat glanced at Diesel, then diverted his gaze. "You can grab a pair of my gym shorts from the suitcase in the bedroom."

"Oh, right."

When he returned, Mat removed a box from one of the stools at the kitchen island. "You look refreshed."

"The shower was great."

Diesel saddled up onto the empty seat beside him. "Looks great. What is it?"

"Mrs. Callahan's frozen chicken pot pies."

"Frozen?"

"Well, they were frozen. I microwaved them. They're horrible for you . . . loaded with sodium. But they're tasty. I'm not much for processed food but in a pinch, you do what you have to."

"Delicious," Diesel said through a bite.

"After we eat, I'll pack you some things for your trip to Salem. I've got some extra clothes in the truck."

"Wait, Mat. I really think we should head out in the morning."

"But I thought you wanted out of here."

"They brought in a witch, Mat. God only knows what spells she cast. Plus, the White Queen must know about you if she sent Lena. Nighttime can be dangerous for a human. We don't know what's next."

"I'm a Metanormal. They can't get to me." He poured Diesel more milk from an open carton on the counter.

"That witch could have hexed you or something. We don't know."

"She just knocked me around."

"And broke your rib."

"It's just bruised." He touched the torn shirt Diesel had wrapped around him. "I've broken a rib before. This is nothing." He flinched. "It only hurts when I breathe."

Diesel smirked. "In the morning, I can see if Elio can help you."

"What's he going to cry over this time?"

"Good point. He'll be pissed."

Mat took his empty plate to the sink. Diesel drank the rest of his milk and walked to the other side where Mat rinsed the dish.

Diesel flipped open the lid to a box on the counter. "What's in here?"

"Oh, that's Trinity's. Some of her family's memorabilia."

"Yahtzee?"

"It's a game."

"Games. I love games." He fumbled through the box and took out another.

"Ants in the Pants?"

Mat chuckled. "I haven't played that one in a long time."

Diesel took it to the living room.

"Gosh your back's all cut and bruised. Lie down, and I'll fix you up before we go." Mat went into the bathroom and returned with ointment. He sat on his haunches over Diesel's back. "God, they really did a job on you."

"That's nothing."

"Nothing? I'd hate to see what you'd look like really injured."

"Oh, that feels good. Can you rub right there? Yeah."

Mat massaged Diesel's back.

"Oh, man. This is delightful."

Mat kneaded harder.

Diesel groaned. "What's that?"

"It's your deltoid muscle."

"Not what I meant. I think you've got . . . ants in your pants."

Mat jumped off the couch.

"Hey, don't stop. I was just..." Diesel rolled over, then caught a glimpse of Mat's sweats. "Kidding."

"We should go before it gets too dark." Mat headed for the bedroom.

Diesel went to him. "Mat, it's okay." He touched his arm. The electricity was palpable. "If we wait till morning, it'll be easier."

They stared.

"Do you want to play Ants in the Pants?" Diesel asked.

THREE ROUNDS OF THE game—all of which Diesel lost—and a sleeve of Oreos later, Mat packaged up the box. "I'm beat," he said.

"Me too." Diesel yawned. "I can take the couch."

"Don't be silly."

Diesel hitched an eyebrow.

"There's another bedroom." Mat pointed.

"Nah, I wouldn't want to mess it up. That's for Trinity, ain't it?"

Mat nodded.

They used the bathroom and got water.

Diesel fixed the blanket at the couch.

"Hey, Diesel?"

"Yeah."

"Maybe we should sleep closer to each other."

Diesel looked up.

"Not like we're going to . . . I just think it might be safer. You know, if something were to come during the night."

Diesel dropped the pillow. "Your protection over me, you mean?"

Mat stammered a few unintelligible words before nodding. "Yes."

"I'd appreciate that."

Mat's bed squeaked as they nested and propped pillows. After a couple of throat clears and gyrations, they quieted. The throbbing cadence of crickets filled the room.

"Can I ask you a question?" Mat asked.

"Sure."

A rustle of the sheets appropriated.

"Are you straight? I mean . . . do you like women? Female humans that is."

"Can I be honest?"

"Of course," Mat said.

"I've never been with a human that way."

Mat rolled onto his side and Diesel faced him.

"Did you ever want to be full-on human?"

"All the time. I hate shifting. I hate magic. It's always trouble. You don't know how good you have it."

"The grass is always greener."

"What's that mean?"

"It's a colloquialism for things seem better from a distance, from another vantage point."

"Hm." Diesel lay on his back. "I hate my father. My stepmother is horrible. When I was at UPS, we would watch human artistic programs, as part of our studies for Human Culture. I always admired your ideal families. *The Brady Bunch* was one of my favorites."

Mat propped up on an elbow. "They taught you *The Brady Bunch*? I wouldn't say that is a likely example of family life for humans, much less art."

"Maybe not, but I liked it."

"Me too, actually."

"I wrote a paper on how it tied in with your peace movement from the 1960s that surrounded it."

"Meaning what, exactly?"

"The 1960s were a very pivotal time for you. Many Metanormals were believed to have spawned from that era. I think the Brady's were all Metanormals."

"How so?"

"Just a hunch."

Mat rolled onto his back. The crickets grew louder in their silence.

"My real mother died in childbirth. I used to wish she was a human, and that maybe that was how I became what I am . . . my lust for humanity." Diesel faced him. "I mean, I lust to be one."

"Maybe your father mated with a human."

"While I fantasize about my real mom's true nature, I can't imagine my father ever having mated with one, so that really throws my fantasy a curveball." He faced Mat. "It is curveball? I got that saying correct, right?"

"You did. How'd did Honoree meet Jezebel?"

Diesel rolled onto his back. "Jezebel. She was my mother's best friend, which doesn't say much for my mother's choice in friends, but I'll cut her some slack. Cut slack?

"That's right."

"Jezebel then married my father."

"Do you think they were having an affair prior to? And maybe you're her real son."

"God, I hope not! No, I don't think so. She doesn't really seem all that attracted to him, but maybe that's what happens over time. Plus, I look nothing like her. So, tell me about Mat Kwan."

Mat tugged the covers up some. "I told you already. My family perished in a fire."

"No, not that." Diesel adjusted the hem of the sheet. "Are *you* straight, as you call it? Do you prefer women? Are you and Trinity mates?"

Mat laughed. "Trinity and I are friends. At one point, we thought we could be romantic, but it didn't work out. She's going through a lot. Her parents' death. She's raising her kid brother who's into drugs. We met online through a virtual grief counseling group. I recently came out here . . . to Maine . . . about a month now. Gosh time flies."

"Time flies. I like that one."

Mat chuckled.

"You came out here for her?"

"Nah. I've been traveling, escaping the past and California. I couldn't deal with wildfires, earthquakes, and mudslides anymore. Besides, I needed a fresh start. Maine sounded good, plus I knew Trinity."

"So, you quit your job and moved to Maine."

"I left the forestry last fall. Rented my house out. It covers the bills. I've been living on the road ever since. I'm a simple man. Don't need much."

"Simple man. I want to be a simple man. I admire you, Mat."

"I admire you too, Diesel."

The crickets silenced.

"You didn't answer my question," Diesel said.

"About?"

"About being straight . . . or not."

Mat stared at the ceiling.

Diesel turned onto his side. "I've always wanted to be with a human . . . intimately."

"You're what your pack calls a humansexual."

"Yes."

"I can't say I've ever thought about having sex with a wolf-shifter."

Diesel reached over and tugged the man's crotch. "I think you have."

CHAPTER TEN

NEPRC

JEZEBEL'S FILL OF MAGIC from Witch Lena leaked out like one of those old tires on Diesel's horseless carriage. She stood beside Mitsy—in the rows reserved for women in the back of the assembly area. Before them, the Board of Directors prayed in their meeting's commencement.

Mitsy's cuticle bled, and she sucked her finger to stop it.

"That's so unbecoming," Jezebel said to her, but Mitsy didn't seem to hear her and picked at her nailbed further.

"Praise Darthius," Honoree said, head bowed at the center of the board of director's table. "May he help us coalesce our magic to rid the world of good."

"May Lord Darthius," Buck added, "help us stop humanity in its tracks before they take over the Kingdom and prevent evil from spawning. For the betterment of supernatural kind, may he hear our prayer."

"Lord, hear our prayer," the congregation recited.

The Board of Directors sat.

Honoree banged the gavel. "Let the record be stated, the Board's emergency session has officially begun."

Mitsy leaned into Jezebel. "What do you mean Witch Lena didn't work out?"

Jezebel held her hands close to her chest. "Don't worry," she whispered. "I have a plan."

"What about Diesel? Did he get out?"

Jezebel shook her head. "He's at the human's cabin." Jezebel's hands smoked, and she stashed them under her armpits to prevent the wisps from being visible.

"Jezebel, what's wrong with you?"

"I've taken to cigarettes is all."

"Cigarettes? You're lying to me again."

To the right of the Board of Directors, a tawny wolf-shifter positioned a cardboard graph onto a floor-standing easel.

The audience silenced.

"The New England Paranormal Research Centre is King Winston's pride," the wolf-shifter said. "It is an experimental group designed to detect Metanormals from normal human beings."

"We already know we have one," shouted a vampire from the crowd, "we don't need high-paid consultants to tell us that."

"Order!" Honoree shouted. "Let the director state his case."

The wolf-shifter pointed to a diagram depicting humanity's evolution from a unicellular being into a multicellular one, then to a being that created advanced civilizations. "If NEPRC has its way, Homos will not advance into magical beings. He drew an X over the question mark at the end of the evolutionary line. "NEPRC claims to rid any confusion about the Homo sapiens' rise. NEPRC is on the verge of creating a supernatural being that can not only detect Metanormals but kill them."

"Just kill all humans and be done with it!" shouted a wolf-shifter in the audience.

"Killing all of humanity is a rather drastic measure," the presenter said.

"Drastic times call for drastic measures!" the dissenter added.

Ketch faced the protesting wolf-shifter. "And you propose we feed on moose and deer for the rest of eternity?"

As he rose, Honoree's chair pushed back with a thunder. "Citizens, please! We are taking matters under control. We need your support."

"Yeah, like that witch really helped," shouted someone else. "The poor thing is dead now, because of your wife."

Mitsy's head wobbled, and her eyes closed as if she were about to faint.

Jezebel elbowed her. "I told you, I've got a plan."

"You promised me Lena wouldn't be hurt." Mitsy clutched her belly. "She's dead? Is that why your hands are riddled."

Jezebel wrung her hands. "I caught a little bit of that Metanormal's spell. I'll be all right. He is very dangerous and needs to be stopped."

The Board of Directors vetted the decision to hire NEPRC further.

"They can send a wizard over immediately," the treasurer said. "We can use our emergency funds. That's what our magic bank is for."

"I still don't know why the White Queen doesn't use her own magic currency for this," the secretary said. "They're loaded with magic."

"It's a deposit. You know how miserly they are with magic. I shall see to it that our tokens are reimbursed when we're successful," the treasurer said. "This will be a good opportunity for our clan to show its commitment to the Kingdom and prove our worth."

"And we have King Winston's support?" Buck asked.

"We do. He'd rather us not involve his wife at this time."

The audience was silent.

Buck called for board approval, and the motion passed unanimously.

Mitsy wedged her way out through the row of female shifters. "Pardon. Excuse, please. I feel a wave of morning sickness coming on."

A LOUD KNOCK SOUNDED from the living area, and Diesel swept the blanket off his head.

"Damn it." The sun shone in his eyes. "We overslept." He nudged Mat.

Mat swallowed a snore. "Huh."

Diesel stepped into a pair of the man's discarded underwear on the floor by the foot of the bed. The knock repeated. "Someone's here."

Another thump from out front sounded, and he crept closer to the bedroom door.

Mat sat up with a painful grimace.

"Diesel?" Mitsy's voice rang out. "Are you in there?" She knocked louder.

Diesel heaved a sigh of relief. "Relax. It's just my sister."

Mat stretched and winced.

"You're still pretty banged up from that witch," Diesel said to him.

"Um, more from another banging." Mat grinned.

"Did I hurt you?"

"After the third time, it grew a little easier."

"Sorry."

"Diesel?" Mitsy rapped again. "I know you're in there. I can smell your musk."

"Coming!" He opened the door, then faced Mat. "Get dressed. I'll introduce you."

Mat tossed him his sweats. Diesel put them on and went to the front door.

On the front porch, Mitsy held her hands in the pockets of her cloak. "What are you still doing here? You need to get out."

He motioned for her to come in. "I tried getting out yesterday, but the portals are locked."

"The Board hired a bounty hunter. You haven't much time."

Mat stumbled out wearing the gym shorts Diesel had gone to bed in. He waved, went into the bathroom, and shut the door.

"Is that the Metanormal?"

"Yes, but don't believe all you hear about how bad—"

"He killed Witch Lena, Dee."

Diesel furrowed his brow.

"She's gone. Now what am I supposed to do about my baby? Her potions were to get me through." She clutched her stomach, and Diesel led her to the couch.

"You walked all the way over here in your condition?"

"I'm already feeling sick without her potions. If it wasn't for your friend …" She sniffed. "Did you …?" Her eyes grew wide. "You mated with him."

"Three times." He grinned.

Mitsy sat gingerly, hands on stomach. "Without Lena, I'm not sure I'll make it full term. And with no witches left in the community, what am I going to do?"

"We'll figure it out, Mits."

"*We* won't. You need to go. Jezebel says she can work her way with the White Queen for the baby, but she caught a hex from your friend."

"He's trying to protect me, Mits. I have a plan to get us out of here. I haven't heard from Bence, and I'm getting concerned."

She clutched her belly and winced, and Mat came out from the bathroom.

"Mat, I'd like you to meet my sister, Mitsy. Mitsy, Mat Kwan."

Mitsy refused his hand.

"Mits, he didn't do it on purpose. He saved me from the pack who were trying to take me back."

"Do what?" Mat asked.

Mitsy glanced his way. "The witch couldn't penetrate your power, and her spell kicked back and killed her."

Mat sat in the upholstered chair opposite her. "She threw a bolt of light at me that slammed me against the well. I tried getting up, then got hit again. That's all I know."

"It wasn't his fault, Mits."

She sighed. "I told Jezebel it was too dangerous. Even she got hit some."

Mat stood. "Can I get you a glass of water?"

Mitsy nodded. "That'd be nice, thank you."

Diesel, sat on the arm of the couch, brushed a strand of hair away from his sister's forehead. "Maybe I should stay around to help you through."

"No!" Her hair fell back. "You need to go. I want you to go. Set the course for your new nephew, maybe one day you'll free us all from this cage."

Mat returned with the water and handed it to Mitsy, who drank it readily.

"Another?"

"No, thank you." She gave the glass back to him, and he set it on the coffee table beside the Ants in the Pants game.

"What is that?" Mitsy eyed the box.

"It's a form of human entertainment. It's fun. You want to play?" Diesel moved to the couch cushion.

"There isn't time for fun, Dee. The Board approved the New England Paranormal Research Centre to come in and eradicate Mat."

Diesel stood. "King Winston's experimental group?"

"Uh huh. They're sending a wizard over. He should be here any moment now."

"We should go, Diesel." Mat rose.

When Mat shut the bedroom door, Mitsy faced her brother. "I can smell your scent all over him. I can't believe you two had sex."

Diesel rolled his eyes.

"You know the Lord says it's an abomination to lie with a human."

"Duh Mitsy, you know I'm a humansexual."

"I know but . . . in the forest, he could be watching you here and punish you."

"You know how I feel about the scriptures."

"Okay. Okay." She put her hands up. "Religion aside. Having sexual relations is a big step, Diesel. You just met him. You're the one who told me how delicate humans are. You could hurt him emotionally if you're not vested. And you do have a tendency to—"

"You sound like Elio."

"The human is not another Bence you can play around with."

"He needed to discover his sexuality, and I've never been with a human. So, it was a win-win."

"Win-win?"

"It's a saying Mat taught me."

Dressed in jeans and a tight-fitting polo, Mat returned from the bedroom carrying a rifle. He raised the gun. "Just in case."

Mitsy got up clutching her belly. "I think I'm going to be ill."

Mat handed the gun to Diesel and led Mitsy toward the bathroom. He touched her shoulder, and she froze. "I'm sorry. Did I hurt—"

She looked up at him, then Diesel. "My nausea. It's gone. It went away when you . . . when you touched me."

IN MAT'S SUV, THEY drove toward the wolf den with Mitsy in the back and Diesel holding the rifle upfront.

"I told you I could walk. This is too dangerous. You need to get out of the forest," she said.

"I'm not letting a pregnant woman walk a mile and a half." Mat turned the vehicle down the narrow path Diesel pointed to.

"Don't worry, Mits. He'll protect us. I told you humans aren't bad."

"Well, just drop me off at the clan's edge. It's not too far of a walk from there."

The vehicle bounced its way over bumpy, dirt roads and through thick woodlands choked with maple trees, sumac, and buckthorn.

Mitsy leaned forward. "This truck is a lot quieter and more comfortable than the old diesel rigs you fixed up."

"It certainly is." Diesel eyed the colorful display on the dash.

"It's a hybrid. The engines are a lot quieter than gas-powered ones."

"Hybrid?" Diesel replied.

"It's not a diesel, Diesel. Hey, is that how you got your name? From your trucks?"

"When I was a kid, I would play in the junkyard with all the old beat-up cars. My favorite was a blue truck with a diesel emblem. My buddies, Bence and Luke, nicknamed me after it. My real name is Daniel, but not many people call me that."

"You can let me out just around the bend," Mitsy said. "The thicket clears some there. It's close enough to the den."

Diesel touched her hand that sat on the headrest. "Are you sure you're going to be all right?"

"Yes, big little brother. Especially now that my mornin' sickness went away. Even the cramps—"

Mat slammed on the brakes.

Honoree and Buck stepped into the middle of the dirt road.

"Damn it!" Mat threw the transmission into reverse, but an obese man with a safari hat and a dart gun stepped out from the pines.

"Run!" Diesel flung open the door. He pointed the rifle at the rotund man while Mitsy got out.

Buck grabbed her. "Are you all right, my little lady? Did that human hurt the baby?"

Rattled, she shook her head.

"Son, you're coming with us," Honoree said.

"Not if I can help it." Diesel fired the rifle at the bounty hunter, but he caught the bullet with the tip of a wand he pulled out from his coat pocket.

Mat climbed onto the hood of the SUV to get to Diesel, and Honoree stepped back.

Two golden arrows shot out from the man's dart gun. One snaked around the left of the vehicle and struck Mat in the shoulder. The other wound around the other side and hit Diesel in the neck.

Part Two

Magic

CHAPTER ELEVEN

Wand

THE MAGIC JEZEBEL HAD gleaned from Witch Lena faded further, and she longed for more.

Bingham chased a blue and green dragonfly darting by the lake at the base of the dragon lair. The sun shone brightly. The water glistened, and the grass at its edge danced in a subtle breeze.

Elio lumbered down the hill toward the boy. *Click, click, clack.*

Bingham, with the dragonfly now beating on his finger, nodded. "Okay. I stay here."

Elio cooed and flew off over the lake, sending the dragonfly to scurry in his wake.

Bingham chased the insect up the hill toward the cave, when Jezebel stepped out from the thicket and followed.

She stayed behind so he wouldn't see her and watched him gimp along. "Oh, what a waste, you poor imperfect child."

The dragonfly pivoted. Jezebel ducked behind a pine tree, and Bingham hobbled back down to the lakeside.

"Ah, now the deformed boy is out of my way."

The dragon's cave was cool and dank—a welcome respite from the hot early-fall afternoon.

She waved a hand in front of her nose. "Nothing smellier than an Emphilothepy's cavity." She worked her way deeper into the cave using the sparks from her fingers to guide her. "What little magic I did gain can be of some use."

She advanced down a narrow corridor and off it, into a hollow not much wider than the width of her body. There, she clawed at the compacted ground. "This was definitely not a good week for a manicure."

After a few false attempts at locating where she had left it, she unburied her witch medallion. She clutched the round metal disk etched with necromantic carvings to her chest. A kiss ignited it, and it glowed a soft red light.

She placed the chain around her neck and let the totem's powers absorb into her heart until it stopped glowing.

She wiggled her fingers, and bright arcs snapped out. "Oh, magic is like a good orgasm." She moaned. "That feels much better. This, at least, should get me through the night." She removed the chain, kissed the medallion once more, and returned it to the ground with a pat. "Charge up some, my ancient friend. Once I do just a few more things, I shan't use up your fuel."

Jezebel wiped dirt from her hands when a scuffle from the corridor won her attention. She peered around the hollow's edge.

Bingham shuffled down the corridor, then braced against the wet walls when he saw her.

"Hello, Bingham."

"Who . . . who you. You no belong here."

"Oh, but I do. Perfect timing. I love how Satan creates such opportunities." She moved toward him with a grin so wide it pained her cheeks. "I can finally fix you."

Bingham backed up shaking his head.

"Bingham, you can be my miracle baby. I can repair your deformities and have my full powers returned. I've been aching to do this for a long time. Now's the year."

Bingham hit up against a wall. "N-no, no."

"This won't hurt too much, Bingy. I bet you'd be a rather handsome wolf-shifter all fixed up. It's a shame you're stuck the way you are." She grimaced. "It's rather embarrassing. But I can make you into a perfect male wolf-shifter, one the Lord would be proud of."

She advanced, and he trembled.

"It was supposed to be that way all along. Now, I have the power to correct you"—she smirked—"and help myself a little in the process."

Bingham shook violently as she neared.

Jezebel flung sorcery from her hands and at the boy, unleashing an assault that lit the cavern. Its damp walls sizzled. The boy convulsed in the golden light, then the magic burst back knocking Jezebel from her feet.

She crawled up onto all fours with her bun unraveling in her face. "Son of a—" On her knees, she rubbed her hands, hoping the magic hadn't subsided, but there was none left. Her heart pounded and head spun.

Except for the pool of urine at Bingham's feet and fear that wrought over his face, he stood unchanged.

"A waste of a day's magic." She rose and combed back her tresses. "Did that Pure get to you? Did he!" Jezebel feared the Metanormal's touch infiltrated her magic.

Bingham quivered. The corridor darkened.

Jezebel spun around. Bingham ran to Elio, whose blackened silhouette obscured the corridor's entrance. He welcomed Bingham in his arms, then protected the boy by setting him behind him.

Elio hurled a thick flame at Jezebel, which raced down the narrow tunnel too small for him to fit.

She ducked into the crevice where her totem lay, and the flames shot past farther down into the tunnel's depths.

"Okay . . . okay you win this time! I'll leave."

As Elio stepped aside, the light returned to the hallway. Jezebel peaked out. Hidden, Elio clicked and clacked forcefully.

She worked her way up the incline. When she reached the top, Bingham slid out from behind Elio's tail.

"I'm not done with you, son," she said on her way out.

Elio growled.

"Oh, did you not tell him that he is my son? How could a goody-two-shoes Emphilothepy keep such secrets from the boy?"

Bingham peered out from behind dragon's tail.

Elio heaved a torrent of flames from his nostrils, and Jezebel ran.

*A*T THE END OF *an alley, far from where music spilled out into the street, Mat's cell phone lit his face, and he smoked a cigarette.*

He leaned up against a brick wall and raised his foot to it. "Hi, Maxine, I'm just returning your call . . . checking in."

"Checking in, huh. Nice of you to do so."

Mat rubbed the back of his neck. The cigarette glowed a bright orange. "I'm on a break."

Maxine was silent for a time. "The news reported a breakout near us, but you firefighters probably already know that."

"It did? No, I . . . no, we didn't hear. We've been too busy."

"It burnt through the canyon a few hours ago."

Diesel stirred. His head felt heavy, like having drunk too much whiskey in an attempt to shake off a tough shift. He recognized the old, abandoned witch's hut. He hadn't been in it since that time he and Luke cast a spell on the portal to try and break free and were held up there. He laid his head back against the wall.

Mat wore a red, long-sleeved shirt, black jeans, and black boots. The dumpster along the opposite brick wall read San Francisco Bay Hauling.

"How's Ty? Is he still upset over the sneakers?" He took a drag of his cigarette.

"Ty's fine," Maxine said. "And I'd rather not talk about the sneakers."

A tall man with a large, gold belt buckle stepped into the alley's entrance, and Mat motioned for him to wait a minute.

"Maxine, tell Ty I love him."

Diesel tried to speak, but it pained to open his mouth. Mat lay across from him on a cot with a thin, gray mattress pad.

In a chair on the other side of the bars, the bounty hunter snored. The brim of his safari hat tilted onto his brow, and his clasped hands rested on his belly, which rose and fell in cadence with his heavy breath.

Mat and the man with the gold belt buckle returned to the club. Loud music blared and men in tight-fitting clothes played pool and drank beer. At the corner of a rectangular bar, they downed a shot of something brown, then carried beers to a darkened area where men in leather congregated.

A shirtless man rose above the onlookers' heads and gyrated in front of them, while patrons stuffed dollar bills into the waistband of his underwear.

Diesel lifted his head from the wall, and a jolt of pain shot through his eyes.

Mat moaned. He roused, but his leg was chained to the cell's bar.

Diesel's eyes were heavy, and he grew dizzy.

In a vibrantly lit diner, Mat sipped coffee in a booth with cracked, orange vinyl seats. He still wore the red shirt and black pants from earlier. The television above a glass case of pies, piled with meringue, showed a fire-ravaged neighborhood.

Mat called Maxine's number, but it went right to voice mail. He raked a hand over his face, placed a twenty on the table, and left.

Motion returned to Diesel's left foot, then right. "Son of a—" he murmured, crawling now on all fours toward Mat. When he reached the cot, he rested. "Mat?" he whispered with eyes trained on the obese man.

He shook Mat, and the human whimpered.

Gray ash covered the concrete slab of Mat's home. He fell to his haunches; head hung low. Helicopters flew overhead. He wept.

The sounds of neighbors crying as they returned to their devastated homes filled the air. Under a pile of charred boards, most likely the cellar stairs, he pulled out a safe and removed its contents: eight-hundred dollars in cash, the will, his wedding band, and photographs of better times.

Mat opened his eyes.

"It's okay." Diesel rubbed his shoulder. "I've got a plan to get us out of here."

Mat braced up on an elbow, then fell back down.

Diesel recognized the gold ring on Mat's left hand as the one pulled from the safe. "It wasn't your fault, Mat."

"Huh?"

"The fire. It wasn't your fault."

Mat propped back up. "How do you . . . ? What are you talking about?"

The hunter choked on a snore.

"I saw what happened," Diesel muttered.

Mat tried to sit up, but the cuff prevented his movement.

"Easy."

"I was dreaming about the fire," Mat whispered.

"I know." Diesel reached under the cot and pulled out a pin. "I . . . I can't explain it. But it's like I read your mind." He picked at Mat's cuff with the barb. "That's never happened to me before."

"What are you doing?"

"Getting us out of here." He picked more. "Luckily, us rambunctious teenagers were good at aiding future, sorry-ass convicts." The cuff released. He grinned and held up the gib.

AT THE CELL'S LOCK, Diesel inserted the pin. "This . . . one's always . . . a bit . . . more . . . diffi . . . ah!" The lock disengaged. He returned to the cot and knelt before it. "Let's leave it for the next pris—"

"Uh, Diesel," Mat said.

Diesel dove for the exit, but the bounty hunter was already there pointing his wand at the door.

"Not so fast, boys." Gold rays emitted from his wand, and the cell sealed shut. When he finished, he pulled a red bandana dangling from his pants pocket and wiped it clean.

"A wand wizard," Diesel said, "is that all you are?"

"You don't know all that I am, Daniel."

"Oh, and you know my name."

"I know who you are." He returned the wand wrapped in the bandana to his pocket.

Diesel rushed the gate and grabbed the fat man by the scruff of his shirt. The wand fell out of his pocket and rolled away from the cell beside bookshelves stacked with hardbacks—titles written with runes on their spines.

"No!" the wizard yelled.

Diesel jerked him closer, until his chubby face was wedged between the bars. Diesel bit back his anger, else he'd shift and be useless.

When he drew the wizard onto his knees, Diesel faced Mat. "Your belt. Give it to me."

Mat took it off while Diesel flipped the man so that his back was against the bars and wrapped Mat's belt around the wizard's neck.

"Get the wand!" Diesel yelled to Mat. "The wand. Get it!"

Mat slinked on the floor with his arms underneath the cell. "It's . . . too . . . far. My arms . . . They're not long enough."

"Don't . . . do . . . this . . ." The wizard kicked his feet, attempting to push the wand even farther. His hands gripped the strap around his neck.

Diesel tightened, and the man coughed and choked. Red-faced, he drooled, and snot pooled on the floor where his face leaned.

With a free hand, Diesel pulled Mat closer to him. "Hold him."

Mat took the reins.

"Please, wait," the wizard said, under Mat's looser hold. "You don't understand."

"Oh, I understand very well." Diesel reached for the wand. "You're a pathetic excuse for a wizard. Wand wizards are the lowest rung of them all. And they sent *you* after a Metanormal?"

"This is just a gig . . . to pay off a gambling debt I owe to Winston."

Diesel stretched farther—right shoulder pinched against the lower bar. He reached the wand but not before catching the wizard's boot to his face.

"No, don't!" the man said.

"Without this you're nothing." Diesel aimed it at him.

"No, please!" The man retracted his foot.

Diesel pulled the wand into the cell, aimed it at the lock, and the door plunked open. Diesel hitched up his pants. "I didn't know I had it in me."

"No, you can't!"

"I just did." Diesel removed the bandana from the wizard's pocket. "You talk too much." He gagged him with it. With Mat's opened cuff, he chained one of his wrists and used the belt to tie up the other.

The wizard gibbered unintelligibly through the binding.

Outside the cell, with Mat by his side, Diesel held the wand over him. "Oh, do you want this back?"

The wizard nodded. Tears wet his cheeks.

Diesel snapped the thin, wooden wand over his knee and flung it at the wizard. "I hate magic. Nothing good ever comes of it."

"It got us out," Mat said.

"There are always consequences."

CHAPTER TWELVE

Paranormals

To the left of Mat's RAV4, an orange and purple glow flickered through a grove of pines, as the morning fog rose in a blanket of ferns beneath the trees.

"His Joindrr profile was perfect," Mat said at the wheel. "He wanted to be discreet and wasn't looking for a commitment, and I just wanted to test the waters."

"Now that you tested them, what do you think?"

"Well, Gold Belt Buckle and I did nothing. I chickened out."

"I meant, after testing them with me."

Mat wet his lips with the tip of his tongue. "I think I'm gay." He faced Diesel. "Thank you for helping me realize it."

"I knew you needed it."

Mat glanced back at Diesel. "Needed it? What, am I some kind of experiment for you?"

"I didn't mean it that way. Damn, Mitsy and Elio were right: humans are emotional. I should know better."

"I suppose you're right. I did need it." Mat chuckled. "I'm still aching."

"Sorry about that. I lose control sometimes."

"What about you? Are you gay?"

"I'm a humansexual. I never really thought I needed to choose between a human man or woman. I never thought I'd get that far. To me it's about your essence . . . spirit, regardless of gender."

Mat smiled. "That's beautiful."

Diesel laughed. "Who am I. I'm just a dumb wolf-shifter. Not a poet or anything."

"No, I meant the sunrise. Look." Mat veered east.

"Oh."

Mat placed a hand on Diesel's knee. "I'm sorry. What you said *was* beautiful. It's just . . . it's just I'm not sure I'm ready for a relationship."

"Okay."

"Honestly, I just want to screw your brains out," Mat said.

WITH THE SUV PARKED haphazardly on the side of the road and the windows steamed up, Diesel splayed one hand against the headliner and clutched the headrest with the other. He cried resoundingly and climaxed.

Mat checked his appearance in the rearview mirror and wiped his mouth with a napkin from the glove compartment.

Diesel breathed heavily and buttoned his pants. "That thing . . . with your tongue . . . how'd you . . . ?"

"Just comes natural . . . I guess." He started the car and tore gravel as he pulled back out onto the street. "It smells like a locker room in here." He rolled down the windows.

Wind swept through Diesel's hair and cooled his sweaty forehead. "We're almost there." He placed his baseball cap back on.

Mat bit his lower lip. "I lied to Maxine. I told her I was working overtime fighting the Donlan Fire, when all along I had the weekend off." He faced Diesel. "I just needed to get away."

"It's all right. I get it. Stuff happens."

"I should've been there, Diesel."

"Had you been there, you couldn't have done anything."

"I could've got them out. That's a regret I'll have to live with for the rest of my life."

Diesel took his hand. The sun's rays radiated through cumulus clouds over a canopy of maples. "It is beautiful."

"It's beautiful that I'll have regrets for the rest—?"

"No, silly, the sunrise."

At the town line, they stopped. Diesel got out of the truck first and went to the barrier. An electric field of blue walled off the exit. It carried up into the sky where it disappeared behind clouds. "This is bubble number one. It was first laid down after what your realm calls the Victorian era."

"I don't see anything," Mat said.

"Humans can't see it. They can get through without any problem. The great Dr. Dolessenbee placed it over the area when Sam Winston, our king, settled here in the 1800s. Winston chose Central Maine because it was close enough to food sources and remote enough not to be detected by Pures."

"Pures?"

"Humans."

"Oh, right. I forgot about that."

"Winston gathered a group of supernatural and paranormal beings and transported them to the States . . . to this abandoned swath of land . . . to fight the advancement of humans. When Dr. Dolessenbee found out, he placed a bubble over them to prevent them from getting out and dominating America. There are a few portals around the edges to allow us out for feeding."

"Feeding."

"Dr. Dolessenbee prevented vampires from siring, but they still need to feed. Over time, Winston discovered propagating the various supernatural species extended the barrier, as it naturally grew to accommodate a burgeoning population."

"Propagate. Is that why they want you to mate with a she-wolf?"

Diesel nodded. "Over the past few centuries, Supers have dwindled, especially wolf-shifters. The rise of humans . . . we call it the Rise of the Normals, and people like you—no offense—who are immune to our threats, cause us to die off."

"Now I feel bad."

"Don't. Shifters, especially wolf-shifters, are among the lowest rung of the supernatural ladder. We only have one power: turn into a wolf. We've been dying off for a long time. It's the more powerful beings—witches, mages, and wizards—who are most threatened by you."

Mat followed Diesel who walked along the line. "There are other types of shifters?"

"Oh yeah. Some can turn into a lot of things. Me." Diesel touched the barrier and his hand shot back. "I'm just a bottom-of-the-barrel wolf-shifter. That is right, 'bottom of the barrel?'"

"Uh huh."

"Most Supers are evil," Diesel said. "When they lost World War II—"

"What do you mean lost World War II?"

"Supers were behind the rise of your realm's Third Reich." Diesel waved a hand just inches from the barrier's bluish haze. "Interesting, because *Reich* translates in English to realm . . . sort of. Never thought about that."

"Okay, this is getting too weird. I'm not sure I can absorb all this right here, right now."

"When Dolessenbee learned about the ability of the barrier to extend, he placed another over it. That border is about a mile from this one. Your friend's cabin is in between. Winston was grateful to get it last year when the border extended. He'd been after the Hawkins for some time."

"Why?"

"Why did he place the second one?"

"No. Why the Hawkins?"

Diesel shrugged. "Fresh meat?"

"The barrier, the original one, effectively locked us in time. The King and Queen abhor anything to do with humanity's progression, and they disseminated their disgust to the forest's inhabitants—banning anything post mid-nineteenth century. I learned a lot of this at university. Bence and I were rebels, dressing in twenty-first century clothing, and got our hands on discarded cell phones and computers in the Trash Heap."

Mat tilted his head, curiosity etched across his face, but Diesel pressed on.

"It's not all bad though. There are some good Supers. There's a faction of us who believe Supers and humans can coexist. There were very few of us in Hubbard Forest. With Bence gone, I'm probably the last. I learned about most of this at university."

"You were liberated?"

Diesel snickered. "The conservative a-holes that run this place are nuts."

"So, there's hope."

"Without hope, what else do you have?"

"Good point."

"The Monitors are a subset who believe humans will bring lasting peace."

"Monitors?"

"It's a group headed by a powerful wizard named Dr. Dolessenbee. Monitors watch over humans, like you, and shepherd you through to magichood."

Mat walked back toward the truck. "This is just way too weird."

"I'm sorry. I just wanted you to be aware."

"Are you my . . . my shepherd?"

"No! Monitors are highly skilled and trained. You have to be chosen by Dr. Dolessenbee."

"All right, brain overload. Too much info. The entire reality I thought I knew is falling apart."

Diesel placed a hand on Mat's shoulder. "Sorry, buddy. I'll stop. Let's see how we can get over to the other side."

Mat walked through the barrier with ease and held his hand out for Diesel who took it. As Diesel neared the edge, the field's electric charge knocked him back.

"Are you okay?" Mat went to him.

"I'm good." Diesel shook his head. "I think. Let's try another way."

Mat gave Diesel a hand to help him up on his feet.

"Perhaps you need to envelop me," Diesel said.

"Hug you through to the other side?"

"Yeah, maybe trick the barrier into thinking it's letting through a human."

At the edge, Mat held out his arms. Diesel wrapped an arm around his neck and jumped into them. "You're . . . not . . . the lightest thing I've ever carried."

"Go ass first."

Mat pushed his rump through the force field. When Diesel's body touched the grid, he shot out from Mat's arms and landed face first in front of the SUV.

"I don't understand how I can so easily get through and you can't. Then again, I don't understand a lot of what's going on here."

Diesel used the vehicle's bumper to get up and leaned onto the hood with his head hung down.

Mat rested next to him. "What if we drive through?"

Diesel gazed up.

About a half mile from the barrier, Mat revved the engine. "Ready?"

Diesel nodded.

The wheels spit gravel, and the vehicle barreled toward the line.

"Woo hoo!" Diesel yelled. "This may very well work."

"It better. That barrier better not ruin my car."

"We'll get you a new one if it does."

"Oh, yeah? With what currency? Super dollars?"

"We have tokens."

"Backed by what? Gold?" Mat asked.

"Magic. The root of all evil."

As they neared the line, electric sparks from the field shot out as if detecting Diesel's presence from afar.

Diesel beamed. "Faster! Faster!"

"I'm going eighty for God sake." Mat's hood sizzled. "I can see the energy now."

They crashed through the barrier with a heinous clatter. The truck shimmied.

Silence suspended them.

Blue sparks filled the cabin, followed by a burst of white. The automobile barreled through, and they blasted out the other side.

Mat slammed on the brakes. The vehicle smoked in its sideways turn, and they both jumped out.

"Holy shit!" Diesel laughed. "That was awesome!"

Behind the SUV, the barrier cracked like a vertical frozen pond.

"Uh oh." Diesel cupped his hands on the brim of his cap.

"I thought you said it was awesome."

"That's not good. Come on. The other barrier isn't too far from here."

They drove farther and stopped near where Luke had originally discovered the tear.

Diesel rushed out of the vehicle. "The rock is in the forest a bit deeper."

They plodded through a thick blanket of ferns and progressed past moss-laced pines.

"Dr. Dolessenbee, the guy who heads up the Monitors, manifested the barriers to contain the New England Paranormal Research Centre from expanding," Diesel explained. "I learned about Dol, as they call him, at university. Fascinating stuff."

"Dole? As in the pineapple?"

Diesel laughed hard. "No. But I know what you're talking about. I had canned pineapple at school."

While they walked farther, they discussed the history of the barrier system.

"The Great Wizard War, huh?" Mat said, codifying his understanding. "It started in the fifteenth century?"

"Yes, in human time. Fought between Dr. Dolessenbee and Sam Winston. It was said to have ended in your realm's period of 1969 or thereabouts, but from what I gather the battle continues."

"The sixties?"

"In the sixties, humans advanced further, spreading peace and love throughout the world. Supers were hell bent on stopping it but lost. Dol gained more magic . . . as humanity's rise stokes his power."

Mat kicked a pinecone. "This battle has been fought over humans? One side fearing their rise and another encouraging our supposed magic?"

"Uh huh. He supposedly lost a lot of his power over the last decade or two, and used most of his remaining magic to create a group of Monitors—"

"Monitors."

"Yeah, shepherds, if you will, who watch over humans, especially those brimming with potential and guides them through to what he calls 'mag ichood.'" He faced Mat. "Maybe you have one."

"Me? A shepherd? Who?"

Diesel shrugged. "Then again, from what I've learned, they're kind of scarce. Dolessenbee needs more magic to spread his mission further."

"So, this Dolessenbee wizard laid down the law with a second barrier . . . to stop them from getting out. And we just broke one."

"Yeah, that's not good." Diesel pointed to the lichen-covered boulder. "The tear in the second is behind that rock."

Diesel knelt at the rock's base. "I can scoot underneath it. We can try calling Bence with your cell phone on the other side. We should have better reception there."

Mat tapped his pockets. "I must've left my phone in the car."

Diesel scooched through. "That's all right," he shouted through the other side. "Meet me at the end of the road. You should be able to drive through no problem. We can call him from the truck."

MAT DROVE SLOWLY AROUND a bend.

Diesel stepped out from the thicket, waved, and jaunted over to Mat's open window. "Did you find your phone?"

"No, they took everything." Mat set the Toyota in park. "They even pilfered the extra clothes I packed for you."

"The scents along the trail are overwhelming. Apparently, more Supers knew about the tear than I thought. There's a hint of vampire, wolf-shifter, and more. I lost Bence's scent just a few yards past the rock on this side of the barrier." He took off his baseball cap and tossed it through the RAV4's window, then removed his shirt.

"What are you doing?"

"I need a better sense of smell to track him down." He unzipped his pants and shucked them off. "Hold these."

Mat took the clothes and placed them on the passenger seat.

Diesel ran naked toward the forest, dove into it, and shifted midair.

"Wait!" Mat got out and scurried after him.

By the time he found him, Diesel had transformed back and held the body of a blond man dressed in jeans and a dark-brown leather coat. A duffel bag clung to his arm. Diesel wept.

Mat knelt beside him. "Bence?"

Diesel wiped tears with the back of his hand. "He . . . he was clutching my totem." His voice hitched with emotion. "It's all my fault. I should've gone with him. If I had done what I wanted to do . . . what I really wanted to do . . . neither you nor he would be in this predicament."

"Shh. Shh." Mat knelt and hugged Diesel. Without knowing him, Mat still sympathized with the man's plight—trying to escape, off into a new world, and being thwarted before even starting. His features were striking, even in his death.

Diesel sobbed more. "Who would do this? Why?"

Across from them, a cage, of sorts, had been forced open and hung by ropes from a tree. "Was . . . was he in there?"

Diesel nodded. "I lost his scent, then saw him in the cage dangling from the tree." Diesel cried more.

"Did a human do it?"

"No, it's magic. There's no physical trauma." Diesel kissed Bence's forehead.

"Why?"

"I don't know, but I'm going to find out." Diesel lifted him and carried him to the road.

They placed Bence's body in the rear of Mat's SUV.

Diesel dressed by the side of the car. "The return into the forest might be a little bumpy."

"We're going back in? I thought the purpose was to get out."

He poked his head through his shirt. "It's probably best I drive."

Diesel drove a bit farther south at first to gain speed, turned around, then crashed through the barrier. The truck shuddered. The passenger side mirror flung off.

Diesel didn't slow. "Sorry about that. I'll repay."

"You don't have to. That's what insurance is for."

Diesel sped for the next barrier. "We need to bury him before the evil spirits discover him. We need to set his spirit free in a proper burial."

"Why couldn't we have buried him in the human realm? Wouldn't he be safe—?"

"Stop asking me questions!" Diesel tugged the brim of his ball cap. "I'm sorry. I . . . I don't know. I . . . I keep getting these intuitions to tell me what to do. Ever since that bounty hunter shot us."

"Maybe we shouldn't follow them then. Maybe they're trying to get us to do something for their benefit. They can't be trusted, Diesel."

They approached the next barrier.

"I . . . I can see the second barrier, well the first depending on which direction you're coming from," Mat said.

Diesel gunned the engine.

Mat held onto the dashboard. "It's like a bluish haze with a web-like pattern. And cracks running all along it."

"We damaged it . . . severely. Elio warned me." Diesel accelerated even more.

When they collided with it, the vehicle slowed as if it were confined by a net. The center console's bright lights flickered, and the air conditioning went out. The engine shuddered, then they snapped through to the other side. The vehicle spun, but Diesel gained control.

Behind them, the wall collapsed, shattering like glass. From the heavens above, another pane descended to take its place. Cracks veined across its surface, and the whole structure quivered, alive with unease.

Diesel engaged the four-wheel drive. "Welcome back, Bence."

THE VEHICLE'S AMENITIES WERE more modern than the 1993 Ford F-150 Diesel was accustomed to. He hunted for the right button to lower the windows.

"It is a little warm in here," Mat said. "The a/c went out."

Diesel pressed another button. The window grinded and slowly lowered. "We need to be quiet." He snapped off the driver's side mirror that had been banging against the door.

A black cloud darkened the road ahead.

"Wh . . . why is it getting so dark? It's high noon."

"Bence was left for possession." He rolled up the window.

"Oh, and I suppose you're telling me the possessor is coming to claim him."

"An unburied body is up for grabs. First taker wins."

"And we're going to offer him to this possessor?"

"Not if I can help it. But I'm gonna find out the mo'fo who did this and we're going to bury him properly before they can get his soul."

"We?"

They drove farther.

"How do you shut off the lights?" Diesel asked. "We need to be stealthier."

"Flip the button next to the . . . yeah, that one."

The car shimmied and sputtered. "For a modern vehicle you think this thing'd handle a few scrapes and scraps."

"Toyota didn't make this model to be driven through the supernatural world, Diesel."

A wail bellowed.

"Damn, they're getting closer."

"They?"

"The lost souls. They've discovered us and want to claim Bence's spirit. They like the company of others and don't want him to fully cross over. They're a jealous bunch and hate to see others get what they want."

"On top of vampires, mages, wizards, and wolf-shifters you have . . . ghosts?"

"Oh, there's far more supernatural and paranormal creatures than you can . . . shake a stick at? Is that—?" Diesel slammed on the brakes, and Bence's body slid forward with a thud.

"What's the matt . . . —?"

In the road, a gray mist cleared, and a pale girl stepped out. She wasn't that much brighter than the cloud from which she emerged. Hair covered her face, and she wore an ashen colored gown dotted with blood, dripping from a large wound on her neck. Her head wobbled, as if only a shred of tissue kept it from falling off.

In a sudden burst, she dashed up onto the hood of the car.

Mat screamed.

Her teeth were pointy and black. She gnawed at the windshield. Her head lobbed.

Diesel flipped the wipers on and squirt the sprayer. "Damn pests." She flew off.

Mat cowered.

The SUV crept forward. Diesel placed a hand on Mat, which spooked him. "We'll be all right. The burial ground isn't too much farther. Once we get him in the ground, they'll dissipate."

Another entity, this time an older man with no limbs, thumped a stump on Diesel's window. And another, a little boy, hovered by Mat's side.

"How, exactly, are we going to bury him with ghosts picking at us? Did your rambunctious teenage buddies leave a barb to get us out of this one?"

"No, but I've got a plan."

Behind them, a bastion of grayish women wailed. They rattled the rear of the car.

"Is one of these . . . or all of these . . . the killer?"

"I doubt it." Diesel accelerated the car, and the entities flew off. In a cacophony of squeals and snarls, they rushed after them. Diesel banked the vehicle right. The car vibrated loudly with the uptick in speed. The engine whined. Diesel banged the steering wheel. "Come on you modern contraption. Just a little bit more."

"I'm gonna need a new car."

"Sorry 'bout that. I'll get you one from the Trash Heap."

"I prefer hybrids."

"Not sure 'bout them, but I'll see what I can find."

The center console flickered. The lights went out, and the vehicle stalled.

The gaggle of ghosts approached. They clawed at the windows. A finger crept in through the ventilation.

Mat hollered and climbed into the back seat.

A head popped out from the vent on Diesel's side. He smashed it.

"They're getting in." Mat kicked at a head working its way through the speaker.

"They can't get to you. They just try and scare you."

Diesel opened the door and whistled with his fingers to his mouth.

By the time Mat opened his door, Diesel had already lifted the rear's hatch and took out Bence's body. Diesel whistled again.

A thunderous whoosh swept the ghosts and darkness away, but they quickly flowed back.

Diesel hoisted Bence's body over his shoulder. "Follow me."

They ran.

Another whoosh pushed the beings away, and, again, they leapt forward.

A deafening roar blared. A flame burnt away the darkened clouds. The ghosts shrieked.

The ground quaked, another flame burnt away another onslaught of paranormal beings, and Elio emerged from the clearing. Bingham hobbled over to Diesel.

"We haven't much time," Diesel said.

Elio moaned upon seeing Bence's body. He belched out another, more ferocious flame, and the ghosts evaporated.

Diesel set Bence onto Elio's back. "Climb onboard," he said to Mat.

"Wh-what?"

"We haven't time." Diesel hopped up and put out a hand for Mat. The ashen girl with the pointy teeth snapped at Mat's foot, and he rushed up onto Elio's back.

Elio mouthed Bingham and placed him beside Diesel.

"Hold on!" Diesel said, and they pelted off into the air.

Diesel hadn't ridden Elio in years. From above, the forest's vastness came into sight. But having ventured out beyond Hubbard Forest for university, the acres of land didn't seem as big as he remembered from childhood.

The wolf dens occupied the smallest component of the forest, and vampire cabins dominated the region. Former witch huts—now confiscated by mages, wizards, ogres, and fairies—were situated north of the wolf dens.

Above, the crack in the barrier they made spanned outward. Along the horizon, black specks—Malificious dragons—hovered around Hubbard Mountain, and a few buzzed around the castle's spire.

The paranormal cloud gained ground beneath them.

"Elio!" Diesel shouted. "Set down here." The Trash Heap's abandoned vehicles, human bones, and discarded riffraff emerged. "We can bury him where we met." Diesel swallowed hard and kissed the top of Bence's head.

Elio's wings softened the blow to the ground. Bingham slipped off first. Diesel handed him Bence's body and, he too, slid down.

Stunned, Mat stared and clung to a bony spike protruding from Elio's spine.

"Mat. Mat." Diesel touched him, and the man flinched.

The cloud of entities loomed.

Diesel yanked Mat off. A wet spot stained his pants.

"I . . . I'm afraid of flying," Mat said. "I . . . I've never even been on a plane." He glanced at Diesel.

Elio hurled flames at the approaching, now bigger cloud of paranormal activity. He hoisted up onto his rear legs, fanned his wings, and flung more flames. The ghosts cried and hollered.

Bingham dragged Bence to a clearing. Diesel rushed over to a fence edged with weeds and rusted out vehicles. He yanked a hubcap off an old Volkswagen Bus and rushed back to Bingham who had already started digging with his paw.

With two hands on the hubcap, Diesel dug.

Behind them, Elio roared. Ghosts cried.

"This is going to take forever." Diesel dug faster.

"Not much time," Bingham said.

Elio's roar quieted. Next, the dragon clawed at the ground and with two or three scrapes the hole was wide and deep enough to accommodate Bence's body.

Diesel spun around.

Mat stood with his back to them, and his hands splayed out. The paranormal cloud bounced up against him and shrieked. When they tried to work their way around him, he batted them back like a tennis ball, and they volleyed off into the forest.

Diesel removed Bence's totem from around his neck and returned it around his friend's. "Goodbye, Bence. I'll see you in the afterlife, buddy." He and Bingham lowered him into the hole.

Elio helped Bingham back out and, when Diesel stepped out, pushed dirt on top of the body.

"Wait!" Diesel jumped back in. He retrieved his own totem still clutched in Bence's rigor-mortised hand. "I have a persnickety feeling we might need this." He stepped back out. When Elio fully covered the body, the ghosts quieted and evaporated.

"They can't get him in there." Diesel lowered his head and prayed.

Elio's flames had set the surrounding trees on fire. They crackled and radiated heat. Mat fell to his knees.

Bingham lowered beside him. "Good job. Good job."

Elio moseyed over to Diesel. *Click, click, clack.*

"You think you can put the fire out?" Diesel said to the dragon. "The forest is pretty dry."

Elio clacked, set Bingham on his back, and flew off.

Diesel placed his totem around Mat's neck. "Something tells me this is safer with you rather than with me." He helped Mat up. "We're not done here."

Chapter Thirteen

Marksman

Jezebel slammed the cell door, and the man chained to it shuddered. "How could you let them get away!" She paced by the witch's cauldron. "What kind of bounty hunter are you? You are no doubt one of Winston's useless minions."

Sweat beaded on his forehead, and he mumbled.

She huffed. "I can't understand a word you're saying." She went to him and removed the bandana from his mouth.

"Oh, good Lord. Thank you." He breathed heavily. "They snapped my wand."

Jezebel picked up one half of the wooden stick beside him. "This teeny thing?" She twirled it. "Are you telling me you're a meager wand wizard?"

"Winston took my powers decades ago. That's all I've got left."

"Hm. We have something in common." She released the strap that held his right arm above his head. "Does your little stick have any juice left in it?"

He sighed with relief and grabbed the other half of the wand. A gold smear of magic plopped out like gel from a well-worn tube of toothpaste. "Perhaps a little."

Jezebel returned to the cauldron's hearth and removed a ring of keys from a hook embedded into the cupboards beside it. "If I unlock you . . . and you give me a little bit of your magic . . ."

"What are you suggesting?"

She dangled the keys from a finger. Her heels clicked along the wooden floor as she wandered over to the opposite end of the small cabin. "If I unlock you . . ." By the bed, she stepped onto a creaky board, stopped, and tapped it with the tip of her shoe. A hollow sound emitted.

"Jezebel, if you unlock me, I might be able to share some of the wand's magic."

She spun around. "How do you know my name?"

"I've done my homework. I may just be a wand wizard, but I've come prepared. You can call me Marksman."

"Marksman." She moseyed over to him, twirling the keys again. "What else do you know about me?"

"I know you're a hexed witch."

She cocked her head. "Winston told you that?"

He nodded. "Interesting. I didn't think he knew about any former witches in his dominion."

She went into the cell, knelt, and unlocked the cuff. Before he could rise, she slammed open the cell and exuded her dominance by banging it up against him.

"Easy!" He rubbed his side where the gate smashed into him. "I'm not going to do anything tricky."

"Let's keep it that way." She shut the cell's door behind her and returned to the creaky floorboard at the foot of the witch's bed.

Mark rose to his knees and tried to piece the two halves of the wand together. "You got any duct tape?" He sat down on the rocking chair, and the tip of the wand drooped.

"Tape? You need tape to keep it erect?"

"You'd be surprised at what modern inventions can do."

Jezebel pried open the floorboard and pulled out a black velvet satchel. "You say you lost your powers?"

Marksman nodded, but his eyes were trained on Jezebel's find. "What's that?"

"It's from the old witch who used to live here before The White Queen had her removed to Salem."

Mark eyed the medallion she pulled out from the bag. "A witch's amulet. Why didn't she take it?"

"Queeny wouldn't let them take anything. Most have been confiscated unless you know where they're buried. Interesting, Marksman . . ." She walked over to him. "Why did you lock my stepson and his lover-boy in a witch's cell?"

"Honoree and Buck told me this was the safest place to contain them." He snapped the wand back together, and it glowed red.

She stepped in closer. "Is it fixed?"

He licked a finger, touched the wand's tip, and it sparked. "Ouch." He looked to her. "I think so."

"Give me some of it." She grabbed for it.

He rose and held the wand up in defense. She stopped. "Why should I trust you?"

Jezebel smiled. "You shouldn't." She set a hand to her hip. "But I do know a way you can find the boys and get your bounty. How much are they offering you for their capture?"

"It doesn't matter."

"Tell me. I don't bite. I'm not a vampire for hell's sake."

He retrieved the bandana from the floor and wiped the wand with it. "Winston said it could grant me my powers back."

"Oh, well then. Capturing the boys must be very important to you."

He nodded.

Jezebel wandered over to the hearth. An open stack of shelving flanked its right. A small, circular tin of talc caught her attention, and she pocketed it. From the middle shelf, she pulled down a ceramic cup beside a dusty hardback *Book of Shadows*. "Shall we see where they are?" She tipped the cup onto her free hand, and a crystal globe rolled out.

"Does that thing work?"

"Only if I have my magic."

"That amulet. If I empower it, you can get the crystal orb to show us where they are?"

"Would I lie to you?"

AT THE METANORMAL'S CABIN, they hunted through the garage.

"It's gray and sticky," Marksman said.

"Does it look like a duck?" Jezebel tore through a box by the lawn mower.

"No. Duct. D-U-C-T," he said. "If we can keep it together long enough, I can charge your amulet and you can get the crystal ball to show us where they—" He pulled out a roll of tape.

Jezebel stared at it. "Oh, not at all what I imagined."

Once Marksman repaired the wand, he shot a ray of light at the amulet dangling around Jezebel's neck. It glowed red, stars burst into the air, hovered around Jezebel, and she inhaled them like an addict snorting a narcotic powder.

She tested his operation with a flick toward the dilapidated well across the lawn, and its rock base crumbled into the hole. "Not bad. Marksman, I may, very well, have to keep you around."

"Can you get the crystal to—"

"How 'bout you remove these shackles first?" She held out her wrist. "They bind my powers."

When Marksman pointed his wand at them, they heated and glowed red. "Satan in Heaven!" she yelled.

The tape around his wand's base melted, and the tip smoldered. "I think the curse is too powerful." The stick burst into flame. "Son of a—!"

Jezebel watched it fizzle to ash on the ground. "Is it broken?"

"That would be an affirmative."

"Sorry about that, Marksman. Perhaps the king can grant you a new one." She tossed the crystal globe into the air. "At least we have Witch Bazomella's ball." It hovered, then sped across the lawn. "Wait up." She chased after it.

MARKSMAN ATE POTATO CHIPS from a bag he had confiscated from inside the cabin. "How much longer till you get it under control?"

The crystal ball flew haphazardly about the front yard. Jezebel flung hooks of light at it to try and rein it in. "I haven't had my powers in decades. I'm just a little rusty is all."

"You shot that well up pretty good."

She set her shoulders back and reset locks that had dislodged from her bouffant. "Give me two more minutes."

"You sure you don't need any more help?"

"I can do this on my own, Marksman." She chased the crystal. "Witch Bazomella wasn't the most becoming of witches. I'm not familiar with her settings."

"I'm gonna make another sandwich." Marksman munched the rest of the chips. "The Metanormal's got some pretty good food in there."

"Blessed, finagled thing." Jezebel reached for the crystal, but it flew from her approach.

Marksman watched as he devoured another bag of potato chips. He removed a pocket watch—a sleek gold gadget looped through a buttonhole in his vest.

The crystal hovered with a soft buzz in front of Jezebel. "There," she sighed, "I told you I'd get it eventually. Bazomella was a horrible witch, that fat old maid." She cupped her hands around the floating orb. "Ah look, what have we here? It appears the barrier . . . it can't be."

"What?" Marksman returned his timepiece to its pocket and rushed to her side, leaving the empty snack bag in his wake.

"They've cracked the barrier. The magic's leaking out."

Marksman stepped closer to her. "The second barrier should contain them."

Jezebel showed him the crystal. "That other barrier is damaged too."

Chapter Fourteen

Fire

T HE FIRE HISSED AND snapped with an intensity Mat hadn't heard since being in California. He carved out a path through the dry grass and exposed the soil beneath to prevent flames from skipping over into the nearby field.

"We need to call in the Forest Service!" Mat yelled.

Diesel dug alongside him. "If they come, the vampires will get them. They'll be of no use."

Elio stamped out flames with his paws.

"We need water!" Mat shouted.

"The lake is too far from here."

Elio thrust Bingham onto his back.

"Where are you going?" Diesel asked the dragon, but he flew off without explanation.

"We need to contain the fire," Mat said. "Keep digging a trench."

"Without Elio it isn't easy."

"We need a scratch line to prevent it from jumping." Mat yanked out a few weeds within the widened path they had carved. "Get it down to the soil."

"I'm trying. I'm trying. Elio's flames don't typically cause such devastation. It's like the magic is leaving the forest."

"Well, I don't know about your reality, but in the human realm torching dry brush causes forest fires."

Diesel stopped. "That's it! Human reality is leaking in. That's why it's worse near the town line."

"Huh?"

"The breaks in the barrier . . . your reality is sinking in." Diesel looked up. Beyond the smoke, air plumed where the crack lay. "Elio was right. He knew crashing through it wasn't the right thing to do."

"I don't know about that. Oxygen is fanning it."

They worked the ground, extending the control line farther. When they surrounded the perimeter, Mat pointed to a cluster of dead trees within the hot spot. "We need to knock 'em down to prevent them from catching. Leaving them up is like playing a game of dominoes with matchsticks inside a tent of fireworks."

Flames licked nearby as they kicked at the bases of the dried-out trees until they gave way. When they finished toppling down the last of the bunch of trees, they hopped back over the control line and rested in the center of the field.

"There's not much more we can do right now."

"Do we just let it burn?" Diesel caught his breath.

"We need to pace ourselves. There's only two of us. Overworked, we're useless. We need backup." Mat stamped out a glowing flake that landed nearby.

"Elio will be back soon."

"Where did he go?"

"Most likely to get Bingham out of harm's way."

"He's been gone for a while." A cloud darkened over them. "Is that the paranormals coming back?" Mat asked.

Diesel jumped up. "No, I don't think so." He held a hand to his forehead. "It's . . . it's Emphilothepy!"

"Emphilo-what?"

"Emphilothepy. Green dragon. It's Elio! He's back with others. Elio! Over here!" Diesel waved.

They ran toward the control line.

Above, Elio dove and lifted his leg, and a cadre of dragons behind him did the same.

"Get back!" Diesel said to Mat and ran the other way.

"What—?" A golden shower rained down on Mat.

Diesel laughed, hands on haunches.

Mat held his arms out. His shirt dripped with dragon urine. "It stinks." He ran out of the way as another dragon squatted above the flames.

The dragons clicked and squeaked, like an aerial ballet of dolphins at SeaWorld.

"They're drinking from the lake, then peeing on the fire." Diesel cheered on Elio as a line of dragons, headed by Elio, flew away to refuel.

"Brilliant! Have them work their way in from the edges, where the scratch line is."

Diesel whistled at a trio of Emphilothepy with their backs to them like men at a line of urinals. "Guys, over here!" He pointed.

Mat and he ducked, as dragon urine zoomed overhead.

"Good. Nice aim!" Diesel said.

After the dragons extinguished the fire, Mat and Diesel rested in the middle of the field and watched them pirouette out of sight. A soft wind rustled burnt-out trees, and the acrid stench of urine mixed with smoldering wood pranced in the air.

"You need a shower," Diesel said.

"Dragon piss isn't the most becoming of colognes."

"I'm exhausted."

"Me too."

For a few minutes, the men basked in the afternoon sun until a high-pitched, onomatopoeic chirp alerted Mat.

Diesel rose onto his elbows. "What is that?"

The noise grew closer.

Mat stood. "It's Trinity."

"The redhead?"

"That's the sound of her Volkswagen. There can't be too many of those around here. She must've called me and grew worried when I didn't answer or call back."

"She shouldn't be here."

"I know. I tried to tell her not to come up for the weekend. She must've called out. It's not Friday yet."

"Called out?"

"She's a teacher. Last I talked to her, she wanted to pull in a sub and take a few extra days off to come see me."

"A sub?"

"I should go to her. Before the vampires do."

"You have some time. The fire will mask her scent. Do you want me to come?"

"It's probably best I do this on my own."

"Right."

The engine's sputter grew louder.

"I should check in on Mitsy and make sure the wolf den didn't get damaged in the fire."

"Or drenched in dragon urine."

Through a cluster of trees on the other side of the field, Trinity's blue Beetle sped past.

IN BED, MITSY CLUTCHED a wooden statue of the deity Baphomet and prayed. Her windowless den was warm and stale.

"Let me take you to Mat," Diesel said.

"I'm too weak," Mitsy replied.

"I can carry you."

"No, I need rest."

"But his touch helped you."

"Only temporarily."

"He can make you well." Diesel tried to pick her up, but she flinched and grabbed her belly.

"It's too much, Dee. I just need to relax some."

"Even if it were just temporary, he might be able to make you last through to full-term."

"I have Lord Darthius. Please, go. You shouldn't be here. Buck and Honoree will be back any minute."

"Where are they?"

"Looking for you. They're mad at what you did to the NEPRC wizard."

"He's a lowlife wand wizard."

"Diesel! Enough. The Lord says we shouldn't judge."

"He drugged us and chained us up."

"Buck and Honoree will find your scent here. I'll have to cover for you. Again."

"Don't worry. I washed in the lake to reduce my body odor and rolled around in pine needles to smell more natural."

"Good."

"I did something bad, Mits."

She huffed. "What now?"

"I broke the barrier."

She moved to get up but winced in pain and remained flat. "Is that what caused that fire?"

"Well, yes and no."

"I'm not sure I want the details. The less I know, the better I am."

"Bence is dead."

She was silent.

"I found him after we crashed our way out. I brought him back and gave him a proper burial."

"What!" This time she rose, pain and all. "What about the paranormals?"

"Elio kept them back, then Mat."

"I'm going to be sick. Quick. Get me a—" She vomited off the side of the bed into a bucket.

Diesel got a cold washcloth and placed it to her forehead. "You've got a fever, Mitsy. I'm worried."

"Sunday, the night Bence escaped"—she pressed the cold compress against her cheek—"Buck was late coming back for the bonfire. He and Elder Bainbridge showed up long after the first bottle of cognac."

"You . . . you don't think they did it? Do you? Why?"

"There's been scuttlebutt about the need for a sacrifice." She threw up again.

THE WASHING MACHINE SQUEALED in its spin cycle, and Mat—freshly showered, shirtless, and dressed in Trinity's loose-fitting, earth-tone yoga pants—removed a soda from the fridge.

The stack of deli meat on the top shelf had been opened and half of it gone. "Were you hungry?" he asked Trinity, who sat in the living room.

She wore blue faded skinny jeans with a tear in the right pocket and a yellow-flowered, off-the-shoulder blouse. She sat with her legs tucked under her small frame and shuffled through photographs with the box of memorabilia beside her.

"Trinity?"

"Oh . . . what did you—?" She inspected him and burst out laughing. "Those yoga pants are just stunning on you."

"Ha. Ha. Very funny. Well, the tight pink ones would've been a little X-rated."

She set the pictures down on the coffee table. "Thanks for all you've done around here." She pointed to the boarded-up window he had patched from Witch Lena's hurls of magic. "Shame about the window, porch, and well. I'll have to get it repaired before putting it on the market. But other than that, the place looks great."

He considered lying about how the damage occurred but instead remained silent.

She rose off the couch and pressed out an inconspicuous wrinkle in her jeans. "After their death, I couldn't bring myself to come up here alone." She leaned against the island. "We used to come here in the summer. The place has been in my family for generations. I hate to sell it but—"

"Maybe you shouldn't sell."

She went to the fridge. "It's either this place or the house in Elk. I still can't believe my parents had such a high mortgage on it. If I sell this, I can pay off their debts and keep the main house. Plus, the house in Elk is closer to civilization. There's not much out here."

"You have no idea what's out here."

She cracked open a can of naturally flavored seltzer. "Like the person who stole your car."

He pointed to her drink to avoid further lying about the absence of his Toyota. "No more Coca-Cola?"

"You know I don't drink that stuff."

Mat furrowed his brow. "There was a six pack of Coke in there. There are only two left."

"You think I'd drink that sugary crap?" She slurped and returned to the couch. "I brought a bunch of groceries." She held up her drink. "And my seltzer."

Mat scratched his head. "Maybe Diesel . . ."

"Diesel?"

"He's the guy you saw on the phone the other day."

"The hot one?"

Mat chuckled and folded his arms across his chest. "Yeah, that one."

She hugged her knees. Her sandals lay on the floor beside a book of Mad Libs. "Oh, do tell."

"Tell what?"

"I can read it all over your face, Mat. You like him."

"Trinity."

She rose. "You do." She walked to the kitchen area. "Are you guys . . . an item?"

"No. We're not . . ." His face flushed. He slid open the partition to the closet off the kitchen, removed his clothes from the washer, placed them in the dryer, and turned on the machine.

Trinity, sitting on the counter, strummed her feet along the lower cabinets. "I'm waiting."

"Waiting for what?"

"The details."

Mat huffed. "All right. We did it."

She jumped down. "What? You guys had sex?"

"Shush." He beamed.

She hugged him. "Oh, Mat! I knew you were gay. I'm so happy for you."

"Happy? What about . . . us?"

Trinity pulled away. "I have a tendency of falling for not-so-straight men. I knew it from that time in the back of the Beetle when you couldn't—"

"Let's not . . . go there."

While clothes clanged in the dryer, Trinity made a snack of celery, carrots, pita chips, and hummus from her stash, and they ate from a shared plate at the timeworn table in the center of the kitchen. Blue distressed cabinets surrounded them, and a rusted refrigerator with a pull-down handle hummed beside her.

"So, have you had any more visions?" Mat asked.

Trinity licked hummus from her thumb. "In a meditation the other day, I got the sense that Fragrance was a dragonfly."

"Fragrance?"

"Ginny, my kid sister. We nicknamed her Fragrance. She was a brilliant blue dragonfly with green, iridescent wings. I'd never seen anything so beautiful. I got the warmest feeling about it. It buzzed all over." She gazed at the ceiling, then glanced at Mat. "Have you seen any more . . . vampires?"

"No. Just werewolves."

Trinity suspended a celery stick over the dip, then laughed. "Good one."

"No, really. There was an injured wolf I saved."

"Oh, you mean a real wolf."

"There's a pack in the forest."

"You should be careful. They can be dangerous."

"Diesel is . . ." Mat bit a chip.

"Hm?"

"Diesel is good with them. The wolves."

Trinity nodded.

Mat swallowed. "Do you believe in magic?"

"What are you saying?"

"It's just . . . all these weird coincidences. Like us meeting online. Me wanting to move to New England. You, living in Maine."

"What does that have to do with . . . magic? New England's a big region. It's not all that coincidental that we met. Facebook is, after all, a global app."

"I felt compelled to quit the forestry and come here."

"Okay." She picked a baby carrot off the plate. "And I felt compelled to welcome you into my life . . . be it in whatever form our relationship took."

"Ty came to me again. He told me I should 'save the dog.' I think he meant wolf, because he had never seen one, and Diesel's wolf kind of looks like a big dog."

"Diesel has a pet wolf?"

Mat sighed. "He is a wolf."

Trinity dipped the carrot into the hummus. "Were you . . . drinking by any chance?"

"I gave it up."

"Good for you. I should keep the wine coolers I brought in my bedroom."

"Ty meant I should save Diesel. It's a little confusing, but Diesel is . . . the dog . . . or the wolf rather."

Trinity sipped seltzer. "Oh, I brought you your anti-depressants. You left them in the spare bathroom."

"You think I'm crazy, don't you?"

She touched his hand. "No, Mat. I don't think you're crazy. I guess, it's not as crazy as me thinking Fragrance is a dragonfly buzzing about Hubbard Forest."

"She was flying around here?"

"She loved dragonflies and loved coming to the cabin." She pinched the bridge of her nose. "It's just my mind trying to make sense of all that's happened over the last year."

"I get it." Mat nodded. "Trinity, I lied about being away fighting the fire when Maxine and Ty died. I was at a gay bar in San Francisco with a guy I met on Joindrr."

She reached across the table and grabbed his hand. "Why didn't you tell me? Or the group when we all shared our stories?"

"I couldn't tell myself. I couldn't admit it. Till now. Diesel helped me . . . it's a long story."

"Well, thank you for sharing that. It must feel good to get it off your chest."

"It does."

"So, when do I get to meet Diesel?"

"He's at his sister's. She's pregnant."

"Oh, how sweet. He's going to be an uncle." She snapped the lid back on the hummus and a clip onto the chip bag. "We shouldn't spoil our appetite. I brought salmon. We can cook it in the pit for dinner."

"It's dry around here. We should be careful with a campfire."

"Speaking of that, there was a fire along I-95." She placed the hummus back in the fridge.

Mat turned around. "You saw it?"

"Yeah, they were dousing it from overhead."

"Did you . . . see the dragons?"

She froze—chip bag in hand and an upper cabinet open. "Let me get you your medicine."

I N A REMOTE AREA of the forest near the lake, an enormous pine tree grew through the center of Elder Bainbridge's den. The oldest, known, living wolf-shifter lived in a hollow below the tree.

Diesel dabbed pine sap to his neck to mask his scent. He rubbed some on his wrists, under his arm pits, and—after looking over his shoulders—put his hands down his pants and applied some to his testicles.

As he approached, the door to Bainbridge's hovel opened, and Buck came out. Diesel ducked behind the tree and waited for him to walk, down the wooded path, out of sight.

Diesel opened the door. "Elder Bainbridge?" he shouted, knowing the man was hard of hearing. "It's me, Dan Diesel Cade. Bainbridge?"

The elder shuffled out from one section of the den and into its center. He used a cane to aid his step over to a rocking chair and removed a shawl from the back of it.

"Excuse me. Elder Bainbridge!" Diesel said.

The wolf-shifter turned in his direction. He sniffed the air. A long, gray beard, pointed at the tip, hung from his thin face. Bushy eyebrows hooded his blue, glaucoma-ridden eyes. "Who's there?"

Diesel stepped closer to him. "Elder Bainbridge. It's me Daniel Cade."

"What . . . what are you doing here?" He placed the wooly, gray shawl over his shoulders. "Do you know your father is looking for you?"

"I do, sir. Please, may I have a minute?"

Bainbridge lowered to the seat—revealing bony knees in the process—and rocked. "The last time you were here, I told you to go off to school and study Humanity."

"I appreciated that, sir. It helped my father and stepmother make their final decision. Did you know I graduated with honors?"

"I heard. Have you learned to defeat them?"

Diesel dragged over a stool and sat. "About that."

"That is why you studied humans after all, right? Why else would a Super learn about humans?" Bainbridge rocked and stared ahead. Wiry hairs wormed out from his ears and nose—the latter, wriggling with each whistling exhalation.

"I went to UPS in Yorkshire to study and learn all about them." Diesel knew, even back then, the only way to get approval to major in such an oddity was to acquiesce to their foul notions.

"Then, why are you trying to leave the forest? Honoree and Buck tell me you tried to escape again. We are in our greatest time of need. Your father has no male heir. You can't abandon your flesh and blood. You have an obligation to this pack."

Diesel gazed at the ground. Tears welled. "I . . . I can't do it, Elder Bainbridge. I'm a freethinker."

"Religion is the way. Devotion to the Lord will set you free."

"Is it the only way? My instincts tell me different—"

"Your totem is your instinct. It's your destiny!" Bainbridge's voice grew phlegmy. "Your way will be revealed at the Howling Moon of your twenty-first year." Bainbridge gazed a cloudy stare Diesel's way, hunting for the amulet.

Afraid the man may see through clouded eyes that he wasn't wearing it, Diesel leaned back in the stool. "I want to live beyond these walls. I want to live with humans and be just like them."

"Daniel! You belong here!" Bainbridge's whistling nose revved into a higher pitch. "What about your poor sister, raising her son? And your friend there . . . that dragon . . . not sure what you see in him, but what would they do without you? Do your duty. Your father will find you a nice she-wolf."

"The girls laugh at me."

"Because you wear funny clothes and hang out with that frilly, orphaned Bence boy."

"About Bence . . ."

With the aid of his cane, Bainbridge rose, shuffled over to a closet a few yards away, and removed a moose hide from a hook. "This is your grandfather's cloak." A few bald spots mottled the gray fur, which hung belong Bainbridge's knees as he shimmied back. "He wore it in his final battle during the Peace Movement."

"Honoree II?" Diesel met him halfway and took the wrap.

"He was your grandfather. A great fighter that man." Bainbridge returned to the rocker with a sigh of relief and his nasal passage quieting to a faint whistle. "Go on, put it on. She-wolves don't like men who wear clothes from the human's modern realm, Daniel. I don't know how many times we must tell you. No woman wants to be with a pure-like man."

"I will."

"Humans don't believe in magic. That's their species greatest downfall."

"Some do."

"Very, very few, Daniel Cade. And we need to keep it that way."

"Maybe magic isn't all it's cracked up to be."

"Cracked up to be?"

"It's a human saying . . . maybe magic isn't so great after all. In school, I learned about concrete reality: time, space, and evolution. I'd rather know what's really real and live from that place."

"Things are only real because those who interpret it as such think it is so. Think about that, my son. If enough were to see it and agree on it, then it would be, as you call, real. I call it magic."

"Bence was killed outside the second barrier."

Bainbridge rocked. "A shame. He was a good-looking boy. Could've made some nice cubs. What was he doing outside the barrier and how did you find him?"

"He was escaping, sir."

"And in your leaving you discovered his body?"

"Yes."

"Those humans. They're treacherous." His nose whistled. "Homo sapiens have grown stronger over the centuries. It must've been that Meta—"

"I don't think it was a human who killed him."

Bainbridge blinked.

"He died the other night after the hunt. I heard you and Buck were late in joining for the ritualistic bonfire afterward." Diesel, with his grandfather's hide in hand, returned to the stool.

"My memory's a bit foggy these days. When was this?"

"This past Sunday. You were handing out cloaks for the shifters when we returned."

"Ah, Buck and I had some business to attend to."

"What kind of business?"

"What do you want to know, Daniel Cade?"

"Did you know anything about Bence's disappearance?"

"You two were off by the fence refusing to hunt."

Heat swept across Diesel's face and neck, embarrassed the Elder may have known about them with the *PEOPLE* magazine. "How did you know we were there?"

"The fence was jangling."

Diesel tugged the brim of his ballcap down. "We were just . . . killing time . . . waiting for the portal to open."

"Bence left a bag behind."

"That's right. He did. He later went back to—"

"Ketch put something in it."

Sweat trickled down Diesel's neck, and his body tingled. "Ketch? What did he put in it?"

"That's the business I was attending to with Buck. Apparently, the king asked for a tracking device on your friend."

"A tracking device? What for?"

Bainbridge's nose simmered to a low hiss. "I don't know."

Chapter Fifteen

Fate

At the crest of Hubbard Mountain, the vegetation thinned out to scrub brush, and an ocean of autumn colors decorated the panorama below. Marksman's Jeep traversed a dusty, dirt trail.

Jezebel checked her appearance in the visor Marksman had lowered for her. "I guess some horseless carriages are of benefit. Even dragons don't come equipped with passenger mirrors."

They parked in a dirt-scratched area at the castle's foundation and made their way to a portcullis, a vertical, opened gate with a wooden-lattice grille and rods along its base designed to lock into holes beneath them. The rusted, unguarded entrance gained them access.

Jezebel went to a set of dank rock stairs that spiraled up along the castle's large, block wall. "Go get your little wand fixed," she said to Marksman and pointed to a hallway opposite her that led to a repair shop.

"It shouldn't take too long." Marksman twiddled the remaining piece of his wand.

"Well, then go play pool and drink beer with all the other indolent men. I need time with Her Majesty," she said with a hint of indignity, "to plead for a little more juice to fix the barriers." She took off her high heels and ascended the stairs.

When she reached the top, out of breath, she clutched a green, velvet drape stitched with a gold border that hung at an opened window and wiped the soles of her feet with it. She checked her appearance in the gleam of an armored suit nearby.

A tinny voice echoed. "Miss Jezebel?" One of The White Queen's sprites flew down from the grand hallway. Her eyes, the size of two black grapes, appeared oversized and insect-like for her small head. She flitted about beating large, purple wings that matched her gauzy dress, adorned with white feathers.

"Does the queen always leave this place so unfortified?" Jezebel asked. "Do you know that the NEPRC bounty hunter and I walked right in here unaccompanied?

"Miss Jezebel, the king and queen fear nothing here. There's no reason for guards, and they let us roam freely."

"And where are you and all your colorfully dressed friends? Shouldn't you be scouting about the forest looking for those of us who might need assistance—like acquiring a Malificious instead of riding in some Satan-awful NEPRC truck? Do you know how long it took us to get here?"

"I'm—I'm—"

Jezebel flung a hand at the sprite. "Enough of you. Send me to The queen."

The sprite led her down the hallway. A large, azure runner with gold fleur-de-lis covered part of the white marble floor and marked the way. "Where is Witch Lena?" the sprite asked. "She and I are supposed to paint our nails tomorrow morning. I picked out a beautiful shade of lilac to match my—"

"She's dead."

The sprite flew back and bounced up against a picture of King Winston in his younger days, wearing a suit of armor and brandishing a large wand with a forked spike. Her bottom lip quivered.

The White Queen napped, head slung forward, on her throne. The king's empty chair was positioned several yards opposite her.

"Your Majesty," the sprite said, flying near her face to wake her.

The queen stammered. "Jitsu, you know . . . you know it's my nap time."

The sprite leaned back, as if catching a whiff of foul breath.

"Why are you bothering me?" The White Queen caught sight of Jezebel. "Oh."

Jezebel grinned and offered a poor attempt at a curtsy. "Good afternoon . . . Your Majesty."

"What brings you back here? And where's Lena?"

"Oh," Jezebel's heels clicked forward, "I just broke the news to your little faerie. She didn't make it. The Metanormal killed her."

The queen shot up from her throne. "I don't believe you. You killed her."

Jezebel laughed. "I did not. I'm telling you the Satan-honest truth. She did, however, leave me her powers." Jezebel chose to hold aside the details of her waning magic and slung a ray of golden light past the queen and buzzing sprite.

The queen and Jitsu flinched as a picture, behind them, fell to the floor. "The shackles, I see, still bind you," the queen said, with an air of dominance.

"You need to remove them, so I can have my full powers and kill the Metanormal."

"Ha." The queen bosom bounced along with her laughter. "I can't do that."

Jezebel rushed forward. "You can't? Or you won't?"

The queen dismissed Jitsu with a flick of her hand and when the sprite flew off, closing the heavy, paneled double doors behind her, the queen resumed placement onto the throne. "Jezebel, you know very well the shackle's removal is not a woman's job."

"What *is* a woman's job?" Jezebel asked, not expecting a reply and receiving none.

"When you killed the wolf pack, you substantially hurt the region's growth."

Jezebel stepped onto the queen's dais. "It was fifty years ago! They deserved to die."

"They were wolves, Jezebel. Your witch-baby was an inferior being."

"They didn't need to kill it!" She went to the alcove of windows behind the throne and gazed out at the forest.

"You know the Lord's stance on such deformities." The queen joined her at the window. "They'll weigh us down, marring the growth of our kingdom and the expansion of the barrier system. Our ecosystem only grows with healthy genes and strong magic. She didn't stand a chance, Jezebel."

Jezebel clenched her teeth. "Do you know what it's like knowing there are better ways . . . faster ways of magic? Do you know what it's like living for over fifty years . . . fifty long years with your only trick being to turn into a she-wolf?"

"That was your punishment for causing the population's demise. What happened to Lena, Jezebel?"

Jezebel faced her. "She hexed the Metanormal. Her magic flung back and killed her."

"And she gave you her remaining charm?"

Jezebel nodded.

"A transfer of magic, from witch-to-witch, is short lived, you know?" The queen moseyed over to the picture on the floor.

Jezebel, still leaning on the windowsill, dropped her head. "It's already vanished."

"Then this outburst that knocked down my picture of Fluffy from the wall." She hung it back up. "Explain."

"Your husband's wand wizard lent me more."

The White Queen spun around. "Wand wizard? What are you talking about?"

"After Lena's demise, the clan called in NEPRC. They sent a bounty hunter named Marksman. He's not very good, but he did have some magic in his pathetic, little wand."

"Marksman? A bounty hunter? What in the heaven is my husband up to these days? Men. He's still in Yorkshire wrangling support for the Rise. He must've sent in a lowlife. Perhaps he doesn't know how serious this is. Jitsu!" The White Queen opened one of the French doors. "Fetch an orderly. Have them inform King Winston that a Metanormal has breached the forest. We need more power."

In her pocket, Jezebel snapped open the tin of talc she lifted from Witch Bazomella's.

The White Queen rambled on about the king. She addressed his empty throne, as if he were present. "All this mumbo-jumbo about humans. Who cares about them? We're supernaturals. We reign supreme." She faced Jezebel. "Do you know he's been building these new tracking devices to monitor the supers?"

"No, I didn't." Jezebel cupped a scoop of powder in her hand, covered her mouth, and pretended to sneeze. "Oh, excuse me." The bewitching talc floated through the air till it evaporated near the queen.

"Jezebel, are you catching a cold?"

"Allergies. The pollen's been incredible."

"Mm." The queen dusted the top of King Winston's throne. "The more we grow, the more the barrier does to support our species. We mustn't let Diesel leave. We expanded the barrier almost a quarter of a mile in circumference last year. Only another decade and we'll reach civilization. But we need healthy males, Jezebel, to grow more. Males who want to be with females. You know this. And your daughter, as feeble as she was, wouldn't have been able to bear a child."

Jezebel, now closer to the queen, sneezed again. This time, the powder made a direct hit.

"Oh, Jezebel. All that sniffling and sneezing is most—" The queen sneezed, then wobbled. "It's most un . . . be . . . coming."

Jezebel tore off to her side. "Queenie, if I can trap that Metanormal and keep Diesel inside the barrier, maybe the king will realize the importance of witches and women."

The queen's pout exposed interest.

"Retrieve the sprite," Jezebel said. "We don't need a man to do this. Do we?" She grinned.

"No. No, we do not. I shall do so indeed." The queen flung open the doors to the grand hall. "Jitsu! Jitsu!" She leaned around the corner. "Jiiitsuuu!"

Unable to contain her hatred for the queen any longer, Jezebel's fangs shot out, and she charged at her. She slammed the doors with a partial paw. Took out the bewitching powder's tin and shoved it in the queen's face, smearing the reaming talc to her mouth.

"Oh. Oh." The queen's reluctance turned to an eager want for the remaining talc, and she licked the insides of the tin as if it contained a sugary snack.

Jezebel's transformation retreated, but she still trembled with anger. "You will do as I say." Recalling her eaten-alive daughter, her rage intensified. "You . . . you had that wolf pack kill my daughter." Jezebel's voice hitched with emotion. "You . . . you single handedly made me live out my days as a friggin' lowlife wolf-shifter to teach me a lesson. Ha! Well, guess who's teaching who now? Grow the species for the benefit of the kingdom, my ass! I'll do it to take over."

The doors unlatched, and the sprite buzzed back in. "Yes, Your Majesty."

Jezebel backed away from the queen, grinned, and returned the empty tin to her pocket. "Jitsu." She curtsied.

"Never mind about bothering King Winston," the queen said. "He'll just send over another wand wizard. We can handle the situation on our own. Can't we, Jezebel?"

"Indeed." Jezebel held out her wrists. "Loosen me up a little. I'll need full power for this."

"Oh?" The queen cocked her head, and a reluctant frown wrought her face.

Jezebel huffed, fearing the bewitching talc's expiration. "The barriers need repair. The human and *my* stepson have done some awesome damage to it."

"Oh, my. Jitsu, some pixie dust, please."

Jitsu hovered, wings beating a purple haze. "But, Your Majesty."

"You heard me! Unleash her!"

WITH A GOLD TETHER around their wrists, Jezebel led The White Queen and Jitsu down the grand hallway.

The White Queen stumbled, shook her head, and sneezed.

Jezebel tugged the rein, as if leading a pack of poodles farther. "I shall hold you hostage till King Winston gives me my way."

The White Queen sneezed again, a bit more ferociously, and halted. "Jit-Jitsu?"

The sprite buzzed closer to her and whispered into her ear.

"Come on you two!" Jezebel yanked the lead.

"Wh . . . what?" The White Queen reeled back. "You-you bewitched me!" She flung her hands up in the air, breaking Jezebel's teether on her and the faerie and encroached Jezebel's space.

"Damn, I knew I should've checked the powder's expiration."

"Who do you think you are?" The queen's eyes glowed red. "I am Queen! You are, at best, a peasant witch!" She hurled a ray of magic that slammed Jezebel in the gut.

Jezebel floundered backward. "Oh, the old lady has a bit of gumption in her after all. I have my powers back, you bitch! Let's just see who's stronger." Jezebel conjured a spider, larger than Jitsu, and it shuffled toward the queen who screamed. "I know your fears."

The queen backed away, bumped up against a suit of armor, and it toppled. Jitsu picked up the headpiece, flung it at the spider, and it evaporated.

Jezebel shot out a gold thread from her fingertips and throttled the sprite at the neck with it.

"Jezebel! Let her go!" The White Queen said.

"Why should I?"

The queen slapped Jezebel in the face. "Because I said so."

Jezebel placed a hand to her stinging cheek. "You bitch!"

Jitsu freed, darted toward her, and yanked out Jezebel's coiffed bouffant. "I know your fears too."

"Stop! Stop!" Jezebel swatted. Her long, black hair fell in disarray to her face and shoulders.

Jitsu tore at Jezebel's dress. "Who are you calling a bitch? I'll show you who's bitchy." The faerie's little wrists pummeled Jezebel's face till blood dripped from the witch's nose. "There, bitch!" Jitsu punched an upper cut, and Jezebel fell flat on her back.

Dazed, Jezebel rolled over and rose upon her knees.

Jitsu zoomed back on her and yanked her hair back.

"Enough, Jitsu." The White Queen clapped her hands. "Thank you." She conjured a rope and tied Jezebel to the stairwell's post.

Jezebel tugged at the rope. "Look, I'm sorry."

"Sorry? You betrayed royalty," the queen said.

Jezebel leaned up against the post and hung her head. "I need my magic." A tear mixed with the blood from her nose and blended into her red dress. "I need to save my child."

"Your daughter is dead." The White Queen stood over her, hands on hips, and Jitsu flitted by her shoulder.

"Not her." Jezebel sniffled. "I had another."

"What? When?"

"I had a boy. I wanted to birth a male to get my power back. I wanted to fulfill my mission and provide a male heir for Honoree."

"Where is this child?"

"His name is Bingham."

"I didn't ask for his name. I asked for his location."

"He's in hiding. I told Honoree it was his child, whilst I carried it, but when it was born . . . " She wept. "It was so deformed. I knew the pack . . . and you!"—Jezebel's snout emerged—"would have it killed. I told the pack that it died in childbirth."

"Was no one witness to the birth?"

"You don't know male wolves. He and Buck were off drinking."

Outside, the sky sparked in nightfall.

"What in evil hell is happening out there?" The queen went to the window with the thick green, velvet drapes.

Jezebel wiped blood from her nose. "The barrier is broken. I told you."

"You must not be serious? It can't break. It's been in existence for centuries."

"Well, I told you: Mat, the Metanormal, and Diesel busted through it trying to escape."

"That's right. It's a wonder I remember anything after being drugged with witch talc. Honestly, Jezebel."

"Human reality will settle in," Jitsu said. "Our magic will evaporate. We must fix it."

"How?" Jezebel lifted her tied up hands. "Even for me, just a peasant witch, it's too much."

Thunder boomed, lightning flashed, and another much louder and brighter one followed. The castle shook.

"Jezebel," the queen unfurled the magical cord that bound her, "if you so much as blink the wrong way, I shall curse you bald." She released the final knot. "And you know I can." She wandered down the hall. "Quick, there isn't time. We must fix the barrier. Jitsu! Come."

The three rushed down the hall to a doorway at the far end. Behind the egress, they took to a set of stairs.

The White Queen grasped the hem of her dress and began her ascent. "Jezebel, I hate to break it to you, but, even without your shackles, witch power is not of much use in Hubbard Forest anymore."

Jezebel stopped. "What do you mean?"

"Winston insisted upon removing all the witches or hang them. I chose to banish them to Salem."

"Why?"

"For one, your scrummage with the wolfpack didn't help set a good precedence." She stopped and caught her breath. "More so, women were becoming too powerful."

"But not all witches are female."

"True, but even the males—the few that we had—were sympathetic to their plight. He let me keep one, Lena, as we need someone with bewitching capabilities, and he trusted my decision to retain her."

"That's why Witch Lena's powers didn't last very long. And my own, when I used my amulet in the dragon's den . . . I should've been able to get more out of it."

"You have your amulet? I asked for them to be taken."

"Since when do I listen?"

They climbed farther.

"Why didn't he throw me out too?" Jezebel asked.

"You are . . . or were . . . cursed as a wolf-shifter. Duh."

Jitsu, who was several steps ahead of them, flew back. "I'm beginning to feel ill. It's worsening. The human realm is settling in. Hurry!"

The White Queen clutched the other side of her dress and climbed higher. "If we kill this Metanormal and get Diesel past the Howling Moon, I guarantee I can get the king to remove the hex on witches."

"How?" Jezebel asked.

"A woman has her ways."

"And my powers would fully return?"

"Fully."

They rounded a bend in the stairs.

"Did you know I wanted to be a seamstress when I was young?" the queen said.

"A seamstress? What for?"

"I love clothing. Once we get this barrier fixed, I'll tend to that dress of yours."

When Jitsu reached the top, she budged open the rusted metal door, and the trio emerged out onto the castle's turret.

Above, the barrier sparked.

Jitsu's coloring faded to white. "I'm weakening."

"Girls, on the count of three!" The White Queen held her arms out to the sky—Jezebel and Jitsu complied. "One! Two! Three!"

The trio unleashed fireworks that lit up the sky. Another round shot through the center of the barrier, directly above the castle's flagpole.

"Good shot," the queen said. "We need to get through the hole and repair the outer one first."

"Again! One. Two."

The outside barrier illuminated blue. A web of white codified broken ends.

The trio unleashed another. And another. Then, tended to the interior barrier.

The quarter moon's glow blurred as the shield of the two barriers sealed.

After the trio's grand finale, they each took to a parapet and leaned up against it, rumps on the cement.

Jezebel combed loose strands of hair away from her face through her fingers. "I've never really taken to smoking, but now feels like a good time for a cigarette."

"Ladies, we mustn't rest." The White Queen rose, went to the center of the turret, and removed a cover from a crystal ball. "We must capture the Metanormal."

"But he's stronger than us." Jezebel rose.

"Humans are emotional. If we hurt what they love, they're putty in our hands." The White Queen cackled, frizzy hair bouncing with each belch of laughter.

"Diesel?" Jezebel smirked. "You can't hurt him though. You can't get to him if that Metanormal is around him."

The White Queen cupped her hands over the crystal ball. It glowed green, and the moon reflected on it. "Jitsu, fetch your faes. I have a plan."

CHAPTER SIXTEEN

Faeries

THE MORNING SUN SHONE into the vampire's cabin. Pedro wore sunglasses to prevent exposure. "I'm telling you I don't know where Ketch is!" he shouted.

Diesel's nose and mouth transformed into a wolf's snout, and he snapped at the vampire.

"Get away!" Pedro kicked him. "Get back you damn mutt!" Pedro jumped up onto his bed, springs squeaking.

Diesel howled.

"Since when do you shift, anyway? I thought you didn't believe in using magic." Pedro bore his fangs and hissed.

Diesel transformed his muzzle back, hopped up on the bed, and pinned the vampire to the headboard.

"All right. All right. He's probably at the castle. He's been working with King Winston."

"What's he been working with Winston on?"

"Honestly, I have no idea."

Diesel slammed him up against the bed's backing.

"Truly, Diesel. No idea. Ketch and I are close, but he does his own stuff."

Diesel, gripping the vampire by the collar, read his honesty and let him go. He sat on the edge of the bed. "Do you know anything about Bence?"

"Bence? Your wolf-shifter buddy?"

"Yes. How many Bences are there in the world?"

"Well, I don't know how many there are." Pedro slinked off the side of the bed. "What about him?"

"He's dead, Pedro."

"Oh."

Diesel sighed. Oddly, he sensed the man was telling the truth.

"Are you going to just sit there naked on my bed? If someone comes in . . ."

"I didn't want to ruin my clothes. You're not worth it." Diesel got up and went to the door where he had disrobed in anticipation of a full-wolverine onslaught. "If you see Ketch, tell him I need to talk to him."

"Yeah whatever."

Diesel penned him up against the hall's wall. "You heard me. I need to talk to him."

"All right, all right. Geez. Take it easy. Testosterone a little high or something? Maybe you do need to mate."

Beyond the vampire cabins, the field opened into a pasture of tall grasses that swayed in the breeze. Diesel considered hollering for Elio's aid to make the trip to the castle faster, but he knew the dragon was out of reach. His head ached from shifting at Pedro's but changing back to his wolf side would be quicker than walking.

As he began to unbutton his shirt, to leave Mat's clothes in a safe place for his return, a girl stepped out into the field on the opposite end. He stopped. "Hello?"

When she saw him, she ducked back into the forest.

"Wait!" He ran after her. "Who are you?" When he reached the location where she had been, a drastic change in temperature made his nipples erect. He refastened his partially undone shirt. "Hello?"

A twig snapped behind him, and he turned toward it.

"Diesel." Her voice was soft, almost melodious. She was shorter than he, wore a loose-fitting dress—white with purple flowers and a tie around her waist—that settled just above her knees. Her long, red hair hung in front and masked small, perky breasts. "Diesel," she intoned again.

He recognized the face. "You're . . . you're . . . Mat's friend."

She giggled and ran back into the open field.

"Wait!" He chased after her.

She disappeared into the tall grass.

"Trinity." He ran toward her.

When he reached the center of the pasture, he found her lying on her back with her hair splayed in a crown-like fashion around her head. She undid the first of three buttons along the top of her dress. "Diesel."

He fell to his knees at her open legs, which she raised, exposing a pair of white panties.

An arousal swept over him unlike any he ever had. He moaned softly.

She reached up and pulled him down on top of her.

Diesel's groin felt as if it were going to explode. He began to undo his pants. He had to release.

She kissed him.

His loins boiled more.

He kissed her again, this time sweeping back a strand of hair along the side of her face. A pointy ear stuck out. "What!" He rose onto his knees.

She cackled, baring sharp, black teeth.

When he shuffled back, she tugged him forward—no longer the beautiful Trinity. "Enter me!" she yelled. "Give me your seed."

"A . . . a fae!" he shouted.

The faerie no longer resembled Trinity. Rather, it bore bulging, red eyes, horned ears, and a nose disproportionately large for her small face. Atop her head hung an orange and brown headdress beset with jewels and loose bands of cloth accompanied by a high forehead.

"Ah!" Diesel manifested his wolf snout and bit her hand.

She shrieked. "You lech!"

He bolted for the open field.

Above, a band of other faes—equally ugly—descended. They were flanked by smaller, colorful sprites. The leader, a purple one, yelled. "Charge!"

He was no match for them, even had he fully shifted. His eyes grew weary.

"I read his mind! I tricked him." The beads on the fae's headdress clattered in her laughter. "He wants the redheaded human. I knew it."

"Good work." The purple sprite hoisted a suit of armor's shield and slammed it up against the side of Diesel's head.

Everything went to black.

IN A CHAMBER IN the castle's cellar, Jezebel tapped her foot with arms folded across her chest. "He likes real humans not you hideous faeries."

A parade of faes masquerading as the redheaded human descended—for the seventh time—upon a naked Diesel gagged and strapped to a bed of concrete. His lack of interest in the faes, as evident by his flaccid phallus, irked them.

"And all this time I thought he favored boys."

The White Queen held up a long needle. "If he's not going to give us his seed in a natural way, we'll have to extract it in an alternative manner. Flip him over."

"No! No!" Diesel yelled through the gag.

Jezebel rolled her eyes. "Can't we just get the Metanormal first? The Howling Moon isn't for another couple of days. You're going to have to put that stuff on ice, or something, for it to be any good."

"Shush, Jezebel!" The White Queen stepped back as the sprites and faes untied and retied Diesel onto his stomach. He writhed. "If he fights anymore, knock him out again."

"My pleasure," Jitsu said.

"You had your choice, big boy," The White Queen said. "Spread 'em girls."

While the sprites held his butt cheeks, the queen inserted the needle up his rear and tapped his prostate. Diesel screeched.

"Grab his totem!" the queen hollered over Diesel's cries.

Jitsu yanked the chain off from Diesel's neck, and he fell face forward when the queen removed the needle.

At the examining table, the queen snapped open the cap to the totem and removed the scroll inside it. "What is this? This isn't his."

"What?" Jezebel advanced to the table.

"Bence Deringer? Jezebel, what is this?"

Jezebel's mouth fell open. "Bence is his boy . . . his friend."

The door to the chamber slammed open, and Marksman wobbled in. "It's fixed!" He held up his wand and wobbled. "It didn't take long, as you thought." He hiccupped. "Afterward, I took you up on your suggestion and had a few pops with the guys."

"Oh, for Satan's sake." Jezebel set a hand on her hip.

"What's going on?" Marksman slurred.

"If you must know, we're capturing Diesel's seed so the queen can perpetuate the wolf-shifting species and keep her husband, and the region, in balance," Jezebel said. "There's one slight problem, my stepson's totem is not his own."

Jitsu pulled Diesel, face up, by the hair. "Where is it, wolf-boy?"

Diesel headbutted her, and the sprite tumbled off the side of the cement bed.

Marksman stepped closer. "Jezebel, your crystal orb. With my wand fixed," he hiccupped, "we can locate his totem."

The White Queen and Jezebel exchanged a look and shrugged.

"Unfortunately, Marksman," Jezebel said, "I left it in that poor excuse of yours for a mode of transportation."

He smiled and pulled it out of his pocket.

She smirked. "I knew I kept you around for good reason, even if you do smell like a brewery."

Jezebel tossed Witch Lena's crystal in the air, and Marksman balanced it with a ray from his wand. The globe displayed an image of Mat with the totem around his neck. "Oh, how cute. He's lent it to his new beau."

"No! No!" Diesel's muffled cries shot out.

"I can get it," Marksman said, "but I'll need a dragon to get there."

CHAPTER SEVENTEEN

Dol

Trinity closed the door to the Beetle with a soft snap and grabbed her seatbelt. "Are you coming?" she asked Mat, who stood beside the open passenger door. He looked back at the cave on the hill before getting in. "A dragon's lair, huh?" she asked, turning over the engine.

The car sputtered, and Mat strapped himself in. "I know it sounds crazy, but Elio and this boy Bingham live here. They must be—"

"Mat, you promised me." She unlatched the glove box where she had placed his medicine. "I drove you to the wolf . . . errr . . . wolf-shifters' den then to try and find your car and nothing."

"The car. I can't remember exactly where we were. The forest is so huge." Mat sighed. "And the den, we just dropped off Mitsy, so I don't really know—"

"Mat." She eyed the prescription bottle lying on its side in the compartment; Mat's name was on the label.

He took it out. "Fine."

Trinity released the parking brake. "It's nothing to be ashamed or scared of. It's common when you go cold-turkey from your medicine to have adverse reactions, some of which may be hallucinations."

Mat toyed with the bottle in one hand and held Diesel's totem around his neck with the other before tucking it in his shirt for safekeeping

"You've been stressed out," she added. "We both have been. I'm trying to hold onto two houses and keep my kid brother from going to rehab and you . . . you've been through a lot."

Mat twisted off the cap and slid out a pill. They drove away from the cave and sat in silence for the fifteen-minute trip back to the cabin.

When they arrived, Trinity parked on the ribbon driveway in front of the garage's open bay.

"We should probably shut that. We don't want any critters getting in." She killed the engine.

"I'll get it," Mat said. As he reached up to close it, he noticed the contents of a box by the seated mower had been fumbled through, and a roll of duct tape left on the cracked floor beside it. "Were you in here?"

Trinity shoved her keys into the back pocket of her jean shorts. "No, I haven't been in here in years." She wandered over to a box marked *Toys*.

An empty bag of potato chips rattled in the corner of the garage as if it had been blown in from the breeze. Mat picked it up. "I bought this on my way in and never opened it."

"My Dad liked them. It's probably been there for years."

Mat examined the bag for an expiration date when a shadow, to his right, caught his attention.

Behind Trinity, a dark shade slid over the Beetle then disappeared above the garage. Mat glanced at her to see if she saw it, but she was more interested in the contents of the box. He dropped the bag, went out, and gazed up. "Not a cloud in the sky."

"Expecting rain?" Trinity held a naked Barbie doll. "Maybe I should roll up my car windows."

A dark spot appeared again, but Mat saw no evidence of its origin.

"Let's get in the house." Mat placed his arm around her, and they advanced to the cabin.

"I can make us some tea." She tossed the doll in the air and caught it. "I brought the Earth Goods brand you—"

Mat turned to her. An arrow stuck out from her right shoulder. She dropped the doll, and Mat grabbed her before she, too, fell.

Above the garage, a sneering black dragon hovered, and Marksman deposited his bow in a satchel on its side.

THE DRAGON BELLOWED AND landed by the firepit with a thud that shook the ground. He whinnied like a disobedient horse, and Marksman tugged the reins.

"Get back!" Mat shouted. His stomach soured and his legs quaked. "I'm a . . . I'm a Metanormal. You . . . you can't hurt me." He shielded Trinity—whom he had rested up against the Volkswagen's wheel well—and stretched out his arms to protect her.

"I'm not going to hurt you." Marksman slid off the dragon. "I'm here for Diesel's totem." He wore khaki pants with suspenders. His waistline rested far above where his belly button should be. The top of his pants held back a large, protruding tummy. He slid up glasses that had sagged down his long nose.

Marksman edged toward Mat with his hands raised. "Trust me. I'm not going to hurt you."

"Why should I trust someone who shoots first and asks questions later?"

Marksman snickered. "I didn't think I was asking any questions."

The dragon whinnied, but Marksman kept his eyes trained on Mat.

"Why are you here? What . . . what do I have to do with Diesel's totem?" Mat pretended not to feel the wolf-shifter's amulet tickling the hair on his chest.

"You're the one with the questions." Marksman stepped closer. "If you must know, Diesel's been captured."

Mat's stomach turned more.

"He's at the castle with the queen and Jezebel."

"Jezebel?"

"We need his totem, and I know you have it." Marksman slid out his wand. The tip of his red bandana revealed itself in his right front pocket.

Mat shoved out his hands, hoping for rays of magic to stop the advancing man but nothing happened. "I . . . I don't know what you're talking about."

"I know you have it. I'm a wizard. I know these things."

"A wand wizard."

Marksman tilted his head. "That's partially true, but there's more to the story I didn't tell you." He stopped at the driveway's border.

"I see you fixed your stick."

"Indeed."

Mat blinked. "I . . . I don't care about your story. I want my friends . . ." Mat swallowed. "I just want my friends, Diesel and Trinity, to be free and safe."

"My full powers were taken from the king," Marksman said, ignoring Mat.

Mat stepped back, bumping up against Trinity's foot. "I thought this was just a side gig for you, working for NEPRC."

"Ah, you *were* listening." Marksman scratched his chin. "But that's not entirely true."

"Determining what's true has been quite a challenge these last few days."

"What I didn't tell you is that my magic—what little of it there is—is not exclusive to wands." He tossed the stick in the air, where it hovered, and he clapped his hands. The arrow in Trinity's arm flew out. She banked right, and Mat lowered to her side to prevent her from landing, face down, on the gravel.

The arrow glided over to the dragon and dropped into the satchel. "I was holding back for good reason," the bounty hunter said.

"And . . . and what's that good reason?"

"My real name is Dol."

"Dole? I don't suppose you mean as in a can of pineapple."

The man squinted. "Dr. Dolessenbee. People call me Dol for short. Marksman was something I made up, on the fly . . . shooting arrows like a marksman, you know? That's what the wolf pack expected of me." He chuckled. "I thought it was rather clever for some quick thinking."

"Dol . . . Dolessenbee." Mat recalled his conversation with Diesel when they discovered Bence's body. "Dr. Dolessenbee."

"I was once a very prominent wizard but lost my powers in a battle with Sam Winston, the now king, about fifty years ago. I've been trying to fully restore them ever since."

Mat swallowed. "You're the one who created the barrier system."

"Ah, so you know. I'm happy to hear my name is not complete mud around here."

"Well, I would say the jury's still out on the Double Bubble."

Dol chuckled. "Is that what they call it?"

Mat nodded.

"Well, you boys did quite a number on it. My powers were too weak to fix it. I had to get a couple of witches to mend it, hence my delay." Dol, who had advanced, stopped in front of Trinity's car.

"Witches?"

"The queen and Jezebel."

"Jez . . . Jezebel is a witch? She's Diesel's stepmother."

"It's a long story. I infiltrated the clan's request to NEPRC. They think I'm a wand wizard sent to hunt you down and get . . . and get Diesel to mate. That's why I shot you two. To make them think I was on their side . . . well, and a little more. But, right now, the most important thing is I need your help."

"My help."

"Jezebel and the queen think I'm on their side."

"You said that."

"I did? Oh, yeah, I did. What I meant to say is that they're putty in my hands." Dol chuckled. "I had them repair the barrier back to near perfection. Jez thought I was getting my wand fixed. The whole time, I was spying on them. I didn't need the wand repaired at all, but I *do* need more power. Mine is weak and even weaker in Hubbard Forest."

"If you're the Dr. Dolessenbee Diesel told me about, you're supposed to be very powerful."

"Here, only one wizard's power can reign supreme."

"And who's power would that be?"

"King Samuel Winston. When I put the first barrier up, that was the price I had to pay—to leave him dominant. Magic always has a price."

"So I hear."

"Winston's wife, The White Queen, is pretty powerful too. Winston banished all the other witches so she could hold most of their powers."

Mat pressed a palm to his forehead. "My head is aching trying to comprehend all this stuff. Magic. It can't be real."

"In your realm, it's considered fictitious."

"Ya!" Mat checked on Trinity.

"She'll awaken momentarily." Dol moved his head toward the dragon. "A Malificious might have freaked her out a little. I didn't put as much juice into it like I did for you and Diesel." He stooped over her. "She's just a little thing, cute as a button."

"I've . . . I've been trying to get her to believe me about the forest."

"The forest brims with magic. Without the barrier, it weakens."

"We saw that during the fire."

Dol placed his hands on his wide hips. "Diesel is in danger. I need your help." He pointed to Trinity. "Let's bring her inside. I'll explain more."

In the cabin, they laid Trinity on the couch. Dol rested on a bar stool while Mat covered her with a blanket.

"Oh, sorry about your food. I was a little hungry earlier."

"That was you? What were you doing here?" Mat rose.

"I was with Jezebel. I should've returned the groceries, but I had my hands filled with her. I spiked the talc she found in the witch hut and even had her fetching a crystal ball like a puppy chasing its tail. I got quite a kick out of it." When he laughed, his stomach jiggled like a bowl full of Santa Claus's jelly dessert.

Mat smiled weakly.

"She hadn't a clue it was me, dodging the thing around like a tennis ball." His laugh was wheezy. When he stopped, he snapped a finger and a sack of groceries, with a bag of potato chips sticking out of it, appeared beside him. "Told you; I'm not really just a wand wizard. I had led Jezebel here to not only play the part, but I was also hungry." He rubbed his belly. "It takes a lot of work to keep my figure."

Mat removed its contents and placed a package of deli meat in the fridge.

Dol opened the bag of potato chips and took one out. "I lead a group of monitors in France."

"Monitors. Don't monitors watch over Metanormals to help them realize their magic?"

"Ah, yes how do you—?"

"Diesel."

"I'm glad the university taught the boy some good."

"Are you my . . . my monitor?"

"No, you haven't been assigned one," Dol said, munching a chip. "We're a bit of a start-up, only in operation for a little over one hundred years. The Rise of the Normals is growing too fast. I can't keep up with demand. Plus, I haven't enough magic to grow our organization."

"Diesel mentioned your magic has been waning."

"Creating barriers and watching over humans uses lots of energy. Manifesting a bag of groceries is easy. Fighting a civil war is another."

"The Civil War was centuries ago."

"Not that one. One amongst the supernatural. Hubbard Forest is isolated. Living in a bubble." He laughed. "An actual one."

"Two."

"Indeed. I stand corrected." Dol chuckled. "In what your realm calls Europe and England, there's a growing faction calling for the end of humanity."

Trinity groaned.

Mat moved closer to her. "Trin?"

"Mat?" She propped herself up on her elbows, and the blanket slid to her waist revealing a white top with puffy short sleeves laced with floral eyelets. "Who are you?" she asked, eyeing Dolessenbee.

"Ms. Hawkins." He extended a hand.

"Wait, how do you know who she is?" Mat asked.

"A doctor?" Trinity added. "Are you a psychiatrist?"

"How do you know her?" Mat repeated.

Dolessenbee rested his thumbs in his rainbow suspenders. "Oh, no. I'm an MD in Artificial Intelligence."

"Oh. You look like a shrink."

"Most humans say I look like a movie star." His belly jiggled but stopped when neither Trinity nor Mat showed appreciation for his humor. "Well, Ms. Hawkins, we have some explaining to do."

"We?" Mat sat beside her. "I want to know how you know her name. I never told you."

"Let's say we lunch, and I'll explain. I could go for some more of that deli meat."

After Dolessenbee scoffed down half a sandwich, the teakettle whistled, and Mat poured hot water into Trinity's mug.

"Your parents weren't killed in a hiking accident," Dolessenbee said to her.

Trinity blanched. Mat overfilled her cup and yanked a rag from the oven's handle to clean up his mess.

"I don't mean to shock you. But I don't know any other way to tell you. They were removed."

"Kill . . . killed? Removed?" Trinity paid no attention to the water dripping onto the floor from Mat's pour.

"They were *arevealized*, our word for moving a being elsewhere, from this very cabin to Acadia . . . to make it look like a human accident, away from here."

"They . . . they were murdered?" Trinity said. "They came here last summer. It was the last time anyone was here."

Dol clucked. "Hm. That makes sense. That's about the time the barrier shifted."

"Barrier?" Trinity asked.

"I'll explain later," Mat said.

"There has been a rationing of missing people in Central Maine. It started last year." She blinked, as if processing the details.

Dol licked mayonnaise off his thumb. "That's why they brought them to Acadia to dump the bodies there and not cause concern. Winston's NEPRC, that is the New England Paranormal—"

"Research Centre," Mat added, rising from the floor where he had been dabbing his spillage.

"NEPRC," Dol bit into his sandwich, "they were quite fearful of them."

"Fearful of my parents? Why? Wait . . . what? Paranormal research centre? What are you talking about?"

"Trinity, like I was trying to tell you, this place is strange."

Outside, the dragon neighed like it was anxious to leave.

Dolessenbee took the last bite of his sandwich and licked a thumb. "We need to get going. I'm afraid the Malificious may catch wind of my dissention to the queen." He pushed back the chair with a squeak against the floorboards.

"I . . . I need to tell Chip." Trinity fumbled with her phone to call her brother.

"It's probably not something to tell him in a call, Trin," Mat said.

"Mat is right," Dolessenbee added. "We've been watching over you since. He's safe."

"We?" she asked.

"My team of monitors."

"She has a monitor"—Mat rose—"and I don't? Is she . . . is she a Metanormal too?"

"Indeed."

"I'm a what?" Trinity touched her chest. "This is all very strange. But maybe the dreams of the blue dragonfly and my parents speaking to me make sense now."

"They've been coming to you?"

"Yes."

"Was there anyone else present?"

"A man. A man dressed all in white, with a goatee. He's old, with gray . . . white actually . . . hair."

"Winston."

"Winston?" Mat asked. "The king?"

Trinity, deep in thought, went to the kitchen island. "He kinda looks like the KFC guy." She chuckled.

Dol went to her side. "Did he have a cane?"

"Yes," she said, mouth agape.

"That's him."

"I . . . I thought he was God letting them into heaven."

The dragon whinnied again. This time louder.

Dol moved to the window and pulled back the curtain. "We haven't much time." He removed his wand. "Mat, we need to keep Diesel's totem in a safe place. He tapped the tip of the wand to his finger and an identical looking amulet appeared. "Wear this one."

Mat removed Diesel's totem from around his neck, withdrew his prescription bottle from his pocket, and undid the cap. He had dumped the pills when Trinity wasn't looking.

"Sorry I didn't believe you," she said.

"No worries." Mat placed the totem inside and twisted the lid back on. "I wouldn't have believed me either."

OUTSIDE, WHILE DOL ATTENDED to the dragon, Mat shut the door to Trinity's car with her inside and leaned against its open window. "I hate leaving you like this, but it is the best strategy. You'll be safer outside the forest, and you can break the news to Chip back home."

Trinity, still shocked, locked the prescription bottle in the VW's glove box as they had agreed. "I . . . I don't know why the necklace needs to be out of the forest," her voice was soft, "but I'll . . . I'll take it with me."

Mat touched the decoy dangling from his neck. "I'm not entirely sure its replacement will pass at the castle, but it's worth a shot, like Dol says."

"Quiet!" Dol yelled. "The dragon can hear you."

When Mat turned, the Malificious rose on his hind legs and knocked Dol to the ground.

"Trinity," Mat faced her, "go. Go now!"

"Wait!" Dol rolled onto his side with so much effort that his reddened faced. When he stood, he rushed over to the car with wand in hand. "Where is it?"

"Huh?" Mat asked.

"The totem. Where is it?"

Trinity pointed to the glove box. "It's locked in there inside the empty bottle of anti-depressants."

"Good." Dol tapped the roof of the VW with his wand and a gold shield covered the vehicle, then evaporated, as if the car had absorbed the energy. "You're good to go. Go home to Elk. Trevor will—"

"Trevor?" Trinity said. "Chip's friend?"

"Trevor is the monitor I assigned to watch over you two."

"Trevor?" Mat asked, his mind racing back to the two boys smoking weed in the backyard. "The pot head?"

"Pay no worries to that. It's all a cover. He's a good witch."

"Witch?" Trinity started up the engine and released the parking brake.

The dragon's lead, tied to a nearby pine tree, broke free.

"Go!" Dol yelled.

While Dol wielded a white tether and reined in the dragon, Mat stood, hands on hips, watching Trinity drive out of sight. The dragon's growl masked the VW's chirp, now barely audible.

"Uh oh," Dolessenbee said holding the limp end to his new rope.

"Uh oh?" Mat advanced toward him. "What do you mean, 'uh oh'?"

The dragon sped off in the direction Trinity had gone. The other end of Dol's magical white rope dangled by its side.

They rushed to the edge of the property line, by the dilapidated well, when a firestorm erupted above the trees.

"Trinity!" Mat yelled.

A cacophony of growls echoed followed by a burst of silence. The faint sound of Trinity's car returned. Then, the Malificious' limp body traversed through the sky and landed with a deafening crash onto the road. Its carcass skidded up and onto the lawn and stopped by the firepit, but not before toppling the rocks that lined it. Blood dripped from its snapped neck. Smoke billowed from its nostrils, smudging the side of the garage with soot.

Next, a green dragon burst out above the trees.

"Elio," Dol muttered.

Mat faced him. "You know Elio?"

Dol didn't answer. Instead, Elio settled on the road. An angry look wrought his face.

"I'm so . . . sorry, Elio. But it was the only way."

Mat frowned. "What . . . what was the only way?"

"I'll explain later." Dol chirped at Elio, and the two argued back and forth for a time until Elio acquiesced, lowering onto all fours. Dol harrumphed his way atop the dragon and extended a hand to Mat. "Let's go."

Mat, steady as a frequent flyer, ignored his aid and climbed aboard.

Chapter Eighteen

Castle

J EZEBEL, CROSS-ARMED, STRUMMED HER fingers along her bicep.
"Your call," she said to the queen. "Do you want your little faerie to
live or not?"

"Jezebel," the queen stammered. "Diesel, let her go or . . . or . . . or we
shall hex you."

Diesel held Jitsu by the throat. The gag was loose around his neck, and
he wore only a pair of jeans, unbuttoned at the top. "I'll rip her wings off,
one by one. I swear." His breath was heavy. Sweat dripped down his heaving
chest.

"Shall we?" Jezebel asked of the queen.

The queen nodded.

Diesel tugged one of Jitsu's wings, and she shrieked. "Don't hurt me!
Stop!"

"What's a couple of witches to do?" the queen asked.

"We could kill him," added Jezebel.

Diesel gaped. "Witch? Jezebel?"

"Oh, you didn't know?" Jezebel set her hands on her hips. "I hate to break it to you, step-sonny, but yes. I'm not just a bitch."

"Shall we place him in a sleeping curse?" the queen asked Jezebel. To protect them from his wrath, she steadied her hand to maintain the magical protection screen that she had manifested when Diesel captured the faerie. "A Sleeper may be best to lure the Metanormal with anyway."

Jezebel smirked. "I like it. I haven't done a sleeping curse in eons."

"Then, we can more easily commence conversion therapy and remove his humansexuality."

Flummoxed, Diesel dropped his guard, and, with a small charge from her cane, the queen took the opportunity to free Jitsu.

He raced to grab back his hostage, but when he bumped up against the protection shield, its electric force jolted him back.

Jitsu rushed to the queen's side. "You big brute," she squeaked back at him. "You're nothing but a . . . but a mongrel. A big 'ol wolf . . . the lowest of the ladder . . . the lowest of all shifters and supernatural creatures!"

Her red face clashed with her purple attire, and Jezebel told her to give it a rest. "He's not really a mongrel; otherwise, we wouldn't be going through all this fuss."

Jitsu stammered. "I guess . . . I'm just . . ."

"I call him that, yes," Jezebel said. "It's . . . it's just a saying."

"There, there, Jitsu." The queen petted her faerie. "Now, Daniel," she turned to Diesel with a scowl. "I have a proposition for you. You behave. Agree to mate with a she-wolf, as is your wont, and you can live a very happy life here in Hubbard Forest. What do you say?"

"The Heaven with you!" Diesel spat.

The queen flinched, then righted her tiara. "I have your seed, Daniel. And your totem is on its way." She faced Jitsu, who cowered beside her like a puppy. "Now, why don't you go see if you can find out where that bounty hunter is? Go. Shoo."

Jitsu flew off, cast an evil eye at Diesel by the exit, and left.

The queen shut the door behind her. "We'll be able to use his sample in the king's lab. Not the ideal situation, but under extenuating circumstances a test-tube wolf-shifter may be allowed. We'll pray to the Dark Lord to forgive any indiscretions in using science versus nature."

Diesel's chest hair bristled as if about to shift. "Tell me, who killed Bence?" he said through grated teeth.

"I told you, I know nothing about that. I have no control over my husband's business."

"Why was there a tracking device?"

"Winston. Boy's play," she said dismissively. "I don't know all my husband is up to. Now, I want to know about your totem. Is that why you wore the gay boy's? To honor him in death?" She turned to Jezebel. "Bence Deringer was, after all, the gay boy who refused to mate?"

"Yes."

The queen reset a large, green ring on her finger that had twisted inward. "Well, we must exterminate poor genes from our creation pool."

"Poor genes? Creation pool?" Diesel said. "Is that all you care about?"

She thumped her cane to the floor. "I care about the welfare of our kingdom, Daniel Cade! Apparently, you do not."

"I care about . . . I care about kindness and compassion. And letting people choose how they want to live, and who they want to love!"

The queen held a stoic look for a few moments, then she pealed in laughter. "These young ones . . ." she held her stomach and caught her breath " . . . are so full of hope. Aren't they, Jezebel?" Her laugh morphed into a cough.

Jezebel offered a weak smile to her.

"You," Diesel said to Jezebel, "you've been masquerading as my father's wife."

"I am your father's wife, unfortunately. And since when do you care about him? If you did, you'd give him cubs."

Diesel stared off. "You're a witch."

The queen butted in. "For hell's sake, Jezebel, don't torture the boy."

"Torture? Look who's talking. You made me a wolf-shifter. Turned a perfectly powerful witch into a lowlife."

"Made her a wolf-shifter?" Diesel said, still stunned.

The witches argued about the queen's role in her hex: "Not my idea. I was just following orders."

"But you ultimately drew the potion."

"What's a witch to do when her husband is king and insists?"

"We're witches. We should have each other's backs?"

"I just carried out his orders."

Diesel rubbed his face. "Wait, what?"

"Don't worry your pretty little head," the queen said. "You'll be asleep in a moment."

"Who killed Bence! I want to know." Diesel stepped up to Jezebel, hands on his hips. "What do you know about it?" He sniffed. "You stink of guilt."

Jezebel splayed a hand across her chest. "Moi? Why would I harm an innocent, good-looking boy?" She smirked.

The queen manifested a small, blue energy source in the palm of her hand. "It is the Great Lord's opinion, and mine for that matter, that an inferior gene pool weakens our kingdom." The ball hovered a few centimeters, pulsated, and grew. "You, unfortunately, have a healthy background." She chuckled. "Bence Deringer's family was nothing but inbred tramps. It's a wonder they were born able to shift with all that co-mingling."

Jezebel added her own, smaller energy force to the queen's, and their concoction thundered like a miniature rainstorm.

Diesel stepped back. "What are you?"

A bolt of energy shot out from the tiny weather system, which rained golden flakes. The witches gathered its yield in the palms of their hands. When the cloud stopped flaking, they blew the powder in Diesel's face.

"What the—!" When it reached Diesel, he collapsed, hovered in the air, and his head drooped to the side.

The witches, with outstretched hands, brandished a bed of golden magic to settle him back onto the concrete slab.

"A nice sleeping curse that only true love's kiss shall break." The queen covered him with a blanket. "Perhaps one day a she-wolf will find him."

"Who would want him? They all think he's some freak. A humansexual."

Elio landed beside the NEPRC truck. The near-full moon, with only a sliver shadow on its left, hung above the castle's spire. Mat and Dolessenbee slid off Elio.

"NEPRC has a Jeep?" Mat eyed the centre's logo displayed along the vehicle's side. "I didn't think they allowed modern things in."

Dol chuckled. "I did it for spite."

"Funny."

"Wait here," Dol said to the dragon, who groaned with dissatisfaction.

The pair rushed toward the portcullis when Dol stopped. "Wait. We need to make this look a little more official."

Mat, who had run ahead, stopped.

Dr. Dolessenbee removed his wand. "This won't hurt. Well, maybe a teeny bit, but we need to have it look legit." He tapped the wand and shackles appeared on Mat's wrists and ankles.

"I . . . I can hardly walk." A large, metal ball, strapped to a chain on his ankle, rolled down the incline. He stopped it before it pulled him down. "If you say so." He lifted the ball with a grunt. "Good, God. This is heavy."

"Fight me."

"Huh?"

Dol cleared his throat. "Metanormal!" Dol said authoritatively. "Do as I say! Into the castle!" He pointed behind Mat.

When Mat turned, two guards stood at the portcullis. The larger one donned a long, black cape that partially covered his ripped, red body. A pair of curled horns protruded from his forehead. The other guard was wispy, thin, and gaunt. The slippers she wore hovered a few inches above the ground. Mat swallowed.

"What have we here?" said Wispy, in a snippy, alarming tone.

"I am the bounty hunter. I've chained the Metanormal much to the queen's delight." Dol yanked the totem around Mat's neck and glanced at him. "Sorry. I promise this'll be brief." He eyed the odd pair. "The queen wants this. I need to give it to her."

"I shall take it." Wispy sped over. The larger one stomped forward.

"No," Dol said, "I must explain the Metanormal's peculiarities to her."

"Let me go!" Mat said. It felt fake, but he hoped it would add credence to Dol's request.

"Hm. Very well." The wispy, ghost-like being stepped aside and glided toward the castle. They followed.

Inside, the vestibule's dank air chilled Mat.

Wispy walked through a wall by the spiral stairs, then poked her head back out. "Mephistopheles, take them up to the lab. The White Queen awaits."

Mephistopheles grabbed Mat's ball and carried it in his clutch with little effort. Behind the tall, red man, Mat struggled to keep up, and Dol touched the small of his back in a reassuring way.

When Mephistopheles passed a barred window, Elio's large eye peeked in.

"Shoo," Dol mumbled.

Mephistopheles spun around, clanking Mat's chains. His black robe had a large, stiff collar that rose to his ears. He grunted, but Elio had disappeared.

"Move it!" Dol pushed Mat forward, which appeared to satisfy Mephistopheles, and they proceeded.

At the landing, a familiar voice rang out. "It's about time." Jezebel stood, cross armed. "Marksman," she said, stepping forward, heels clicking as she stepped off the carpeted area, "I see you've captured the Metanormal. Good job."

"I have," Dol tugged at Mat's necklace. "Brought him totem and all." He smiled diabolically.

Mat shivered, not knowing if it were Dol's acting or the cool night air that caused him to do so.

"Excellent," Jezebel said. "Follow me."

At the end of the long hallway, at a T-section, they walked through a glimmering shield of blue on their left and into a bright, windowless lab.

The queen looked up from a microscope she had been using. "Ah, Marksman. Finally."

"I bear your wants," Dol said. "He's a little friskier than normal. It took some time."

"Mephistopheles," the queen said to the red man, "that'll be all." She waved a dismissive hand, and he left.

Dol ripped the necklace from around Mat's neck and held out the totem to the queen in the palm of his hand. He bowed. "At your request, Your Majesty."

The queen studied the totem. "Hm." She held it up to the fluorescent fixtures embedded in the ceiling. "Let me check its authenticity."

Mat cleared his throat nervously, and Dol elbowed him.

The queen returned to the microscope, and Jezebel peered over her shoulder. Annoyed, the queen stared at her, and Jezebel stepped back hands splayed.

The queen placed the totem on a glass slide, donned a pair of glasses dangling from her neck, and examined it through the instrument. "Ah. Very well. Daniel Cade." She peeked up, over her glasses. "Nice work, Marksman. I believe we owe you a reward."

"Indeed." Dol licked his lips.

The queen unlocked a file cabinet and, from a seemingly endless drawer, pulled out a small blue velvet satchel. She tossed it Dol's way.

Dolessenbee caught it greedily, smiled, and untied the gold thread cinching its apex. He buried his nose inside and snorted its contents like an addict would a pile of cocaine. He levitated. His face reddened. "Merciful heavens!" he exclaimed and shook his head. "Woo hoo!"

"Evil Satan," Jezebel said. "There's nothing worse than seeing a wizard snorting a high."

"We've got work to do," the queen said to her. "Come now."

"What about the Metanormal?" Jezebel asked her.

"Marksman's got him." The queen reset her glasses to the bridge of her nose. "Marksman," she said to him. "Take his soul to my husband. Ketch will drain his blood and dispose of his corpse in the Trash Heap with the others."

Mat's eyes darted between Dolessenbee and the queen.

Dolessenbee wobbled drunkenly. "Yes, Your Majesty." He carried the ball clasped at Mat's ankles. They exchanged no words until they reached the hall's T-section.

"Dr. Dolessenbee?" Mat said. "Are you . . . are you okay?" He empathized with the alcoholic-like change in personality.

The doctor nodded slowly.

When they reached the landing to the staircase, which they had traversed earlier, Elio chirped at the window to gain their attention. He pointed a sharp claw upward, as if indicating the way, and flew off.

Voices echoed from the vestibule below. They peered over the edge. Mephistopheles and the wispy woman argued with a large, stocky bald man.

"NEPRC sent you?" Wispy asked, seemingly bewildered.

"Yes, I'm telling you. I'm the bounty hunter," the bald man exclaimed. "Winston sent me. We just got word of the wolfpack's need."

Mephistopheles grunted.

"But . . . but that can't be," Wispy said. "The Metanormal's been captured already. We just sent him to the queen. Show your credentials!"

"Quick!" Dolessenbee, having shaken off his high, released his wand and whisked off Mat's shackles.

J ITSU CARRIED A POT of tea and biscuits on a tray through the lab's side entrance.

The queen hovered over Diesel's totem lying in the center of a metal tray. "Again," she said to Jezebel.

"But the faerie has arrived with tea," Jezebel said.

"Again!" the queen demanded.

Jezebel sighed. "My nails are fried. There's got to be some sort of spell on it that won't let us open—"

"Again!" the queen repeated, this time with more authority.

"Fine." Jezebel splayed out her hands over the tray.

"On the count of three," the queen said.

Jitsu set the tea on a round table beside them. "Is everything all right, Your Majesty?"

"Jitsu," the queen said, annoyed, "leave us be. It's nothing two strong witches can't handle."

"There's some scuttlebutt going on downstairs. You should probably—"

"I don't care about scuttlebutt!" The queen wiped away a bead of sweat with the back of her hand. "Mephistopheles and Grim are probably fighting about who's Lord Darthius's favorite again."

Jitsu poured tea. "I think it's a little more—"

"One!" The queen yelled. "Two! And three!" She and Jezebel unleased a charge that electrified the metal tray, and it rattled atop the counter. The totem glowed and, like before, spit back a force that shocked them. A beaker of green liquid beside it shattered.

"I have had enough!" Jezebel patted her hair bun. "This Satan forsaken totem is hexed."

"The Howling Moon is tomorrow. It's my window of opportunity to substantially grow the clan. If we can get Diesel's magic into a she-wolf, the bubble will expand."

Jezebel sighed. "This bubble-growing thing is such a slow process. It's been over 150 years, and we still haven't conquered New England. At this rate, we'll be 5,000 years old before we take over the planet."

"It's Dolessenbee's curse."

"I realize that. Perhaps we should have let the bubbles collapse instead of repairing them."

"Oddly, those bubbles protect us, Jezebel. Else, we'll wither away into some fictitious human reality. My husband's magic keeps this place running."

The servant's door behind Jezebel burst open.

The queen splayed a hand across her chest. "Good, gosh. Doesn't anyone knock around here?"

A faerie in yellow clothes hovered beside a tall, bald man with bulging muscles. "I found him," she said, buzzing about, raising her eyebrows to the delight of her catch.

The queen cocked her head. "Found whom?"

The yellow faerie made way for the man to enter.

The bald man lowered his head in respect of royalty. "Sorry, Your Majesty, but I came as quick as I could." He spoke with a thick, British accent. "But with your husband's absence, NEPRC only now got word of the wolfpack's need for someone to hunt a Metanormal." He wielded a shotgun. "I came as quick as I could."

Jezebel blinked. She and the queen exchanged a glance. "You?" Jezebel said to him.

He nodded nervously. "I may not appear as much, but I'm very good at what I do."

"No, that's not what I . . ." She stepped closer. "You're the bounty hunter? Where's Marksman?"

"Marksman?" His wiry brows furrowed. "I know of no Marksman."

Having frantically searched for Diesel in all but one of the many rooms off the castle's upper floor, Mat and Dol reached the end of the long hallway. Mat flung open one last door. "A closet. Damn it!"

Dol, catching his breath, leaned against the window. The break of dawn through the hall's only light source cast an eerie shadow upon the surrounding hard surfaces. The window's bars were thick, much more so than seemed necessary for a window its size. "Uh oh," he said, peering out.

"Uh oh, what?" Mat's speech was hitched. He stepped beside him. A horse-drawn carriage was posited by the Jeep. "Who is that?"

"The real NEPRC bounty hunter."

Elio's face, upside down, filled the window. *Click, clickity, clack.*

"There's another floor?" Dol asked exasperated. "How . . . how do we get there?"

Elio, now hovering upright, shrugged. *Clack, clack.*

"All right, I'll come." Dol gripped the bars on the window; it was too small for anyone to get through.

"Wait," Mat said. "We can't fit through there."

"Not in this form I can't. Animus!" he shouted, and a crow cawed on the small ledge.

"Dol?"

Caw, caw! The bird flew out the window, and Elio disappeared.

"What the hell? What am I supposed to—?"

From the other end of the hall, a door swung open, and a slice of light infiltrated through.

"Shit." Mat ducked into the closet and softly closed the door.

He recognized Jezebel's voice and the click of her heels traversing the hall's wooden floors. "I can't believe I've been had," she said.

"That makes three of us," said someone who sounded like the queen.

A man's voice followed. "I saw the NEPRC Jeep in the lot. I thought maybe Winston sent in another scout, using modern technology to lure the human. I apologize for any mix up."

"Mix up!" the queen shouted, heels clicking. "You're saying he's a traitor."

Mat's stomach churned. A sudden urge for a drink overcame him, but when he pressed his back to the wall, it opened, and he fell back. "The hell?" he muttered, tripping up against a set of stairs. He crab-walked up a couple of steps, and the wall he had pressed up against slid shut. He ran up.

The trio's onslaught hastened; their footsteps echoed down the hallway.

Mat scurried up, taking two steps at a time, until he reached a landing. "Dol?" he whispered.

At a window matching the one Dol's animus flew out from on the lower floor, Elio's face popped into view.

"In here?" Mat pointed to an arched door in front of him, where the dragon's shadow cast on its wooden slats.

The dragon nodded vigorously.

The door creaked open. Dol, back to his chubby self, greeted Mat with a somber look. Behind the door's inswing, Diesel was arranged on a rock bed. Mat rushed in, and Dol locked the entrance's iron brackets. "Is he . . . is he . . . dead?"

Dol locked the door. "I . . . I don't think so."

"You don't think so!"

Outside, Elio whimpered and gripped bars to a window larger than the ones in the hall. His nostrils sizzled as tears rolled down his snout and wet the floor.

"What's . . . what's wrong?"

"I'm . . . I'm not really sure," Dol said.

Mat leaned his ear to Diesel's chest. "He's . . . he's not breathing!"

Dol paced but stopped short when the knob to the door rattled.

"Let us in!" Jezebel yelled. "We know you're in there."

Elio clawed at the stonework along the bars, as if trying to work his way in.

Dol placed a hand on Diesel's forehead and removed his pocket watch.

"What are you doing?"

"Waiting."

"For what?"

A shot rang out from the other side of the door.

"We haven't much time," Mat said.

Dol shut his watch. "Hm. He's under a spell."

"Your watch told you that?"

Dol ignored him and placed a hand over Diesel's heart. "A sleeping curse."

"Like in *Sleeping Beauty*? That was one of Ty's favorite movies. The prince kisses her and wakes . . ."

Mat and Dol exchanged a look. "Only true love's kiss will awaken him," Dol said.

Mat stepped back. "Me? But I . . . we just . . . met. I don't know if . . . I'm certainly not a prince."

The door clattered louder.

"Kiss him!" Dol said.

Elio ripped out a bar, and one of the stones crumbled to the floor and another outside.

"Mr. Marksman!" The real bounty hunter's voice was only slightly muffled by the thick door. "You are in violation of several NEPRC policies. You must let me in."

"As if I care," Dol muttered, then pointed, authoritatively, to Diesel's body. "Now. Before it's too late. I know you two have been . . . intimate."

"Okay. Okay!" Mat lowered over Diesel. Oddly, while he and Diesel had engaged in sex, they hadn't kissed. A subtle scent of pine clung in the wolf-shifter's hair. Mat traced his own lips across Diesel's face, then kissed his soft yet cool mouth long and hard.

On opposite sides of the slab, Dol and Mat waited for a sign of life.

Another shot to the door caused Mat to flinch, and Dol removed his wand and fired back.

"Satan!" the bounty hunter yelled, sounding as if Dol had injured him.

Dol fired another shot, and Jezebel shrieked. Dol, returned his attention to Diesel, and tapped his face. "Come on, boy. Come on."

"It's not working." Mat caught Dol's eyes. "I . . . I . . . must confess. I like Diesel . . . a lot. But . . . but I don't know if I . . . if I love him . . . that way."

Another, much more powerful blast shattered a board on the door, and Witch Lena's crystal ball, which had been sitting atop a table nearby, rolled off. Dol caught it before it shattered onto the floor. He gazed into it. "Criminy!"

Another boom to the door splintered it further.

"What's wrong?" Mat let go of Diesel's hand and moved to Dol's side.

Dol looked up. "Your friend."

"Trinity?"

"She didn't leave."

"What?" Mat took the crystal from Dol, and in it Trinity stood in the cabin's kitchen holding a box. "She went back for the memorabilia. Damn it, Trinity."

Dol stopped at the head of Diesel's bed. "Wait."

Elio ripped out another bar, leaving an egress now wide enough for them to escape, and clacked at the wizard, as if encouraging him.

"I hear you, El. I hear you. I just thought it'd be better off if someone else—"

Elio screeched.

"Fine!" Dol leaned over Diesel and kissed his forehead.

Diesel shuffled.

Mat's jaw slackened.

"Yes. Yes!" Dol's eyes widened.

Mat jerked his head back. "You have the hots for Diesel?"

"It's . . . it's complicated," Dol said with a downward glance at Elio.

Another door board shattered. Mat left the crystal ball on Diesel's bed and helped him down.

"What's . . . going on?" Diesel moved with Mat's aid but froze when he saw Dol. "You?"

"Wait! Wait!" Mat said to him. "He's not bad. He's here to help."

"Help?" Diesel's hair bristled. He sneered.

"Don't shift," Mat rubbed his back. "Look, Elio's here." He draped a discarded shirt over Diesel. "If he trusts him, we can."

The door to the chamber blew open. They scurried over to the opening and jumped aboard the dragon.

T HE BOUNTY HUNTER FIRED a shot out the window after Elio flying off into the forest. The White Queen stood by his side.

At Diesel's empty lair, Jezebel picked up the crystal ball. "Oh," she said, raising an eyebrow.

"What is it?" The queen came and grabbed the crystal. "A redhead, huh? And what in Satan's evil earth is she driving?"

"A blue buggie of sorts," Jezebel said. "Let me after her. I have an idea."

"Jezebel, you've done enough damage. The bounty hunter is perfectly capable of—"

"Is he?" Jezebel asked, looking at the man scratching his head at the gape in the chamber's wall.

"What do you need?" the queen asked.

"My powers."

"I told you. Witch powers are limited in the forest. Jezebel, I saved you by making you a wolf-shifter."

Jezebel blinked. "Thanks?"

"The wolf-shifter hex wasn't just my concoction. Jitsu may have lifted your shackles, but you're still limited. Witches—"

" . . . can only do limited things here," Jezebel said. "I know. Since I can't arevealize over to her." She seized the crystal back from the queen. "I'll need a dragon."

Chapter Nineteen

Trinity

A New England dawn, on the verge of autumn, made for a chilly ride aboard the dragon. But the temperature wasn't top on Diesel's mind, only a pesky backdrop that caused him to put on the shirt, Mat's shirt, someone grabbed for him prior to exiting the castle.

He argued with the rotund man holding Elio's reins, who Mat stated wasn't really Marksman or a bounty hunter, but none of it made sense. "All right, I won't throw you overboard if you tell me who you really are," Diesel said. "And did you have something to do with my buddy's death?"

"I know nothing of your friend's death, but I promise to help you find the truth."

Mat leaned in from behind. "We tricked Jezebel with a fake totem that he . . . he made out of thin air. Yours is safe with Trinity. We think."

Diesel looked back at him with a furrowed brow.

"We tried to get her to leave," Mat said. "But she went back to the cabin for some family stuff."

"We think she stayed the night at the cabin," the driver, whom Diesel formerly knew as Marksman, said.

"Who are you? You didn't tell me your name."

"Dol."

"Wait. What? Something tells me you don't mean a can of pineapples."

Dol's face creased. "What's with the pineapples?"

Mat placed a hand on Diesel's shoulder. "He's Dr. Dolessenbee."

Diesel glanced at him, then at the driver. He chuckled. "Wait. You're *the* Dr. Dolessenbee, head of the Monitors . . . creator of the Double Bubble?"

"In the flesh." Dol smiled. "Double Bubble . . . funny," he muttered.

"No way."

"Way," Dol said.

Elio clacked.

Diesel straightened. "He is?" he replied to the dragon.

Dol patted Elio's neck. "Thank you, Elio for your vote of confidence."

"You . . . you know Elio? And you speak dragon?"

"We go back some. And, yes . . . yes, I do know him."

"Elio, why didn't you ever tell me?"

The dragon exchanged a glance with Dolessenbee, then—in a series of clicks and chirps—reminded Diesel he was over 400 years old.

Diesel digested the news in silence for a moment. "This is a lot to take in, but what's more important is Bence. I need to get back to the castle to get Jezebel. She knows something about his death, I can tell."

"Can you?" Dol asked. "That's good."

"Well, then turn Elio around and let's go—"

"After I shot you with my arrow, have you experienced anything . . . shall we say new?"

Diesel blinked. "I . . . I don't know what you're—"

Mat chimed in, "Remember, Dee, you read my dreams."

"Yes, I did." Diesel faced Dol. "That was you . . . your arrow? Some sort of potion in it?"

Dol smiled with a slow nod. "Ah, it worked. After all this time, the magic is still in you."

Diesel arched an eyebrow. "Explain."

"You are more than just a wolf-shifter, Diesel." Dol caught his eye.

"But . . . but I don't even like magic. I just want to be like a human. Normal. Magic is fraught with issues."

"There's more to it." Dol quieted the chirping dragon with a rub to its neck. "For now, we need to know where Trinity is and get your totem. She was to take it out of the forest, out of harm's way from other magical creatures. Where is she?"

Diesel jabbed a thumb to his chest. "You're asking me?"

"Tap into your psychic powers."

"Psychic . . . is that what I am?"

"And more."

"I don't want to be more. I want simplicity. I want the regularity of a human life. Like . . . Bence and I planned." He turned to Mat.

Mat nodded. "I get it. I understand."

"I don't want to be a psychic. I don't want to be magical!" Diesel said.

Dol placed a hand on his knee. "It's not a choice, my son."

The man's touch was electrifying. An image of him, younger and thinner, swam in his head. Diesel moved away. "I need to find out who killed Bence. Elio, let me down."

"Your totem," Dol said. "We need your totem first."

"I don't care about my totem. Never have. Elio, now!"

The dragon groaned.

Along the horizon, a black speck shot out from the castle, and Diesel's mind lasered upon it. He sensed Jezebel onboard. "It's her," he muttered.

Dol shielded the glare from the rising sun to look over at the black speck flying off. "You can tell? Is that Jezebel who's on that dragon?"

"Yeah. Yeah. It is," he said defeatedly. "So, I'm a . . . psychic? Your arrow made me—?"

"My arrow only awoke what's been in you since birth."

"I'm confused."

"More about that later." Dol jerked Elio's reins.

"The cabin's this way." Mat pointed as they flew in the opposite direction.

"Jezebel's crystal," Dol said. "It's still locked on Trinity. She must've left the cabin."

Diesel closed his eyes and placed a hand to his heart. A vision of the beautiful redhead driving her car, heading for the forest's exit, coalesced. His eyes shot open. "Trinity is nearing the gate. My totem is safe in her glovebox."

THE MALIFICIOUS FLEW AWAY, leaving Jezebel in the woods near the road. According to her crystal, the little blue car carrying the totem would be rounding the bend momentarily.

Ketch, donning sunglasses, seemingly working his way back toward the vampire village after his nightly feed, stopped when he saw Jezebel. "What have we here? A she-wolf out without her husband?"

"Zip it, bloodsucker," Jezebel said.

"Ouch. You're a little feisty for a beautiful morning."

Jezebel switched hips from the one she was leaning on. "Ketch, it's high time the village knows I'm more than just a wolf-shifter. In fact, I'm really not one at all."

Ketch lowered his sunglasses a tad down the bridge of his nose to inspect her, but the sun proved too much, and he slid them back up. "This will have to wait for another time. I must hear." He moseyed on, then stopped. "But be careful, it appears there's another Metanormal in the forest."

Jezebel perked.

Pedro stepped out from the depths of the thicket. "Some redheaded chick. Staying at the cabin where Ketch here lost his chop-ahs. We didn't dare go near'a."

"How . . . how do you know?" she asked.

"Look, you may . . . or may not . . . be a dumb shifter," Ketch said, "but us vampires have a strong penchant for these types of situations. Her blood smells just like the other one. I could tell."

"Yeah, we didn't botha' with'a," Pedro said. "C'mon, Ketch, the sun's rising. We gotta head home."

The vampires vanished, leaving Jezebel alone with only the sound of the redhead's car nearing.

"And now," she said to herself and rushed toward the road. She tousled her hair in the process, to make the effect more compelling. When she reached the road, she waited to see the car round the bend and dashed out in front of it, hands splayed. "Excuse me! Can you help?"

The little blue car braked with a screech, stopping just a few yards in front of her. The town line's web sent off a wave of electricity behind, warming Jezebel.

The evaporating morning dew cast clouds at the road's shoulder, and Jezebel approached the driver's side. The girl's breath fogged the windows, and, in the glass, Jezebel noticed the reflection of a green dragon hovering behind her. "Elio!"

"The name's Trinity." The girl had cracked her window. "Is everything all right?" Her mouth gaped as she gazed behind Jezebel.

Jezebel turned and shot a golden rod at the approaching dragon with Mat, Diesel, and Dol aboard. Her sorcery tore flesh from Elio's right wing, and he crashed into the thicket.

The door to the car flung open and hit Jezebel causing her to fall to the road. Trinity ran for the forest where the dragon had crashed. "Mat!" she yelled, seemingly having seen the other Metanormal onboard the Emphilothepy.

"Not so fast little girl." Jezebel, on her back, released a web that caught her. She got up on her knees, dragged her closer, and bound her hands with shackles, similar to the ones Jitsu had removed from her. "Oh, you're an easy catch. Your Metanormal-ness must not have materialized yet."

Trinity fought, but the web and shackles were too strong.

Jezebel tied the end of the magic web to the car's bumper and went inside the vehicle to search for the totem. Her crystal lit up near the glovebox. "Ah hah." When she went to open it, it sent out a charge that zapped the tips of her fingers. "Son of a witch!" She struggled through the pain, desperately trying to unlatch it. The car shook. Her nails smoldered. "Dah!" She gave up.

"Trinity?" a voice yelled from the forest.

Jezebel hurried over to the girl, untied her, set her in the passenger seat, and closed the door. "Evil Satan, I haven't driven one of these since Hitler was in charge." She slid into the driver's seat and futzed with the stick shift. "How in . . . ? How do you get this into reverse?" Finally, as the boys emerged from the woods, she ground the gears into first. It bucked and coughed, but she swung it around the shoulder and sped off in the opposite direction.

In the rearview mirror, as she shifted into second, the distance between her and the approaching boys widened until they disappeared. She turned left onto a dirt path and barreled down the bumpy trail.

"Who are you? And . . . and where are you taking me?" Trinity asked.

"That need not concern you at the moment." The vehicle bucked. "Ah, like driving a bicycle . . . never forget." The car settled some as it trudged over a clearer path.

The girl looked out the window. "Are we going to the dragon's den?"

Jezebel turned to her. "You know. How smart. Did you intuit that? Is that your power?"

"Huh?"

"Never mind."

"I need you to open that glovebox."

"I . . . I can't."

"You can't? Or you won't?"

"There's a . . . a protection spell on it." The girl shook her head as if she couldn't believe what she was admitting.

Jezebel rubbed the tips of her fingers. "No wonder." She took another left. "I definitely picked a bad week for a manicure." Branches scraped the roof, and the car jostled over stones.

When they reached the open field, she banked left, gunned the engine, and drove up the hill toward the mouth of the cave.

Inside the lair, she killed the engine, got out, went to Trinity's side, and hauled her out.

"Easy, bitch!" Trinity said. "You hurt me, and Mat'll have your ass. Do you know he knows karate?"

"Karate, huh?" She dragged her toward the passageway.

Trinity, with arms behind her back, jumped up and kicked Jezebel in the chest. "Yes, I taught him."

Jezebel landed on the curved hood of the automobile, rolled off and onto the dirt ground.

Trinity, on her back, struggled to get out of the magic bind.

"M-M-Mom?" Bingham's crooked paw came into Jezebel's view.

Jezebel panned up, his half-human, half-wolf face was wrought with concern. "What you do?" His mouth struggled to form the words.

Jezebel's heart sank. "Did . . . did you call me, Mom?"

"What you do with pretty lady?"

The morning sun shone in, revealing a blue dragonfly buzzing around Bingham's head. He extended a human-like finger, and the insect landed on it. He took it back outside babbling something about the bats getting it.

"The totem. My totem." Jezebel rose and dusted off her dress. She strengthened the bind around Trinity's wrists and dragged her toward the passageway.

I N THE WEDGE IN the rock corridor, Jezebel clawed at the ground. The tether that clung to the girl hampered her some, but she didn't let that get in the way.

"What are you doing?" Trinity asked.

"You ask too many questions." Jezebel felt the medallion's cool metal. "Ah. I've got it."

"What are you digging for?"

"Again. Too many questions." Jezebel rose and with amulet in hand, worked her way out from the crack in the wall. "That's better." She held the medallion to the scant light leaking in from above.

"Mom." Bingham crawled his way down the incline.

"For Satan's sake, Bingham! I told you to go off and play."

"You my real mom." His mouth contorted, and he stuttered, "Elio t-t-told me, after you l-l-left last time." He scooted, on his rump, down the incline toward them.

Trinity and Jezebel exchanged a look.

"Well . . ." Jezebel said to him. "That's not important right now."

Bingham, now closer to the two, stood and embraced Jezebel. "Momma. I al . . . al . . . ways wanted to know my mother."

Arms fixed at her side, Jezebel gaped. The weight of her child's body clinging to her made her a little unsteady. She raised her arm to avoid falling and dropped her amulet. She spun around to catch it, but it, and Bingham, slid down the slick rocks and into the dark depths of the crevice.

"Mom!" Bingham's voice trailed off.

"You son of a bitch!" She cursed. "You made me drop my amulet!"

"Mom?" Bingham groaned. From the sound of it, he had fallen a few feet below and onto the ledge.

"Listen to you." Trinity shuffled down the incline after the boy. "Who's the bitch?"

Jezebel grabbed her by the hair. "Where do you think you're going?"

"After your son! The poor thing only wanted a hug. What the hell kind of mother are you?"

"Listen you, Pure!" Jezebel tightened the slack to Trinity's tether. "You don't know the half of it. He's deformed. He's not welcomed in our society."

Trinity, who had wedged herself steady to the rock wall, let her foot go, and she slid down. "*You* shouldn't be welcomed."

Jezebel fell onto her face as the tie to Trinity pulled her downward. They landed in a clump beside Bingham.

"Mom?"

"What?"

"I f-f-forgive you," Bingham said. "I l-l-love you."

The air carried a pungent, musty odor.

Jezebel rubbed her thumb and forefinger together and manifested a flame. She lit a small torch embedded in the wall. A few bats flew from the light.

"Did you hear what he said?" Trinity asked. The fall had loosened the tie around her wrists. She yanked the strap, and the other end whipped off Jezebel's arm with a forceful tug that startled the witch. Trinity stepped closer to her face. "You don't scare me."

Jezebel breathed in the girl's scent of strawberries, smelling far better than bat guano. "I heard him." She stared into the girl's ocean-blue eyes. The flickering of the torch's flames reflected in them.

"Who the hell . . . what the hell are you?"

The girl's demands infuriated Jezebel. "You ask too many questions."

Trinity broke her stare and tended to Bingham. "Are you okay?" She helped him up.

"I . . . I'm fine." Bingham smiled at her. "Th . . . thank you." He caught Jezebel's stare and smiled tightly at her.

When the boy lumbered closer to Trinity, Jezebel's amulet came into view, and she rushed toward it.

"Not so fast!" Trinity stepped on it. "What *is* this thing?" Trinity picked it up.

"Let . . . let it go. It's . . . it's of no use to a Pure . . . even a Metanormal."

Trinity moved backward into the dark, swinging the chain from her finger. "You didn't answer my question. And why should I give it to you? I don't know if I can trust you."

"It's my amulet!" Jezebel said quickly. "It's my totem. If we are to get out from this bat-stinking hole, we're going to need a little magic." Next to her, she pointed at the chute they slid down. "We can't very well climb back out."

"Hm. And this thing'll do it."

"I . . . I can use it to levitate us out of here."

"Your totem, huh?" Trinity inspected it and rubbed her hand over the intricate carvings. "Funny, it doesn't look like the other one."

"Diesel's?"

"The one the doctor put in my glovebox. Is that Diesel's? Why do you want his so bad?"

"I don't. I want my own." Jezebel reached for it, but the girl stepped back. "Give it to me."

Trinity held it over a ledge to her left. "Apologize to your son first."

"Don't . . . don't drop it. It's our only way out."

"You heard me. Apologize to your son."

"I'm . . . I'm sorry, Bingham." The confession released a wave of emotion she hadn't expected. She cleared her throat.

"What happened?" Trinity asked.

Again, the questions. "What happened with what?"

"You and . . . Bingham?"

Jezebel tried to chase away thoughts of abandoning the boy, but the sensation of love was too strong. "I . . . I did my best," her voice hitched unexpectedly. "I did what a mother is supposed to do . . . with a . . . with an imperfect child."

"Is that what he is to you?" Trinity patted the boy's damp hair with her free hand.

Watching Trinity comfort her only child spiked jealousy and guilt. "I did what I was supposed to!" The confession slipped from Jezebel's tongue too quick for her to retract and years of remorse spilled forth. She closed her eyes to hold back the tears but felt their warmth trickle down her cheeks. "I don't know about your world, but here only the strong are allowed to live. Only . . . only superior beings . . . strengthen the clan. I set him loose."

"Survival of the fittest. Hm," Trinity said. "Well, in my world we take care of all . . . or at least try to. Every breathing organism has the right to live freely."

"I did set him free." Jezebel looked away. "To be . . . to be food. That's what I'm supposed to do."

"Says who?"

"Questions!" She paused. "The scriptures."

"Hm. Religion. I guess it gets in the way here too."

Jezebel recalled Elio coming to her to inform her he had rescued the child and later being upset with her when she never came by to visit. "He would've been eaten by the other wolves or have the blood sucked out of him by a vampire."

"Would have?"

"God, you ask lots of questions."

"God? Does he live here? It doesn't sound it in this hell hole."

"Enough!" Jezebel turned her back to them, using the privacy to wipe her tearstained cheeks and dab her eyes. "The dragon . . . Elio . . . rescued him, else he wouldn't be here."

"I l . . . l . . . love Elio!" the boy said.

Jezebel's shoulders shook. "I know . . . son. But we can't let the others know you're here." She faced them again. "They'll kill you."

Trinity stood with her arms crossed and a hand to her chin. "It must've been difficult for you."

The emotion welled up again, but Jezebel staved it off like she had for years. "I muddle through. Now, give me my totem. I can hover us the hell out of here."

"I'm a professional rock climber. We don't need this."

"We do! I do!" Jezebel dove toward her. The girl slipped and dropped the totem.

"Oh, shit," Trinity said. "I . . . I didn't mean."

"You!" Jezebel fumed. "You!" She screamed.

CHAPTER TWENTY

Mom

B Y THE TIME DOL finally caught up with Mat and Diesel, the Volkswagen had long been gone.

The wizard leaned against a tree to catch his breath. "Elio . . . his wing . . . is pretty bad. I haven't the power to repair it."

"Why not?" Mat asked. "You are more than just a wand wizard, after all."

"He can't fly. He's following after us, but insisted I go ahead," Dol said.

The two argued for a time.

Diesel knew he had to chase after Jezebel. His quest was for Bence, for sure, but a dull ache told him there was something more to it. "Elio," he muttered. An image of the poor dragon limping toward them, sniffing the ground, and following their scent snapped into his mind. Then, a calmness overcame him: a sense of clarity and knowing. He removed his shirt.

"Are you going to shift?" Mat asked.

"I'm going after Jezebel." He tossed one boot to the side, then the other.

"You don't need to do that," Dol said, his breath a little steadier now.

Diesel shucked his pants. "No?"

"You're a shifter."

"I know. And every time I shift, my clothes become rags. A good pair of jeans are hard to come by in this forest."

Dol opened his mouth, as if to say something, but didn't.

Diesel, using his nascent psychic powers, couldn't penetrate the man's mind.

"You're young, very young," Dol said. "But very powerful." He smiled.

Mat collected his clothes.

Diesel's body shuddered, and the involuntary urge to morph began. His jaw snapped, and his body writhed. His canine brain locked onto the scent as he lowered onto all fours, but this time he held onto the words of the wizard: 'psychic' and 'very powerful,' swam in his wolf-mind unlike any time before.

He turned back and looked up at Mat and Dol. They spoke, but, as usual, he couldn't interpret in his wolf skin; yet this time, unlike any other, he could sense his manly self still with him. He raised a paw, expecting it to look something like Bingham, half-and-half, but his forelimb was pure animal. His tail swept behind him as it typically did, but this time he was aware. Aware of his true self within the body of a wolf.

Mat lowered to his level. He muttered something, but Diesel only caught the emotions as the man scratched his ear: *concern*. Dol lowered too: *pride*.

An overwhelming sense to save Trinity from Jezebel overcame him, and he rushed off into the direction the Volkswagen had traveled. *Volkswagen?*

He slowed. *How does a wolf know what a Volkswagen is?* His hyperawareness tripped him up, and he stumbled some, then tossed away any resistance his mind caused, and his full wolf took over. He ran, faster and faster, for a time as the lingering scent of the car grew stronger.

Follow the gasoline, he thought. *Wait? How can a wolf know . . .?* His awareness slammed into him, as if he had left his true essence, his spirit, back in the trails, and it just now caught up with him. He expected to involuntarily shift back, but a blue dragonfly flew by and led him farther.

He followed it until he reached the base of Elio's den. Then, with a growl, he darted up the hill and skidded into the mouth of the cavern beside the car. No one was around.

The dragonfly landed on the open hood of the Volkswagen, and a yellow rope was tied to the car's bumper.

Volkswagen. He sniffed the ground, holding his awareness of self and the wolf in harmony.

Jezebel. He noted the scent of her leather high heels. *Trinity?* An aroma, almost orgiastic, caused him to ache with want. He thought of the fae's spell in the woods, to trick him into making love to a poor version of her. *Trinity.* The clarity overwhelmed him, and he followed the strawberry fragrance toward the corridor.

"I T'S HELPFUL TO KEEP rappelling gear in the trunk. You never know when it'll come in handy," Trinity said.

Jezebel, unsure why the human would help, secured the rope around Bingham's waist as the girl had instructed.

"You got it, big boy," Trinity said to Bingham. She had pulled her hair back into a ponytail, and her face now hung over the ledge above.

"Think I got it." Bingham gripped the rope as best he could with his half paw.

Jezebel led Bingham toward the rock chute that Trinity, without the aid of any gear, had easily rappelled up to earlier. "Why did you come back?" Jezebel asked.

"Huh?" Trinity tugged the rope.

"When you climbed out of here, I didn't expect you to come back."

"Don't get all sentimental, lady. I came back for the kid. It's just something in me. I can't leave someone stranded who can't fend for themselves." Trinity's face disappeared, and Bingham rose.

Jezebel pushed him up from behind. "What . . . about . . . me?" she asked through grunts.

Trinity was quiet. "Give . . . me . . . your hand," she said, but it was for Bingham. "Work your back legs. There you go!"

"I made it!" Bingham said, sounding surprised.

Jezebel leaned against the wall. She looked over at the ledge where her totem had fallen. She wondered what life as a witch would be without it when the yellow rope she had placed around Bingham came down for her.

"Grab it, M-M-Mom," Bingham said.

D IESEL FOLLOWED THE YELLOW rope and the strawberry scent clinging to it down the rock corridor. Now that he had given up fighting his true self, his wolf brain—or a mishmash of all of him—comprehended the moment with profound clarity. *Yellow rope. Strawberry.*

Midway down, he stopped, still panting from the run, and caught Jezebel's scent by a crack in the wall.

A little farther, he eyed the redhead tugging at the rope. *Beautiful girl.* Beside her, Bingham peered down into the depths of the shaft. A small ray of light pierced upward.

"C'mon, Mom. You can do it," Bingham said.

Mom? Diesel thought. *Bingham doesn't know his mother.*

Trinity's cut deltoids flexed as she hauled up something with the rope, and Bingham reached a paw out to help. When their catch came into view—black hair, olive skin, and red dress—Diesel growled.

Startled, Trinity turned and shrieked upon seeing a wolf. The lead slipped. Bingham pitched forward. Diesel lunged, shifting back, to catch the boy before he slipped farther.

Trinity yelled louder upon seeing Diesel— now naked—and let go of the rope.

Jezebel fell down the chute and landed with a thud.

"Mom!" Bingham leaned over, but Diesel pulled him back.

Trinity gaped, then turned away.

"Diesel," Bingham said, "you have to h-h-help us s-s-save her."

"What . . . what are you doing? Why are you calling her mom?"

"I see it's a surprise to you too?" Trinity said, careful not to take in too much of Diesel's nakedness.

"Oh." Diesel placed a hand over his groin.

Bingham removed the oversized shirt he wore to hide his twisted chest. "Here, Diesel, wear this." He pointed a crooked paw to Trinity. "She nice lady."

Diesel put on the shirt, and its tails covered his private parts. "What are you two doing down here? Bingham, you know this area is off limits. It's not safe."

"Jezebel took us down here," Trinity said, staring at him. "You're . . . you're the guy from the phone."

Diesel furrowed his brow. "The . . . phone?"

"Never mind. You know Mat."

"Yes."

"Is he safe?"

"Yes, he's on his way."

Trinity's shoulders relaxed, and she let out a sigh of relief. Then, as if remembering, she turned back to the slackened rope. "Jezebel?" She lowered herself down.

"Wh . . . wh . . . why are you saving Jezebel?" Diesel asked. "She's a witch."

"I can't leave someone stranded who can't fend for themselves."

"She's my mom." Bingham smiled at him. "Jezebel's my m-m-mom. I have a mom!"

Diesel cocked his head.

"Elio told me so." Bingham was too excited to question. "She came the other day. Try to fix me, but it didn't work."

"Fix you?" Trinity and Diesel both said, then exchanged a tight grin in recognition of each other.

"You don't need to be fixed," Diesel said.

"There's nothing wrong with you," Trinity added, keeping her eyes trained on the chute. The light below went out. "Jezebel? Are you okay?" After a moment of silence, she wrapped the yellow rope around her waist. "I'm going down."

"Wait!" Diesel touched her shoulder. It was electrifying. "Are . . . are . . . you sure? She could be up to no good."

"I can handle women like her." She disappeared into the dark.

"Wait. I'm com—" Diesel lost his footing and slid down the chute after her.

Darkness heightened his senses. The rock ground was cold, damp, and . . . "Eww. Bat guano." He recalled having been down there, years ago, for a romp with Bence, prior to any bat's having taken over. "Elio," Diesel muttered, thinking of the dragon's fondness for flying mammals.

"Diesel," Trinity said, "over here."

He followed her voice, clinging to the right side of the wall to avoid the ledge he knew existed opposite it. "We need a ligh—"

A small flame from a match lit Trinity's face. She reached up, tippy-toed to the torch in the wall, took it out, and lit it. "Helps to be prepared." She pointed it down another corridor. "There's blood. She's injured."

"There's an opening at the end of the corridor," he said, recalling his times with Bence.

"Jezebel?"

When they reached the opening, they found her sitting up against a rock in the center of the hollow. She held her forehead, and blood dripped between her fingers.

"Laura," she said, eyes glazed. "Lydia." She looked at Trinity, then turned to Diesel. "Daniel."

Diesel took the torch from Trinity, who tended to her, and lit another torch in the wall.

"Jezebel, you have a concussion. We need to get you help," Trinity said.

"I don't need help. Who would help me? I'm just a banished witch set to live out her life as a wolf-shifter."

"Come with me," Diesel lowered beside Trinity. "Look, I know we've had our differences. But you are my stepmother, and I respect that. I can carry you out."

"You're not . . ." She stopped, as if trying to find the words.

Diesel cocked his head. "Not what?"

"You're not who you think you are."

A cold wave came over Diesel. "What do you mean?"

"While I may be your stepmother, Honoree is . . ." She lowered a bloody hand and set it in her lap. "He's not your father."

Diesel smirked. "You're delirious."

"A concussion will do that," Trinity said. "Let's get you—" Trinity went to put her arms under Jezebel's, but she stopped her.

"I found you here." Her head fell back against the rock, palms up to the room. "Laura, Lydia, and I were pregnant at the same time."

"Laura? My mother?"

"She was not your mother."

"What?" Diesel inched closer to her.

"Laura, Lydia, and Lena. They were witches. Triplets actually, though they didn't really resemble one another."

"Lena? Witch Lena? My sister's midwife?"

"That one. She is . . . was . . . the queen's favorite. She was spared. The rest of us were cursed to live out our lives as wolf-shifters and grow back the species after a pack . . ." Her face wrinkled, and she cried. "After a pack killed our children back in the motherland!" She convulsed into tears.

Diesel stood and pressed a hand to his temples. "My moth . . . Laura was a witch?"

"Laura wasn't your mother. I don't know who is . . . or was."

"In Europe, after the fall of Hitler," Diesel said, for Trinity's benefit, "the pack was decimated after a brutal witch hunt. My ancestors were brought here to thrive and grow, protected by the magic of the area and unite with the British extension at the castle."

"And those of us witches . . . were cursed to be what we killed," Jezebel's words slurred, and her eyelids drooped.

"The . . . war? World War II? How old are you?" Trinity asked Jezebel.

"180," Jezebel said.

Trinity slinked back, then rose joining Diesel. "This is too weird. I can't believe all this. Maybe I'm the one suffering a concussion." She wiped her brow, as if looking for blood but only brushed away a smudge of dirt.

"Witches age slowly here," Diesel offered.

"Uh huh. Are you . . . a witch?"

"Now, I don't know what I am. I'm a wolf-shifter, at least that's all I've ever known." He returned to Jezebel, who stared off beyond the rock wall she faced. "How do you know Honoree is not my father?"

"Laura's baby died in childbirth and mine was premature . . . deformed."

"Bingham was your child?" he asked, and she slowly nodded. The facts hit him in the gut with startling clarity. He knew, somehow, she was telling the truth.

"Elio looked after him as you, too, were left here to be looked after. There's nothing more caring than an Emphilothepy." A hint of disgust swam in her last sentence, the real Jezebel glinting through with jealousy. "Afterward, Elio came to me . . . for me to see Bingham, but I couldn't bring myself to do it."

"Where did I come from?"

She ignored him. "If the queen found out about Bingham, he'd be killed. If I were to repair him," her eyes widened, "I'd be considered a great witch, and the king would want to restore my full powers."

"You just found me here?"

Jezebel's head wobbled, and she looked up at him. "It wasn't uncommon for women to come here and leave an unwanted child. The wolves won't come here with the dragon."

He knelt beside her. "That's why Elio always has imperfects around here."

She held a hand to his face. "But you were so perfect, I don't know why someone would abandon you. Laura's birth was difficult, and she and her baby died. I lied to Honoree and told him the baby survived."

"Why?"

She sighed. "In her honor. None of us could hold a healthy baby full term."

"You stole me from here and brought me back to the pack . . . to Honoree?"

"I had . . . no . . . mate," Jezebel slurred. "My pregnancy was not sanctioned."

"Jezebel, who killed Bence?"

She shielded the torch light from her eyes, and her head fell back against the rock.

A voice in the hall infiltrated the room. "Diesel? Trinity?"

"Mat!" Trinity ran out after him.

"Jezebel?" Diesel shook her chin, but her eyes closed.

Diesel laid out Jezebel on the ground by the front of the Volkswagen, and Dr. Dolessenbee tended to her wound with his bandana. "I'm only doing this because the girl insists," the doctor said.

"She's a living being," Trinity exchanged a look with Mat, exhibiting their disagreement. "I have my reasons," she added, eyeing Bingham who spoke with Elio by the cave's entrance.

Dol tapped his wand to Jezebel's forehead.

They waited—Mat, Trinity, and Diesel leaning over Jezebel's outstretched body.

Dol, on his knees, pulled back one of the witch's eyelids and shined his wand's light into her eye. "Nothing."

Diesel lowered and placed an ear to her chest. "Her heart's beating."

Bingham lobbed over, in the process he had wandered to the back of the cave and returned holding a jar.

"Bing," Diesel said.

The boy held the glass jar out to Dol. "Elio's tears . . . they fix my mom."

Diesel turned to the opening of the cave where Elio sighed and looked away. "That's his emergency backup."

"Uh huh," Bingham said.

Dolessenbee opened the jar, looked to others for confirmation, then poured its contents onto her head. Jezebel's wound repaired, and her eyes snapped open.

"Evil Satan! What in the devil's sake are you doing?" She wiped Elio's tears from her face and stood.

"Easy." Trinity held a hand toward her, but Jezebel wanted nothing of it.

Jezebel rose, dismissed Trinity's aid, then headed for the cave's exit. "I have places to be . . . things to do."

"Wait!" Diesel rushed to her and grabbed her by the arm.

She stared at him. "We need not mention what went on here."

"What about Bence?"

"He was a good boy. Handsome. It's unfortunate he's gone."

The reality hit Diesel hard: she knew nothing of Bence's death. The truth swam in his blood, nipped at his bones, and stung his core.

Jezebel combed fingers through tresses dangling along her forehead. "Don't tell Honoree or Mitsy about what happened here." She looked back into the cave. "Honoree would be devastated, and your sister's too troubled with her pregnancy to bother her with such matters."

"Mitsy?"

"She's his only child."

"But she—"

"Sometimes the truth is best left unsaid, Diesel." She had never called him by his nickname.

"Why did you marry Honoree?"

She shrugged. "What's a wolf-shifter to do?" She wandered down the embankment and partway down shifted into a wolf.

Chapter Twenty-One

Ketch

Dol helped Trinity pack up her rappelling gear into the Volkswagen. "The Howling Moon is tonight. Keep the totem in the glovebox. Trevor will care for it and take it back to safety."

Diesel was indifferent about the plight of his totem. He hadn't believed in the practices everyone followed and why they were so revered, but something tugged at him. "Where will it go?"

Dol faced him. "To the Monitors' headquarters in France."

"Why there?" Diesel asked.

Dol looked down. "It's safer there."

"It's my totem. Shouldn't I . . . ?" He didn't know what he thought about it.

"On your twenty-first year, it's best kept off site."

"Why? I'm not who I think I am." He placed a hand on the open passenger door to the Beetle. "Will it tell me who my parents are . . . were?"

Dol didn't answer right away. "I don't know."

"It's noon," Mat said to Trinity. "You should get back before too long."

"I don't feel right leaving you all." Her eyes met Diesel's. They stared for a bit until she broke it and lowered the Beetle's front hatch.

"Wait." Diesel pointed to a metal barb dangling from her bag of gear. "Do you mind if I borrow this?"

Trinity paused. "Sure."

Diesel pocketed it and headed for the exit.

Mat went to him. "Where are you off to?"

"Business to attend to."

"I can give you a lift," Trinity said.

WHEN THE BEETLE REACHED the bottom of the embankment, Diesel pointed right for her to retrace the path she had come down. At the fork in the road, they went left toward the Trash Heap.

"You've really been here for twenty-one years?" she asked, picking up on their polite conversation thus far.

"I was away at boarding school in London since I was a teen. I came back from time to time and then attended, what you call university, back in England. I graduated this past spring."

"And now you're back."

"Sort of."

They sat in silence for a bit.

"I live about an hour south of here in a town called Elk. My family has had this property here for generations. I hadn't come up here in years."

"Mat told me. Sorry to hear about . . . about their passing."

She nodded and shifted into third gear.

"I like your car."

"Thanks. It was my dad's pride and joy. The bank repossessed the SUV and the Subaru. Now, they're threatening to foreclose on the house."

"That sucks."

"It does. What about you? What does a wolf-shifter do for a living?"

"Well, it's not quite like that here. We're taken care of, in a way, by the queen." He leaned his elbow on the chassis of the open window. Air blew the traces of hair sticking out from his ball cap. "My buddy and I were trying to get out of here. Heading to Salem."

"Massachusetts?"

"Yeah."

"My parents went to school there. Salem State. That's where they met."

Diesel nodded. "In Salem, Supers and normal folk . . . people like you, can live freely."

Trinity turned to him while shifting into a lower gear. The car bucked. "You mean like witches."

"And shifters, mages, vamp—" He stopped when she chuckled nervously, and he recalled his lectures about Normals and their fear of the supernatural. "It's a lot to take in, I know."

They drove on.

"So, you and this friend are off to Salem?"

"We were, but he . . ." He spared her the details. "Something happened to him that I need to follow up on. What do you do?"

"I teach special ed."

"Special ed.?"

"I'm a teacher. I work with kids who have physical and intellectual disabilities." She inhaled slowly. "It doesn't pay much, but it's rewarding, at times. And challenging."

"I bet. You were really good back there . . . with Bingham."

She nodded. "I majored in Environmental Education. Passion is nature, the woods, rock climbing, but I love kids."

He didn't want to get her too close to the Trash Heap for fear she'd freak upon seeing human remains. "You can let me out here."

She slowed. "You sure?"

"The road is thick with brush. You won't be able to get through," he lied to avoid her seeing any atrocities.

The car came to a stop, and she yanked up on the lever between the seats with a tick. "I guess this is it."

He wet his lips and bit his tongue. "Maybe . . . one day . . . we can . . ." He scratched the back of his neck. He wanted to ask her out. "We'll see an end to all this craziness," he said instead.

"I'm happy for you and Mat."

Diesel smiled. "Yeah." He recalled the delicacy of human emotions from class. They weren't as sexually permissive as Supers. He tapped the dash above the glovebox. "I should let you go."

A S WAS COMMON FOR a vampire, the house was boarded up tightly for midday.

Diesel rapped on the door but, knowing it wouldn't wake the vampire from slumber and that a vampire wouldn't readily answer the door on a sunny fall afternoon, he used the shiv he borrowed from Trinity to let himself in.

"Ketch, rise and shine!"

The vampire slept prostrate—hands clasped across his chest. A pair of sunglasses rested on his bedside table for the occasional wake in the middle of the day.

Diesel tapped Ketch's cold nose. "Ketch." When he didn't wake, he flicked his finger harder, and the vampire stirred. "Wake up!"

Ketch's eyes, shot through with red vessels, shot open. "For the love of Satan!" He snatched his sunglasses and quickly placed them on. "Diesel, what in the frig' are you doing in here?" He looked over to the window where a bit of sunlight peeked out from the edges of the black shade. "You know better than to wake a vampire during the day."

"What do you know about Bence?"

The vampire smirked. "Bence? He gave good head."

Diesel slapped him hard across the face, and his sunglasses flew off.

"Jesus!" Ketch held a hand to his face, shielding his eyes from the glare.

Diesel picked up the glasses from the floor and held them out to the vampire. "Want these?"

Ketch reached for them, but Diesel held them back. "Dee! Give me them!" the vampire shouted, hand to face.

Diesel walked over to the window and leaned up against the sill. "Tell me about Bence."

"I don't know nothing!"

"Yeah, you certainly don't know nothing, you lug." Diesel twirled the sunglasses. "I suspect you know why he was placed outside the barrier system . . . dead!"

"I don't. I don't."

Diesel attempted to use his newfound psychic abilities to test the vampire's truth, but his anger got the better of him. The buzz of alignment he felt when he had read Jezebel was gone. "I smelled your scent outside the barrier," Diesel lied, he hadn't been able to specifically detect Ketch but didn't want to let on. "The stench of foul play was prominent."

Ketch lay face down on his pillow to shield his eyes. "C'mon man, give me my sunglasses. Better yet, get the hell outta here!" His words were muffled.

"Bence, Luke, and I were the only ones who knew about the tear in the wall."

"All right! We followed him. After the Metanormal broke my friggin' teeth, Pedro and I went hunting and traced his scent."

"How'd you get through the tree portal?"

Ketch held his hand out. "Come on, man, give me my sunglasses!"

Diesel tossed them on the bed.

The vampire rolled onto his side, put them on, then sat up on his haunches. "Jesus. You're friggin' relentless."

"I am. I want to know about Bence's death. Why were you out there?"

Ketch sighed. "Look, the king gave Ped and I a special key. He's sympathetic to us vamps. We can get out . . . sometimes . . . if we're good . . . for something to eat other than deer and muskrat blood."

"Payment for putting those tracking devices on people?"

"How'd you know about that?"

"I have my ways." Diesel placed a finger in the blackened shade's ring pull. "What else?"

Ketch glanced over at Diesel's hand on the shade. "Look, why don't you—"

Diesel tugged on the pull, knowing the full onslaught of sun beaming in would prove too much for a pair of sunglasses to shield. "What do you know?"

"We saw him. All right? We saw him by the big ol' rock. We saw him slip out behind it."

"And?"

"And that was it."

Diesel peeled back a sliver of the shade and peeked out. "Beautiful New England day."

"No! Don't!" Ketch's voice was muffled, his face back in the pillow.

"I could pull the shade up and let you catch a glimpse. Or?"

"Okay! We followed him. We wanted to know. We didn't know there was a way out."

"So, you followed after him. Why did you kill him?" Diesel fumed.

"I didn't! We didn't! I swear."

Diesel inhaled deeply and closed his eyes. He reached for that place he felt earlier, when he had better control over his emotions, and could sense the truth, but he couldn't find it. "What do you know?"

"I promised not to tell."

Diesel opened his eyes. "Who?"

"She threatened to tell the castle, then King Winston would take away our special passes."

Diesel quivered. "Who!"

Ketch watched with interest as the wolf-shifter's hand touched the base of the shade. "We need more than moose bits."

Diesel tugged the shade, and it spun open with a clatter.

"Ah!" the vampire yelled. "All right! All right!"

"I'm waiting."

"Shut it! Please!" Ketch dove under the bedding.

Diesel closed it again, and Ketch, fumbled under the covers, apparently for his sunglasses that had fallen loose in the process. "He wasn't dead when we left. I swear."

"Who?"

Ketch pulled back the covers. The vampire's black hair was disheveled, and he held up a hand. "I honestly don't know what happened or if . . ."

"If what?"

"If she did it. I don't know why she would."

"She?"

"Your sister."

Part Three

Advances

CHAPTER TWENTY-TWO

Wolf Den

J EZEBEL AND HONOREE STROLLED through the ward's empty assembly area. Fair-weather clouds shaded the sun's warmth, making the cool, fall air bite hard.

Jezebel, opting for clean-and-subdued over glamorous, wore her hair down, past her shoulders. She donned a royal-blue, mid-length dress, which was tucked under her bust and had a square neckline.

Meeting notices, tacked to a cutout in the middle of a pine designed for such things, flapped in the subtle breeze. One announcement "The Howling Moon Celebration Tonight!" flapped loudest with only one pin holding it.

They walked past rows of empty benches, appearing larger with no one occupying them.

Beyond the assembly, they entered the traditionalists' row where wolf-shifters nestled in the root system of mammoth, magical pines.

One of the reasons Jezebel married Honoree was for his more opulent, modern home on the opposite side of the assembly area—a cabin with windows. Her friend Linda, Honoree's ex-wife who died in childbirth, had insisted upon it. If a witch were to live out her life among the lowest rung of the supernatural species, she might as well have the best, and Jezebel took her spot.

Honoree held her arm. "I'm glad you're back. I was beginning to get nervous."

"I had some thinking to do. Things to take care of."

"Diesel?"

She nodded. "Maybe you should let him go."

Honoree stopped. "What are you saying?"

"The queen was able to get a sample. We can raise his offspring scientifically."

The Alpha scrunched his brow. "Science? What about tradition? The scriptures say—"

"Sometimes things just need to evolve naturally."

"Exactly." He let go of her. "A lab baby is not *natural*."

She retook his hand; maybe she could make a go of this wolf-shifting world after all. Without her amulet, there was no witch life to go back to. "What I mean, Husband, is that times have changed. The world has evolved. We should accept things," she bit her lower lip, paused, then went on, "and stop trying to make them fit into a reality they weren't meant for."

"Diesel is my son. I need my son to have a family, settle down."

Jezebel placed a hand to his bearded face. She didn't have the heart to tell him the truth. That Diesel wasn't his. Not yet. "Mitsy is with child. Your daughter is having a boy. You should be grateful."

He took the hand that caressed his beard and held it to his chest. "What's gotten into you?"

She shrugged. She honestly didn't know.

They walked to Mitsy and Buck's hollow hand-in-hand. Elder Bainbridge opened the door.

From the entryway, there was clear sight to the home's one bedroom where Mitsy lay feverish in bed.

A stench of sulfur hung in the air, and Jezebel held a hand to her nose, breathing in the scent of lavender from her bath. The smell concerned Jezebel, but she knew not why and ignored the matter by removing a perfume bottle from her purse. She sprayed, discretely, as they walked down the small stoop and into the home.

At Mitsy's bedside, Buck dabbed a dingy rag to her forehead. When he saw them, he stood. "Honoree. Jezebel. Thank you for coming."

"We need a witch." Elder Bainbridge tapped his cane behind them in the home's center room.

Jezebel set her purse on the couch, took the perfume with her, entered the bedroom, and spritzed, quietly, again. "Mitsy," she said. "What's wrong with her?" she asked the elder.

"Her fever won't break. She needs bedrest." He used his cane to feel his way through the bedroom's entrance.

"She needs air." Jezebel sat on the bed, opposite Buck. "I'll take over," she said.

Mitsy's head sank back into the pillow. "You? You're going to take care of me?"

"Look, if it wasn't for me, Witch Lena would be here to coax you through. It's the least I can do."

In shock of the offer, Mitsy propped up on elbows, but Jezebel shushed her and made her settle back down.

"Get me some fresh linen," Jezebel commanded Buck. She yanked off the thick blanket. "This heavy thing is making matters worse."

Buck whisked past Honoree who remained by the door.

"Honoree," she added, "get me some water and a fresh cloth so I can wash her down."

"Jezebel?" Mitsy said, while putting her hands up to let Jezebel remove her wet nightgown.

"Quiet. You've done enough for me over the years. Cleaning my nails. Fixing my dresses. It's the least I can do." Jezebel stopped when she saw her husband still standing by the door. "Honoree! Bainbridge! Fetch me a bucket of cool water."

When the men left, she finished removing the girl's nightgown and tossed it to the floor. "And a pair of fresh pajamas!" she yelled to the closed door. "Buck?" she said, when she didn't hear a reply.

"Yes, ma'am."

Mitsy chuckled. "He doesn't know where I keep the fresh clothes."

"Men." Jezebel went to the chest of draws against a windowless wall and opened the top one.

"The bottom drawer is mine," Mitsy said.

Jezebel opened it. It was empty. Surprised, she placed her hands on her hips and faced Mitsy.

"They must still be out on the line."

Jezebel opened the door as Honoree approached with water and a cloth. Buck stopped short behind him carrying sheets, and Bainbridge lowered onto the couch. Jezebel took the offerings and told Honoree to go back to their home to gather fresh towels and some of her nightwear.

When she closed the door, Mitsy already fared better. Her complexion was less sweaty and reddened.

By the time Jezebel finished bathing the young girl and changed the bed linen, being careful not to move her too much, Honoree had returned with fresh clothes.

"Thank you," Mitsy said, donning a warm, cotton gown. She snuggled down into the sheets.

Jezebel went to the living room to retrieve her purse, only to find the men drinking, apparently content that Jezebel was taking care of things. "Why don't you make yourselves comfortable?" Her sarcasm didn't faze them, and she returned to Mitsy.

From her purse, she took out fresh herbs and set them on the bedside table. "Lavender to help ease the pain." She wasn't sure why she had brought them from her home—something told her too. She spritzed more perfume. "What is that stench? We need to get you a housekeeper or—" Jezebel caught sight of the wooden statue of Baphomet, previously hidden by Buck's presence. She went to it. "What is this?"

"Ba . . . ba . . . Baphomet." Mitsy quivered.

"I know who it is, but why is it here? Where did you get this?"

Mitsy didn't answer.

"Mitsy, where did you—?"

"Witch Lena."

"She gave you this?"

Mitsy was quiet.

"Why? Why did she give you this?"

"To . . . to protect my baby." Mitsy placed a hand on her belly.

"The sulfur." It hit her hard. "That's the smell of guilt mixed with . . ." Jezebel said, recalling the dark magic. "Mitsy, what did you do?"

The pregnant girl burst out crying.

"It's the decaying aroma of the Dark Lord." Jezebel stood open-mouthed.

While Mitsy confessed her incantations and deeds for Lord Darthius, Jezebel only half listened. A wide grin pinched her cheeks, and she burst out of Mitsy's bedroom with such a clatter that Bainbridge's cane flew into the air.

Honoree and Buck choked on their drinks. "Where are you going?" Honoree asked, wiping mead from his mustache.

Jezebel headed for the door without answering.

"What about Mitsy?" Buck asked. "She needs your help."

Jezebel clutched the Baphomet figurine in one hand and stopped at the stoop with a free hand on the knob. "She's your wife. *You* take care of her." Her mind schemed with possibilities. "I have an appointment to get my nails done," she said and left.

CHAPTER TWENTY-THREE

Fragrance

THE AFTERNOON SUN DESCENDED into the tops of pines, maples, and birches that dotted the forest. A colorful display of purple, blue, and orange painted the horizon.

"Witch Lena told me to pray to Lord Darthius for the health of my baby." Mitsy smiled. "And . . . he spoke to me! He called upon me, Diesel. He called upon *me*." She thumped a thin wrist to her chest. "The one who has been shunned by her friends and even by her own husband. He spoke to me," her voice warbled.

Diesel's truck idled at the edge of the assembly area where he had stopped when he saw Mitsy alone, sitting in a pew.

"I came early for him," she added.

"Who?"

"Lord Darthius." She had posited herself up front, in a bench reserved for males. "Buck uses me. He doesn't love me." Her lip quivered with vengeance. "He never has. The only thing he loves is that he's having a son."

"Mits." Diesel shook his head. He couldn't think of anything else to say. Truth, as hot as the sun, radiated from his sister. It didn't take his nascent clairvoyance to detect her raw candor.

The wind whipped, and a notice tacked to the bulletin board loosened from its pin. It danced along the ground and traveled off into the woods.

"What did he tell you to do?" Diesel feared her response but needed to hear it.

"Help him exterminate the weak."

"Mitsy." He sat beside her. "Tell me you don't believe that. Tell me you know that is wrong."

"It is written."

"It's wrong, Mits!" He never raised his voice to his sister, but she was no longer there. It was as if he spoke to a shell of the fun-loving kid he used to know.

She whispered with hands clasped in prayer.

"Bence. You didn't. We used to play as kids. The three of us." A tear slid down his cheek. It's warmth somehow welcoming, freeing. And another. Still more. Tears dripped down his neck and soaked the collar of his shirt, while Mitsy prayed.

"The Lord is my savior," she mumbled. Her eyes glazed. Her lips chapped. "The meek shall be exterminated from inheriting the Earth, and one day the daemons will rise again. Superior."

"Mitsy." Diesel placed a hand on her bony shoulder. Her skin was cold yet burning at the same time. She shivered. He took his jacket off and draped it over her.

"The Dark Lord is my shepherd. He shall comfort me in my time of need. Lord Darthius is my savior. I welcome him. I pray for him." She lifted her arms, and the jacket slid off. "I pray with him. I do his tidings. I am his vessel."

When she finished, she turned to Diesel. "Bence was a weak omega. He was no good to the pack if he wasn't going to procreate."

"What? Mitsy, you're deluded. You're feverish."

"Lord Darthius has informed me." She beamed. "He chose me. Little ol' me. He told me the pack has turned impotent. Those who won't procreate are dragging us down."

"Did . . . did you kill Bence?" He needed to hear her confession.

"Yes."

Diesel shook her. "Mitsy, no! Please tell me you didn't."

She stared off in the distance, as if seeing beyond the darkened forest and setting sun. "I followed him that night."

"Bence?"

She nodded. "Witch Lena lent me a pass to get out of the portal, and I followed him. Lena knew you two were able to get out."

"You told her." His rage boiled. "I told you that privately. You're my big sister. I thought I could trust you."

"King Winston needed to prove your ability to leave with science and created a new detection system."

"Ketch," Diesel muttered, understanding the vampire's involvement with the device. "But why? Why kill Bence?"

"Witch Lena put the cage out there to trap him. Like the dog that he is." She sneered. Her snout partially forming.

He shook his head. He couldn't believe what he was hearing.

"The trap was set for him to walk into it and lock him in. I just had to sprinkle him with the Soul Death dust Witch Lena had created."

"But . . . but . . ."

"Tonight. Upon the Eve of the Howling Moon. The Dark Lord shall rise and possess his carcass."

"Possess his carcass? That's worse than the empties." Diesel thought of the paranormals who chased Mat and him before the burial, seeking to snatch his spirit.

"Upon the seventh day, the spell will fully mature."

"What are you talking about?"

"Upon the seventh moon after the killing, the body will be ready for taking. That's how the Soul Death works, according to Lena."

"You betrayed me."

"Diesel . . ." Mitsy's face scrunched, and she convulsed into tears. "He wanted you. Lord Darthius really wanted to take *your* body." She wiped snot from her nose with the back of her hand. "I pleaded with Witch Lena. Bence was the consolation. I saved you, little brother." She smiled, eyes wide with craze.

"To hell with Lord Darthius!"

"Diesel!"

"Mitsy, this is nonsense." He backed away, trembling.

"During the Howling Moon, Lord Darthius shall rise again. My sacrifice proved my devotion to him, and for it, Witch Lena promised me he would see to my having a healthy baby boy." A pain seized her, and she clutched her stomach.

He returned his jacket to her shoulders.

"It is written. It is law. It is the Lord's way."

Diesel stepped back from his sister. The betrayal was too much. He raked a hand through his hair.

"You must leave, Diesel. You promised me you would leave for Salem. If Darthius finds you here tonight, there's no telling what he might do."

"I was to leave the forest with Bence . . . not alone."

"It doesn't matter. He's gone. When Lord Darthius returns, he will go after you if he finds you here."

"Why?"

"He wanted you after all. That's why I told you to leave. I was protecting you, Dee."

"You killed my best friend! That's not exactly looking out for your little brother."

"I had to do it, Dee. For the betterment of my baby and for the future of the pack."

"For Christ's sake, for that matter I'd'a had a child."

She looked out at the setting sun. The moon peeked out along the horizon. "It's too late. Witch Lena mentioned your twenty-first year was important."

"Yeah, it's important for all male wolf-shifters. That's when we become adults. But I'm already twenty-one."

"The Howling Moon is of special significance. The next won't be here for another twenty-one years."

"When your baby . . . my nephew will be twenty-one." He remembered how he wasn't really blood to Mitsy but now was not the time to bring it up. It was too much to comprehend.

"Lord Darthius created us all. He made us in the image of Satan."

"That's a myth."

"It is written in the—"

"Yes, Mitsy. I know what's written in the scriptures! I studied them at school. They drilled it into our heads, but I don't buy that hundreds-of-thousands-of-years-ago, multi-translated bullshit!"

"Diesel! Take that back."

"Darthius can suck my fat one!"

She gestured the sign of horns across her chest and mumbled for his forgiveness. "Before humans walked this planet, Darthius created the supernatural, and evil reigned over the planet until man's rise."

He wasn't into debating her.

"That is why," she said, "we must infiltrate the minds of humans and turn them to the dark side."

"There's also a faction of Supernatural, Monitors for instance, who believe humans are the Resurrection. Why do you think we won against evil in World War II? Dr. Dolessenbee's army saved them. Humans were leaning toward Lord Darthius's side and we—"

"And we lost that battle!" said a voice from behind him. "Unfortunately."

Diesel spun.

Jezebel stood wearing a full-length, black gown with a high, scalloped collar. Her hair was poised eloquently in a bun on the top of her head, and in her manicured hand, she held the Baphomet statue. "While Dolessenbee's army may have been behind the taking down of Hitler by aiding and abetting silly humans, we haven't given up. Nor did we give up during the human's so-called American Civil War. Unfortunately, slavery was abolished. A beautiful thing that was." She stepped forward. "We were this close." She pinched her forefinger and thumb together.

"Jezebel," Mitsy said. "Thankfully you've come around."

"I see Witch Lena taught you my spell."

"What!" Diesel said.

"I taught Witch Lena the Soul Death spell." She kissed the figurine's head. "I'm so pleased she left behind this damnation." She raised it skyward. "With Darthius's return, witches can reign at full strength once again."

Upon seeing Diesel at the bottom of the embankment, Bingham traipsed his way toward him. "Dee!" the boy shouted. To his right, Trinity's blue Beetle was parked at the edge of the pond, and she sat cross-legged by the water's edge.

"What's going on?" Diesel asked when he approached. "She was supposed to head off to Elk."

"I know," Bingham said. "Dr. D-D-Dolessenbee's pissed."

At that point, Diesel caught sight of the doctor, arms extended, arguing with the crouched redhead.

"Why is she still here?"

"She talk to my dragonfly," Bingham said exuberantly.

"Huh?"

"The blue dragonfly. Fragrance. It's her sister. She can speak to it, like me."

"Is she crazy?"

"No. Wait. You think I'm c-c-crazy for t-t-talk to bugs?" Bingham said.

Diesel ruffled his surrogate brother's hair and progressed toward the pond. "It's just that not many humans talk to insects."

"Fragrance is s-s-special," Bingham said.

"She is." Diesel recalled how the Odonata had led him to the cave to find Trinity, Jezebel, and Bingham earlier.

"Heel is back!" Bingham said as if having forgotten to tell him.

Elio's partner of 200 years—also an Emphilothepy—had been away in England for some time. "When did he arrive?"

Bingham limped along. "C-c-couple hours ago. He says the How-How-Howling Mo-Mo-on is to be fierce."

"So I hear." When Diesel reached the pond, the blue dragonfly hovered beside Trinity, and Dol pleaded with her to leave.

On the hill, Elio and Heel emerged from the cave. Heel clicked and clacked in recognition of Diesel who acknowledged him with an enthusiastic wave.

"I told you to drive the totem to Elk," Dol said. "It's best that it's out of the protective area tonight. Trevor will watch over—"

"And, as I mentioned several times," Trinity said with a hint of irritation in her voice, "Fragrance tells me otherwise. I'm a woman who follows her instincts, Dr. Dolessenbee. Maybe you should too."

"A dragonfly is not your instinct."

"This dragonfly is my sister. It's her spirit speaking to me from . . . from where or how I do not know, but I have a profound sense of clarity that it *is* her. She wants me to stay. To keep the totem here."

Dr. Dolessenbee walked away shaking his head. "I swear, I'll never fully understand humans," he said to Diesel.

"What's going on?" Diesel sat beside Trinity at the edge of the pond. The dragonfly landed on the brim of his ball cap.

"She likes you," Trinity said. "I know everyone thinks I'm crazy, but this is Ginny, my kid sister who was killed alongside my parents. They had nicknamed her Fragrance when she was a baby because she smelled so cute."

Trinity paused. Tears welled in the corners of her eyes. "Even Bingham called her that. So, I'm not entirely nutzo. She spoke to him too."

Diesel looked back at the dragon couple and Dol. There was a strange comfort among the three, as if they had known each other for eons.

"She likes to hang out by the water. The bats in the cave are pretty scary for her."

"Makes sense."

"She's telling me there's a storm coming."

Diesel closed his eyes. His core buzzed with something that he could only recognize as *purpose*.

"I remember that she always liked dragonflies," Trinity said. "She must have been able to put her spirit into one." Trinity shook her head and picked at a blade of grass. "So weird. I can't even believe I'm talking like this. After I dropped you off, I followed her here."

"Children are better at remembering their true selves, more so than grown-ups," Diesel said. "We adults tend to get too hung up in the reality of time and space and forget about the mystical realm. We get disconnected from our source energy, whereas children haven't spent enough time living reality to veer away."

Trinity nodded slowly and played with another piece of grass.

Mat wandered down the embankment carrying something in his hand.

"What's Mat think of all this?" Diesel asked.

"He knows that when I get something in my brain, I'm like a dog on a bone and won't let it go."

They played with Fragrance for a bit. Bingham showed them how she was able to do tricks, leaping from one hand to another without the use of her wings. They laughed.

Mat approached. "Got it." He held up a photo of Bence.

"You took that from my room?" Diesel stood.

"Sorry," Mat said, not taking his eyes off the photo. "Bingham told me it was in there."

Diesel looked at the others, who now all stood staring down at it. "What . . . what am I missing? Why are we staring at a picture of Bence and me?"

"Fragrance spoke to him," Trinity said.

"What!" Diesel said.

"He's not quite entirely dead," she added. "Yet."

Diesel took off his hat and ran his hands through his hair. "Mitsy. She . . . she told me she fed him a soul spell. The Soul Death spell . . . or something like that. I never heard of it, but Jezebel had."

"What's Jezebel got to do with this?" Trinity asked.

"Her transformation into Goody Two-Shoes didn't last long. I'm not surprised." Diesel set his baseball cap on backward. "She's back to her old tricks again. Apparently, she taught Witch Lena the spell. Something about Baphomet."

Trinity and Mat exchanged a look of confusion, then shrugged it off when Dol approached.

"Did I hear something about Baphomet?" the doctor asked.

Diesel explained to the group what Jezebel had told him about the seventh moon, Mitsy sacrificing Bence, and Lord Darthius's return.

"Criminy!" Dol shouted. "We need a witch."

"I don't think Jezebel's gonna give us a hand here," Diesel said.

"No." Dol scratched his chin. "But in that old witch hut, where I had jailed you two, there were several dark magic books in there."

"That's Witch Bazomella's old place," Diesel said. "It's been abandoned for years, ever since King Winston ridded the forest of witches."

"I recall seeing a *Book of Shadows* there," Dol said. "Runes down the spine."

"I do too," Mat said.

"Heel!" Dol shouted.

Elio's husband lumbered down the embankment. Elio with a bandaged wing followed behind.

"Heel, can you take me to Witch Bazomella's?" Dol asked.

Mat stared at Bence's picture. It had been snapped using a Polaroid camera discovered at the Trash Heap. In the photograph, Bence rode on Diesel's back—both shirtless, about to dive into the water.

"Mat?" Trinity elbowed him. "Mat."

"Huh? Oh, sorry." Mat lowered the picture. "What are we doing?"

"Yes, what *are* we doing?" Diesel asked. "Can someone fill me in? I feel like I missed a couple of chapters in a good suspense novel."

"Mitsy murdered Bence with the Soul Death spell," Dol said. "Well, sort of murdered."

"Sort of?"

"Yes, the spell is very strong and, because of that, it takes several days to maturate. If I recall correctly, seven days."

Diesel counted on his fingers. "That would be tonight."

"So I feared. Perfectly executed for the Howling Moon," Dol said. "And if what you're saying about Lord Darthius's return—"

"Wait," Diesel interrupted, "you knew Bence was killed? Did you have anything to do with it?"

"I did not kill your friend," Dol said. "I knew Mitsy needed to summon the Dark Lord's arrival with a sacrificial offering. He likes to test a creature's allegiance to him."

Diesel sighed. "Lord Darthius. I thought he was just a myth. Please tell me this is all concoction."

Dol swallowed. "Not a myth entirely. All myths start with an element of truth. All concoctions start with an idea, and the Dark Lord is the master of spinning folklore into reality."

"So, he's . . . he's resurrecting . . . tonight?"

"He's here to take over. I killed him centuries ago."

"You . . . you killed him?"

"At least I thought I had. The reason I came back here . . . to Hubbard Forest . . . is I heard about his supposed return. Apparently, your sister—"

"She's not my sister."

"Apparently, Mitsy," Dol corrected himself, "summoned him with deep dark magic, the likes of which I didn't know even existed. And all this time I thought it was Jezebel."

"Why do we need the *Book of Shadows*?" Mat said.

"The book at Witch Bazomella's. It struck me as dark magic. I haven't seen a book like that since . . . well, since Lord Darthius roamed the planet. We must retrieve it. In it, there may be an antidote for Bence and to stop the Dark Lord."

Diesel's core buzzed, like it had when he sensed Jezebel's truth earlier. "Jezebel didn't know about this . . . not at first. Witch Lena taught the spell to Mitsy, promising her a healthy baby in exchange for the sacrifice. Lena must've wanted the witch powers that King Winston had thwarted to be returned. Now, Jezebel's all over it. She's up to no good."

Dol nodded as if it were all finally coming together for him. "When Mat killed Witch Lena, Jezebel assumed her powers."

"You killed a witch?" Trinity asked her friend.

"I didn't mean to."

"Lord Darthius will favor Jezebel," Dol continued. "He'll sense Lena's essence, her powerful magic, in Jezebel."

"Is that why my mom's totem didn't work?" Bingham asked. "When she tried to fix me, it didn't work."

"Precisely," Dol said. "But now that she's aware of what's going on, she's more powerful and if we don't interrupt Darthius arrival, the two of them will wreak havoc." He boarded the dragon. "Mat, you and Trinity need to retrieve Bence's body."

"R . . . retrieve?" Mat muttered.

"A Metanormal's protection may stop Darthius."

Trinity opened her car door. "Come on."

"*May* stop?" Diesel said. "Wait, I'm going too. It's too dangerous."

"No," Dol said. "I need you with me. Hop on."

Elio clicked. He and Heel rubbed noses, then conversed.

"Elio is going to follow you," Diesel said interpreting for Trinity who had already started the VW, while Mat hesitated.

Bingham opened the passenger door. "I'll show them where the Trash Heap is." He got in the back.

"Doctor D., are you saying there's hope for Bence?" Diesel asked. "That he may be resurrected?"

"Hoping, yes," Dol tugged the reins, "but not with certainty."

Diesel boarded Heel.

Dol turned to Mat. "We'll meet you at the burial ground. Use that photo." He pointed at the picture that Mat still clutched. "Bence's soul will need guidance, a remembrance of its form from this reality in order to reenter it."

Chapter Twenty-Four

Baphomet

I N A SPOT ATOP an overturned, halved pine log—where a placard typically sat for Honoree III during board meetings—a small, raised altar, decorated with runes, was assembled. In its center, a warped, tin dish containing sprigs of hemlock smoldered. Three red jasper stones, one for each millennium past since Darthius's prior resurgence, dotted the tray. At the altar's base, two black candles and one red votive flickered in the breeze. And in the middle, beside the burning hemlock, rested the Baphomet statue.

As the sun set, Jezebel and Mitsy occupied the front pew and chanted from the *Book of Shadows* taken from Witch Bazomella's.

The urine-like scent of the burning poison made them cough, but they kept—as best as possible—from allowing it to impede their mantra.

The dusk air grew cold.

"Sou Lalin kriyan sa a, se pou li leve. Se pou li ante Latè ankò. Se pou lonbraj Seyè nwa a egzamine prezans nou yon lòt fwa ankò. Seyè Darthius se sovè nou an. Li se ewo nou an. Kite l leve!"

The moon hinted at a massive presence along the horizon, and a wind began to whip.

"Let the Dark Lord's shadow hex our presence once more. Lord Darthius is our savior. He is the Antichrist. Let Him rise!"

Mitsy coughed. "The hemlock." She spat. "It's too much."

"Shush! Just chant."

Mitsy grunted and clutched her belly.

"Upon this Howling Moon . . ." Jezebel went on with the chant. "Let the Dark Lord rise. Sou Lalin kriyan sa a, se pou li leve. Se pou li ante Latè ankò. Let Him rise. Let Him haunt the Earth again. Let him torture."

"Upon . . . this . . . Howling Moon," Mitsy muttered, suppressing a cough. "Let. Him. Rise" She cleared her throat and wheezed.

Jezebel flipped the page back to the Haitian text. "Sou Lalin kriyan sa a, se pou li leve. Se pou li ante Latè ankò. Se pou lonbraj Seyè nwa a egzamine prezans nou yon lòt fwa ankò. Seyè Darthius se sovè nou an. Li se ewo nou an. Kite l leve!"

A breeze flipped the book's pages.

They chanted and chanted until the sunset dipped below the tree line. The wind intensified, and Jezebel held the pages down to continue to read and not miss a word. Her hair whipped around her head.

A dust devil emerged from the forest.

Mitsy cramped again, gripping her stomach. "Oh, it hurts."

The mini cyclone slowed.

"For Satan's sake, Mitsy! Toughen up! We must chant through to the moon's rising."

"Sou Lalin kriyan sa a, se pou li leve," Jezebel said, and the pregnant she-wolf joined in partway. "Se pou li ante Latè ankò."

The wind increased.

"Let the Dark Lord's shadow hex our presence once more," they said. "Lord Darthius is our savior. He is the Antichrist. Let Him rise!"

"Ah!" Mitsy clenched her jaw.

The Baphomet figurine toppled in the tray.

"Satan," Jezebel cussed and elbowed Mitsy.

The dust devil neared.

Jezebel smiled. "Come on, Darthius. Come on. Momma isn't going to hurt you."

The Baphomet statue vibrated.

"It's working. It's working!" Jezebel said.

The figurine levitated a few inches from the altar. The whirling windstorm approached, and the statue spun in harmony.

"Let the Dark Lord's shadow hex our presence once more." Jezebel nudged Mitsy to continue, and the girl did. "Lord Darthius is our savior. He is the Antichrist. Let Him rise!"

The cyclone consumed the Baphomet, and the candles blew out.

"Let the Dark Lord's shadow hex our presence once more," they shouted over the shrieking wind. "Lord Darthius is our savior! He is the Antichrist! Let Him rise!"

The cyclone grew larger.

A few curious stragglers graced the edges of the assembly.

The twister whipped the components of their altar to the side, and the cyclone swelled even more. Its sound, like a locomotive, intensified.

Mitsy grimaced, gripped her belly, and gritted her teeth.

The cyclone stopped—and the ear-shattering sound with it.

More of the ward's residents approached the outer edges of the area.

The whirlwind, which had suspended in a photographic-like still of itself, hissed. From its edges, thousands of forked tongues slithered out, as if tasting the air.

The residents dispersed.

"He's . . . he's looking for Bence's body," Jezebel said. "To reanimate it."

"Darthius." Jezebel cleared her throat. "We had a bit of an . . . incident. The body has been buried at the Trash Heap. We can take you—"

Then, in a hair-blowing-back explosion Jezebel and Mitsy were flung backward and landed a few rows behind the pew and into the benches reserved for females.

The dust devil regained motion and sped off into the forest, snapping and toppling trees in its wake.

Mitsy vomited.

CHAPTER TWENTY-FIVE

Retrieval

DIESEL CLIMBED ABOARD HEEL, who waited patiently outside Witch Bazomella's hut. "Now what?" He put a hand out to Dol to help the rotund wizard up.

"I know I saw the *Book of Shadows* there earlier," Dol said, after he settled in. "It was on the third shelf, right beside the crystal that . . . Jezebel!" he said, realizing the culprit who took it. "She's up to no good."

"I don't think good and Jezebel have ever mixed well in a sentence." Diesel chuckled.

"We need to stop Darthius from possessing the vessel," the wizard said, ignoring Diesel's pun about the witch.

"The vessel?"

"Your friend. Bence. He's the vehicle, if you would, that your sis . . . that Mitsy chose to be the Dark Lord's medium."

Diesel grabbed the reins. "Mitsy said he spoke to her. The Dark Lord that is. He really wanted me, and she, in her deluded mind, spared me and chose Bence."

"Lord Darthius was after you?" The concern in Dol's voice was profound.

"Yes, and why is that such a surprise? According to Mitsy, he just needed a healthy body. I do say I'm rather fit. Though Bence is too, so—"

"The level of fitness is only one aspect. There are other properties the Dark Lord seeks."

"Like what?"

"Later. We must find Bence before the Dark Lord's return."

Diesel jerked the lead. "Let's go, Heel. To the Trash Heap."

When they gained altitude, the moon's glow revealed a path of downed trees. "What the hell happened? It looks like a tornado swept through," Diesel said.

"Shit."

"You cuss?"

Dol ignored him. "Darthius is here."

"In the form of a twister? What is this? *The Wizard of Oz*?"

"Now's not the time for jokes, Diesel. He's on the hunt for the body."

"Bence?"

"Yes. Bence," Dol said with a hint of irritation. "Let's get to the burial ground before he does."

Through the web-like barrier, near the spot where Bence had been hung, a cluster of trees shimmied.

"He's over there." Dol pointed to the area.

"That's where Bence hung."

A deafening roar echoed throughout the land.

"Uh oh," Dol said.

"'Uh oh' isn't a very comforting statement coming from a powerful wizard."

"We must get to the burial spot before he sniffs him down."

Heel picked up speed for the Trash Heap.

"Apparently the barrier is impervious to the Dark Lord," Diesel said.

"There's not much that stops Darthius. Mitsy was smart in hexing him out there, so the paranormals wouldn't pull his spirit out first. Darthius needs a freshly discarded body."

The roar intensified. The cyclone crashed through the barrier, and it splintered.

"Uh oh." Dol's head arched back as the crack raced upward.

ELIO DUG AT THE edges of Bence's grave, careful not to hurt the body. His broken right wing rested in a sling-like contraption the size of Mat's California king-sized sheets he and Maxine used to sleep in.

Trinity discovered Bence's hand, and she and Mat unearthed the rest of the body.

Except for the dirt that covered Bence's face, the body looked rather intact. "He hasn't decomposed."

Elio clacked, but Mat couldn't understand him.

Bingham, who had tried to help as much as possible, knelt atop the hole. "Elio say . . . sp-sp-spell . . . it not fu-fu-fully taken over."

"Let's get him out," Trinity said. They used the yellow rope that was attached to the Volkswagen's bumper to hoist him out. Trinity climbed up beside Bingham, while Mat stayed in the hole.

The body wasn't as cold as he had expected. He hugged the man around the waist and set the rope under his arms, as Trinity instructed.

"Careful," she said. "Not too tight."

"Got it."

Trinity, Bingham, and Elio pulled while Mat pushed. When they successfully got him out, Heel approached.

"Dad!" Bingham shouted, excited to see his other surrogate father.

Trinity helped Mat out just as Heel landed.

"You got him!" Diesel slid off the dragon.

"Good job." Dol chose any easier path to disembark, using the dragon's neck and lowered head.

The ground rumbled.

"The hell is that?" Mat asked.

Trinity froze.

"Lord Darthius," Diesel said.

"Shit," Mat said.

Trinity packed up her gear in the Volkswagen's front hatch. "Dol, are we resistant to the Dark Lord?"

"We?" Mat added.

She shut the hood. "We are Metanormals after all."

"But . . . but he's the Dark Lord," Mat said.

Trinity walked over to the Beetle's passenger side, opened the door, and closed the glovebox.

"Wait." Dol opened the door wider. "The glovebox. How did you—?"

"That's where the lever is to open the trunk. How else was I supposed to get my repelling gear?"

"I had sealed it."

Trinity, annoyed, held up a key with the VW logo on it. "And I have this."

"Shit."

"You're cussing again," Diesel said. "Wait." He moved beside Dol and peered inside the car. "Can you open that again?"

Trinity inserted the key, turned it, and it popped open.

Dol made a stink, but Diesel ignored him. "My totem." He reached in and took out the prescription bottle but struggled to open it.

"Allow me." Trinity put out a hand, and he gave it to her. She unscrewed the cap, pulled out the large tooth by its strap, and offered it to Diesel. "Something told me this would come in handier here than in Elk." She eyed Dol impishly.

"Hold up." The wizard placed a hand on Diesel's forearm. "Maybe you shouldn't—"

Diesel nudged him away and walked toward Bence with the amulet. "I trust her. She's right. It is better here." He turned to Dol. "I can feel it in my bones."

Diesel took the tooth in his fist, placed it over his heart, and beams of golden light radiated from between his fingers.

"Uh oh," Dol said.

Diesel turned to Mat. "It's you."

A chill ran down Mat's spine. "What . . . what do you mean?"

Diesel loosened his grip on the tooth and lifted the totem to the moon—the base of which was now visible above the tree line. The totem glowed and pulsated. Diesel stood for a time in silence, eyes closed.

Dol lowered his shaking head.

Diesel opened his eyes and looked over at Mat, who now stood beside Trinity. "You're here for him," the wolf-shifter said. "You're his . . ." He put the totem's strap around his neck and crouched beside Bence's prostrate body. Diesel closed his eyes again, inhaled, and touched the totem to his heart. When he opened his eyes, he faced Mat. "You're here for Bence."

"Wh . . . what?" Mat asked, but he knew. His core vibrated. The hair on the back of his neck stood. Gooseflesh covered his arms. He practically felt the heat of the Polaroid in his front pocket.

"You're his soulmate," Diesel said. "You're that ol' dirty dog's soulmate." A satisfactory smile lit up his face.

"I . . . I am." Mat looked to Trinity as if apologizing, but the grin filling her face told him it was unnecessary. He smiled back. *Save the dog*, Ty's voice spoke to him, and it all came together. The reason he came into Diesel's life these past few days was to lead him to Bence—the other dog. *Save the dog*, Ty said again. Mat had never felt anything so right in his life. "But he's dead."

Diesel touched his shoulder. "Not if we can help it."

Then, Darthius's cyclone burst out from the forest with a reverberating pulse that rippled the ground.

Dol lost his balance and fell against the side of the Volkswagen. "Quick. He's here for Bence."

"Wake him!" Diesel shouted at Mat.

"Me?" Mat asked. "How?"

"Kiss him," Diesel said, as if the answer suddenly came to him. "That's what the *Book of Shadows* would have told us. The antidote is a soulmate's kiss."

"You're . . . you're right!" Dol shouted over the roar of Darthius's approach. "A true mate's kiss will return the soul from the dead!"

Trinity tugged Mat's arm. "Kiss him, Mat."

Mat fell to his knees beside the dirt-covered body.

The vortex of Lord Darthius's cyclone spun only a few yards away.

Mat kissed Bence on the lips.

Darthius's cloud stilled. Forked tongues—thousands of them—slithered out from its gray edges. "I have come," it hissed in a long, drawn-out whisper.

Bence's eyes flickered. His mouth twitched.

Mat peppered the man's lips, face, and forehead with more kisses.

"I shall rise," Darthius murmured, long and slow. The black tongues peppered the cloud, and plumes of green mist emerged from their numerous mouths.

Mat gagged from the sulfuric stench.

"You shall not rise!" Dol shouted, then to Diesel said, "Show him the totem."

"Huh?" Diesel said.

"The totem. Show it to Darthius."

"Wh . . . why?"

"Just do it! If he realizes who you are, he'll stop."

"What do you mean, 'who I am'? Who am I?"

"Just do it!" Dol yelled.

Diesel shoved the large, wolf tooth up to the hissing, stinky cloud, and it jumped back.

Bence opened his eyes. "You," he said to Mat.

The cyclone roared. The tongues retreated into their mouths, and the smell of rotten eggs dissipated as the twister slinked back.

"Diesel." Bence sat up.

"Bence!" Diesel rushed to his side, helped him up, and hugged him so hard he lifted the man off his feet. "I love you, you ol' dirty dawg. I love you! And missed you! I'm so sorry. I should have gone with you."

"Dee, your sister," Bence said, as if not knowing how to break it to him about her.

"I know." Diesel continued to hug him. "There's a lot to tell you about." He lowered him.

Bence turned to Mat, smiled, and put a hand on him.

Darthius's cyclone busted down trees as it left.

"That's hardly the last of him," Dol said. "Now that he knows, he won't stop till he finds what he wants."

"Knows?" Diesel asked. "Knows what?"

"Of your existence. He wants you," Dol said.

"Why?"

"Later," the wizard replied, "let's get your friend safe."

The group hovered around Bence, who now held both hands on Mat's shoulders.

"I saw Maxine and Ty," Bence said.

Mat blinked.

Bence faced Trinity. "And you . . . your parents and Ginny. They were there too."

Trinity's mouth fell open, but she said nothing.

"They're fine," Bence added. "They wanted me to let you know they love you."

Trinity burst out crying.

"The dragonfly. It's Ginny, or Fragrance as you call her. It's her way of letting you know they're good." Bence faced Mat. "And Maxine forgives you. It wasn't your fault; she wanted me to tell you that." He wet his lips. "She and Ty want you to live your life . . . to live happily ever after."

Mat felt as if he would pass out. His knees weakened. Trinity and Diesel set him down, and he wept.

"We must go," Dol said. "Darthius isn't going to let up."

Elio placed Bingham on his back and chirped something to Bence who apparently understood dragon. He agreed he needed cleaning up, jumped atop Elio, and tousled Bingham's hair in a welcoming gesture as he sat beside him.

Trinity made a fuss about leaving her car behind, but when Diesel told her no one in the forest cared about vehicles except for him, she boarded Heel and joined the others.

Chapter Twenty-Six

Darthius

Darthius's cyclone crisscrossed the forest while Heel and company followed it. The source of werewolves baying at the moon appeared to interest the Dark Lord, and he pivoted toward their direction.

The werewolves stopped when the cloud burst forth onto the assembly. The gathering crowd dispersed.

Heel landed quietly on the outskirts of the assembly area, just as Darthius terrorized the ward—kicking up trees and benches and throwing aside creatures in his path.

Panic stricken, Honoree and Buck—in full regalia of headdress and wolfskin—emerged, side by side from the wolf dens' coppice. They stopped, in horror, at the cyclone whirling about, casting debris in its wake.

Unfazed by the hubbub, Mitsy stared at the crumbled altar upon the log table and mouthed words undetectable over the vortex.

Darthius's snake-riddled cloud swirled in her direction.

"No!" Buck dashed her way. The regalia crowning his head fell off. The costume of a dead animal hunted for meat was meant to symbolize the control a shapeshifter held over their transformation, as opposed to a werewolf's dependence on the moon and blood thirst. The slight superiority was the only comeuppance the dwindling species possessed. "Mitsy! Run!" he shouted.

"Lord Darthius, save my baby. The Dark Lord is my savior." Diesel could hear her words now that he approached.

"Mitsy!" Diesel shouted before Buck reached her.

She turned to him but said nothing. A grim demeanor spoke volumes of her deep sorrow.

"Darthius!" Dol shouted at the twister, and it stopped swirling.

One of the cloud's many snakes lunged out and aimed, fangs bared, for the doctor, but, before it could bite Dol, Diesel ripped the snake out from the cloud by its neck. It was long—three or four feet at least—and with a quick shift to his wolf snout, Diesel bit the snake's head off. The tail slapped and rattled against his leg. By the time he spit out the head, his face had transformed back. "Bastard," he spat again.

"Darthius, my enemy," Dol addressed the cloud with a pull to his overcoat, "how funny to see you here. I see you're a bit under the weather."

Darthius—or his multiple snakes—hissed, then a voice swung through the air as if from a distance. "So many millennia. So many, Dolessenbee." His words were slow, almost painful. "And I bet you thought you were done with me. You are, after all, a betting man, remember?"

"I remember. I remember you all so well. But I've come a long way since our last encounter millennia ago. You are not welcomed here."

"No?" The snakes shot out from the hovering storm cloud and clutched Mitsy.

"Lord Darthius!" she shouted. "I did as you asked."

"Where's the body?" he hissed.

The vapors, in fluorescent-green clouds, plumed out from thousands of little reeking mouths, and Diesel gagged trying to protect her.

Mitsy cried, kicked, and pleaded. She explained how she and Witch Lena conspired for the health of her baby. "Please save my unborn child. You can take me, but please save my baby. You promised."

"Promises. Promises," Darthius hissed. "I don't want you. I need a man's form." He paused. "Your baby may do just right."

The snakes lifted Mitsy, slinked their way up her face, and wrapped their bodies around her head. She convulsed and recited words in Haitian, when they crept through her ears.

Diesel moved near her but stopped when Dol held up a hand. "Is he possessing her?" Diesel asked. Despite her treason and lack of kindred, he still thought of her as his big sister.

"He doesn't want her. He's speaking to her."

Her lips cracked. Her thin, greasy hair clung to her brow. The largest of the snakes slithered up her nightgown.

"No! Please! Please don't take my baby." She kicked.

"Then kill him!" Darthius's voice grew closer, as if vibrating from the thick black snake. The reptiles evaporated, and she plummeted to the ground, landing on her back.

"Who . . . who do you want?" Mitsy crawled on all fours toward a splintered bench.

"The one I always wanted." The black snakes hissed, and the cloud revolved.

"No," Dol said.

The snakes retreated into the depths of the cyclone, now a black-and-green mist of stink. Mitsy lifted herself up with the aid of the broken pew.

"You know what to do." Darthius's voice echoed but with a hollow, distant pitch. The cyclone rotated slowly. "For the betterment of your species . . . For the benefit of the Supernatural . . ."

With a force and speed like the cyclone's, Mitsy seized a large, dagger-like wooden splint dangling off the bench with such force that Diesel was amazed at her strength. She spun around and shoved the spear into his side.

"You shall not!" Dol rushed toward Diesel, but he collapsed.

Mat caught him.

Buck rushed to Mitsy's side. "Is the baby okay? You did what you had to."

"You. You son of a bitch!" Mitsy said. Fur sped down her limbs and her wolf transformation initiated. "You . . . you Satan freakin' bastard! You only care about a child. Not me!" Her metamorphosis concluded, and she attacked her husband, tearing his gut and clawing out his innards. Lastly, she ripped his totem from his neck.

"Mitsy!" Honoree rushed and flung her off his friend.

She skidded across the dirt path and landed at the foot of the cyclone. Buck's totem dangled in her muzzle, and when she altered back, the totem fell to the ground. Blood trickled down her legs.

Diesel sat up against the dais and held his bleeding wound.

"I . . . I—" Buck muttered. His face grayed and paled. His hair fell out and his skin withered and wrinkled. He transformed into someone much, much older. "I . . . need . . . my . . . totem."

Honoree, who was hovering over his friend, slinked back with his mouth agape, apparently astonished by the transformation occurring before him. "B . . . B . . . Buck?"

Buck continued to age.

Elder Bainbridge with his cane doddered over. "Honoree."

Buck and Honoree looked up at the elder.

"A spitting image of the portrait over the mantle," Diesel said, dumbfounded. The decaying shifter now resembled the Great Honoree I, his great-great grandfather, hanging over the mantle in Mitsy's house—the one cracked in the fight over the laptop.

A voice from behind recited something in Haitian.

Diesel turned to see Jezebel holding open the *Book of Shadows* from Witch Bazomella's. "Sou Lalin kriyan sa a, se pou li leve. Se pou li ante Latè ankò. Se pou lonbraj Seyè nwa a egzamine prezans nou yon lòt fwa ankò. Seyè Darthius se sovè nou an. Li se ewo nou an. Kite l leve!"

The cloud withered to merely a shadow of its former self. Then, with a snap of thunder, it evaporated entirely, and the Baphomet statue dropped out from the air. The figurine spun on the ground from the force of the vortex that had held it, and it came to rest beside Buck's discarded totem.

JEZEBEL TWIRLED BUCK'S TOTEM with an extended forefinger and walked over to his decaying body. "Well, well, well. You are certainly not the stag everyone thought you were."

Mitsy, who had managed to crawl closer to her dying husband, said matter-of-factly, "You're . . . you're . . . Honoree the First."

Jezebel examined the totem. "What magic bound you? Hm." She sniffed the amulet. "A witch's aging spell. All this time you werent' the lech named Buck. You . . . you were the Great Honoree the First." She sniffed again. "Ah. But you're not a witch. You're definitely a wolf-shifter. Someone added a hint of magic. A spell to prevent you from aging, like that of a witch. Powerful. Interesting."

The dying wolf-shifter coughed and gasped for breath.

"You're . . . you're my great-great grandfather?" Mitsy clutched her belly. "I've been impregnated by my great-great grandfather?"

The dying man said nothing.

His grandson, Mitsy's father, Honoree III approached. "Buck? You're not Buck? You're . . . you're my great-grandfather? All this time I thought you were my . . . my friend."

A tear stained the dying man's wrinkled cheek. His teeth fell out, as a purple mist of magic evaporated from him, and the aging process continued. He gummed an unintelligible reply.

"We were charmed, back in the day," Elder Bainbridge explained. "The White Queen and Witch Lena reversed our age."

"Oh, age reversal. Hm," Jezebel said. "Then how old are you really, Bainbridge?" she asked, but he didn't reply.

Dr. Dolessenbee gazed down at Honoree I. "The White Queen charmed him, returned him to his youth, to perpetuate the species," he said, as if figuring it out rather than having known.

"We're all inbreds," Honoree III stated. "No wonder we're dying off."

"That's why they wanted me to bear children so bad," Diesel said. "I'm the last . . . well, they thought I was the last of the line."

Crouched beside his traitorous friend, Honoree III looked up at the man he believed to be his son. "What are you saying?"

"I am not your child," Diesel said with palpable relief. "I have no genetic connection to you."

Honoree III inhaled slowly and looked over at Jezebel.

"Oops." Jezebel walked away, still whirling Honoree I's totem. "At this point, you might as well know the truth. Diesel, or, rather, Daniel Cade, was an orphan I found in the cave. Some she-wolf must've got knocked up and left him there for the gay Emphilothepy couple to raise. It's not uncommon."

"He is not my flesh and blood?" Honoree III rose.

"I only partially lied." Jezebel giggled. "Linda did die in childbirth, but so did her baby. Your baby. I'm sorry," she said, more for her dead friend, and cleared her throat. "I have no idea who this pain-in-the-ass belongs to." She gestured to Diesel, but he was in too much pain to acknowledge her.

Stunned, Honoree III shook his head, stood, and ran off, embarrassed.

Moonlight lit a circle of werewolves in the center of the assembly, and they howled at the sky.

Buck/Honoree I gasped a final breath, and Elder Bainbridge, who knelt by his side, cried. "Farewell my friend." He lowered his head.

Paranormals amassed.

D ARTHIUS'S CYCLONE HAD RUINED most of the assembly's gaze-bo, which had been decorated for the Howling Moon's festivities. Ripped banners flapped in the breeze and clung to busted railings. Petals of ivy and lily—meant to cover the she-wolves in matrimony—were strewn about.

Diesel tore one of the wards' Howling Moon celebratory streamers to use as a corset. He then ripped the shard out from his gut. "Argh!" With blood spurting, he tied the strip around his waist, then fell back against the dais for fear of passing out.

"We have to bury Buck. We have to bury Honoree the First," Elder Bainbridge pleaded.

Dol lowered beside Diesel and tied his totem along his nape. "Son, wear this proudly. It will restore you. It's almost midnight."

"Huh?" Diesel touched the wolf tooth, and in a wince of pain clutched it so tight it pierced his palm.

From the edges of the forest and out from the sides of the garrison—used to store community items, like those for the evening's spoiled celebrations—crept paranormals, hungry for Honoree I's soul.

The little girl, who had earlier jumped on the hood of Mat's SUV, now crept, spider-like, with extra limbs Diesel hadn't previously seen. Diesel recognized the slash to her neck and wobbling head.

Bainbridge covered Honoree I's lifeless body with a Howling Moon banner, as if to prevent the paranormals from seeing his friend. "The empties! They can't take his soul. We've come too far, too long for this."

The ghost of a man shuffled beside Wobble Head. His feet never touched the ground, and he carried an ax. Diesel imagined him being the perpetrator to Wobble Head's injury. The left side of his face was blown out, as if from a gunshot wound.

Diesel was startled when a horde of other ghastly creatures—a tall, woman with a tree limb jutting out from her midsection; a young boy with a bayonet protruding from his eye socket in Civil War regalia; and others—came out from behind him.

Honoree I's spirit lifted from the body. Horror wrought his face—surprisingly young again, like the Buck everyone knew—as he witnessed the creatures approaching him.

Bainbridge clawed at Buck's ethereal mist, trying to protect him, but his hands only fanned the vapors.

Wobble Head descended upon the carcass, kicking Bainbridge to the side. She opened her jaws. Rows of black, pointed teeth extended out and devoured Buck's spirit. The stub of another limb, the tip of which bore Buck's expression in a silent scream, grew. Diesel then noted the faces of her victims upon each appendage.

The Baphomet statue vibrated. Each thud resonated through the earth, deep and strong.

"Uh oh." Dol got up and went to it.

The werewolves circled the dilapidated gazebo and howled.

The paranormals vanished.

Through a hole in the gazebo's still-standing roof, a beam of moonlight illuminated the remains of a pentagram painted on the center of the dais.

"It's midnight." Jezebel glanced at the statue, then at the dead body, and finally at Dol. "No!" She raced to the figurine, trying to beat Dol to it, but both were too late.

The Baphomet pounded against the ground. The tip of a snake's snout cracked the figurine like an eggshell, then an enormous black rattler jumped out like a gag gift.

The crowd screamed and dispersed. Even Diesel found the energy to claw his distance from the body the snake aimed for.

The rattler shot up into Honoree I with such a force that the corpse rocketed into the forest, then pivoted, lighting its way upward with a fiery glow where it cast a shadow across the moon.

Mitsy screamed.

Jezebel's hair blew back.

Darthius slammed back to the ground in the exact spot where Honoree I had lain. He looked nothing like Buck nor Honoree I. His body was naked and red. His nose was a mere slit and his forked, black tongue flicked out, like a snake's. Fur peppered his limbs, and a set of horns, similar to the Baphomet statue, curled upon the crown of his head.

The crowd—save Diesel, Dol, Mat, and Trinity—fell to their knees and bowed.

Jezebel ascended from her genuflect. "Your Majesty." She grinned. "Welcome to Hubbard Forest. I've been waiting for you for a long, long time."

Chapter Twenty-Seven

Gas Lamps

ANOTHER TREMOR SHOOK THE forest, and gold sparks shimmered down from the sky. When the embers hit the land, they sparkled until the ground, buildings, and surroundings absorbed them.

In fear, werewolves, mages, shifters, and ogres fled into the forest. Diesel, too pained to run, observed.

The assembly area's antiquated nineteenth-century trappings transformed. Broken streetlamps now hissed with gas. Bulbs flickered, then glowed steady. Cobblestone paths—which had been covered in decades of overgrown grass and grime—emerged, buffed and new. Even the center's gazebo creaked and straightened behind Diesel, and a missing post returned and supported his spine.

As if having used the earthquake-transformation as a distraction to dress, Darthius, while never having moved, now donned a black top hat, which fit perfectly between his horns.

The creatures, who had left, crept back in awe of their savior.

"What just happened?" Diesel asked, but no one said anything. The crowd stared at Darthius.

The Dark Lord's blood-red face and hands stuck out against his pitch-black suit. Its coat tails furled in the breeze, and he brushed a hand over the suit's velour-like trim, which swirled in fleur-de-lis patterns along lapels.

Jezebel was also redressed. She wore an all-black, full-length gown and bunched up the voluminous laced material to keep the hem from dragging on the ground. She took in its long sleeves, loose-fitting at the wrists, with admiration, then touched the string of pearls around her neck and the accompanying gems on her ears.

The storage facility now shone brightly with gas lamps. Lampposts lit its walkways, and flames flickered in their globes. The soft hiss of fuel sourcing them infiltrated the hush.

"Don't do this," Dol said to Darthius.

"I already have," he replied with a deep and raspy voice, as if his vocal cords had been unused for some time.

Jezebel placed a hand to his shoulders. "I have one request," she whispered. When he ignored her and approached Diesel, she frowned.

Dol stuck out his chest. "I said, 'Don't do this.'"

In an effortless flick of the wrist, Darthius flung the doctor with an invisible force into the brush.

"Daniel!" Dol shouted. "Run!"

By the time Diesel looked up, the daemon slammed into him, snapping his head back. The air escaped from him.

Seconds later? Maybe a few minutes? He found himself on his back with Darthius's face hovering over him. "I needed a body. Any body with a tinge of magic, and Honoree the First's body served that purpose." He inched closer. "Now, to get my real victim." The same sulfuric stench from the snake cloud wafted out from his rotten mouth.

"Dude, you . . ." Diesel struggled under his weight. "You . . . you need a Tic-Tac."

When Darthius cocked his head, Diesel kneed him in the groin.

The monster fell off him with a screech, but as Diesel shuffled to get away; claws dug into his calves and climbed their way up his back, piercing with each stab up his body. Warm blood drenched his clothes.

Darthius flipped him over and sat on him again. "You shall not get away from me this time."

"This time? I never forget a face, even as ugly as yours. I don't recall ever having seen—"

Darthius slapped him.

"Ouch." Diesel placed a palm to his stinging cheek.

Darthius giggled. Spittle tossed into the air and landed on Diesel's face.

Diesel pretended to try and knee him again, but when the monster moved to protect his groin, he poked him in the eye instead.

Diesel used the distraction to shimmy out from under Darthius, but the daemon grabbed him by the chain around his neck. The totem, which had somehow seared into his chest, pulled at his skin.

Darthius yanked him back. "Come to me, you bastard."

Diesel screamed. The pain from the wolf tooth tearing at his chest was too much. He touched the area as it ripped off. The chain and totem then caught around his neck.

Darthius lifted him off his feet.

Diesel choked and gasped. He tried to loosen the chain strangling his neck.

Dol grabbed at his kicking feet. "You can't have him! Let him go!"

"He's all yours. Besides, I would never break our little pact and take your only one." The daemon laughed hoarsely. "That would be cruel. Hm. Then again." Darthius's grip tightened as he laughed more. He shook the wolf-shifter with such force that Diesel felt his neck would snap.

"Let! Him! Go!" shouted a female voice.

Diesel faced the spokesperson. "Trinity!"

She stood, dwarfed by the daemon, with Mat by her side.

Darthius turned to her. His grip on Diesel loosened some, and Diesel welcomed the air.

"Ms. Hawkins," Dol pleaded, "please don't." A look of concern wrought his face.

"Trinity, no," Diesel said. "Get away—"

Darthius's grip tightened, and he lifted Diesel higher.

"I said!" Trinity shouted. "Let! Him! Go!"

"Don't piss her off," Mat added. "She's a force to be reck—"

"Do you know who I am?" Darthius interrupted. "I am the Dark Lord. You're an imp. And you, a human . . . a Black man for that—"

Trinity shoved Darthius in the waist.

Darthius hollered.

Diesel fell to the ground.

Trinity pummeled the Dark Lord in the face. With each touch of her skin to the daemon, he burned. His skin singed, and the air smelled of burning flesh.

He scuttled away.

She and Mat ran after him until he grabbed Jezebel, then they disappeared leaving only a cloud of vapors behind.

HEEL FLEW THEM TO Trinity's to get Diesel's help with supplies she had back there, but, when he deposited them out front, it became clear the property had changed.

Diesel limped with the support of Mat and Dol.

"The hell?" Mat said.

In the cabin's place, a large two-story white farmhouse spanned the area. Only the garage, with its ribboned driveway, and the well were recognizable from earlier.

"This can't be." Trinity rushed toward the house.

A wide porch spanned the width of the dwelling, and a red door welcomed them with two yellow lights burning small flames inside their globes.

"This is the old Beecher house." She went up the stairs gracing the entrance.

Mat stopped. "It's like the painting . . . the one you have over your fireplace back in Elk."

She turned to him. "The Beecher home. It burnt down in the 1800s." She went for the door. "My grandfather later rebuilt the cabin in its place."

They all moved inside where nineteenth-century trappings greeted them: a parlor with dark-green furniture to Diesel's right, thick, matching curtains draped the windows, shiny hardwood floors creaked under their weight, and elaborate furnishings stood upon expensive-looking oriental rugs.

Mat sat Diesel on the couch.

Trinity came out from a small room—presumably the bathroom—with bandages and medicine. "My mother talked about this house when I was a kid. The property is in the Beecher family, my mom's side." She pressed a hand to her temples. "Unless I'm having some weird déjà vu. It had been ravaged in a fire in 1800s and was later replaced with the much smaller cabin. The one we visited in the summer. The one I'm supposed to sell." She faced Dol. "This can't be."

"Are you saying we've traveled back in time?" Mat unfolded a wrap of gauze Trinity handed him.

Dol removed his jacket. "If I were to guess, I'd say it's around the mid-nineteenth century," he said, unfazed.

"What!" they shouted in unison. "That can't be," Mat added.

They spent little time discussing the historical trip and more to the importance of Diesel's wounds.

In a lyre-back chair Mat had set in the center of the parlor, Diesel touched his left oblique where Mitsy had stabbed him. "I guess the totem did do some good after all. The gash is gone."

"Your totem is very powerful," Dol said. "It has the power to heal, but only if you tap into it."

"I didn't think I tapped into anything," Diesel said.

"You have to believe it to see it."

Diesel shook his head. "I'm confused."

"I told you it would help you. You believed it, and it happened."

"Then, why can't I willy-nilly manifest a healed chest or get rid of Darthius with a blink of an eye."

"Doubt creeps in. All magical beings, and even Metanormals, create resistance to their power by overthinking and too much doing."

Trinity motioned to Mat to get more supplies from the bathroom and went back to mending Diesel's wounds.

"What did Darthius mean when he said that I was 'your only one'?" Diesel asked Dol.

Dol hemmed and hawed, saying little of anything intelligible.

Trinity placed a cold, wet cotton ball on Diesel's chest wound, and he flinched. "Son of a—!" Diesel stopped himself from cussing.

She dabbed the swab along the edges of the bloody gap in the center of Diesel's chest. "That's okay. It's not the first time I've been called a bitch."

"I didn't say . . ." Diesel winced as the medicine bit. "It just smarts a little."

"Don't act like a baby."

"A baby? Who are you calling a baby? I just fought the Dark Lord."

"And who kicked his ass?" She arched an eyebrow.

Light from the lantern set upon a marble-topped, walnut table danced in her ocean-blue eyes, and Diesel swooned. "You got me."

Mat came out from the bathroom with more medicine. "This is unbelievable. It's like we were transported back in time. The tank is high above the toilet," he gestured with his hand, "and it says Crapper on it! Does this time shift only in the forest? What about the outside world?"

"It can't escape the barrier system," Dol assured.

Diesel lifted an arm for Trinity to wrap him with the bandages. "So, Dr. D., tell us about this Darthius dude with the bad breath."

"He's the creator of all supernatural beings," Dol replied.

"That's not a myth?"

"No."

"Hm. So how do we send him back to hell."

"Well, it's not really like that. There is no hell, per se. No heaven either."

"Oh?" Trinity rose, satisfied with her nursing of Diesel's wounds, and removed to the couch. A green Victorian lounge, of sorts, with wood trim. She sat on its thinly cushioned edge.

Dol paced. "Look I'm not going to lecture you on the afterlife. We need to stop him."

"First, I want to know what he meant by me being your only one."

Dol took to one of the matching chairs across from the couch where Trinity sat. He chose the one without arms, and it creaked when he lowered. He turned to Trinity and Mat, who had joined her on the couch. "Would you excuse us for a mo—?"

"Whatever you have to say to me, they can hear." Diesel took to the chair beside Dol. He set his elbows on his thighs, clasped his hands, and leaned in toward Dol. "What gives?"

"You're my son," Dol said matter-of-factly.

Diesel baulked, then shook his head. "Come again?"

Mat leaned in. "He said you were—"

"You are my son," Dol repeated.

"That's what I thought you said." Diesel leaned back and crossed his legs. "You abandoned me and left me to be raised by two gay dragons? Not that they weren't great but . . ."

"It's not my proudest moment, but I did it for your own good."

Diesel waited. "I'm listening."

Dol sighed. "We really need to stop Darthius."

"We really need to hear why you abandoned your son." Trinity hitched an eyebrow.

Diesel smiled at her.

"That's why your kiss woke him," Mat said to Dol.

"What?" Diesel said. "What kiss?"

"True love's kiss. The love of a father and his son. It's true love," Mat explained. "Dol kissed you on the forehead when Jezebel and the White Queen put you in a sleeping curse." He gazed out the window. "True love . . . and mine woke Bence."

Trinity rubbed his knee.

Dol rose and paced again. "I am your father. Your mother was a witch. She died in childbirth."

"I'm a . . . I'm a . . . a witch?"

"And part wizard."

"I'm a . . . a wizard?"

"With the propensity to be very powerful." He looked down and tapped a toe against the frame to the adjacent dining room. "More so than me."

"You say that with a tinge of guilt," Trinity said.

Dol faced them. "Look, I left you because I was afraid of you. Plus," he combed a hand through his balding head, "I couldn't raise a child on my own. And . . . I needed my powers back."

"You were afraid of me? I'm just a wolf-shift— Wait, but, I *thought* I was a wolf-shifter." Diesel rubbed the base of his neck.

"Jezebel stole you, thinking you were an abandoned wolf-shifter because of the wolf-tooth totem I left you with. And, since you were raised by wolf-shifters, that's all you knew. That's what your magic was trained to. You learned to be the only thing you knew how to be."

Diesel tipped his head to the side.

"Your wizardry power is nascent," Dol went on. "When I shot you with that dart, I kickstarted some of your potential to help me with Darthius."

"Is that why I was able to interpret Mat's dream? And know when Jezebel was telling the truth?"

"Yes. It's your psychic powers unraveling."

"But I can't access them now." He rubbed his solar plexus, recalling the buzz he had felt before. "I can't read your mind."

"For one, us wizards are very powerful. We can put up shields against such infiltrations. But moreover, you're young. You haven't learned how to access all your potential. And your alignment to wolf-shifting, since it's all you know, lives on. Learning full wizardry takes hundreds of years."

"Hun . . . hundreds?"

"Yes. Hundreds."

"How old are you?" Diesel asked.

"In human years, I lost count somewhere around 15,000. But time doesn't exist. There is no such variable in the equations of the universe."

"Hm. You don't look a day over 1,000." Trinity grinned with her arms folded across her chest. "That's great, Einstein, but I'm still a little hung up on the abandoning part. If you knew he had so much potential . . . why? How can a parent be afraid of their child's potential?"

Dol hung his head. "I'm an addict."

"Huh?" Mat said.

"I'm addicted to magic."

"How can you be addicted to magic if you *are* magic?" Mat asked.

"I can't get enough of it."

"Ah." Mat nodded. "Makes sense. That's why you got so excited when the White Queen gave you that satchel . . . the bounty for finding Diesel."

"My powers are weak," Dol said. "I lost them in a battle with Darthius during the nineteenth century."

"And that's why we're back in the nineteenth century?"

"Or there abouts. I'm not sure what Darthius planned when he returned."

Diesel squinched his face. "'Splain."

"Look we really need to get Darthius. Where's Heel?" Dol went to the window and pulled back a thick, tasseled curtain to look outside.

"He's checking in on his son and his husband, like a good father should," Trinity said.

"And Bence," Mat reminded her.

"And Bence," she added. "He should be right back."

Dol returned to the chair. "All right. In order to defeat Darthius, I had to relinquish my powers to King Winston. We agreed upon the first of the 'Double Bubbles,' as you call them." He chuckled. "Central Maine was their land. Now, with Darthius's return, he has reverted us back here to set the record straight and regain power. When I found out, back in France, that a she-wolf, Mitsy, had reached out to him and that he was to return upon the Howling Moon, I came right away."

"You tricked them into thinking you were from King Winston's research facility," Mat said.

"Precisely. Look, they're in the process of advancing and evolving supernatural beings to fight off the Rise of the Normals."

"The Metanormals?" Mat asked.

"Well, moreover, normal human beings turning into Metanormals. Winston's NEPRC has the power to not only kill Metanormals, but they're working to prevent the *infection*, as they call it, from spreading amongst the regular, normal human beings."

"The meek shall inherit the earth," Diesel muttered.

"I thought Metanormals were kick-ass," Trinity said.

Dol chuckled. "You *are* kick-ass for now, but if Winston gets his way you won't be for long. They're starting with Normals before they turn. That's why I have monitors looking after some of you."

"Like Chip and me?"

"Yes."

"And not me," Mat said, apparently still bitter.

"You've already turned," Dol said to him. "Trinity, not until now, and Chip not yet."

Diesel stared at his totem. It glowed a greenish hue. "If my totem was so powerful and had the ability to heal me from Mitsy's stab wound, why not the other cuts and scrapes?"

"Darthius is stronger."

"And if it could heal me and prevent me from being hurt, why did you want Trinity to take it out of the forest?" He left it to dangle against the bandage around his chest.

Dol stood. "I think Heel is arriving."

"You didn't answer my question." Diesel stood too.

Dol faced his son and sighed. "Upon the Howling Moon, it would become clear you were not just a wolf-shifter. Your true identity would be revealed."

"How?"

"During the mating rituals, it wouldn't work."

"Is that why I'm not attracted to she-wolves?"

"Yes."

"The runic messages along its sides would indicate you were my son."

Diesel looked at the inscriptions along the edge. "Is that what this says?"

"Yes. The White Queen and King Winston must not know you're here . . . as a powerful wizard. They believe you are a wolf-shifter. It's better that way."

"I don't want to be a wizard. I don't want magic. I want to be normal." Diesel caught Trinity's eye.

"This still isn't clicking for me," Trinity said. "He's holding something back."

The wizard paced. "All right! I'm addicted to power. I was afraid I'd consume my son's magic and take the life right out from him."

"No," Trinity said, "that's not all. You abandoned Diesel to gain power. You said Darthius took it all from you and forfeited it to this King Winston dude."

Dol loosened the tie around his neck. "I . . . I did."

"Your mind shield doesn't work against Metanormals, Doc." Trinity winked. "I guess I have psychic powers too, now. You abandoned Diesel to get more magic. If his true identity is revealed to the king, you've broken your promise to give away your magic. All bets are off, and you lose your power again. You came here to collect more magic, not to kill Darthius. Darthius is just a distraction."

"Darthius is not just a distraction! His return could kill off humanity!" Dol, red-faced, breathed heavily.

Trinity studied him for a moment. "That may be, but you wanted Diesel's magic for your own. That's why you wanted me to take the totem out of the forest. I'm glad I trusted my instincts, otherwise Diesel would be dead right now."

The door flung open, and Bence and Bingham moseyed on in. "Hey, all. What's up with all this Victorian stuff?" Bence tossed Diesel some fresh clothes, and Bingham waved to the group.

Dol placed a hand on Diesel's shoulder. "Please forgive me. Son."

Diesel pulled away from his father's touch and put the shirt on that Bence had given him. "Come on, dawg, let's get the hell out of this forest, like we planned all along. I should have left with you for Salem when I had the chance, and none of this shit would have happened."

"Dude, what the hell's going on?" Bence asked.

Diesel stopped at the door and turned to his father. "I don't give a shit about you. Or about being a wizard." Diesel spit on the hardwood floor.

Bence put a hand on his shoulder. "Dee, please."

Diesel left, but Bence went after him.

Part Four

The Human

Chapter Twenty-Eight

Shattered

J ezebel picked calendula from the herb garden behind Witch Bazomella's hut.

The moonlight spilled onto Lord Darthius, who lay beside her prostrate in the grass with his coat and shirt folded neatly beside his top hat.

"If you were a little smaller, I'd take you inside to lie on the bed," Jezebel said.

"I don't need no bed!" He snorted, hooved feet clawing into the ground. "I need that salve." His legs bent inward like a goat or fawn's hindquarters.

Jezebel sprinkled the calendula into the granite mixing bowl set atop the potting bench. "It's almost ready."

"I shall kill that human," he muttered. Burn marks peppered his face.

"I'm surprised Witch Bazomella isn't here. Seeing that you brought us back over a hundred-fifty years, I thought the others would be—"

307

"We don't need the creatures from that era. The only one I need is Dolessenbee and his dopey son."

"Son?" She grasped the pestle and ground the calendula in with the sea buckthorn seeds and beeswax. "Who is his son?"

"You stupid bitch. Who do you think? The one I fought."

She stopped grinding. "Diesel?"

"Finish that stuff! And put it on me. Lather me up, then we shall fornicate. It's been too long." He grunted, then groped himself.

Jezebel cleared her throat and hastened her pace. "It's almost done." She smirked. "However, there is one thing that would make things a little faster."

Darthius moaned and toyed with his crotch. "What."

"My witch powers. They're limited. King Winston and The White Queen hoard and control the real potent magic."

He groaned in self pleasure. An enormous erection tented his trousers. "In good time you shall reign over this forest, my dear."

Jezebel smirked.

"Get me my salve!" He inclined.

Jezebel scraped the thick pestle along the side of the bowl and slid the ointment off its base. "Ready."

With each stroke of the balm upon the creature, Darthius grunted in pleasure. "Oh, yes. That feels good."

"Your Majesty," said a voice from behind.

Jezebel turned to see Ketch and Pedro bowing

"It's an honor to have you hex our presence," Ketch said.

"Yeah, a real hon-ah," Pedro added.

"What are you two doing here?" Jezebel asked. "Being your nosey little selves, I imagine."

Darthius raised a hand. "It's quite all right. I believe one of you is the king and queen's servant vampire."

"Yes, you know." Ketch sounded surprised.

"I know everything," Darthius growled. "Now come here and stroke the Dark Lord with this witch. I shall fill you both with my seed."

"Wh . . . what?" Ketch backed away.

"Get over here!" Darthius roared. He slammed a fist to the ground, and the earth shook. "With my seed you shall prosper."

Ketch eyed Darthius's tenting trousers, then exchanged a glance with Pedro.

"I could use another set of hands," Jezebel said.

Darthius's reptilian nose twitched, and he unbuttoned his pants.

T HE TREE PORTAL WAS in sight.

"I just think you're acting hastily," Bence said for the fifteenth time since leaving the Beecher property.

The ground trembled. Diesel stopped. "Darthius."

It roared again, and a wave of earth rolled out so powerful it knocked them off their balance.

"Why another earthquake?" Bence leaned against a tree for support.

"Don't know. Don't care." Diesel advanced toward the portal.

In the distance, a groan bellowed out, and another tremor bowled through.

"Get away from that tree!" Diesel shouted as a large limb snapped and tumbled down. Bence narrowly avoided it with a dive to the ground. Diesel dove too, and they both lay on their stomachs to ride the wave.

"What the hell now?" Bence said when it passed.

Diesel rose and dusted off his pants. "The quicker we get out of this shithole, the better we are."

"Are you sure about this? What about the others?" Bence asked.

"I've been living my life too long for others. It's time Dan Diesel Cade did what he wants."

Another groan from afar thundered overhead. A fluttering, chirping dark cloud covered the moon and descended off into the night sky.

"Bats," Bence said.

"Thousands of them," Diesel said when their squeaking passed and the moonglow returned.

Then a green missile-like sound whistled from the eastern horizon, and red and blue lights followed.

Silence fell, save Diesel and Bence's hurried breath.

Crackling sounded. Blue, electrified fragments sparked and showered down.

"The barrier. He's breaking the barrier." Diesel scurried. "Come on!"

They ran for cover.

NAKED, JEZEBEL, PEDRO, AND Ketch huddled under Darthius's cover while a blue, mucous-like membrane rained down on them.

Bats flew up from the depths of the forest and escaped through holes pierced through the protection barrier from their magic missiles.

As the barrier collapsed, blue shards plummeted from above and sparked fires in the grass.

A wind howled.

CHAPTER TWENTY-NINE

Slaughtered

UPON SUNRISE, THOSE BURNT and injured from the protection barrier's collapse stretched out across the outdoor assembly. The dead, or soon to be, were piled high along the south. Instead of helping them, an army of devotees to the Dark Lord—a mix of shifters, mages, ogres, and vampires—killed them.

Jezebel wielded a sword Darthius crafted for her. Her fully returned powers, and then some, sped through her veins.

Mitsy watched with mouth agape. Darthius had fashioned her in a pink, floral-printed, lace trimmed dress that hung below her knees. The sleeves were long and had a circle of lace at the wrists that matched the one around her collar. Over the outfit, she donned a two-pocketed apron, the stark white of which accentuated the pallid daisies peppered about the material and her swelling belly beneath.

Darthius patted Mitsy's head. "Little lady. I owe all this to you. If it hadn't been for your devotion, I wouldn't be here. I couldn't affect Earth without a body to do so."

She split her curtain bangs with her fingers. Her mouth quivered. "Why . . . why do we have to kill them all?" She had a rosier, healthier complexion since Darthius's return.

"Not everyone, deary," Jezebel said. "Just the maimed."

"They'll hold us back," Darthius added. "For your reward, I shall see to the health of your baby." He reached for her belly, but she flinched.

"Mitsy?" Jezebel said with a cocked head, and Darthius touched Mitsy's apron.

Mitsy convulsed a bit, then a smile raked her face. She cupped a hand over Darthius's massive one. "The pain's gone."

"He's a fine one," Darthius said. "He'll make a good soldier."

"Soldier?"

"To fight."

"Fight whom?" she asked.

"The humans," Jezebel said. "The Rise of the Normals, duh."

Mitsy attempted to wipe off the bloody handprint Darthius had left on her apron, but it only smeared.

Darthius spun around, coattails flapping. "Everyone!" He removed his top hat and bowed. "I am your creator, and I designed you to rule this planet."

Mephistopheles and Grim cheered, and the crowd followed.

Darthius returned his top hat and advanced toward the gazebo. "Humans are our servants. We are the dominate species in all our variations. Humans shall not rise to our level."

"They already have," Mitsy muttered.

"Shush," Jezebel said.

The group cheered, as Darthius stepped onto the dais.

"The bats I released shall infect the human populous, but it will take time for them to spread their poison around the globe. We need every ounce of supernatural magic to win this war."

The group silenced.

"The sick and the maimed hold us back." He tsked. "The decrepit and weak shall release, on my demand, what little magic they have left in their feeble, pathetic little bodies and hand it over for the greater good . . . or should I say evil." He snickered.

"Yes!" Grim thrust a fist into the air.

Darthius slammed a fist atop the railing, and it cracked. "Let the killings begin!"

Ketch and Pedro, perched atop a tree, descended. Darthius's injection freed them from the need for sunglasses. Their black and bloodshot eyes rolled back as they bit into an elderly couple sweeping the gazebo—Ketch's repaired incisor aided him well.

"They're too old," Darthius said when he saw Mitsy's horror. "Don't need 'em. Only the fit shall remain." He eyed a she-wolf. "And the beautiful." He slapped her rear.

The carnage awed even Jezebel. She stood motionless.

"What's the matter?" Darthius sniffed her neckline. "Cat got your tongue?"

Jezebel broke from her reverie. "No. No. I'm just deciding which victim I want next."

Darthius laughed and went over to Ketch and Pedro.

"I . . . I did this?" Mitsy gazed outward looking at everything and nothing at the same time.

Jezebel set her sword's tip into the ground. "You brought him here." She steadied a trembling hand around the pommel and clasped it with her free one. She was unsure if nerves were the cause of her shuddering, for she had never killed so much, or if it was just the raging of her newfound powers.

"But Witch Lena promised—"

Jezebel pointed to the stain on her apron. "You got what you wanted."

Darthius snacked on the limb of a werewolf. "Let's move onto the infirm." He chomped. "We need only the strong. The rest will hold us back."

Elder Bainbridge, who had lost his cane, crawled toward Darthius. When he reached him, he kissed the Dark Lord's feet. "Lord Darthius, creator of all that is evil, creator of the supernatural." He kissed them again, lifted up at the waist with bones cracking, and bowed for another peck. "Please save me. I shall be devoted to you for eternity."

Annoyed, Darthius kicked the man in the face as he moved to kiss again and nodded his head at Jezebel. "He's all yours."

Jezebel started to ask for clarification, but she knew what she had to do. She cleared her throat. Her shadow cast over the praying Elder Bainbridge, and she raised her trembling sword over his head.

"That's it, my girl." Darthius licked his lips.

Bainbridge turned to her and lifted his arthritic arms in defense. "Religion is not the way if this is what it brings." He gestured to the devastated grounds.

"Devotion to the Lord will set you free." Jezebel grunted and slammed the sword through Elder Bainbridge's chest.

The old man coughed out blood, and it stained his gray beard.

"Jezebel!" Mitsy yelled.

Bainbridge's soul fought to return to its lifeless form, but the paranormals ripped it out.

Ketch, in throes of orgiastic delight, knelt before the dead bodies and gorged on their blood. Pedro snapped the necks of the shifters—two at a time—then moved to an overweight ogre and disemboweled him.

"Be sure to turn a few into vampires," Darthius said. "We'll need extra reinforcements. Vampires make good soldiers."

Ketch and Pedro's mouths fell open.

"Yes," Darthius said, patting them on the back, "your siring abilities have been returned."

Mitsy ran, but Darthius, lightning fast, dashed out in front of her.

"Where are you going, little lady?" He leaned a hand against the garrison.

Jezebel moved over. "I asked her to fetch me a potion to kill these wretched beasts."

Darthius stepped aside, and Mitsy left. "I like wretched beasts," he said. His mouth, near hers, reeked of rotten flesh. "Shall we fornicate again?"

"Shall love to." She smirked. "However, we do have some wiping clear of the weak, don't we?"

Darthius grunted his agreement.

Mitsy came out from behind the shed. She wielded a sword nearly half her size and struggled to lift it.

"No!" Jezebel said.

Darthius spun around. "My little lady, what the frick are you doing with that?" He took the sword by the blade. It cut his hand, but he didn't flinch. "You think this"—he held it up—"is going to stop me?" He laughed; head tilted back. Green vapors plumed from his mouth.

They stood in silence for a time.

"Induce her," Darthius demanded of Jezebel.

"Wh . . . what?" Jezebel said.

"You heard me. Pop the bitch! We can use that baby. I have no need for her. She's just a girl."

Mitsy tried to run, but he stopped her with a bloodied hand on the crimp of her dress. He spun her around, facing Jezebel. "Induce her!"

"I . . . I have another month to carry," Mitsy cried.

He wrenched Mitsy's arm behind her back. The bright color in her cheeks faded, as if he drained away any rejuvenation given to her. Her hair grew limp, and her lips chapped, as if removed of any life he had provided her.

Jezebel blinked and stifled her reaction.

Darthius arched an eyebrow at the witch, and she flung out a perfectly manicured hand at Mitsy's stomach. A green liquid-like ray pitched forth from her fingertips.

Mitsy collapsed in pain. She screamed. "How could you?" The girl faced Jezebel. "My child isn't ready. He's not ready!" She breathed deeply and clutched the grass.

Jezebel gazed a stoic eye on Darthius. She remained composed to conceal any emotion, yet her stomach fluttered.

Mitsy rolled onto her back. "If you're going around killing all the maimed, what about your deformed son? Are you going to kill him too?"

Jezebel's jaw clenched. Her legs weakened. She opened her mouth to say something, but caught Darthius's stare and said nothing.

Mitsy's nostrils flared. "I've seen you scoping out Bingham, at the cave." Her eyes were cold and flinty. "You watched from a distance so the dragons wouldn't see you. But they knew. Diesel taught me dragon. I could hear them chatting about your lack of motherhood. But you care!" Mitsy yelled with clenched fists tugging her apron. "You care! Don't you! You care!"

Tears streamed down her face. "Tell me you care! How could a mother not care about the child she bore?"

Jezebel slapped her.

"You care even though you pretend not to!" Mitsy shrieked. "Diesel, Elio, and Heel care more about him than you do. He just wants to be loved. It breaks my heart." She sobbed.

Darthius rolled his eyes. "Hysterical women. So nineteenth century."

"We are not nineteenth-century women." Jezebel's heart raced.

Darthius was silent for a moment. He moved closer to her and grabbed her by the throat. "Oh, a little spunk." His breath reeked of bat guano. "That's so sexy." He grazed claw-like fingernails along her neck. "Shall we fetch your child? I shall like to see this deformed being of yours that you care nothing about."

"But . . . but your Honor—"

"Let's see this maimed child! If Diesel cares about him, apparently more than you, it could fit nicely into my plan."

"Plan?"

"We shall torture Buzzbee."

"Buzz . . . Buzzbee?"

"Bingham!" Mitsy corrected him. She leaned a hand against the garrison and used it for support to stand. "He has a name even if he can't reproduce or hold a sword. It's Bingham! He's a living being who deserves happiness and a good life."

Honoree approached with blood in his beard and dripping from his hands.

"Bing . . . Ham." Darthius swung the sword he had taken from Mitsy. "We shall torture Bing Ham. It will surely bring Diesel near, so I can possess his enchanted body." He shivered, as if the thought excited him.

"T . . . t . . . torture?" Jezebel swallowed.

"Afraid?" Darthius asked.

"No."

"Good. Think of it as a token of your devotion to me. I want Diesel. Once I'm inside him, I shall halt his magic. I can inhabit his perfect body and rip the precious magic right out of his heart."

"Let me show you the way," Jezebel said.

Chapter Thirty

Freedom

Mat, who had been injured in the barrier's collapse chasing after Bence and Diesel, limped toward the door to leave. "I'm fine. I'm better now!" He pushed Trinity's arm away. "I need to go find them." He approached the wizard. "It's morning. You said that we could leave after sunrise."

Dr. Dolessenbee snapped open the gold timepiece chained to his vest. The watch's Roman-numeral face indicated it was close to eight o'clock.

"Mat," Trinity said, "let's wait just a little longer. It's too hectic out there." She pulled back the curtains and peered out. "I think Dr. Dolessenbee is right wanting us to stay. There are Malificious everywhere."

Dol exhaled heavily as he rested in the armless chair. "We're safer here. The shield I placed over the house will hold for some time. My limited powers could at least do that."

"And if you hadn't run . . ." Trinity reminded Mat for the umpteenth time how his decision to follow after Bence and Diesel, shortly after they had left instead of staying, caused his wounds when the barrier collapsed.

There was a knock at the door, and the three of them froze.

Trinity, still by the window, peeked out. "Oh my God!" She ran for the door, flung it open, and hugged Bence.

Mat ran too but stopped at the foyer. He longed to embrace Bence—not only for being happy to see him but more so to satiate the desire to be close to him. "Bence," he said, keeping his distance.

Dr. Dolessenbee stood and nodded to Mat giving him approval to quell his want.

Bence and Mat lingered in their embrace longer than Mat had anticipated, but he liked it. No, he loved it.

"I was concerned about you," Mat finally said holding Bence out at arm's length. "I went looking for you two, but it was too dark, and I couldn't find you. Then, the sky collapsed."

"Darthius smashed the barrier system," Bence said. "It's gone."

"Yes, we know," Trinity said. "Dr. Dolessenbee says it's pretty bad, but he put a protection spell . . . or something . . . over the house so we wouldn't be harmed." An indignant eye Mat's way served as another reminder of his folly.

"But I didn't listen," Mat added and rolled up a sleeve to show one of his cuts.

Bence winced and touched his arm. The contact was electric yet comforting.

"Where's Diesel?" Trinity asked.

Bence released Mat and faced her. "He left."

Dr. Dolessenbee paced. "For Salem? He can't go just yet." He scratched his neck. "I thought for sure he'd stay," he muttered.

"He's upset," Bence said. "But I couldn't leave." He caught Mat's stare. "I was concerned about you all. And Bingham, Heel, and Elio. Have you heard from the dragons? There are Malificious everywhere."

"We have not," Dol said, "but Emphilothepy are strong, and they're protected in their cave."

"You came back for us?" Trinity said.

"I did, but Darthius has an army storming the castle," Bence said. "From what I heard from those in the woods, they've been instructed to dethrone the queen. We need to get out of here before all hell breaks loose, literally."

"We will. In time." Dr. Dolessenbee returned his timepiece to his vest pocket.

"What . . . what are we waiting for?" Bence asked.

"Good question," Mat added.

There was a scuffle on the porch.

"Diesel?" Trinity went for the door.

"Wait!" Dr. Dolessenbee went to it instead. "She's arrived."

"She?" Mat asked.

"Jezebel?" Trinity added.

Dr. Dolessenbee opened the door. Mitsy had been placed on the porch. Honoree ran off down the lawn, transformed into a wolf, then dashed off into the forest.

Mat ran out onto the porch.

"Mits . . . are you—? You're not okay." Mat placed a hand over her belly and the bloody handprint on her apron. "What's wrong? The baby . . ." He carried her inside and set her on the couch.

She swallowed, as if relieved some by his touch, then caught sight of Bence.

"Hey, Mits," Bence said. "I take it you're surprised to see me alive."

Mitsy stared at him incredulously. "You're . . . you're not dead."

"No. I was saved," he said.

Tears rolled down her cheeks. "I'm sorry. I'm so sorry." She wept. "Please forgive me."

Dr. Dolessenbee checked his watch again. "We can leave now."

"Does that watch tell you what to do?" Mat asked.

The doctor didn't heed his question. "We need to get her to the cave before the baby comes."

"But . . . but she's not due for another month," Bence said.

"Exactly. The cave will be the best spot for her to have her child."

Trinity's lips parted. "You knew she was coming. That's what you were waiting for."

Dol opened the door and whistled with fingers pressed to his lips. "Heel!"

ONLY A KNEE-HIGH WALL of blue haze remained of the second barrier. Diesel kicked it down out of spite, though he could have easily stepped over it. Beneath his boots, fragments buzzed faintly, as if making one last, futile attempt to hold him back—then he stepped into freedom.

The land stretched vast and vacant. Sun blazed. Birds chirped. Clouds drifted across a brilliant blue sky.

Diesel glanced back. The knee-high wall was gone—erased, as if it had never existed. "What the—?"

He pressed forward, climbing the crest of a grassy knoll, the unsettling thought growing that he hadn't just crossed a barrier but into another time.

In the valley below, a horse attached to a wagon neighed, and a man lay strewn in the grass beside it. A young-looking, Black boy in brown trousers and a white shirt was digging a grave.

Diesel sensed the boy's humble, human spirit from afar. "What happened here? Do you need a hand?" he asked upon approach.

The boy—lanky and with a pockmarked face—appeared surprised by Diesel's lack of accusation for the killing. "Neck snapped by a black dragon," he explained and introduced himself as Tobias, a slave escaping from South Carolina for Canada. He stood an inch or so shorter than Diesel.

Diesel dragged the body into the hole, while Tobias fought off paranormals emerging from the forest with a stare and a punch that intimidated the ghasts.

When they placed the last shovel of dirt upon the grave, and the paranormals retreated, they shared water from a canteen in the back of the wagon.

"Saw it happen," Tobias said. "Vampires, ghosts, and werewolves spook these woods constantly." He wiped a bead of perspiration from his forehead. "They're 'fraid of some of us."

"You're human." While Tobias's body looked no more than sixteen and seventeen, his soul seemed much older. "Why do you think they're afraid of you?"

"Not sure really."

"You a Metanormal?"

"Don't know what that is, sir. I ain't had no schooling. Only learning I got was from my mother who taught me and my sister to read back on the plantation before we were separated."

"Sounds like a good mother." Diesel laid a checkered quilt along the driver's seat.

"I'm hoping to find them in Canada. We were separated four years ago."

While Diesel inventoried supplies in the rear of the wagon, the boy educated him more about his plight.

Tobias picked off pieces of grass and dirt scattered atop the coverlet draped over the jockey's seat. "I was hiding under this."

Diesel stepped aboard the rig. "Let me give you a lift."

"We're going in opposite directions," Tobias said.

"That's okay. You said there's a safe house—I believe that's what you called it—nearby."

"That'd be mighty kind of you." Tobias boarded. "There's a house down 'round yonder. I can hole up there for a time."

The horse pulled them over farmland where cattle grazed, and wooden fences flanked a worn path in the grass.

Their empty canteen clanged at the foot of the carriage where copies of the *National Era* and the *Boston Morning Post* lay.

"He was an abolitionist," Tobias said.

"Huh?"

"The driver of this here wagon. The quilt he had hanging off the side of it told me he was safe. The *National Era* is an abolitionist newspaper."

Diesel recalled his Human History class at uni. "Darthius brought us back before the barrier was put in place," he mumbled.

"What you saying?"

"Never mind."

Not too much farther, Tobias pointed to a farmhouse in the valley. A similar patchworked quilt hung, like the one Diesel sat upon, from its window, and smoke rose from a center chimney. "That's it."

Diesel watched Tobias wander down the hill. When the door to the home opened, Diesel waved to the woman at the entrance. Tobias was welcomed inside, and Diesel left.

A mile or two later, at a fork in the road, Diesel slowed the horse. To his right, a sign read *Boston–300 Miles*, and an arrow beneath it pointed south. "Well, the F-150 would be faster, but this old wagon'll have to do." He snapped the reins, and they trooped along.

A brook babbled in the distance. When the horse approached it, Diesel stopped him, shuffled sideways down a slight incline, and filled the canteen at the water's edge.

From a nearby tree, he plucked apples and stuffed them in the pockets of his sweatshirt.

Beside a rock near the wagon, he relieved himself. As he zipped up his fly, he was reminded that his clothes didn't fit the period and considered the need to find something to blend in. Yet, oddly, Tobias hadn't questioned his Red Sox cap and Levi's.

He settled back onto the carriage. As he was about to loosen the brake, a blinding vision of white light struck him, and apples tumbled out of his pockets.

"The hell!" He picked up a McIntosh rolling over the newspapers.

Another revelation besieged him, and Bingham came into view.

"Bing?"

Tears streaked a path along the boy's dirty face, and his lower lip quivered.

"Ah ya!" Diesel shouted at the horse and, with a couple quick tugs, pivoted the carriage around.

Diesel rose into a squat over the wagon's jockey and tugged the reins to quicken the horse's pace. When he passed the Boston signage, he followed the northward-bound one that read *Hubbard Forest*.

Another blinding light burst into view. Diesel lost his balance and tumbled off the wagon.

Inside Elio and Heel's cave, Darthius held Bingham in a vice grip—one arm around his neck, the other held the boy's hands behind his back—and Jezebel stood by his side.

Chained to a boulder and a tree out front on the front slope, Elio and Heel tugged. Blood dripped from their hind legs where the cuffs clamped, and a muzzle was wrapped around their snouts to prevent any fire breathing.

Bence, Trinity, and Mat crouched by a clump of blankets with someone lying on the ground.

'Mitsy?' Diesel thought. He knew he wasn't there. The memory of falling off the carriage was his last one.

"Let him go, Darthius." Dr. Dolessenbee unleashed his wand. The barely foot-long thing looked pathetic beside the seven-foot-tall beast.

Darthius laughed. "Oh, nooo. I'm terrified." He feigned to release the boy then snatched him back before Bingham budged. His maniacal laugh echoed inside the cavern, and Bingham trembled. A wet spot spread across his pants, and Jezebel looked away.

"No!" Diesel woke with his lower half strewn in the brook. The horse licked his face with an apple-smelling slobber. The animal had somehow unhitched itself from the carriage, and Diesel led him back to the wagon where he reestablished the tug.

They rushed northward—past Tobias's temporary refuge, its chimney still pluming. Soon they crossed the place where the protection barrier would one day rise, and faint sparks still crackled in the grass. Diesel slowed, unsettled. The barrier didn't exist yet—not in this time—but its remnants hung like echoes bleeding through from the future.

Visions popped in and out of his head until a particularly strong signal focused, and he slowed the horse to prevent another fall.

"We shall press the boy," Darthius said. "The wizard's son is on his way. I can sense him."

"Bingham is not a witch," Jezebel said, taking her son's arm from Darthius.

"Mom, you're . . . you're not going to hurt me."

"You must show your allegiance," the Dark Lord said to Jezebel. "We must exterminate the weak among us. You know the drill. They'll hold us back." Darthius grimaced. "Look at this pathetic thing. It can hardly walk." He laughed. "He's a twisted wreck. You bore such a calamity?"

Jezebel bit her lower lip.

Bingham quaked.

Outside the cave, Dol was slumped, passed out up against a tree where Heel and Elio were chained. Mat wiped a gash from the wizard's forehead and tried to wake him. Trinity and Bence tended to Mitsy.

Diesel rose onto his haunches and snapped the reins. "C'mon, boy," he said to the horse. Yet the next vision knocked him down onto the jockey.

The blue dragonfly emerged and settled on the tip of the equine's nose as if leading it.

"Fragrance," Diesel muttered, and the vision consumed him.

"Of course I am allegiant." Jezebel tugged Bingham's arm, and the boy winced.

"Good." Darthius snickered and twiddled his fingers, tapping long, claw-like nails together.

Along the slope, Elio lurched forward. A pathetic cry emanated from his muzzle-clad mouth, and Heel tried to assuage him with a tender touch to his shoulder.

The tree they were chained to listed with each pitch forward.

Bence and Mat muttered. Mitsy cried.

"She's having her baby," Diesel said, coming to. The dragonfly beat its wings atop the horse's head. The reins dangled along the fast-moving ground below.

"Give him to me!" Jezebel pulled Bingham away from Darthius. "I shall do it myself. He's my son."

"Finally, seeing reason." Darthius sneered, baring a black-tooth half-grin, and tapped his nails together again. "I hope you understand, I need to see your allegiance to the Dark Lord in order to grant your full powers."

Darthius manifested a witch press—a slab of stone—in the center of the cave, where Trinity had once parked her VW. Resting against the wall was a thick wooden plank and a pile of rocks.

Jezebel set Bingham on the slab. He fought back, but Jezebel's grip was too strong. Darthius settled him with a slap to the face, then placed the board atop him.

"No!" Diesel yelled.

Fragrance looked back at him with a somber yet assuring nod.

Darthius cast a large boulder onto the plank, and Bingham harumphed.

Elio shrieked. Heel stood on his back legs and bent the swaying tree.

Trinity rose. "Oh my God. Bingham! Stay with Mitsy," she said to Mat and Bence.

"Me? I don't know—" Mat's voice was cut off by Mitsy's cry.

Trinity ran up the embankment, toward the cave, as the tree snapped from Heel's tug. Freed, Elio carried the boulder that chained his other foot and stumbled forward after her.

A second, larger stone had been set upon Bingham's plank. Bingham lay red-faced below it, gasping for breath.

Darthius closed his eyes. His nostrils flared as he inhaled. "He's almost here."

"Who?" Diesel asked, then realized the Dark Lord meant him. "Why me?"

The dragonfly sat steadfast with her wings fixed behind her from the force of the rushing air.

Dol awoke. The chain around his ankle was no match for his wand. He unleashed himself, and Heel readily.

Bence and Mat tended to Mitsy while Dol rushed up the hill.

"Why does he want me?" Diesel asked.

"He needs your totem," Dol replied.

Diesel flinched. "Wow, we can communicate this way?"

"It's one of your powers. Son, I need you here. I can't take Darthius down without you. Together we can outsmart the Dark Lord."

"Hey, Fragrance," Diesel said to the dragonfly. "Can you make this thing go faster?"

The horse halted. The supplies behind him lurched forward, and a box marked dishware crashed to the ground.

"I said faster not—"

Fragrance flew off the horse's head, went to the tug binding the carriage to the equine, and it disembarked.

"Ah, that was you. Why didn't I think of loosening the load?" Diesel jumped off the wagon and got on the horse's back. Fragrance sat on Diesel's shoulder, and they sped off.

Darthius fixed another boulder onto the plank. This time, Bingham whelped. Blood trickled from his snout.

Diesel gasped. His body tingled, and he grew dizzy.

Fragrance buzzed. "If you're going to pass out, you'll fall off."

Startled by the dragonfly's ability to communicate—or his sudden fluency in Odonata—stalled his lack of consciousness. "I . . . I didn't know I spoke dragonfly."

"You don't," Dol said. "It's your intuition."

Diesel blinked, and the dragonfly's antenna twitched. Its permanent grin seemed to widen.

"Ah, how's Bingham?"

"Hurry," Dol said. "Darthius blocked off access to the cave. Neither Elio, Heel, nor I can get in."

Diesel studied the dragonfly, and the clarity of his vision deepened.

Beside the dragons, Dol stared—as if in a meditation—into the haze of the electric field preventing their entrance. The boulder hitched to Elio's foot was spotted with blood. Heel clawed at the barricade, and with each scrape his nails smoldered from the shocks.

When Diesel reached out a hand, as if to help, the vision disappeared. The dragonfly and the horse returned to focus.

"You can shift," Dol's voice rang out in his mind.

"Huh?"

The horse nickered. They passed another abandoned wagon, as paranormals consumed the driver's spirit from his body that had been devoured by something hungry.

Fragrance flew out in front of Diesel's face. "Go!"

"You're more than just a wolf-shifter," Dol said.

"Go! It's faster," Fragrance buzzed. She went to the horse's ear and buzzed inside it.

The horse bucked, tossing Diesel into the air. His anger welled, and the urge to shift consumed him. He attempted to right himself for fear of landing on his head and breaking his neck yet throughout each twist, turn, and sting of transformation he seemed to fall farther and faster. The tumble took much longer than it should have for the mere five or six feet he had dropped.

He growled and continued to descend.

The jowls of his wolf form snapped into place with an excruciating ache. Fur covered his body. His spine twisted and cracked.

He plunged more.

A warm, white light consumed him, followed by dark, cool air. A frigid, upward draft seemed to slow his descent, but he still landed with a thud. Pain raked his body.

When he opened his eyes, Elio and Heel's cave came into view, but the room spun like he had drunk too much whiskey.

Darthius laughed. "Ah, he's finally joined us. He's in his canine form, but it's better than nothing."

"Diesel!" Bingham shouted.

Diesel squinted to focus the three Binghams approaching him into one. The boy had been let out of the witch press. Blood dripped from his half-wolf face and his twisted body appeared in pain. Bingham flinched and placed a half-paw to his chest, as if the press had cracked his ribs.

Jezebel gripped her son by the shirt and pulled him back. Bingham winced.

"Your final proof of allegiance." Darthius snickered, and arevealized a flag with three moons. A pentagram occupied the center's full one along with the Stainless Banner of America's Confederacy. "I pledge allegiance to the flag . . ." He laughed. ". . . of the Wicked Confederate homeland with damnation, irreverence, and deathly devotion to the cause for which it stands."

Diesel's stomach turned, and he swallowed vomit. He rose onto all fours but stumbled when he tried to walk.

Darthius yelled for Jezebel to proceed. His voice echoed. The electric sheet that sealed the entrance vibrated.

She trembled, and the sword she held in her hand shook.

On the other side, Heel clawed, Elio pounded, and Dol shot magic from his wand to no avail. Every shot bounced back, and the wizard stepped away to avoid meeting with a ricocheted bullet.

"Sou Lalin kriyan sa a, se pou li leve," Jezebel muttered. Tears streamed down her cheeks. "Se pou li ante Latè ankò."

Darthius shivered, excited with each word she uttered.

"Se pou lonbraj Seyè nwa a egzamine prezans nou yon lòt fwa ankò."

Diesel rose but landed on his face. His paws weren't paws but rather his human hands and feet. "The Hell."

"Prove your allegiance!" Darthius yelled to Jezebel. "And you shall be set free. We shall reign supreme."

"Seyè Darthius se sovè nou an. Li se ewo nou an. Kite l leve!" Jezebel trembled. Her face crumpled. She lifted her blade to Bingham's throat.

"Yes. Yes. Yes." Darthius clapped, giddy with joy.

Jezebel screeched so loud it induced gooseflesh throughout Diesel's body.

Then, as if in slow motion, she sliced the blade across Bingham's throat.

"No!" Diesel snapped back into his human form and rushed toward the collapsing boy. Yet Darthius reached out, grabbed him by his necklace, and ripped the totem off his neck. The force landed Diesel onto his back.

Elio pounded on the electric force shield.

Diesel crawled over to Bingham as the boy bled out.

Elio wailed and pounded louder.

Jezebel fell to her knees, clutched her chest, then giggled. Her hair had become undone, and her eyes were black as coal. Her laugh intensified. She threw her head back, laugh-crying louder, and dropped the sword.

Darthius flew to her, picked her up, and peppered her with kisses. They levitated higher, and her hysterical rant echoed.

They rose toward the cave's stalactite ceiling where, with a thunder, the air cracked. They vanished, and Diesel's totem fell to the ground.

CHAPTER THIRTY-ONE

Totem

WAILING FROM THE DRAGONS drowned out Dol's words on the other side of the wall. Diesel laid Bingham's lifeless, still bleeding body down and moved closer to the barrier.

Walking up the embankment, Mat and Bence carried Mitsy. Trinity rushed over to help.

Diesel placed his palm on the barricade. It zapped him and flung him back beside Bingham's body. "Jesus!"

Dol shouted more nonsense when a mist slid through cracks in the cave's walls.

"Shit." Diesel scurried over to prevent the paranormals' entrance, but it was too late. Wobble Head morphed into form and approached.

"Get back!" Diesel yelled at the ghost trying to get Bingham.

"Diesel! Diesel!" Dol shouted.

He moved closer to the wizard.

"Where's your totem?" Dol asked.

"Who gives a frig'?"

"Where is it?"

Diesel rushed Wobble Head, and she stepped back. "Hey, she's afraid of me." He cradled Bingham's body.

"Where is your totem!"

"For the love of God." Diesel grabbed it from where Darthius had dropped it and held it up. "It's right here." He palmed it, examining its weight. "It's lighter. The gold cap is missing."

Dol shook his head. "Damn it."

"Damn what? What does that mean? Why did he take off the gold—"

"He got it."

"Got what?"

"Your essence. Your spiritual connection is in that totem. That's why it's so important."

"My spiritual connection?" Diesel placed a bloody palm on his naked chest. "My spirit is in here," he said, thumping his hand over his heart.

"True. It's there . . . mostly. But a piece of a Super's true essence is in their totem."

Diesel placed the chain around his neck. "Why?"

Dol harumphed. "For mating and regeneration, but that doesn't matter right now. What's important is he's using it."

"To make babies?"

"To merge with your soul and . . . You said Jezebel and the White Queen took a sample of your . . . you know."

Diesel winced, remembering the pain. "Yeah."

"A dollar to a donut, he and Jezebel are off to the castle. That's why I wanted the bloody thing out of here in the first place. Once they have the full trifecta, he can assume your powers."

Diesel blinked.

"With the mixture complete, he can assume the power you were born to employ."

Diesel guffawed. "Magic. Why do I have to be so special? All I want is to be a normal person."

"Normal. You are anything but." Dol glimpsed behind Diesel. "Watch it!"

Diesel turned. Wobble Head and three other ghastly beings nibbled at Bingham. "Get outta here!" Diesel snapped off a bit of a stalagmite.

The ghosts cowered.

"Hey, I'm pretty friggin' powerful, you asses." He smacked them with the column. It moved through them, but they fled, nonetheless.

"That's . . . that's not what they're fleeing from."

"Huh?"

A mist grew out from the crevice where Jezebel had gone down earlier.

"Did you say Jezebel lost her totem somewhere in the cave?"

The black mist filled the cavern. Diesel choked. "Yeah, she dropped it over the ledge."

"Shit. I . . . I . . . think it's coming back for her."

THE DRAGONS MOVED TO the rear of the cave to try and get through there. Mat, having followed them, returned to Bence and Trinity at

Mitsy's side. "It looks like Heel and Elio are trying to get in some other way. It's their home. They should know their way around."

Bence relaxed his shoulders. "The contractions stopped." He had been so focused on Mitsy's care that he didn't seem to notice Mat had even left. "She's in and out of consciousness."

Trinity combed her hair away from her face. "The baby . . . it's not due for another month."

Bence felt Mitsy's neck pulse. "Apparently, Jezebel induced her."

"She told us, when she was conscious," Trinity added. "Darthius forced Jezebel to show her allegiance to him by hastening the baby's arrival."

"That's messed up," Mat said. "Will it . . . will it live?"

"I think we can save it, if she holds on," Bence said.

"Holds on?" Trinity—pale-faced—leaned back on her haunches.

Bence looked up at her. "I don't think she's going to make it. Her heart rate is too low. I've helped Witch Lena birth a couple cubs before. Losing the mother is hard, but a baby is even worse."

"You've got a good bedside manner," Mat said. "You'd make a good nurse or doctor."

"I used to want to go to medical school."

"Used to?" Mat said.

"Maybe Dr. Dolessenbee can help us." Trinity looked over at the wizard talking with Diesel through the hazy screen.

"Dr. Dolessenbee is an MD in Artificial Intelligence, not an obstetrician," Mat reminded her. "Unless there's some magic in his wand . . ."

"Supers who know AI are in high demand these days," Bence said. "With the Rise and all." He placed a hand on Mitsy's cheek. "C'mon, Mits. You can do it, girl."

Mitsy's breath was labored and sweat beaded on her brow.

"The girl tried to kill you," Mat said, "and here you are trying to save her baby."

Mitsy mumbled. The contractions returned. Mat found it hard to watch. This was nothing like Maxine birthing Ty in a nice, sterile hospital in Eureka. He couldn't watch anymore. Following the dragons was one distraction, he needed another and moved closer to the wall.

A black mist inside the cave billowed. "Is there a fire?" Mat asked Dol. But anxiety consumed the wizard, and he ignored him.

"You need to get out!" Dol shouted to Diesel, whose figure barely showed through the haze and fog. "Elio and Heel are trying to get in through the other side of the cave."

"It's solid rock back there!" Diesel shouted.

"Jezebel's mist will kill you!" Dol banged on the wall. His fist singed when he touched it. He flinched and rubbed a charred hand. His knuckles bled.

Mat reached his palm out to the membrane wall.

"Don't!" Dol placed a bloody hand on his. "It'll burn you!"

Mat pushed him away and touched the barrier regardless. It was hot and required a little force, but his hand slid through the hot membrane with little effort.

Dol smiled.

"Hey!" Mat yelled over to Trinity. "I think we're impervious."

Trinity removed from Mitsy's side and came over to him.

"Diesel?" Mat shouted, halfway through.

"Dee!" Trinity barged in, and Mat landed beside her.

They coughed in the thick smoke.

"Tear down the wall!" Dol said.

Trinity found a broken half of a stalagmite column by the entrance. "Mat, grab another." She slammed the tip of the rock into the force field, and the wall shattered.

Mat kicked over a larger column to the left of the entrance, and the two hammered the barricade until a hole developed large enough for Dol to slip through, and he did.

The mist billowed out and improved visibility.

"Diesel!" Dol walked in. "Son? Where are you?"

Trinity and Mat shattered the wall further, enough to allow the dragons access when they returned.

Trinity rushed to Bingham's body. "Mat, help me get him outside."

"Dan Diesel Cade!" Dol's voice grew distant. "Son, where are—"

TRINITY WIPED SWEAT FROM her brow. She stood outside the cave where they had dragged Bingham's corpse. "Get back!" she yelled at a paranormal.

Mat charged at a ghastly man carrying his head, but the ghost approached Bingham, nonetheless.

"It's not working." Trinity kicked at the spider-like girl with black tresses covering her face, but her foot went through her.

Elio burst out from above the cave's entrance. He roared a flame, and the ghosts tumbled down the embankment into a fiery torrent.

The hair on Mat's arm singed. Trinity cowered closer to him.

The trees gracing the slope erupted into flames. The ghosts' screeches boomed across the land.

Elio rushed to Bingham's side first. Heel soon followed. They sobbed and wailed. Tears showered onto their son's body.

"Dragon tears," Mat mumbled.

"Can they heal the dead?" Trinity asked.

Bingham's hand twitched.

Mat smiled. "I . . . I think they can!"

"Dads?" Bingham muttered.

CHAPTER THIRTY-TWO

Tussle

THE CAVE EXPLODED. ROCKS and dust scattered down the embankment.

Dazed, Mat hoisted up onto his elbows and gazed back and forth at the bottom of the embankment to gather his bearings. "Bence? Trin?" He rose, using a boulder for support.

Atop the rubble of the now-collapsed cave, Darthius emerged. He appeared much larger and towered over the dragons who gathered Bingham, Mitsy, and Bence away from harm.

Darthius held up Dol by the scruff of the neck like a ragdoll and plodded down the rubble, while the wizard kicked and shouted incomprehensible wrangles, drowned by the ringing in Mat's ears.

Mat scurried over toward the trees to avoid a tumbling boulder and discovered Trinity. Dirt and blood covered her face. "Trin?"

She mumbled, and he helped her sit up.

Darthius flung Dol down the rock mound. "I have taken your son's powers." He landed near where the cave's entrance had been.

"You what?" Dol dusted dirt off his vest.

The Dark Lord smirked. "I now have his seed and his totem's essence. Two out of three of the trifecta ain't bad."

"Thank you for unleashing his powers."

The creature scrunched his brow.

"You can't survive, Darthius."

"I just did." Darthius sneered.

"Diesel's essence is potent. And, since my own is mixed in there, by virtue of being his father, you have unlocked mine." Dol arevealized a light saber, and a long, thin ray of white buzzed from the stub in his hand.

"Fuck."

"You know how magic works, Darthius." Dol pitched the sword to-and-fro, as if testing out rusty fencing skills. "You're fictional."

"What are they doing?" Trinity asked Mat.

"Don't know."

Darthius avoided a swipe from the épée. "When I complete the trifecta—"

"If!" Dol thrusted the sword at Darthius's gut, but the daemon jumped back.

Darthius chuckled. "You think you know everything. You think that you can think it, and it is. Like your goddamn humans. The hottest commodity in the supernatural kingdom . . . ha! I am! Not you."

"I *am* the hottest commodity. What I do is what I be." Dol smirked.

"What I do is . . . huh?"

"You, boasting a big body . . ." Dol chastised. "You think that scares me? You think that scares people?"

While Dol and Darthius tussled, Mat tended to Trinity and brushed blood-soaked hair from her brow. "You're going to be okay, Love."

"Love? Who are you calling 'Love'?"

Mat grinned. "I love you, Trinity. You're my best friend."

"You're telling me this now?"

"Not love as in—"

"I know. I get it." She kissed him on the cheek with a waft of her lavender essence mixed with the loamy scent of dirt. "I love you too, Mat, my best friend."

From farther down the embankment, a painful-sounding wail emerged.

"Mitsy," Trinity said, as if reminding herself. "The baby." She got up and ran to Bence's side who cared for the she-wolf protected by the huddling dragons and Bingham.

Mat moseyed up the hill to the arguing Dol and Darthius. "Where's Diesel?"

The two continued their tussle.

"Supernatural creatures are the ultimate species!" Darthius pointed an oversized finger at Dol's chest.

Dol stabbed him in the gut with the light saber, and it singed through the daemon's vest. "Humans are the key to peace on Earth."

"So, I fear."

"I know . . . I know. You don't want peace on Earth. But there are more beings on this planet who do, and that trumps."

"Not if I have my way."

"You don't get to get your way. I do. Human beings do."

Darthius laughed. "Listen to you. Acting all authoritative and shit. You think you can boss me around. Me! The creator of all ev—"

Dol lifted his saber and with a quick, downward movement sliced off Darthius's left hand.

Darthius cried. "You son of a bitch!" Thick, black blood spurted from his amputated wrist, and he bound it with an invisible force.

The severed hand flopped about on the ground like a mudskipper, and Mat gagged.

"Hey, you." Darthius grabbed Mat by the scruff of the shirt before he could walk away. "You're that queer Metanormal."

"What's it to you?" Mat's anger welled. "And where's Diesel?"

"Oh, he's in there." Darthius pointed the stub of his wrist behind him but was caught off guard, as if reminded that he had no digits on his left stump.

"Dol," Mat said, "we have to get him out."

Darthius chuckled. "His father killed him."

"I did no such thing!" Dol shouted.

"You collapsed the cave to prevent me from getting to him."

"You shall not assume his body," Dol said.

"I have the inklings of his soul: his seed. I just need his heart."

"I collapsed the cave to stall you. You haven't time."

Darthius sneered and inched closer to Dol. "His heart's probably still beating somewhere." He paused and listened to the silence. "I think I can hear. Lub-dub . . . lub-dub. Lub." He laughed.

Dol jabbed at him, but he backed away and karate chopped Dol on the back. The wizard collapsed onto his stomach.

"Those who are devoted to me shall live. Those who don't, shall die." Darthius flicked a finger at Mat. "Go tend to your friends. Dr. Dolessenbee and I have some business to take care of."

"I'm not afraid of you." Mat rushed the daemon but slammed up against an invisible shield when he neared him.

"You should be."

Mat trembled.

"Your powers are weakening. Haven't you noticed?"

Mat licked his lips.

"You're not as impervious to me as you once were." His words purred off his forked tongue with gratification, and his lips curved into a wide smile. "You Metanormals are sick!"

Dol stood. "Don't listen to him. It's a mind game." He threatened the daemon with his saber.

"A mind game." Darthius guffawed. "You think everything's about the mind."

The light emanating from Dol's saber lowered. "Your consumption of my son's powers has activated my own. Thank you." He pulled his timepiece out from his vest. "'Bout now." He winked, and Darthius surged backward from an indiscernible power and landed onto a pile of rock. "What's not a mind game now?"

Darthius shook off the sting. Dust billowed about. "I shall conquer humanity. I am converting them to the dark side."

"Not if I have my way."

"Your way. Ha! To Heaven with your way!"

"Indeed."

"I am stopping the Rise," Darthius fumed. "The spell I have set forth shall break Metanormals. It shall ingest them—and the ones you call 'normal'—with the ability to see reason. My reason."

Dol pursed his lips, seemingly surprised.

Darthius returned his top hat to his head. "Your son. He thinks he's been enlightened by studying humanity at university. You, the professors at UPS, and your monitors from your organization are spreading filth about humans and supernaturals coexisting. Rubbish!"

"They *can* coexist. And they do."

"As the scriptures stated, I have risen. That glorious, evil word shall spread." Darthius sat up.

"You are only a figment of Supers' imagination!" Dol shouted.

Darthius trembled with rage, and he clenched his only fist. "Everything's a figment of imagination!"

"Ah. Now you're talking."

"But . . . but . . . I am flesh and blood!" Darthius flew off the debris pile, and his hat slid off as he slammed into Dol at the tummy. They tumbled down the embankment.

Mat stepped up onto the cave's remains. "Diesel! Dee!"

"Where is he?" Trinity stood at the bottom of the rubble.

"Darthius says he's in here somewhere with Jezebel. Dol blew it up to prevent Darthius from getting him. He has more power now." He squatted and moved aside rock. "Dee?"

Trinity climbed up. "He could be anywhere. We must get him out. Maybe Heel or Elio can—" She paused as a dragonfly fluttered up the hill. "Fragrance? Ginny is that you?"

She rushed toward it and the saddled horse that grazed at the bottom of the embankment. Fragrance acknowledged her with a wink, then dashed off into crevices between the rock pile.

"She's looking for Diesel."

CHAPTER THIRTY-THREE

Reign

MOMENTS LATER, A HORDE of Malificious arrived with the queen. A purple-and-white fae flitted beside the queen, who disembarked from a Malificious with the aid of an armored knight.

Darthius, who held Dol in the air, dropped the wizard. "Ah. The queen has arrived." He giggled.

Mat stepped back, leaving Bence and Trinity to tend to Mitsy.

"Lord Darthius," the White Queen addressed. "What have we here? I hear rumor you have killed some of my people, and your plans are to annihilate my kingdom."

Darthius moseyed toward the queen. "Your Majesty, I'm glad you could find the time to make my acquaintance." She waited in silence by the lake at the bottom of the hill for him to make his protracted approach. He stopped a few feet from her and bowed. "Your enabling of the infirmed and weak has ruined this forest."

"The maintenance of my kingdom is not of your concern," she said.

"*Your* kingdom is no longer." He snickered. "It will be *hers*."

The White Queen blinked. The hovering sprites' wings thumped to a gentle beat, then they rested on her shoulders.

"Who?" the queen finally acknowledged.

"I think you know her." He cackled. "Jezebel."

The sprites gasped, yet the queen's face remained composed.

Darthius stepped closer to her. "Jezebel and I have a little thing going on. I think of her as my maenad."

The queen hoisted a staff into the air. "Over my dead body shall *she* reign!"

"If that's what it takes," Darthius said.

She hoisted a staff into the air, and an army of Malificious burst through the cloud cover. Emphilothepy shot up from below the tree line and joined them.

Darthius rocketed into the air after them, causing nearby trees to rustle. Above, the roar from flames thrown mixed with a cacophony of screeches, and several Malificious crashed to the ground.

Dol went to the queen. "Your Majesty."

"So, you are not a marksman named Marksman," she said. Her sprites sneered.

"I'm sorry I had to lie to you earlier, but we should put that behind us right now."

The queen raised an eyebrow. "I've been told Daniel Cade, otherwise known as Diesel, is your son."

"He is."

"And he is not a wolf-shifter."

"While he can shift into a wolf, it is learned behavior. He knows little else of his powers. He is my progeny."

Another dragon dropped. The ground rumbled, and Mat leaned against a boulder to catch his balance. Next, a screeching knight tumbled down, and his cries halted in the splat of his landing.

"As you know, there is only room for one wizard in this forest," the queen said.

Dol nodded. "Yes, I know. King Winston is this forest's wizard. That is why the fleeting powers I do have are weak here. Even your witch powers are far more superior."

"Don't you talk down to witches, Doc."

"I am not. I mean no disrespect."

"I don't like being made a fool of—nor does King Winston. We assumed Daniel Cade would grow our dwindling wolf-shifter species. You've duped us and are using your son for your own advantage."

"With his forgiveness, my full powers will—"

"Your full powers were taken by King Winston over a gambling debt."

"I realize that."

"Your relinquishing of your flesh and blood was part of the bargain. Little did I know he has been under our nose the whole time. How insidious of you to try and trump the king to get your powers back. You knew in your son's twenty-first year his spirit would fully manifest."

A screech sounded, and a Emphilothepy crashed into the forest. Heel flew off after it. Elio, still with broken a wing, dashed off on foot.

Dol checked his timepiece. "Your Majesty, we must put our differences aside and fight Lord Darthius. We both know his return is not good for your kingdom."

The queen pursed her lips. "We don't see eye to eye on the Rise of the Normals, Dolessenbee."

"But we do see eye to eye on the wrongness of Darthius killing off your kingdom to take it over," Dol reminded her. "He plans to assume my son's trifecta. He has already taken the essence of his spirit."

"And his seed," she added. "He and Jezebel stole it from our lab."

Dol nodded. "With a little more time Darthius will become more powerful than your husband and, no disrespect, but much more powerful than a . . . mere witch."

"He's the creator of all supernaturals. How much more does he need?"

"He is weakening."

Above, two Malificious collaborated with an Emphilothepy and hurled flames at Darthius. His coattails caught fire and flames consumed him.

Darthius pitched into a downward spiral and splashed into the pond.

Dragons dove after him.

"I shall take care of Darthius, Dr. Dolessenbee," the queen said. "I do not need your help."

"Where is King Winston?"

"He has returned from Yorkshire. He is at the castle preparing a cell for Darthius. I have come to collect him."

Two Malificious dragged Darthius onto the pond's banks.

"Good day, Dr. Dolessenbee. I think your visit is over." She progressed toward her beckoning sprites, then stopped and faced him again. "Oh, one good thing Lord Darthius did do was burst your bubble." She laughed. "The supernatural shall reign over the human world once again. It's just a matter of time—no pun intended—until the wave of humanity's nineteenth century rolls out, once again, across this land."

"You were wrong."

She stopped with her back to him. "Pardon?" Her sprites proceeded to gather a dragon for her to board.

"You are wrong about humanity. They believe. They can be the force you seek—to right the world."

She moved toward her ride. "The mid-nineteenth century is returning across the land. We shall right their American Civil War and their slavery."

Dol opened his mouth to say something but remained quiet.

"The Emancipation. The Industrial Revolution." She turned, by the head of the snorting dragon, and faced him. "Mankind's fall from evil began then. Their understanding of science, evolution. We shall fix that, Dr. Dolessenbee. They served us better when they were stupid."

She boarded while a team of knights pinned Darthius onto the horns of another Malificious, and the fleet took flight.

Part Five

Species

CHAPTER THIRTY-FOUR

Kiba

MAT AND TRINITY HELD Mitsy's hands while Bence took charge of the baby's delivery.

To their right, along the forest's burning edges, Bingham paced while he waited for Elio and Heel's return. He stopped occasionally to talk with Dol who comforted him.

Mitsy's blood pooled at Bence's knees. "Push, Mitsy! Push!"

The she-wolf's face was pale and her voice weak. "I can't. I can't."

"You can. Your baby's coming," Bence directed. "Your baby boy needs you. You can do this."

She screamed through a push and squeezed Mat and Trinity's hands hard.

More blood soaked Bence's pants. "He's got a good head of hair."

Trinity smiled. "C'mon, Mits. You got this."

Dol came over and knelt beside Bence. They worked together to extract the baby and exchanged a stint of whispers that broke with a collective nod.

Mat shrugged when Trinity looked to him for information.

Mitsy screamed through another contraction. Bence and Dol aided the baby out farther.

"Mitsy, you've got a special one," Dol said.

"Special?" Mitsy muttered. Her body trembled.

"He's a dawdler," Bence said.

Mat and Trinity shrugged. "Dawdler?" Trinity asked before Mat could.

"One more push Mitsy," Bence said.

Mitsy closed her eyes, her head lolled sideward.

Mat tapped her cheek. "Mitsy? She's going out again."

"Mitsy, one more time, hun," Trinity said.

"A dawdler," Dol said, "is a shifter who's born as a cub rather than in their human-like form."

"They're rather rare," Bence said. "Most tend not to shift and remain canine."

"Not always. I've seen some learn," Dol added.

Bence glanced up at Mitsy. "One more time, Mits. C'mon."

Mat brushed back her hair. "You can do it."

Mitsy opened her eyes. "Is he . . . ?"

Bence stared at Mat and smiled. "He's doing great. One more time."

Mat squeezed Mitsy's hand, and she pushed.

"That's it. That's it!" Bence shouted over cries of agony. "Keep it up." A puppy's whelp mixed with Mitsy's labored breath. After a few moments, Bence held up the newborn that resembled a German Shephard or a Black Labrador. An umbilical cord dangled from its belly, and Dol severed it with a buck knife.

More blood hemorrhaged from Mitsy. Bence placed the baby on her chest. Concern wrought his and Dol's faces.

"Kiba," Mitsy muttered. She kissed the placenta-covered pup. "You're my Kiba."

"Dads!" Bingham shouted at the pond's edge, as the dragons emerged from the forest. They and Bingham trotted over.

"It's . . . i-i-it's a-a-a pu-pu-ppy?" Bingham asked on approach. "He k-k-kinda looks like me."

"He's a dawdler." Dol placed a hand on the boy. "It's a special type of shifter, similar to you. Born already shifted."

Bingham lowered.

Mitsy held the pup as best she could while Trinity kept a hand on it for support. "Kiba," Mitsy said. "Please call him Kiba." Her eyelids drooped.

"Mitsy?" Trinity said.

Mat brushed back her hair again. "Stay with us, Mits. Mits?"

Her eyes fluttered. "Thank you, all." She swallowed. "Bence. I . . . I . . . I mostly . . . thank you. If it weren't for you—" She fought back tears. "I'm so sorry."

"Shhh." Bence had moved to her side, next to Mat, and he patted her wrist. "That's behind us. What's important is you have a healthy, newborn child."

She coughed. Scarlett billows wet the ground. Her eyes rolled back.

"Mits!" Trinity shouted.

Bingham cried. "Can't we do-do something?"

Paranormals crept out from behind rocks and boulders.

Dol fiddled with his wand. "I can't. I'm not powerful and, even if I were, I can't stop death."

Mat and Trinity rose and swatted at the paranormals, but it did little good.

Heel shot out a flame, and they scurried.

"She's gone," Bence said. His voice choked. He handed the baby to Bingham who took it to Elio.

Bingham swaddled Kiba. "Dad, I think we might need to st-st-step in," he said to Elio, who was smiling at the cub.

While Heel fought back the ghosts nipping at Mitsy's soul, Bingham nursed Kiba, and the rest dug a hole to bury her in the ground.

Trinity crafted a cross using twigs nearby and set it on the mound.

Then, they all knelt and prayed.

Chapter Thirty-Five

Fall-Front Trousers

T HE SUN GRACED THE treetops, and an afternoon breeze bit the air. Mat removed his coat and offered it to Bence who'd just finished washing in the lake.

The quilted baseball jacket covered the crotch of Bence's damp boxers—the only other garment he wore. Their blue edging was exposed below the coat's hem. "Thanks." He rubbed his hands together for warmth. "We've got extra supplies stashed in the forest. A wolf-shifter's accustomed to needing clothes in a pinch." He started to walk away. "I'll go get them. Come with?"

"Yeah!" Mat cleared his throat, afraid his zeal proved too revealing of his desire to be alone with him.

They wandered off into the sunlight dappled forest. As they progressed, Bence held back branches to avoid Mat being slapped with them.

"You were pretty amazing back there." Mat's hand grazed Bence's on a bent-back bough of a maple.

Bence waved off the comment. His bare feet seemed surprisingly immune to the pinecones, sticks, and gravel littering the forest floor. The acrid scent of the fire that had swept through hung in the air.

"No, really," Mat said, adding to the soft crunch of their stroll. "I was impressed." As Bence hiked forward, the flexing of his muscular wolf-shifter calves roused Mat's attention. "You . . . you should consider medical school . . . again."

Bence shrugged, then pointed to a small lean-to up and off the ground that was nailed to the trunk of a maple tree. "There's the supply box. We've got them scattered throughout the forest. We'll get some blankets and clothes and bring them back to the group."

When they approached the contraption, Bence unlatched its wooden joggle. "Hm." A small set of doors creaked open. Bence peered inside. "Holy shit." He pulled out some clothes.

"'s matter?"

He picked through the garments. "It's like it's the 1800s again." He held up a pair of khaki trousers with a buttoned flap in front. "The stash's replaced with nineteenth-century stuff."

"Darthius pushed back time. The queen was telling Dol about it. Apparently, they want to change the outcome of the American Civil War."

Bence, who had his head buried in the box, popped back out. "That's when Supers believe mankind shifted away from evil."

Mat shook his head. "I doubt it. Dol seemed surprised by it too."

Bence removed the loaned jacket and tossed it to Mat.

Mat caught it and put it on. Bence's musky scent lingered on the jacket's fabric.

Bence shucked his boxers and cupped his genitals. "A little chilly wearing damp underwear. I guess it's commando going forward."

Mat turned away, scratched an imaginary itch on his nape, then peered over his shoulder.

Bence stood with his back to him. His taut glutes were graced with tufts of blond hair. The shifter stepped into the trousers. When he turned around, he caught Mat's eye and grinned.

Bence buttoned the pants' front flap. "They're called fall-fronts. Traditionalists wore them, even in contemporary times." He drew out a forest-green pullover from the box and put it on. His chest hair stuck out from the shirt's embroidered placket. He grabbed a couple of gray woolen blankets and handed them to Mat.

"Ready?"

Mat swallowed. The blond boy looked even more attractive in his historical attire. "You look pretty amazing." The words fell out before he could filter them.

Bence's posture stiffened. He licked his lips, then grinned. "You look pretty amazing yourself."

Mat's heart thudded so loud he feared Bence could hear it.

They inched closer.

Mat inhaled the wolf-shifter's spicy aroma as the man neared, and he closed his eyes. Bence's warm breath graced his face.

"Bence! Mat!" Trinity's voice echoed. "Guys?"

"Yeah. Over here!" Bence yelled. He stepped away, closed the supply box's doors, and secured its dowel.

Trinity emerged through a tangle of branches.

"We . . . we . . . were just getting supplies." Mat dropped the edge of the blanket to cover his arousal.

"Fragrance," she huffed. "She's found Diesel. We need to go."

CHAPTER THIRTY-SIX

Dickens

IESEL WHELPED AND MORPHED back into a man. The agony of shifting—bone crunching pain—was nothing compared to the metal rods pinned through his paws, which now turned to hands. He screamed, and while he felt his vocal cords stretch and the vibration of sound in his chest and throat, he couldn't hear it.

Fastened to the cave's wall, as if crucified, he bled. The torches alongside him lit the chamber where he and Bence used to wander—deep below Elio and Heel's lair—through passageways too small for the dragons to wedge down. Jezebel—delirious and red-eyed—slashed him with another round from her electrified whip. The pain from each lash surged through to his core until he no longer felt it, and his essence lifted.

A ghast of a man carrying his own severed head by the hair approached. His neck nodded, and his face, at his knees, smiled widely. He held up the decapitated head, as if to inspect Diesel closer and sniffed.

The room spun. A wave of nausea, then Diesel vomited on the beheaded being.

Jezebel's head bent back, mouth agape. He couldn't hear her cackle but knew it nonetheless, for she had been raving with delirium with it since she had captured him—forcing him to shift, threatening him with Darthius's return to seize the last of his soul, and finally pinning him to the wall with witch spikes.

"No!" she mouthed and whipped the paranormal, who dropped his own head, scurried off, and left it behind rolling at Diesel's fastened feet.

The amputated skull bounced, flailed, and snapped for Diesel's feet. When it latched onto his big toe, Diesel felt awareness of himself leave his body.

In his F-150, Bence and he pulled up to the junkyard. He needed a fresh battery, as the charge they had received from the electric ogres would only last so long, and the vampires had brought in fresh supplies in a recent kill.

The littered yard contained a cluster of discarded contemporary items—laptops, cell phones, cars, clothes, and more—to pilfer.

"It's a veritable twenty-first century smorgasbord," Bence said.

Diesel opened the hood to a late-model Chevy and unhitched its battery. "See if you can find some new magazines and clothes. I hate wearing these woolen pants. They're hot and itchy."

Bence wedged up behind him, ran his hands around his waist and up to his chest. "Why don't we take them off and have some fun while no one's around?"

Having recently returned from London for Harvest Moon Break, they sported their school uniforms—gray woolen shorts; long, white socks; penny loafers; and starched, white shirts with embroidered etchings of Hubbardston School's logo. Their blue blazers lay cast in a heap in the bed of the F-150, outside the wrought-iron gates.

The Chevy rocked with the force of their thrusts. When Diesel pulled out of the boy, they rested on the blanket Bence had gathered—set upon the truck's bed.

Bence opened his satchel. "You always get hungry after sex. I snatched a loaf from the assembly area's tent when we passed."

From Bence's bag, Diesel pulled out the textbook from their Advanced Shifting class and paged through it. "Bull crap." He tossed it aside.

"We have midterms when we get back. If you fail, you won't graduate."

"I don't want to study magic. It's bull—"

"It's our life!"

"Humans. That's what interests me. Metanormals are said to have the powers of the most advanced wizards."

Bence peered over his shoulder for fear of someone being in earshot. "Human beings are our enemy, Dee," he said in a lowered voice. "Have you been reading the banned scriptures again?"

Diesel picked up the textbook. "There's not one word about human beings in here. Don't believe all this dogma they teach us in school, Bence. It's all one-sided." He set it back in Bence's bag. "They never give us the big picture. Humans are spirit in flesh and bone."

"And we're not? We're flesh and blood too."

"We may be flesh and blood, but our spirits are manufactured through magic and held in totems. Maybe one day, we could be true spirits, like humans."

"You're reading that Dolessenbee crap again."

"It's not crap, Ben. Have you ever seen a human?"

"Just in the magazines you find from the junkyard. The ones the vampires discard."

"Well, I have. You can feel their spirit."

"That's why we're supposed to kill—"

"Don't give into crap. Supers just want to be the dominant power."

"This Rise, as they call it . . . they're supposed to overpower us. And the new ones, the mega . . ."

"Meta. The Metanormals." A buzz of excitement lit Diesel's core.

"Yeah, those things. They're rumored to be impervious to our spells."

Diesel shrugged. "Good. Teach us a lesson."

Bence cut a slice of bread with his knife. "You are way too radical for Hubbard Forest. No, not only Hubbard Forest, for the supernatural world."

Diesel's stomach growled in anticipation of the bread. "That's why I want to study Humanity." He rocketed up. The Chevy swayed. "I want to change the world!"

Bence tugged Diesel's penis, dangling before him.

"Ouch!"

"Get back down here and let me feed you."

"Feed me?" Diesel squatted.

Bence pushed him off balance, and Diesel landed on his rear. "Yes, I want to feed you. Especially one who wants to study Humanity. You'll starve to death. No one goes into Humanity anymore. You don't even need to pass lower school to get in."

"Good! Then I don't have to study the drivel they teach us." Diesel bit a chunk of bread out of Bence's hand. "Arrrgh. I'm ravenous!"

"You're sexy."

Diesel pshawed. "You're too good to me. You'll make a good husband one day."

Bence grinned. "Yours?"

Diesel scratched his jaw and took another bite the blond offered. "You don't want me."

Bence ate some too. "Oh, I do," he said through the food.

"You're a good man, Bence Derringer. Too good for me."

"You're the good man, Dan Diesel Cade. Believing in humanity. Seeing their good."

"Even though I won't make a living."

Bence picked crumbs off the blanket. "Can I ask you something?"

"a'course."

"Luke . . . Luke says you're using me."

Diesel rose onto his elbows.

Bence studied him for a moment. "He's says you're just a horny shifter who can't get it elsewhere and settles for me."

Diesel swallowed. He liked the sex—no, loved the sex!—but his heart didn't feel right with Bence. Yet this had been going on too long to break.

"I don't believe him," Bence added.

Diesel realized he had been holding his breath and exhaled.

"When you make love to me, I can feel it . . . here." The blond shifter placed a hand over his heart.

Diesel licked his lips. "I . . . I . . . I love you, Bence Derringer." He knew it wasn't completely untrue, for they had been friends since forever, and he did love him, like a brother. As was his habit, he caved into what others expected of him and kissed him.

Bence grinned in their lip lock. "I knew it."

"No! Tell him the truth." Diesel's head rested against the cave wall. "Don't lie to him anymore. Don't lead him on."

Jezebel snapped her whip and it split the severed head, still at his feet, in half. A blue, gelatinous cosmic material burst from it, and Diesel's hearing returned. Flames flickered, Jezebel snickered, and a pounding and scraping of rock sounded nearby.

"You think going to Salem and getting out of the forest will solve your problems," she lectured. "You're Supernatural. A human can never love you. A human and Supernatural living together? Sure, it's a sin in the 'scriptures,' but that's not really the problem." Jezebel moseyed over to the center of the room, continuing her harangue which had started long before her restraining him to the wall.

A wave of pain from his wounds surged, and his head lolled.

"Supernaturals are freaks outside this forest." She choked. "I know! I loved one." She wiped her nose with the back of her hand. "Do you know why Bingham is the way he is?"

Diesel raised his head. "Half human?"

She moved toward the hollow's exit. "I fell in love with a hunter from Bangor. When he found out I was a woman who turned into a wolf when she got mad. When he saw me turn into a she-wolf . . . he left me. Yet I was already with child. From the spell, my genetics had already altered from witch to shifter." She stood with her back to him by the egress.

Diesel thought of Trinity. "But . . . but she's already seen me shift. She wouldn't—"

Jezebel looked over her shoulder. "Oh, you just wait till human reality catches up with her. She's known you for . . . what? A week . . . at best?"

"Mat."

"Your other boyfriend too."

"He's not my other . . . boyfriend."

She peeked out into the corridor. "Darthius, where in Satan's evil name are—"

A Black child strolled in. She wore a wreath of fall leaves in her hair and a gauze dress with shimmering stripes of green, tangerine, yellow, and white. A belt of chrysanthemum cinched her waist, and a brown blouse covered her chest. She was chubby but took to the air effortlessly aided by the lift from enormous orange-and-yellow maple leaf wings along her thorax.

She hovered before Diesel and tapped his shoulder with a horn of cornucopia she held. Blue gel, like that from Head Flopper, poured out from his body.

"I am the spirit who was foretold to you." Her pitch was high and melodious.

Diesel felt sleepy. "There was . . . was nothing foretold to me," he mumbled.

"No? Did Jacob Marley not take the stage?" She looked over her batting wings.

"Huh?" Diesel forced through clouded thoughts.

"I am the Ghost of Harvest Moon Present. I believe you just met my predecessor unless he too got sidetracked in traffic along his way to the theatre." She tapped him again, this time on his left shoulder, and the chamber's walls closed in.

T HE CHUBBY GIRL, DRESSED like a fall-fest faerie, popped out into the cold night air beside Diesel. They stood atop a crumbled rock.

"What's going on?" he asked, noting his attire of denim, a New England Patriots' jersey, sneakers, and a baseball cap. He spotted Trinity, Dol, and Bence carrying rocks away from the cave. "Guys, over here!" He waved to them.

"They can't hear you," The Ghost of Harvest Moon Present said.

"Where am I? What is this? Some sort of mirage?"

"It is your present."

He ascended partway down the mountain of rock. "My present? As in a gift?"

"You could look at it like that, but actually you're *my* gift."

He stopped, hands on hips. "What are you?"

"I am the Ghost of Harvest—"

"Yeah, I get that part. But where did you come from?"

"On Earth, I was a slave, murdered by my master's son in 1849. I've been roaming the Earth, stuck here in Hubbard Forest trying to cross over, ever since. You're my chance at being set free."

"*I'm* your chance?"

She nodded.

"No pressure." He descended farther to meet his friends.

"I told you, they can't hear you."

"But I can hear them. What are they doing?" He caught sight of the dragons. "Heel! Elio!"

"I said they—"

"I know but . . ." He slipped on a rock but caught his balance.

Elio and Heel tunneled out rocks. Their paws bled, and a few claws were discarded by the mound, torn off in the process.

"What are they doing?"

"They're looking for you."

He stopped. "But I'm right . . . here."

"Your body is still in the cave's belly."

"Am I dead?"

"Not yet."

Trinity emerged from a rock wall and swaddled something in her arms. Her VW was parked beside a boulder. The engine sputtered.

"What is Trinity carrying?" Diesel asked.

"Your nephew, Kiba."

He spun around and faced her. "Kiba? Mitsy's baby? She had her child? When we played, as kids, she had a stuffed animal named Kiba." He fought back tears. "Spirit, where is she?"

"Come." She tapped his shoulder with her magic cornucopia, and they rose into the air.

Bingham came into view and carried a rock away from the hole where they dug.

"Bingham! He's alive." Diesel yelled.

"For now."

"What do you mean, for now? And what of my sister? Even though she's not flesh and blood she is still—"

The ghost pointed to a mound on the other side of the cave. A cross made of twigs stuck out from the head of the grave.

"Mitsy," he cried.

"Come. We haven't time." She tapped his shoulder again, and they whisked northward. The forest rushed below them. Night was falling, and gas lamps lit the village. Diesel recognized the vampire huts, and the castle in the distance.

CHAPTER THIRTY-SEVEN

Present

MAT DROPPED A ROCK by the pile of others and rested up against the heap. "I'm exhausted."

"Just a little more," Trinity said. "Fragrance says just a few more yards till we break through."

"I can't believe we're listening to a dragonfly," Mat said.

Bence lowered a rock, much bigger than the one Mat had deposited. "Still don't believe in magic, big boy?"

Mat, more wanting to one-up the wolf-shifter and prove his manliness, rose. "I believe."

Fragrance shivered on Trinity's shoulder.

Dol placed a finger out for the dragonfly to hop onto. "Come here, cutie." He set her on the blanket Bence had retrieved from the supply station, then turned up the gas on the lantern beside it.

"Thanks, Doc," Trinity said.

Bingham kicked aside another claw ripped out from Heel's paw from the fervor of his digging. "We're going to need to find another home, Dad, aren't we?"

The dragon chirped back to the boy, and Bingham sighed.

Diesel and The Ghost of Harvest Moon Present charged through the air.

"We must get to the castle. The king's plan . . . you must see. Darthius has—"

He released his hand from hers, turned, and was surprised he could fly on his own.

"No. We must get to the castle. Darthius has escaped the holding cell King Winston made."

Diesel flew southward, and she rushed up beside him.

"Where are you going?" she asked.

"I'm being called back to the cave."

"By whom?"

"I don't know."

"What kind of call? Where do you feel it?"

He stopped. They hovered. He placed his hand over his heart. "Right here."

She beamed. "Your soulmate."

"Hm?"

She let him lead the way. "Love is the most powerful energy any living being—supernatural or human—can have. This is the power of the so-called Rise of the Normals. Humans have love. Supers squander it."

"But I am not human."

"No, but you love."

They returned to the cave.

"Is it her?" The Ghost of Harvest Moon Present pointed to Trinity. "Is she your soulmate calling you? Or is it him?" She pointed to Bence. "Then again, you've been with that one too." She aimed her head toward Mat.

Diesel rolled his eyes. "Listen. I don't need a lesson in monogamy from a little girl."

"I may be little, but I'm over 150 years old. I stopped counting after that, as it was too depressing."

Diesel, on his way over to the group, stopped and faced her. "I'm sorry. I appreciate all you're doing. I promise to help you get your wings."

She flapped the oversize maple leaves on her shoulders. "I already have them. This is a Dickens play, remember? Not *It's a Wonderful Life*."

He remembered his study of vintage film from Human Cultural Studies at UPS and smirked.

"Your study of humanity is critical to the Rise of the Normals, Mr. Diesel."

"You don't have to call me *mister*. And why am I so critical? Because I'm the bastard son of an addict who calls himself a wizard?"

"Partly, yes. You're the perfect mixture. You know of humans. You love them, especially one."

"Which one?"

The spirit shrugged. "That's up to you to determine. Seeing you've got two, plus a wolf-shifter."

"Enough about my polygamy. I get it. I'm just a randy dog."

The spirit and Diesel watched Bence, Trinity, and Mat who continued unfazed by their presence.

Bence turned to Mat. "You and Diesel? You guys . . . did it?"

Trinity stepped between them. "Oh, I'm sorry. I thought you knew."

"Diesel and I go way back," Bence said. "Long before you came around." He shoved Mat in the chest.

Diesel scurried over. "Guys, wait! Please."

The Ghost of Harvest Moon Present shook her head. "They can't hear—"

"Shh!" Trinity said with a hand to her heart. "Did you all hear that?"

"What?" Bence and Mat said.

She shook her head. "Never mind. It's nothing. Let's get back to work before it's too late."

"I think Bence and Mat should be together," Diesel told the ghost.

"They should, but you've interfered."

"I've ruined it. For good?"

"Come." The ghost tapped Diesel's shoulder. "We must go."

Before long, they settled atop the castle's spire and took to the stairwell, which led them into the vestibule. Next, they rushed down another set, which brought them to the basement.

Beside an open jail cell, Darthius towered over King Samuel Winston, a stout man, dressed in an all-white suit.

Black blood dripped from Darthius's snout and oozed through holes in his chest. Stains, the color of his charcoal suit, spotted his white dress shirt.

King Samuel Winston, with his back to him, scratched his white, Van Dyke beard. "If I join forces with you, I shall rule humanity?"

Darthius slithered out his forked tongue. "Indeed." He grinned.

"And it is just her you want?"

Darthius nodded.

"Who?" Diesel whispered to the spirit-ghost. "Who are they talking about?"

The girl shushed him.

The king put out his hand to the daemon. "Deal!"

The Ghost of Harvest Moon Present grabbed Diesel's hand, and they whisked away. Shortly, they landed in a school room. The spirit sat atop a desk in the back beside Diesel, who was crammed into a small, wood-and-metal apparatus to her left.

"Maybe I should sit on top too." He winced as his knee caught on the underside of the desk, and his belly pressed against the writing area.

"Shh." The spirit pointed, and Trinity pushed a child in a wheelchair through the door.

"This is Trinity's classroom," Diesel said. "She's a teacher."

The ghost rolled her eyes. "You're very smart."

Another woman brought in some more children, while others walked in on their own accord.

After settling in for a time, they all listened intently, as Trinity instructed them about the math lesson on the chalkboard.

"What did I tell you, Timmy," Trinity said to a boy who marked frustration at the assignment.

"That I can do it," the boy mumbled.

"What was that?" Trinity held a hand to her ear. "I can barely hear you."

"I can do it," he repeated a bit louder.

"You can do better than that. Kids? Let me hear you."

"We can do it," the class shouted.

"That's right. You can do whatever you put your mind to. Each and every one of you has the capacity to change your world."

The door creaked open. A curmudgeon of a woman stepped in. "Ms. Hawkins, a word please."

Trinity returned the chalk she held to the tray and pointed to her aide. "Sarah, run them through their multiplication tables."

Diesel popped out from his too-small desk and rushed to the door. It closed behind him, but The Ghost of Harvest Moon Present glided through it nonetheless. "Pretty cool," he said to her.

The ghost pointed her chin to the conversation occurring between Trinity and a woman that Trinity addressed as Mrs. Doobie.

"I'm not filling their heads with false promises," Trinity argued over her protest.

She handed Trinity a slip of paper. "I'm sorry. I have to place you on leave. There have been too many warnings, Ms. Hawkins."

Trinity gazed at the paper. "But . . . but the children." She slipped the notice in the back of her jeans pocket.

"Spirit, is this happening now?" Diesel asked. "I thought she was at the cave. Aren't you the Ghost of Harvest Moon Present?

"Relative present. This happened last week and is one of the reasons Trinity was able to come to see Mat early."

Diesel followed Trinity and Mrs. Doobie back into the class where she began packing her things. Mrs. Doobie, the squat woman dressed in green, informed the class that she would take over for the remainder of the week.

The children groaned.

"Trinity doesn't want to bother Mat," the ghost touched Diesel's shoulder. "He's been through enough, according to her."

They sped through the air.

"Where are we going now?"

"Back to the forest."

"What am I to do with all of this information?"

"That is up to you, Dan Diesel Cade. You have one more visitor."

"The Ghost of Harvest Moon Yet to Come?"

She nodded.

"What about you?"

"If you take the right course, I shall be freed."

"No pressure. I suppose you're not going to tell me what that 'right course' is?"

She deposited him in a dark forest with dead trees. "Till we meet again." She vanished.

"Spirit? Where are you? Where did you—"

Beside him, a leafless tree came to life. Frayed, black robes dangled from its limbs and flapped in a gust of wind that lifted Diesel's ball cap. He held it down. "Am I in the presence of the Ghost of Harvest Moon Yet to Come?"

The faceless creature didn't answer.

"Spirit of the future, I have feared you most of all."

Chapter Thirty-Eight

Salem

The photograph of Bence and Diesel shirtless, about to dive into the water sat framed on the mantle of a fireplace. Ornate woodwork trimmed the hearth.

"Where are we?" Diesel asked The Ghost of Harvest Moon Yet to Come, who consumed the room's only couch with his head grazing the ceiling. When he didn't answer, Diesel went to the window beside a television set and pulled back the navy-blue drapes. Automobiles lined the street and brick sidewalks. "Is this Salem? Did we make it to Salem?"

The front door opened. Bence walked in carrying a bag of groceries and a cell phone wedged between his shoulder and ear. He closed the door and tossed his keys into a wooden bowl atop a white sofa table.

"Bence!" Diesel went to him.

"I just got in," Bence said into the phone and walked right through Diesel.

"Bence?" Diesel followed him into the kitchen—a modest room with linoleum floors, gray walls, and white cabinetry.

"When you finish your shift, pick up some beer," Bence said, "and meet us at Winter Island."

"Who's he talking too?" Diesel asked the ghost who had to bend at the waist to fit into the room.

The ghost nudged his head in Bence's direction.

"All right, Dee. See you in a bit."

"Me! He's talking to me? We're in Salem together?" Diesel beamed. "Yeah, yeah. I'll pick up some brewskis, Bence ol' pal," he said, as if he were on the other end of the phone.

Bence hung up.

"We make it? We make it to Salem after all. This is my future. It's not so—"

The ghost pointed the spindly branch of his arm to the room across from the kitchen. Its door creaked opened.

Diesel swallowed; fear raked his core.

A woman, tall with dark hair, and wearing a red swimsuit emerged. "I thought I heard you come in."

"Patti the she-wolf?" Diesel faced the spirit. "What's she doing in Salem?"

The Ghost of Harvest Moon Yet to Come's shoulders sagged in frustration from Diesel's constant questions.

When Diesel turned around again, Patti and Bence were kissing.

Diesel blinked. "Bence? Since when do you like she-wolves? Something's up."

The ghost touched a stick finger to his shoulder. Next, they stood on the beach.

Bence, shirtless and in a blue bathing suit, volleyed a ball over the net.

"Ketch?" Diesel said, recognizing the vampires on the opposite end. "Pedro? I don't get it. Why—?" Diesel asked.

The Ghost of Harvest Moon Yet to Come placed a branch-of-a-hand to his hood and shook his hollow head.

"What are they all doing in Salem? I know. I know. You don't talk."

Patti placed a hand in Bence's back pocket. "Where's Diesel with the beer?"

"He and Jezebel should be coming along any minute," Ketch said.

"Me and . . . and Jezebel?"

An F-150 pulled into the lot, and Diesel gulped, fearing the sight of himself in the future.

The Ghost of Harvest Moon Yet to Come leaned against a sign. His branches rustled as he silently giggled.

"You think this is funny. What's the point of all this?" Diesel pushed the spirit in the trunk of his chest, and it stepped aside revealing the signpost, which he had covered.

City of Salem.

Per order of King Samuel Winston, under section 13.666 of the Winter Island by-laws, this swimming area is reserved for the sole use of Supernatural beings. No humans allowed!

Diesel kicked the sign's pole, but his foot went through it. "This is bull crap. This can't be."

He caught of whiff of human in the air and followed it to the opposite end of the beach. A rope divided it. "They have their own side?"

The Ghost of Harvest Moon Yet to Come ran after him—robes flowing, branches snapping.

Diesel ducked underneath the divider.

On the rocky beach, people argued. Their misery was palpable, yet it wasn't excluded to their segregation from supers. Their blatant infighting marred their souls and resonated in Diesel's heart.

He walked over to a sign at their area's entrance:

City of Salem.

Per order of King Samuel Winston, under section 13.666.1 of the Winter Island by-laws, this swimming area is reserved for the sole use of white humans only.

Diesel trembled, and he stopped himself from screaming. "They've reversed the American Civil War. Specter, am I too late?"

The doors to the F-150 opened and a man slid out, wearing prison-striped board shorts and a matching top. Even from afar, his red skin was apparent.

"Darthius?"

Jezebel slammed the passenger door and yelled, "Diesel, your driving skills are deplorable!"

"Me? That's me?"

As his future-self approached, the curled horns atop his head became apparent—not a cap he originally took them to be. "No! I have merged with Darthius!"

He fell to his knees before the Ghost of Harvest Moon Yet to Come. "Specter! Am I too late? I am not the man I was earlier. I will not be the magical being I was before our interlude. I have changed." Diesel tugged at the ghost's robes. "Are we passed all hope?" He sobbed. "Spirit! Answer me!"

The ghost's branches shook, and his robes billowed.

The beach scene went dark, and Diesel's eyes stung. "Spirit?' He blinked. "Specter, where am I?"

Light filtered through his eyelids, and he blinked again. Dust crystals rained down onto him.

A thud occurred to his right. The chamber came into focus with its torch lights flickering.

A stalactite fell to the floor. Then another. A fissure in the ceiling cracked open.

"Darthius?" Jezebel said, looking up.

The gap in the ceiling grew, and rocks tumbled to the ground. Sunlight shone through.

"Diesel?" He recognized Bence's voice, then Bingham's calling out for him. Mat's followed.

Trinity emerged through the chasm, lowered by a rope.

CHAPTER THIRTY-NINE

Breakthrough

WITH THE YELLOW ROPE tied to the bumper of Trinity's Beetle, Mat and Dol lowered her into the cavern—now that the hole was wide enough for someone to fit.

"Darthius wants to change the course of human nature," Dol said. "He's started by reversing time, bringing us back to before the American Civil War to do so, he wants to stop publication of *Uncle Tom's Cabin*."

Mat loosened his grip on the tug. "Harriet Beecher Stowe's novel that was published in 1851. I know the book. I know it well. Every American does. It would be horrific. If he changes history, the plight of my people . . ." Mat couldn't finish the sentence, the thought too disturbing.

"All people. The plight of all people would be at stake," Dol added. "Not just your race."

"Darthius believes that's where humanity went right . . . or wrong . . . depending on how you look at it. He is manipulative. I fear King Winston will be duped by him. This cage the queen mentioned." Dol shook his head. "Samuel and I have a long history. He's not the brightest bulb on the planet."

"But he's king."

"Since when do politics and smarts go hand and hand?"

"Good point."

"Darthius will roam around, soaking up powers as long as he can. He sucked in Buck's . . . or rather Honoree I's . . . essence, but that only got him so far."

"But he got Diesel's."

"Not all of it. He needs the most important part."

"What's that?"

"The energy remains in Diesel's heart. Tapping into that, he'll fuse with his form and have the power of a great wizard. And being the creator of all evil, he'll know how to use Diesel's powers."

"Unlike Dee."

"Precisely. Diesel is too young. He still has centuries to hone his skills."

Bence approached. "Hey, Doc. You think you could take a look at the dragons? They're pretty banged up from digging." He grabbed the rope, and Dol left.

Mat filled Bence in on the situation below. "She's talking to Jezebel, right now."

Bence sighed. "Look, Mat. I'm sorry about earlier. About Diesel. If you and he—"

"We're not . . . an item. He's not for me."

"No?"

"No. In fact, I think he and Trinity . . ."

Bence's mouth opened, and he chuckled. "You think?"

Mat nodded.

"What about you?" Bence asked.

Mat stared at him. "I have my eye on someone."

Bence smiled. "I do too."

"Guys!" Trinity yelled from below. "More lead."

They lowered the rope farther down. "You got him?" Bence asked her.

"He's hurting, but he'll be okay. I've hogged tied her!" she yelled.

"Jezebel?" Mat asked.

"No, Queen Victoria! Of course, Jezebel. Who do you think?"

Mat gazed at Bence. "I thought our powers were waning over the Supers. That's what Darthius told me."

"Don't believe Darthius. It's all a mind game with him."

Trinity yanked the rope. "Coming up."

The boys tugged.

The ground rumbled.

Dr. Dolessenbee ran over. "What's going on?"

Bingham followed.

The hole enlarged.

"It's ca-ca-caving in!" Bingham yelled. "Wa-watch out!"

Mat found himself sliding down a cascade of rock steps. Bence and he descended until they reached the bottom.

Jezebel was immobilized with her hands and feet tied together. She mumbled through cloth covering her mouth, which Mat recognized as a piece of Trinity's shirt.

Diesel lay prostrate on the ground, readied to be hoisted up by a rope around his midsection. Blood covered his hands and feet.

"He was spiked to the wall." Trinity snapped a whip. "I made her take him down. I can't believe I saved you," she said to the witch." I should've let you die when I had the chance."

Dol stood atop the heap of rock which had created a stairwell of sorts up to freedom. Bingham stepped out from behind the wizard, and when Jezebel caught sight of him, her eyes widened.

"Jezebel!" Bingham shouted. "Heal my friend Diesel. F-f-fix his wounds."

Jezebel trembled.

Trinity staked the tip of the whip into her beltline. "That's right, bitch. Your son is alive."

"I am n-n-not her son," Bingham said.

Tears formed in the corner of Jezebel's eyes.

"Fix him," Bingham repeated.

"You heard the boy," Trinity said.

Jezebel gazed down at her hogties.

Trinity snatched the electric whip, tied it around Jezebel's neck, and motioned for Mat to loosen her limbs.

As Mat untied her, Jezebel mumbled. Trinity removed the gag but tightened the whip's hold.

The witch sighed. "What have I done?"

"A shit ton," Trinity said. "You heard Bingham. Now undo your damage."

Jezebel recited a spell, and the punctures on Diesel's hands and feet vanished.

The ground rumbled again. Dol and Bingham stepped off the tower of rock and out of view. A few rocks cascaded down and landed in front of Mat's feet.

"Uh oh," Dr. Dolessenbee said.

"Uh oh, what?" Mat asked.

A cyclone descended the rocks, and dust filled the chamber. A slow hiss followed, and thousands of snake heads slithered out from the cloud as Darthius—smaller than before—emerged. He held up the severed head of The White Queen. "My Lady, you now reign over this land." He rolled the head over to Jezebel, and it stopped at her feet. "You and King Winston shall have the Americas. I will overtake Great Britain and Europe."

Jezebel trembled, then fell to the ground laughing hysterically.

With a flick of his wrist, Darthius hoisted Diesel into the air. "You are mine. I am you." He slammed into him, and they disappeared.

D OL SCURRIED DOWN THE rock mound, tripped, and slid in an avalanche of rock until he landed at the bottom of the pile. "Diesel," he mumbled. "My son." His voice choked, and he lowered his head with his hands dangling on his knees

Bingham scooted down on his rump.

Elio peered from the hole above and chirped at him to, no doubt, be careful. Heel lowered his tail for his son to hold, but Bingham chose to trudge down the rest of the way unaided.

"I don't have that kind of power here," Dol said, still sitting at the base of the mound. "Not yet."

Jezebel, with loosened ties dangling from her hands and feet, stared at The White Queen's severed head. Blood pooled into the dirt floor where the neck oozed. Jezebel's eyes were wide with delirium.

Trinity rushed her and looped the whip back around her neck, which she had loosened in the chaos of Darthius's entry and exit.

Jezebel didn't flinch. Her eyes remained trained on the head.

"We should kill her," Bence said. "It's all her fault."

Dol cried, and Bingham comforted him, squatting beside him.

"I . . . I am . . ." Jezebel whispered.

Trinity loosened the noose.

Jezebel blinked. "I . . . I shall . . ."

Mat cocked his head.

She rose onto her knees. "I am . . ." A tear streaked her dirty face. "I am so . . . I am so the queen!" She burst upward. "I reign over Hubbard Forest . . . and the Americas!" She grasped the White Queen's head by the hair and lifted it into the air.

The whip around her neck snapped.

"No!" Trinity yelled.

A smirk tugged at the edges of Jezebel's lips. She snapped her fingers and vanished.

Dol crawled over to the spot she vacated. His hands slid in the White Queen's blood. "This is bad. This is very bad."

Mat caught Bence's gaze. "What . . . what do we do?"

Dol removed his timepiece from his vest's pocket. "Trying to control leads to ruin. It always does. I should know better." His face crumpled with anger. "Trying to grasp, we lose." He closed his eyes and inhaled softly. "There is a time for vigor. There is a time for rest." He pocketed his watch.

CHAPTER FORTY

Totem II

Diesel collapsed onto a hardwood floor. Oriental rugs, thick green drapes, and Victorian trappings surrounded him. "Trinity's family's place?"

At the stairwell, The Ghost of Harvest Moon Present popped into view. Her large, fall-colored maple-leaf wings flapped, and the dragonfly—Ginny Fragrance—flew beside her.

"You two? What's going on?" Diesel asked.

"We weren't quite done," the ghost said.

"But I already saw the Ghost of Harvest Moon Yet—"

"We're going off script," she said when the front door blew off its hinges, and Darthius's cyclone whirled in.

Gas lamps burst. Vases smashed. Curtains ripped from the windows in the chaos, and furniture spun into the air crashing through walls. The room caught fire.

The ghost and Ginny flew upstairs, and Diesel followed.

On the second-floor landing, they rushed down the hall and went into the last of many bedchambers. The spirit slammed the door behind them, and Ginny Fragrance hovered nearby. The cacophony from Darthius's chaos softened.

"I forgot to tell you one thing," The Ghost of Harvest Moon Present said.

Diesel caught his breath. "What?"

To his right, a closet door creaked open. Diesel grabbed a pitcher from the washbasin to clobber the intruder. But when the boy came out, he lowered it. "Tobias?" he said.

The roar of the whirlwind in the hall grew louder, as Darthius apparently checked the chambers for them.

"Sister," Tobias said to The Ghost of Harvest Moon Present.

She ran to him. "Tobias! You made it."

After they embraced, Tobias sped to Diesel. At which point, Diesel realized the boy's quick moves could only be that of a spirit. "You're . . . you're a paranormal too? Did. You. Die?"

"I was dead when I met you."

Diesel blinked. "Oh."

"Quick. We haven't time," he said over the thunder of Darthius's approach. "We need you to escape to the North."

"You must remain steadfast to what you love," the spirit, his sister, said.

"What I love. Why? What are you talking about?"

"It's important!" she shouted over the rumble of the cyclone.

"Important?" Diesel pointed to the buzzing dragonfly. "What's the connection between y'all?"

"We all need to cross over."

"And I suppose I'm the salvation." He recognized he was wearing his New England Patriots' jersey and jeans.

"We'd rather not see you naked," the ghost said to his look of surprise. "You like?"

Diesel nodded with narrowed eyes. "I love . . . it. What does love have to do with . . .?" Warmth radiated throughout his body. He couldn't contain his grin. "I love humanity. I love humans. People. I love everything about them." He faced the spirit and Fragrance. "I love the way they look. The way they smell. Eat. Laugh and make love. I love their essence. The kindness that runs through to their cores. It makes me happy. I love it!"

The dragonfly nodded, and the Ghost of Harvest Moon Present giggled. "I think he's got this."

Tobias grinned. "Keep it up."

The door flung open. Splintered wood flew through the room. The spirits ducked.

"You called," Diesel said to the black cyclone.

The tornado slowed. Snake tongues flicked out from it, and Darthius stepped out. He was shorter than Diesel. His horns brittle and his back hunched.

"You don't look so hot," Diesel said.

"You think you can get away?" Darthius asked. "And use your fairies to set you free?"

Diesel held out his hands. "I am not hiding from you, Darthius. Come and get it."

"Your little girlfriends," Darthius nudged his head toward the ghost and dragonfly, "the little shit's snapped you from me just as I merged with your body in the cave."

"They did?" Diesel glimpsed them on the bed. "That explains it."

Darthius plucked a bluish gel from the air around Diesel's head.

"Ouch." Diesel hadn't known it was there but felt it being yanked out from his ear, nonetheless. He tottered and grimaced, as it slinked out from his head.

"Your aura." Darthius slurped the strand like spaghetti. "Ah. You like football. I can taste it." He licked his lips and tugged out another one. "I like eating what you like. It helps me become you."

Diesel winced from the daemon's stench. "Your breath smells of flatulence and rotten bowels."

Darthius laughed, and he harvested another cord from Diesel's glow. "Your spirit makes me strong. You're very yummy." He chewed. "Could use a little salt though." He licked his lips. "I can hardly wait to eat your heart and assume your powers." The vortex behind him intensified. "It shall make me ejaculate with delight."

"That's a pretty sight." Diesel swallowed.

The daemon plunged a fist through Diesel's gut.

Diesel gagged and clenched his stomach.

Darthius ripped out a large red orb from the shifter's core and consumed it readily. "The taste of unbridled, rough sex." He groaned again. "You are a horny little devil." He flung his head back in laughter. "What else do you like?" He punched a fist through Diesel's rib cage.

Diesel clutched his chest and coughed. The room spun. "I . . . like . . . life."

Darthius belched. A scent of rose wafted by.

"I love nature," Diesel added.

The daemon burped and aroma of cardamom and pine floated by.

"I love the milk of human kindness."

Darthius choked and vomited a thick white substance, and it poured out his nose.

"Yes! Yes!" Tobias shouted.

Diesel shoved Darthius back into the cyclone, but it spit him out and evaporated into a cloud of rain, soaking the floor.

"Wee!" the Ghost of Harvest Moon Present shouted as the bed floated and banged up against the wall. The dragonfly glided about. Tobias jumped on too.

"I love Metanormals," Diesel said.

Darthius heaved out Diesel's aura, blue gelatinous substances hurled into the air in a continuous flow from his mouth.

"I love Normals. I love their movies, their plays, their books. I love a human being's laughter. I love that human beings are rising and becoming more superior to Supers."

The daemon fell to the floor, and on all fours, crawled out into the hallway.

The Ghost of Harvest Moon Present splashed her way over to Diesel, and Fragrance buzzed beside him.

"Hey, Ghost of Harvest Moon Present, you know what I love?" Diesel asked.

She smiled. "What?"

"I love you! And I love Ginny Fragrance."

Darthius belched green bile. "Stop it!"

"You're human, Ghost of Harvest Moon Present. I love that about you. Tobias and Fragrance too. Even though you're all dead. Your spirits are beautiful and still human."

Darthius writhed, clutched his gut, and shit on the floor.

Diesel laughed. "I love Bingham too! Who is also part human!" The glow and intensity of his aura grew in his rampage of appreciation.

Darthius crawled down the stairs—farting, belching, and shitting with each step.

"I love! I love, love, love, love, love!" Diesel chased after Darthius. The daemon stumbled down the steps barfing and spewing more of Diesel's glow, as it appeared to grow within him.

"I appreciate how people care for one another." Diesel soft-shoed down the stairs. "I love people who help others! Hey, Ginny, isn't there a Carolyn Sohier song along those lines?" He scratched his head.

Darthius convulsed and tumbled down the remaining stairs. The fire still raged below, though it had been partly subdued by the cloud's release upstairs.

The Ghost of Harvest Moon Present handed Diesel his totem.

"What is this?" He held it up.

"Your tot—"

"I know what it is. It's my totem, but what am I supposed to do with this?" Diesel inspected it.

At the gaping hole left from the front door's demise, Dr. Dolessenbee emerged on the front porch. Trinity and Mat flanked him. Her Beetle idled on the front lawn.

The doctor pulled out his pocket watch and gazed at it. "Now!" He returned it to its pouch.

Mat and Trinity gazed at each other.

"Give it to me!" Dr. Dolessenbee said to Diesel.

Diesel grimaced. "What?"

"Your totem. Hand it to me."

Darthius rose onto his elbows.

Diesel kicked him. "I love humanity!" he shouted at the daemon, and more blue gel swirled.

Darthius seized and foamed at the mouth. The aura consumed the daemon, and his red sheen grew faint.

"People! I'm a people lover!" Diesel shouted at him. "I'm a humansexual and proud of it!"

Darthius gyrated and shuddered.

"I love humans! I love humanity! I love society. I love cats, dogs, animals, and even some supernatural beings." He winked at Dol.

Darthius's appearance grew paler.

Diesel held out his arms. "Love! Love! Love! Love! I love . . . I love Trinity Hawkins!"

Silence fell save for the swish of flames, and Darthius withered into an orange, red vapor.

Dr. Dolessenbee plunged into the air holding out Diesel's totem and landed on his belly with a harumph. Darthius's hazy vapor spiraled into the hollowed-out wolf's tooth with a vacuum-like force. Dol rolled onto his back and from his pocket, drew out a gold seal, and snapped it over the totem.

"Quick!" Mat shouted. "The fire!"

They rushed out into the yard as the house was engulfed with flames.

Elio and Heel scurried up from the road. Bingham sat on Heel's back, and Bence strode beside the dragons swaddling something at his chest.

Diesel hurried over to his friend. "Is that my nephew?"

Bence removed the cub from it swathe. "This is Mitsy's baby, Kiba."

"Yes, my nephew."

Bence handed the baby to him. "I heard you and Mitsy weren't actually blood."

"Family isn't about blood." Diesel kissed the cub's head.

Bence smiled. "Kiba, meet Uncle Diesel. Dee, meet your new nephew."

Diesel held the cub in the air. "He's beautiful. Is he a dawdler?"

Bence nodded.

"I love him. It doesn't matter who or what he is." Diesel kissed the cub's snout. "I love you, Kiba."

CHAPTER FORTY-ONE

Bells

THEY GATHERED NEAR THE road's edge and watched as the house burned before them. "Ginny!" Trinity yelled. "Fragrance." She lowered her head.

Diesel put his arm around her.

"My baby sister." She edged toward the house, but Diesel held her back and she acquiesced to his clutch. "Ginny."

Mat opened his arms. She went to him and cried more.

Bingham came over to Diesel. "Did you get r-r-rid of the mo-mo-monster?"

Diesel nodded. "You'll be okay, my friend." He swaddled Kiba who whelped. "We'll all be just fine."

"We've got n-n-o home," Bingham said.

"We'll find a new place. A better one. That ol' cave was getting kind of drafty and smelled of bat poo."

Bingham chuckled.

Diesel ruffled the boy's hair.

The Victorian's roof caved in. Mat insisted everyone move out onto the street, then got in Trinity's car and repositioned it on the road out of harm's way.

Dr. Dolessenbee approached Diesel, who stood by the rear of the Beetle.

Diesel acknowledged the doctor's presence with a head nod.

"Good job in there," Dol said.

"Nice dive bomb yourself, Doc."

Dr. Dolessenbee remained silent for a moment, then broke it with a clearing of his throat. "You know . . ." He looked down at his feet. "I'd love it if you called me *Dad*."

Diesel stared at his father. "It's . . . just all so new to me."

"Oh, I get it. I don't mean to pressure you."

"Okay."

Another portion of the house collapsed, and Trinity turned her back to it. Mat spoke to her about heading back to Elk.

"You said something in there." Dol pointed a thumb toward the house.

Diesel furrowed his brow. "I said a lot of—"

"Toward the end, just before I captured Darthius." He held up the totem and shook it some.

"What did I say?"

"In your tirade, you said you loved *some* supernatural beings." Dol cleared his throat again. "And you winked at me."

Diesel bit his lower lip. "I was just . . . just on a rampage."

Dol nodded slowly. "I . . . I kind of hoped it was the truth."

A bell rang from Dol's direction.

Diesel looked at him. "What was that?"

Dol removed his pocket watch. "It's almost time for me to leave." He clicked a button on the watch's side.

Bingham traipsed over. "Time for vigor, as you say? Or time for rest?" he asked the wizard.

"Time for action," Dol replied.

The timepiece chimed again. Then again.

Bingham smiled. "I once heard that when a b-b-bell rings, a spirit c-c-crosses over to the other side."

Diesel grinned. "I told you that."

Bingham held up his crooked paw and smiled. "Three bells."

"That means they all made it," Diesel said. "I think I know which spirits."

Bingham's eyes widened. "Is one of them G-G-Ginny Fragrance?"

Diesel nodded, and the boy ran over to Trinity and conveyed the news with enthusiasm. "She can now reunite with your parents," Bingham told her.

Trinity appeared comforted and told Bingham she was happy Ginny had fulfilled the mission that kept her locked on this side.

Dol opened the face of his timepiece. "You know, Daniel Cade, this isn't over." He closed it and returned it to his vest's watch pocket.

Diesel sighed. "Jezebel, right? She's got reign over the forest."

"King Winston and she will make, however odd, a very powerful pair. They'll reign over the Americas and without Darthius, probably overthrow Europe too. We need to do something."

"We?" Diesel shushed the baby who fussed.

"I'm afraid your job is not done, son."

Bence came over, took the baby from him, and returned to Mat's side. The two cooed at the cub and laughed, and Kiba stopped crying.

Dol resumed their conversation. "Darthius has reversed time."

"It's still mid-nineteenth century?"

Dol nodded. "I doubt it's reached too far outside the forest's borders. Time reversal, well, takes time, but needs to be contained, nonetheless. A change of course could not only be the Rise's ruin but humanity's demise."

"I saw it in my vision of the future. The Ghost of Harvest Moon Yet to Come showed me Salem as an apartheid state."

"We must act," Dol said.

"Again with the 'we.' I'm not sure I'm liking the sound of this."

"Darthius removed the protection barrier. Before I leave," he held up the totem, "to take care of him for good. We need to put up a new one."

"How?" Diesel asked. "You don't have your powers."

"Exactly."

"And I'm a nascent wizard who only knows how to turn into a wolf . . . and maybe a little psychic. What can I do?"

"Forgive me."

"Huh?"

"Look, I know I was an idiot, abandoning you as an infant. But together, we're very powerful. More so than Jezebel and Winston. With your forgiveness, my powers will be restored. I can return the veil over the community, and it'll contain the time shift to the forest. We can potentially save humanity."

"All I have to do is forgive you?"

"Yes, but it has to be sincere."

"Then, why did you leave me?"

Dol looked down. "Honestly? Because I was a fool."

"There's more to it than that."

"You were better off without me. I wanted you to live a good life. Elio and Heel could give that to you. I didn't bargain on Jezebel snatching you from them and raising you as a wolf-shifter. I thought you'd figure out your wizardry with the help of the dragons."

"Is that all?"

Dol sighed. "And I wanted magic. Keeping you meant I wouldn't have an inkling of power. Giving you up, King Winston gave me a wand."

Diesel studied him. "Okay. I believe you."

Dol smiled.

Diesel placed a hand on Dol's shoulder. "I forgive you . . . Dad."

A NEW VEIL GLISTENED over the smoldering Victorian, like a mid-day view of the aurora borealis. The late fall air hinted at the winter soon to come, and the group huddled together on the cobblestone sidewalk.

Dol held up the totem. "I will take this back to Phare du Petit Minou, France for safekeeping in my lab. With my powers back, I can recruit more Monitors to watch over, protect, and shepherd humans into their magic-hood."

"You sure things are contained here?" Trinity asked.

"No one can be sure, my dear."

"Well, now I know how my great-great grandparent's house burned down. Unfortunately, there's been no cabin to replace it, seeing we're stuck in 1850. Looks like I'll have to sell the house in Elk. If it's still there."

"I doubt the time spell has reached too far."

"Trin, no," Mat said. "That's your parents' house, your home, Chip's home. We'll figure out something."

Diesel went to Dol, who futzed with a portal he had arevealized. "I appreciate you showing me the value of magic. I shall work on my skills."

"If you need me, Son, just call." Dol handed him a cell phone. "I know you like technology."

"I didn't think there were cell towers in 1800s."

Dol chuckled with a jiggle to his belly. "Outside the forest, there are."

Diesel hugged him. "Thank you."

"After I leave through the portal, it will be set for Salem. It'll get you and Bence there safely."

Diesel nodded. "Will I see you again?"

The portal's light stopped flashing and streamed a steady, green ray. "That's up to you," Dol said. "Thank you, son." Dol faced the group. "And thank you all," he added, stepped in, and vanished in a haze of smoke.

A gust of wind caught the brim of Diesel's baseball cap, and he held it down at the crown.

When Dol's cloud cleared, the portal glowed red and orange. Diesel detached a note from the exterior's metallic covering.

Next stop, Salem, Massachusetts.

One-way for Bence Derringer and Daniel Diesel Cade.

"Now's our chance," Bence said. "The new veil won't allow us out otherwise."

Diesel recognized a weight in his back pocket and pulled out a wallet. "What's this?"

Bence pulled out one too and tore it open. "A Massachusetts drivers license." He flipped through scores of bills inside. "And a ton of money! We can start anew . . . as real humans!"

Diesel studied his too. "There must be over a thousand dollars in here." He held up a one-hundred-dollar bill. "We're legit citizens of the human world." He rummaged through it more. "And an American Express card!"

"Gold even." Bence held up his credit card. "Thanks, Dr. Dolessenbee!" he yelled into the portal's cavern. His voice echoed back.

"What's going on?" Mat said, meandering over. "What is that?" He pointed to the portal's note, as Diesel reattached it.

"It's our ticket out of here." Bence beamed.

"I see," Mat said, soberly.

"You and Trinity should be able to drive out on your own accord."

Mat nodded. "So, I guess this is it."

"This is just the beginning!" Bence said. He looked down at his clothes: fall-front trousers and a nineteenth-century blouse. "However, I can't go looking like this."

Diesel pointed to the floor of the portal's cavern. "There's more." Bence went to it and pulled out two duffel bags. He tossed the green one to Diesel and kept the blue one.

"He's thought of everything. Even knows our favorite colors." Bence pulled out a fresh pair of clothes and ducked behind the portal to dress.

With the rear lid open and engine sputtering, Trinity walked over from her car. She wiped grease off her hands with a rag. "What's all the fuss?"

"They're leaving," Mat said. "They're taking the portal to Salem. We can drive out. We'll have to use your car since mine is shit, and I can't even recall where in the hell it is."

"Once Dee and I are out of here, the four of us can connect!" Bence yelled from behind the portal. "Be friends. Go out for beers. Go bowling."

"Bowling?" Trinity said.

Shirtless, Bence poked his head around the corner. "Or go to Red Sox games at Fenway Park."

Trinity smiled. "I like baseball over candlepins."

"I like big balls," Diesel said, straight-faced. Silence fell as he stuffed the wallet to his pocket.

They all laughed.

Diesel's face flushed, he feared it matched the portal's red glow. "Big-ball bowling, that is. You know, the large, heavy ones you can grip by the . . . never mind." He chuckled.

CHAPTER FORTY-TWO

Heal

W HILE WAITING FOR THE portal's light to turn green, Diesel held his duffle bag by his side.

Bence rifled through his own and discovered more gifts from Dol—a timepiece like the wizard's, a book on witch spells, and a new amulet.

Mat and Trinity worked on the Beetle . . . something about the carburetor's idle.

To Diesel's right, at the end of the road, Heel and Elio spoke in coos and chirps. Beside them, Bingham held the baby.

Deciding to investigate further, Diesel unzipped his duffle. It was featherlight and less bulky than Bence's. In it, he found a manilla envelope and pulled it out. A note, written in cursive, was scratched on the front:

. . . or you could stay

Inside the envelope was paperwork for an assignment at NEPRC along with a book of passes stamped for travel in and out of any of the forest's tree portals.

The dragon's chirping grew louder, and Heel flew off and up over the tree line. Bingham set Kiba in a swathe around Elio's neck. Bingham shuffled over toward the group with his face somber. Elio limped behind him.

Trinity stepped closer to him. "What's going on Bing? Why the sad face?"

"My dad had to leave."

Trinity eyed Elio—limping over, walking gingerly on a still-injured paw. "He left without us getting a chance to say goodbye?" she said.

Diesel comforted Bingham with a shoulder hug. "An Emphilothepy is not very good with goodbyes," he said for Trinity's benefit.

"I can understand that," she said.

Bingham shuffled beside her. "My dad works for King Winston. They've summoned him to return to the castle for duty in Yorkshire."

"Yorkshire? England?" Trinity said. "I thought y'all couldn't leave the forest."

"There are tunnels under the castle that connect to other supernatural worlds," Diesel explained. "That's how Heel and Winston get to Europe."

Bingham looked up at Diesel. "NEPRC is going full force on stopping the Rise."

"The Rise . . . of the Normals?" Trinity asked. "Wh . . . what are they doing?"

"When Darthius broke the barriers, he released thousands of bats," Bingham said.

"And?" she asked.

"They're laced with a virus to kill humans."

"Kill humans." Trinity placed a hand to her chest.

Diesel's stomach soured. "That's why Darthius aligned with Winston." He shook his head. "The New England Paranormal Research Centre has been working to develop creatures that are superior to Metanormals for centuries."

"Centuries?" Trinity said.

"Now, it looks like they aim to slow humanity's evolution with an infection," Diesel added. He looked at the assignment he still held in hand. It appeared authentic, but something told him it was a forgery—like the one Dol had used to infiltrate the castle as a marksman.

"Dol said NEPRC was responsible for my parents' and Ginny's deaths," Trinity said. "This infection . . . I need to get to my brother."

"It's flashing green!" Bence yelled. "Dee, come on!"

ELIO HUNG HIS HEAD before Diesel. Mat swallowed a lump in his throat. He had enjoyed making new friends and wondered if they would all meet up as planned—or would it be just another one of those things you say in the moment but never comes to fruition.

"Oh, El," Diesel patted the tuft of red hair between the dragon's ears.

The dragon bawled. Tears showered over the group and puddled at his feet.

Mat stepped back to avoid getting wet.

"Dad!" Bingham shouted. "Your claws are growing back in the puddle." But it didn't faze Elio, and his sobbing continued.

The portal's light beckoned imminent departure with the pace of its green flash hastening. "We've got about two minutes, Dee," Bence said.

Mat took the chance and rushed over to Bence. "Uh, Bence."

"Hey, Mat." Bence smiled and held the portal's door open with his right hand and a blue duffle clutched in the other.

"Before you go . . . I just wanted to . . ." Mat pinched the bridge of his nose. "I want to let you know . . ."

Bence pressed his back against the door, reached out, and hooked his pinky finger around Mat's.

A sense of calm enveloped Mat, and he exhaled softly. "There's nothing really waiting for me back in California. Here, I need to help Trinity and Chip get settled some, but after that . . . maybe we can . . ." He hadn't asked someone out in a long time, and his heart thumped with anxiety. "Perhaps we can get a bite to eat for dinner in Salem . . . or take in a movie."

Bence's cheeks dimpled. "I'd like that."

Mat edged closer to him. The green flash beat rapidly, lighting Bence's face with a jade hue. Mat drew him even closer.

Bence's breath smelled of peppermint, and he kissed him.

Behind, the group cheered, and Elio cried louder.

WHILE MAT AND BENCE planned their meetup, Diesel approached Trinity, who slammed the Beetle's lid with a clatter.

"Need a hand?" he asked.

"Nope. I'm pretty proficient with this thing." She went over to the passenger door and opened it.

"So, you live not too far from here, don't you?"

She paused just about to open the glove box. "Yes."

"That was a stupid line," he said.

She sat down on the passenger seat with her legs dangling out. "I live in Elk, about an hour from here. There's a gas station not too far from the park's gates, if you're worried about us getting there."

"Nah. Uh. Yeah. Well, that's good, but what I was . . . What I wanted to say was . . ."

The green light flashed faster, encasing her car with its glow.

"One minute, Dee!" Bence shouted.

Diesel cleared his throat. "Maybe we can get together sometime. You know? Like a date or something?"

She drew her neck back. "You're asking me out?"

"Yeah, I know. It was a silly idea." He turned.

"I'd love to go out with you, Dan Diesel Cade."

He spun around and soaked in her smile. "For real?"

"For real." She opened the glove box and popped opened the front hood.

Diesel rushed to the portal. "Bence, I can't go!"

"What? Now's our only—"

"You go. Look, as a friend, I love you more than anything." He placed a hand on his shoulder. "You're my best friend, and I want you and Mat to have a good life. I have business to finish here. You don't need me. I need to look after Kiba, Bingham, and find a new home for Elio and Heel." He looked over his shoulder. "And some other things."

"But . . . you're always doing for others."

"This time's different. I want to do for others." He held up the NEPRC assignment.

"What's that?"

"I'm going undercover. NEPRC is creating a supernatural being that can kill Metanormals." That part of the assignment he knew was true. His gut told him so. "I want to fight the enemy. It's what I want to do."

"Will I ever see you again?"

"Of course." Diesel stepped out.

The portal's light turned a steady green. It buzzed, then vanished in a cloud of vapor.

Trinity screamed.

"What's wrong!" Mat yelled and ran to her.

She stood by the front of the Beetle's open hood and held up an unzipped yellow duffle bag by the strap. "There's . . . there's over a hundred thousand dollars in here."

Diesel hurried over.

She held a note with handwriting like that on Diesel's envelope. "It's remuneration for . . . for the loss of the cabin." Her mouth dropped, and she stared at Diesel and Mat. "The exact amount we were going to list it for." She rummaged through the bag and found another envelope. She handed it to Mat.

"It's . . . money to replace my RAV4," he said, rifling through the bills.

Mat laughed and hugged her, lifting her off the ground. The bag dropped, and Diesel picked it up, zipped it, and handed it back to her.

"Wait. What are you doing here?" Trinity said to Diesel. She eyed the spot where Bence and the portal had been. "You missed your chance out."

"I've got another chance. A chance to make a difference."

Trinity furrowed her brow.

"He's staying behind," Mat explained.

Bingham clasped his arms around Diesel's waist.

"But you . . ." Trinity cocked her head. "You always wanted out of here."

Diesel held up the passbook. "I can come and go as I please." He ruffled Bingham's hair. "Plus, help out this little man, a dragon couple, and my new nephew."

"That's really sweet. But I'm still holding you to the date." She winked.

CHAPTER FORTY-THREE

Home

ELIO HOVERED FAR ABOVE the forest. Before them, the new veil glistened.

Diesel clutched Kiba against his chest. Despite the cub being secured in the sling around his neck and back, being hundreds of feet in the air kicked in his paternal instincts.

Below, the Beetle's headlights lit the road and beamed at the forest's exit.

"They're almost out," Bingham said, sitting beside Diesel, strapped to one of Elio's bony protrusions.

"Aaaand . . . they . . . are . . . out!" Diesel pumped a fist in the air.

Behind the car, the barrier shimmered and sealed shut.

"They're going to be okay," Bingham said.

Diesel stared at him. "And so are you. So are we."

Elio chirped.

"All right, El, head west," Diesel said. "Let's find a place that suits our family just perfectly."

A burst of brilliant orange, blue, and purple colors canvassed the sky, and Elio flew toward it.

THE END

Want More Diesel?

I F YOU ENJOYED *THE Rise*, don't miss the next installment in *The Rise of the Normals* series. Get exclusive content, sneak peeks, and behind-the-scenes insights delivered right to your inbox.

Join Rick Bettencourt's email list today:

https://rickbettencourt.com/signup/

You might even get a *PEOPLE* magazine pic Diesel and Bence would approve of.

Discussion Topics

R EADY TO SHARE *The Rise* with your book club friends? We've made it easy for you by providing a list of book club questions to get your group to chat about it. (Wine and cheese not included.)

1. **Being Normal:** *The Rise* explores the idea of being "Normal" in a world of Supers. How does Diesel's struggle to live like a human reflect real-world themes of identity, belonging, and societal pressure to conform?

2. **Tradition vs. Progress:** Diesel faces intense pressure from his father and his community to uphold supernatural customs and "mate" to preserve the species. Discuss how the novel portrays the tension between honoring tradition and forging one's own path.

3. **The Rise of Humanity:** Metanormals are presented as a potential threat to the supernatural order. Discuss whether the rise of humans with magical potential is something to be feared, cel-

ebrated, or better understood. How does this relate to power dynamics in today's society?

4. **Forbidden Love and Identity:** Diesel and Bence are mocked and marginalized for being "humansexuals"—Supers who are emotionally or sexually attracted to humans. This term is weaponized by their peers, yet it also becomes a powerful marker of identity and resistance. How does the story use the idea of forbidden love to reflect real-world experiences of queerness, interracial relationships, or nonconforming attractions?

5. **Choose a Bud:** If you could hangout for a day with a buddy from *The Rise*, who would you choose: Elio the dragon, Jezebel the fashion-forward sociopath, Diesel the hot af shifter, Bingham the half-shifted sweetheart, or someone else? Why?

6. **Gaslamp Fantasy Reality:** Imagine your hometown suddenly got the Hubbard Forest treatment: no electricity, magic-only transportation, and a religious mandate to mate during The Howling Moon. What would you do first—panic, rebel, or order something scandalous off Amazon?

7. **The Fashion Police:** If you had to pick between Hubbard Forest's strict 19th-century fashion or Salem's anything-goes vibe, what would you wear? Who in the book is most likely to start a fashion blog? (Be honest—would Diesel's shredded Levi's qualify as "cottagecore"?) Bonus: Who in the book has the best fashion sense—and the worst?

8. **Power and Tradition:** Hubbard Forest enforces strict cultural

rules rooted in tradition, such as forced mating rituals and rejection of modernity. What parallels can you draw between these supernatural structures and real-world systems of control (religious, political, familial)?

9. **Modernity vs. Preservation:** The supernatural society is locked into a "gaslamp" aesthetic and cultural period, resisting any move toward the modern. What do you think the novel is saying about cultural nostalgia and the fear of progress? When does preserving tradition become destructive?

10. **The Many Forms of Love:** *The Rise* explores romantic love, platonic devotion, sibling loyalty, chosen family, and more. Which love story (or non-love story) affected you most? What does the novel say about how love evolves—and how we evolve with it?

About Rick

Rick Bettencourt writes fiction that collides magic, identity, and desire in strange, often hilarious, always human ways. A lifelong New Englander, he sets much of his work in shadowy corners of the region—where vampires gripe about their diets, wolf-shifters fall for humans, and forbidden love might just be the strongest magic of all.

To connect with Rick and get exclusive character art, backstory guides, and series updates, visit rickbettencourt.com

Also By

Other books by Rick Bettencourt include:

Summerwind Magick

Tim on Broadway

Marketing Beef

Building Us

Soulbound

One Nightstand

Not Sure Boys